Fundamentally

A Novel

Nussaibah Younis

Tiny
Reparations
Books

An imprint of Penguin Random House LLC
1745 Broadway, New York, NY 10019
penguinrandomhouse.com

Book design by Daniel Brount

LIBRARY OF CONGRESS CATALOGING-IN-PUBLICATION DATA
Names: Younis, Nussaibah, author.
Title: Fundamentally: a novel / Nussaibah Younis.
Description: New York: Tiny Reparations Books, 2025.
Identifiers: LCCN 2024027430 (print) | LCCN 2024027431 (ebook) |
ISBN 9780593851388 (hardcover) | ISBN 9780593851401 (ebook)
Subjects: LCGFT: Novels.
Classification: LCC PR6125.O96 F86 2025 (print) | LCC PR6125.O96 (ebook) |
DDC 823/.92—dc23/eng/20240809
LC record available at https://lccn.loc.gov/2024027430
LC ebook record available at https://lccn.loc.gov/2024027431

Printed in Canada

1   3   5   7   9   10   8   6   4   2

The authorized representative in the EU for product safety and compliance is
Penguin Random House Ireland, Morrison Chambers, 32 Nassau Street,
Dublin D02 YH68, Ireland. https://eu-contact.penguin.ie

Mum, to the moon and back

Fundamentally

Prologue

September 2019

IT WASN'T IDEAL, NAVIGATING THE ZAGROS MOUNTAINS ON a freezing September night, wearing a trouser suit and ballet flats. The cracked corpse of a river marked the way through the Iraqi–Turkish border.

My handbag slipped off my shoulder as I struggled over uneven ground. I gripped it close with one hand, my other arm outstretched, grasping balance out of the hazy mist.

It had been a thrill, six months ago, buying a designer bag for the UN job. I'd studied the handbags like museum pieces on their backlit pedestals before selecting a buttery mauve tote, holding my breath when I tapped my credit card.

I've since revised my definition of thrilling.

As I stepped onto a rock, it disintegrated into a spray of gravel and I fell, cutting my palms on stones. I turned over, my back against the dirt, the black heavens enormous overhead, covered in millions of tiny stars. The specter of an omniscient God strengthens in moments like this. If you exist, I silently prayed, do me a favor and take it down a notch?

"You is fine, Nadia?" shouted Darban. Twenty meters farther up, his black silhouette was cut out of the sky. The outline of a stiff kaftan, baggy pants, and turban: the traditional dress of Kurdish freedom fighters turned profiteers.

"I'm OK," I said.

I looked down the valley at my burden. She rose through the gloom like an apparition, cloaked in a black abaya and headscarf, that bundle tied to her back.

"How you getting on, Sara?" I called out. The frigid breeze spun my words into echoes that reverberated from the stony surrounds. She paused mid-clamber.

"Bruv," she said into the dark route between us, "you should've got an ISIS smuggler. Man's got us on fucking Everest!"

"Are you dense?" I levered myself back to standing. "An ISIS smuggler would have shot me in the face and recruited you again."

"They're sick smugglers, though, you gotta admit." She hoisted the bundle higher up her back.

"I swear to God, Sara, if you stay a fucking fundy after all this, I'll sell you into sex slavery myself."

Her laughter filled the night air. That's the kind of thing she finds funny. It's one of the reasons I love her.

It does not justify what I have done.

1

Five Months Earlier

I T'S NOT LIKE I WAS EXPECTING STALINGRAD, BUT BAGHDAD took the piss. Arriving for the first time, tucked into a UN car, I watched as the city lights refracted through the bulletproof glass. Floodlights hovered over a pickup football game, square lamps up-lit the National Museum, fairy lights dripped down palm trees beside the Tigris River. Why was it so . . . nice? What happened to the rolling blackouts? The electrical transmission network supposedly ravaged by war? Hadn't I donated to help Iraqi women giving birth in cowsheds lit by the flame of a single candle?

Car after car parked along the river's banks: sparkling Audis and BMWs among older Toyotas and Hyundais. I'd thought I was a high roller, leaving London halfway through a monthly Travelcard. Young men unloaded foldout chairs, shisha pipes, and portable barbecues, setting up by the water's edge. I could almost smell the marinated baby chickens, the flattened carp smoldering over charcoal, but the driver stopped me from rolling the window down.

"Security," he said, tilting his head toward rooftops empty of snipers.

I spotted a huddle of teenagers watching TikTok, trying to imitate a dance, before pushing each other over, their laughter subsumed by the honking traffic. Rosy and I used to dance like that.

A convoy of cars started beeping frantically, and my back tensed up as I anticipated a critical incident ahead. Then I saw white ribbon stretched over the hood of a Mercedes, a bride stepping out, her lace dress draped over marble steps as she entered a five-star hotel. Was this fucking *Midnight in Paris*? I'd signed up for cluster munitions, not glitter bombs. I spluttered with the indignity of it.

"Everything OK, ma'am?" The African driver looked over his shoulder. What had brought him here? A carefully weighed decision, no doubt. Not juvenile heartbreak, like me.

"I'm fine, thanks. You can call me Nadia." I deserved to be called a lot of things, but *ma'am* wasn't one of them.

"Ah, it's like Nadia Buari, big actress in Ghana." He nodded at me with approval. "And why you came to Baghdad, Nadia?"

"Oh, I'm here for a job. I'm creating a deradicalization program for ISIS brides. Yeah . . . don't ask."

The driver raised his eyebrows but stayed silent. I checked my phone, hoping for a message from Rosy conveying immense pain at having me ripped from her life. But my SIM card, flabbergasted at having been brought to Iraq, had malfunctioned.

Returning to the window, I strained my eyes, searching for burned-out cars and bullet holes, something to undermine this tableau of festivity, anything to force Rosy into irrelevance. But in the falling darkness, the jollity glowed only brighter.

We entered the Green Zone, a fortified district where international organizations and government agencies hid from the population they claimed to serve. My new home.

My driver deposited me in the car park of the UN compound. He stepped out of the car and lit a cigarette, staring hard at my chest while I heaved my suitcase out of the trunk. Shouldn't misogyny have an equal and opposite chivalric force?

"Over there." He pointed toward a security cabin, his burning red tobacco dancing against the darkness.

I dragged my suitcase over the ground, the evening breeze a warm relief after the intense air-conditioning in the car. A generator rumbled on the far side of the car park, the smell of diesel repelling insects through the air, the stars obscured by a thin gray smog that hung between the city lights and the night sky.

I entered the security cabin, caught my foot on the lip of the doorway, and fell inside. It usually took more than ten seconds to humiliate myself at a new job, but here I was, already achieving a personal best.

A lean Iraqi man in a blue uniform stepped away from his prayer mat and crouched beside me. "You OK, Doctor?"

I was comforted by his use of my title; status gives you scope to absorb minor failures. I hoisted myself up.

"I'm Farris," he said, his Iraqi accent strongly Americanized. He picked up my suitcase and put it on a trestle table that bisected the room. "You must be Dr. Nadia. You're very welcome here."

I watched in horror as he snapped on latex gloves and unzipped my suitcase.

"Real sorry I have to do this," he said, shaking his head. "It's just protocol."

He used his hand condoms to remove every item in turn. A copy of *Cosmopolitan*, the headline screaming: "Everything You NEED to Know about Rimming!" Scores of enormous black underpants interspersed with a few sexy transparent ones. A lilac bullet vibrator, which he unscrewed until a AAA battery shot out. A backup pack of AAA batteries. I pulled out my nonfunctioning phone and pretended to text, my ears throbbing with shame.

My ears were familiar with the feeling. When I was a teenager, my mum found a *Just Seventeen* magazine hidden in a Quranic exegesis textbook in my bedroom. She lay in wait as I returned from school.

"This is disgusting, Nadia." She waved the naked torso of Pacey from *Dawson's Creek* in my face. "How can you read such filth?"

I don't read it; I look at it while holding an electric toothbrush to my clit.

"It's the other girls at school," I said, inching back toward the door. "I'm only trying to fit in. I don't enjoy it." Evoking the mysterious dangers of peer pressure normally worked on Mum.

"If they jumped off a cliff, would you follow?" she said. It was her favorite retort, but also the most idiotic. I obviously did a risk analysis before deciding which of my friends' behaviors to imitate. Mum was trying to tear up the magazine, but she kept getting the glossy pages tangled in the staples.

"Muslim friends only from now on," she said.

Mum had been a born-again Muslim ever since my father died

when I was a toddler. After the magazine incident, she invested heavily in my indoctrination, until I became deeply religious. A total dork, I loved nothing more than planning my revision time-tables, and being religious was like having a revision timetable for life, the day of judgment being the final exam. I lived as a paragon of Islamic virtue until I went to university, where relentless intel-lectual challenges and social seductions thawed my devotion to naught.

"Good to go, Doctor," said Farris, zipping my suitcase back up. "Look forward to hanging sometime."

His prayer mat lay in the corner, an image of the Ka'ba woven into the fabric, but when I looked at his face, it was warm and free of judgment.

He handed me over to a staffer whose white headscarf and blouse produced the combined effect of a shroud—albeit a shroud destined for paradise. It felt strange being around Muslims again, after my godless life in London, and I wondered if they could smell the apostasy on me.

Shroud led me through a grassy outdoor quad, the air fresh against my matted hair, and into a two-story building, where she tapped a key card against a bedroom door. I stepped inside. The room was tiny, which made the furniture look huge. A single bed pushed against the wall, an incongruously ornate wardrobe, a desk covered in blue pen marks, and a flimsy foldout chair.

Shroud held the door open, one foot in, one foot out, and handed me a bundle of items, including a lanyard, a map, and a schedule for tomorrow.

"You have question?" she said.

Dozens of questions collided in my brain, canceling one another out.

"No." She was gone before my mouth completed the "oh."

I stood in the middle of the room, suitcase next to me, its metal handle standing high, ready to be reversed out of this world. What cunty-bollocking madness had possessed me to come here?

I remembered the taste of Peroni on Rosy's tongue, the sweaty jasmine smell she'd leave on my sheets.

I'd thought I could evade my pain, dump it at Heathrow like lost baggage and fly away. Yet here I was, the exact same person who'd left London twelve hours before, my breathing shallow, the oxygen laced with loss.

I persuaded myself to unpack, told myself it'd make the place feel more homey, but ten minutes later, my suitcase was empty and the room remained indifferent to my presence. For the third time in my adult life, I was trying to create a home on hostile terrain. Your mother doesn't want you, the love of your life doesn't want you, well . . . how about a random failed state? Is it possible you belong here?

In the ensuite, I sat on the toilet tracing the cracks in the tiled floor with my toes, my body too tense to wee. It took a concentrated visualization of Niagara Falls to summon a trickle. I undressed and got into bed. Feeling the rough polyester sheet against my back, I realized it had been a decade since I'd slept on anything other than Egyptian cotton.

"Princess Nadia," Rosy would have said, "can you feel a pea beneath your hundred soft mattresses?"

Easy for her to say, Bubble Wrapped by her doting parents,

taped in the protective seal of a country to which she unequivo-cally belonged. For years, I'd only had her.

Now I was three thousand miles away, lying in a single bed in Baghdad, clinging to the bedspread despite the heat. My fingers held so lightly to life, I could have shut my eyes and let go, my body evaporating, the world unmoved by such a tiny shift.

2

I STEPPED OUTSIDE INTO THE BRIGHT MORNING SUN, FRESHLY showered, inhaling the scent of my strawberry-infused shampoo. Standing in the middle of the quad, clutching my map, I could see the grass being watered by thin black tubes, the ground beyond parched and dusty. I squinted up at the buildings, turning the map around and pointing it in different directions. If that's there, then I must be . . .

"Are you lost?" said a deep Geordie voice behind me.

Only physically, emotionally, and spiritually. I turned around and was confronted by massive pectoral muscles pressing through a khaki-green T-shirt. I looked up. He must have been six foot four, his blond hair lit with streaks of gold, his jaw large and angular, his shoulders enormous. Holy mother. Imagine coming back to London with this specimen on my arm. His leg was bigger than an average man's torso.

"It's science that women haven't got space awareness," he said.

So, I'll have to gaffer tape his mouth shut. He'll still be impressive.

"You mean spatial . . . anyway, hey." I fluttered my eyelashes. "I'm Nadia, it's my first day. Can you help me?" And then fuck me blind?

"Tom." He stepped toward me, his gorilla-like stature blocking out the sun. He plucked the map from my weak feminine fingers. "Where you trying to get to?"

"The cafeteria." I sucked in my tummy so I looked like the type of girl who rarely ate. In fairness, I'd eaten nothing since a piece of Gouda and some oat crackers on the plane. Maybe I'd return to London svelte as well as worldly.

"If the camels die, we die," he said.

I looked at him, perplexed.

"Sherif Ali, in *Lawrence of Arabia*," he said. "It's my favorite film."

"Do you identify with Lawrence, as a fellow blond savior in the Middle East?" I winked.

"Yes," he said, without a trace of humor.

We walked together between two buildings that cast large, overlapping rectangles of shade. Every step we took summoned little dust explosions, coating the bottoms of my trousers in rust-colored dirt. "Can't you even stay clean until breakfast?" Rosy would have said.

We reached a squat sandstone building with wonky flagged steps and small windows armed with metal bars. After the UN's first base was bombed in 2003, the new compound had crouched in a defensive posture. The UN mission, meant to be temporary, was now sixteen years old and larger than ever. Instead of becoming a beacon of democracy, Iraq had lunged from one civil war to another, and the UN had twisted around the carcass like knotweed. And I thought I could make a difference? A heartbroken, foreign academic, showing up after nearly two decades of international failure. The hubris of it.

The cafeteria was smaller than I'd imagined, like a basic greasy spoon. Wipe-clean tables with wooden caddies in the middle, stacked with cutlery, condiments, and napkins. Swirls of moisture glistened from the recent swipes of a wet dishcloth, and the smell of incinerated toast was so strong I half expected to see a cloud of charcoal hanging in the air. I picked up a sticky brown plastic tray and joined a queue of people perusing platters of eggs, fruit, and cheese. One of those conveyor belt toasters was at the end, next to a basket of bread. I picked up a boiled egg, but Tom took it out of my hand and shook it gently by his ear. He placed it on his own tray, picked up another egg, shook it, and handed it to me.

"Childish!" he said to two men giggling at a table that faced the buffet.

"Fun spoiler," said one man in a French accent.

"It's spoilsport," said an African man sitting next to him.

"Spoilsport," repeated the Frenchman.

"Charles and Pierre"—Tom tilted his head toward them—"think it's hilarious to hide raw eggs in with the boiled ones. It's no bother to me, I chug raw eggs before training."

A gray-haired man sitting on the far side of the room tapped an egg on the table edge, and a membranous slime exploded over his suit. He screamed and stood up, a yolky puddle sliding to the floor as gulps of laughter escaped from the vertical brown trays that Charles and Pierre had hidden behind.

I stifled a smile. "Gosh, thanks for saving me from that, Tom, I'd have been so embarrassed."

"You're welcome, doll," said Tom, the lilt of his Geordie accent a perfect complement to his physique.

We sat opposite each other, and I buttered a piece of toast that was burned on one side and completely uncooked on the other. Tom cracked three raw eggs into a tumbler and downed them while I repressed a gag.

"You'd never guess it," he said, "but Pierre's proper fancy like. His dad's French ambassador to America, and his granddad was before. Pierre just pisses about, though, spends all his time hosting parties for journalists. He chats a lot of shit, but, if you ever need info, sometimes he gets decent gossip about what the Iraqis are up to."

Charles had returned to the buffet for seconds, and I watched Pierre throw an open sachet of mayonnaise at his back before ducking under a table. Charles spun around, leaped over a chair, and dove toward him, crushing a hash brown into his face as they wrestled on the floor.

"Quai d'Orsay royalty?" I said. "How unlikely."

"Quesadilla what?"

"It's the French foreign ministry . . . never mind. So, what's the deal with Charles?"

"He's South African, bit of a dark horse . . . can I say that, or will I get canceled?" He sniggered, while I gave the side eye to my bowl of fruit.

"Nah, he's a good lad, Charles." Tom poured milk into his glass, raw egg residue clinging to the sides, and sipped slowly, savoring it like a rare whiskey. "We train together every day; he spots my bench presses. Got a hell of a front squat on him. He's real clever like, something about space rocks and why they don't hit Earth that much. Got a big prize for it."

I squinted at Charles from across the room. He was stocky, well built, his bald head a smooth velvety black. "Asteroids? He's a physicist? What's he doing here?"

"Ah, some family shit back home, just wanted out. His dad's a top politics guy, used to work for Mandela or something."

Why were they all from such eminent families? I thought of my mum teaching the kids at the local mosque. Unless it went very wrong, it was not a career of global significance.

"How's about you, doll? What brings you here?"

I swallowed. "Erm . . . I'm leading a program to deradicalize ISIS women, to help them return to their homes."

Tom whistled and leaned back in his chair. "No shit, that's you?"

A boyish white face suddenly appeared above Tom's head. Pierre.

"YOU?!"

I forced a smile. "Yep." My fingers trembled as I peeled my boiled egg, whole chunks of white coming off with the shell, leaving me with only a jagged yolk.

Pierre pulled up a chair and craned in close, as though expecting to find qualifications tattooed on my neck.

"*Excusez-moi*, mademoiselle, but . . . who are you?"

"Dr. Nadia Amin," I said in my stiffest voice. "I'm a lecturer in criminology at UCL and I've taken a sabbatical to do this job. I was headhunted, actually, to lead the deradicalization program."

"Headhunted," scoffed Pierre. "As though they have no qualified candidates here. *Merde*, the disrespect. I guess you've only been a lecturer for ten minutes, *n'est-ce pas?*"

I looked down at the breadcrumbs on my plate. He was right; I was an infant lecturer, had got the job a mere six months prior.

"Knob off, dipshit," said Tom, putting an arm around me. "She's an expert, this lass is, about criminals. What was it you said, love? Crimolology?"

He was sweet, this simpleton. An anti-Rosy, perhaps, his masculinity free of queerness, his brain free of complexity, his morality free of nuance. What a nice change.

Pierre pushed his chair back and stormed out of the cafeteria.

"Pay no mind," said Tom. "He's just pissed off he didn't get the job, like. You're his boss now."

I covered my face with my hands. "Pierre works for me?"

Tom pushed up his sleeves. "Any disrespect, you come to me, pet. You hear me?"

See. A darling.

"Got any idea who else works for me?"

"It won't be Charles; he's at UNICEF, the agency that helps kids. Oh, it's probably Sherri. Bonkers redhead. She's irritating, not gonna lie. A right Goody Two-shoes."

"Great, that's just perfect. I can't understand why they hired me, Tom. I don't know the first thing about the UN, I've never managed a team, never run a program. I'm just a theorist; the practice is a mystery to me."

He looked at me with sympathy. "I get you. It's like, you cane iron in the gym, but when the shit hits the fan, have you got the aggression?"

I sighed and checked my watch. It was only 8:40 A.M., and I was already exhausted.

"My first meeting's with my boss, Lina Khoury. Know anything about her?"

He raked his fingers through his blond curls. They sprang back into place with a whimsical beauty worthy of Adonis himself. "She's a tough nut, icy, but you'll be all right, you're a smarty-pants, you can handle her."

"Christ below." I sipped orange juice so sour that it made me wince.

He looked at the juice and put his hand on my knee. "How about I take you for a proper drink tonight? *Dr.* Nadia. Give you something to look forward to."

I was flattered. This majestic man could have anyone, and he'd chosen me. Admittedly, I'd yet to see another woman on base, but still, it was a win.

"Yeah? That would be nice."

"Sweet, I'll meet you at the tiki bar."

"There's a tiki bar? What's the dress code? Grass skirt?"

"I'd like to see you in a grass skirt, you sexy little native," he said.

I'd like to sit on your face. Partly to stop you from talking.

We stepped out of the building into the sun. It was like walking into a migraine, our eyelids half-closed against the light, the smell of generator fuel acrid in the climbing heat. Tom walked me to Lina's office.

"Here you go, doll. See you at eight." He folded his body in half to kiss me on the cheek, then disappeared around a corner.

I pulled out my now-functioning phone, only to find zero texts from Rosy. There was a message from my mum: Salaam. You arrived ok? Have you eaten?

Mum's messages had grown more frequent since I'd announced my move to Iraq. It baffled me, her concern for my physical safety after years of emotional neglect. It was better than nothing, I supposed.

All good here, had an egg, I typed. It was 8:51 A.M., and I was determined not to knock on the door a minute before our scheduled start at nine.

I wondered whether Lina would be like my boss back at UCL, Professor Sophie Fletcher: snappy and high-strung, but ultimately a mensch of the highest order.

After my PhD in criminology, Sophie encouraged me to pursue academia, but the sclerotic job market relegated me to temporary and appallingly paid adjunct roles. "You're bloody brilliant, on your good days anyway," Sophie would say. "Academia's just clogged up with ancient men hogging all the jobs." So, I struggled on, teaching for my supper, praying for a plague.

One Tuesday, I had an hour before teaching my seminar, An Interdisciplinary Approach to Homicide, and I was browsing *The Guardian* online at my desk. My keyboard cut a narrow path to my computer, crowded by stacks of half-completed grading.

"Got any actual research to show for yourself?" said Sophie from behind me. I jumped and turned around.

She was standing in the doorway of my tiny office. A room previously considered fit only for a photocopier now crammed in two adjunct lecturers. With one sly hand, I grappled behind me, trying to close my browser. *The Guardian* disappeared, but there was a game of online chess lurking behind it.

"Yes, lots of progress!" I lied. I wished Lydia, my officemate, was there to dilute the scrutiny. Lydia had produced nothing in eighteen months, except for a child, much to the distaste of the faculty.

"It's finally happening," she said. "Jim's worse: He's on a ventilator now. He's done for."

I tried to suppress my delight. "I'm sorry to hear that. Professor Humphrey was always kind to me."

"Don't be obtuse. You'd better publish the best journal article of your life pronto. You and Lydia are in the running." She chewed an arm of her spectacles and leaned against the doorframe. "I wonder how much his house will go for," she mused. "He's got a four-bed in Islington, bought it for ten grand in olden times, the jammy bastard. I'm head of faculty and I'm still renting. . . ."

My heartbeat grew louder, and Sophie retreated into a blur as I realized that every single one of my article ideas sucked.

Over the next few weeks, I became mired in a shit soup of unimaginative concepts, desperate to find something bold enough to land me the coveted lectureship.

Remarkably, given her total disinterest in my career, my mother came up with the solution. I'd missed a few of her calls and decided to ring her while walking to the Tube. Ten minutes with a hard stop was ideal—enough time to catch up, but insufficient for the lambasting of all my life choices. I also preferred to talk to my mother while in motion; it reduced my stress response.

"Are you eating well?" she asked.

No, Mother, everything I eat is deep-fried because that's the crap you raised me on.

"Yes," I said.

"When are you coming to visit? Did you get the wedding invitation from Saif?"

"Yeah, it was fancy with the pop-up gazebo thing inside. How much do you reckon that cost?" I'd left the glittery abomination on my and Rosy's kitchen table. We'd been using it as a coaster and it was now soaked in red wine.

"They could afford to be extravagant with the invites, since it's a small wedding. It's his second, remember?"

"Oh yeah, his first wife ran off. That was exciting."

"Don't be rude, darling, it was terrible for the family."

"Did they ever figure out what happened?"

She paused. "I shouldn't say, *especially not on the phone*, but she went to Syria."

"Syria?! She joined ISIS? I thought she eloped with Malikah from Zumba. For real, someone we know joined ISIS?" A couple of pedestrians stared at me and I realized I was speaking very loudly. I dipped my head and skirted past them.

"Hmm . . . we still have questions about Malikah. Anyway, there were a lot of groups in Syria, other than that one." Mum is allergic to saying the word *ISIS*. She's one of many Muslims in denial.

"Holy shit. Sorry, I mean, *Yah Allah!*"

"Don't use foul language. I never swore in front of you, I can't understand where you learned to be so hideous."

"From the TV, obviously."

"I knew it! The devil's box. So, are you coming to the wedding? If you spend a week in Leicester, you could come to the Mehndi too."

I would rather fuck seven emaciated hipsters from Hinge in seven days.

"Sure," I said.

It was 2018, and ISIS had lost 95 percent of its territory, not that I'd been following the news. I was exhausted by the reflexive defensiveness I felt when parsing media coverage of bloodstained machetes, overgrown pubic beards, and creepy children yelling "Death to the West!" I hated having to defend a religion I didn't even believe in. Al-Qaeda, al-Shabaab, Boko Haram, ISIS . . . these small bands of men waving around their phallic weapons, ruining it for everyone. How unoriginal.

But, thinking of Saif's absconded wife, I began to research women who'd joined ISIS, and found myself gripped. Watching the propaganda videos, I could see they'd been flogged a wet dream (only to be flogged for real when they turned up). Armies of macho men strapped into bondage-style suicide vests, marching toward a heaven full of virgin pussy. I suppose it's nice when a man has clarity of purpose. If I were younger, I might have been persuaded, but I was in my thirties and I'd had enough sex to know that devout Muslims have tedious chat and give crap head.

As ISIS lost battle after battle, thousands of women flocked to refugee camps, where they were detained while their countries of origin debated what to do with them. Many of them had barely left the house during the caliphate, and their ongoing detention raised big questions. What's the appropriate punishment for ISIS brides who didn't commit any violent crimes? Can we detain people just because of their beliefs? Should we try to change their beliefs? Or can we create behavioral change without shifting ideological commitments?

It was the perfect subject for my article: topical and fascinating, with profound implications for the entire field of criminal rehabil-

itation. Over the next six months, I put together an article proposing techniques for the deradicalization of ISIS brides and it was
published by the best journal in criminology. I argued that forced
religious reeducation could trigger a backlash and inadvertently
strengthen radical beliefs. Instead, a deradicalization program
should focus on creating positive psychological and social conditions for behavioral transformation. If ISIS brides received psychological help, particularly to deal with their PTSD, and if they
reconnected with moderate and supportive families and communities, they'd be unlikely to reoffend, even if their beliefs remained
unchanged.

British and international media outlets reported on my proposals, mostly excoriating them, but my department was delighted
both by the prestigious publication and by the media attention. I
was a shoo-in after that. A couple of softball interviews later, my
senior colleagues awarded me the lectureship vacated by Professor
Humphrey's death. When I heard the news, Sophie was waiting in
my office with a bottle of champagne, while Lydia wept in the
bathroom.

"To women helping women," she said, as we toasted.

3

LINA'S OFFICE WAS AN EXEMPLAR OF NORDIC DESIGN. A dove-gray sofa faced a supple teak desk, two granite-colored armchairs perpendicular on either side. In the middle was a triangular coffee table, its curved walnut base visible through the glass like a piece of modern art. Had she literally imported furniture for a two-year stint here? From what I'd seen on the airport drive, what passes for high-end furniture in Baghdad involves copious gold molding.

The window overlooked the compound's solitary patch of grass, as though the earth itself had blossomed beneath Lina's gaze. She beckoned for me to sit without taking her eyes off the desktop computer. Her navy jacket and silk blouse, understated at first glance, were cut as perfectly as couture. I stared down at my unflattering beige trouser suit. I looked like Angela Merkel.

"Yes?" Lina rolled her ergonomic desk chair to the left so she could see me unobstructed.

"Um, yeah, I'm Nadia." I shook and nodded my head, as though unsure of my own name. "I'm supposed to lead the deradicalization program. I just arrived last night. My agenda said to come here."

"Ah, good. Hope you're ready to dive in." Her accent was Lebanese but filtered through an expensive international education. "We've finally got sign-off from UN HQ to set up the rehabilitation program. There are only a couple hundred women in the ISIS women's camp up in Ninewah, locals and foreigners, but you realize this is just a test case. If we succeed here, we'll be ready once ISIS is fully defeated in Syria. So, we're under pressure to make this work. You need to get started ASAP, as soon as you've got permission from the ministry. Other UN agencies want to shut us down, so there's no time to waste. Got it?"

I hadn't even managed to get the lid off my pen, and in my blind panic, I had already forgotten everything she'd said. "Right, yeah, of course."

Squawk, squawk!

I jumped and spotted a luminous green budgie in a cage at the back of the room. What the . . . ? Come to think of it, the room had an earthy, pet-shop smell.

"My Bulbul," cooed Lina. She rose from her desk and walked to the cage, opening its door. The bird flew out and flapped around the ceiling, and I instinctively covered my head. I'd just washed my hair; the last thing I needed was to get shat on. But what if I was offending her? I'd yet to meet a woman in a position of power who had a real baby, but substitutes abounded. I gingerly lowered my hands to my lap.

"That's a beautiful bird," I said. "Quite a . . . sound."

"She's gorgeous." Lina smiled, lifting her arm. The bird landed on her suit jacket and she stroked its back with her forefinger.

My mouth was half-open as I stared at them, afraid to interrupt their reverie.

"Will that be all?" Lina was looking at me and her smile had vanished.

How could that be all? She'd barely said anything! On paper, I may have been an expert, but I didn't know how to do this job. I'd never met an ISIS woman, knew nothing about Iraq, couldn't navigate my way around the compound, let alone the UN system.

"Er... it'd be helpful to understand your priorities. If you were me, where would you start?" I said.

She checked her silver bangle, which had a watch face attached.

"Pull your team together, visit the refugee camp, and get sign-off from the Ministry of Humane Affairs. Don't let me down, Nadia."

I scribbled the words on the back of my agenda: *team, camp, ministry.* Then I stood up and grabbed my handbag. "Understood, Lina, I'm on it."

As I walked toward the door, Lina began to sing in Arabic to the squawking budgie, creating a demented soundtrack that perfectly accompanied my new life.

I rushed over the quad back toward my bedroom, glancing at my phone. Our meeting had lasted seven of the scheduled sixty minutes. I sprinted up the two flights of stairs, tapped my key card nine times before my door unlocked, and slammed the door closed behind me. Dropping my bag onto the unmade bed, I paced the room before resting my palms and forehead on the wall, trying to breathe.

"Well done," Rosy would have said. "Your fate's in the hands of a birder. I told you not to go."

Scrambling around in my cosmetics bag, I found a bottle of Rescue Remedy and squirted a couple of drops under my tongue. Predictably, the crushed-up dandelion essence had no impact on my mental state. I needed benzos, but the sleepy oblivion they induced was so delicious and so moreish that I'd long since committed to abstinence.

I pulled out my laptop, resorting to the millennial lullaby that is *Friends*.

"Pivot!" yelled Ross from the screen, as Rachel and Chandler tried to wrestle a sofa up the stairs.

The familiar dialogue washed over me, distracting my toddler brain and soothing my anxiety. Whatever shit goes down, that purple New York apartment stays the same, its tales repeated like parables, the comfort of small loves, small conflicts, small lives.

I reached for my agenda and looked at the next item: team meeting. Perhaps I could win them over. I'd make a wry comment about Lina's idiosyncrasies, and they'd laugh, drawing closer around me. They'd help me decode the UN system and lay a path toward our shared victory. I imagined us, one day in the future, gathering for a nostalgic drink, marveling at what we'd achieved during those heady days in Baghdad, a family forged in battle, forever bonded by the experience we'd shared.

I WAS LOST AGAIN. THE GROUNDS WERE COMPLETELY SILENT BEneath the clear midmorning sky, and tiny sparrows darted overhead. It was absurd to think I was in the second-largest metropolis in the Middle East, but the city had been clawed back, left crashing against the seven-foot walls protecting the Green Zone.

I wandered through the compound, the mismatched buildings united only by their cheap utilitarianism. A man in gym clothes walked toward me, and I asked him for directions so pitifully that he personally escorted me to the correct place.

The conference room was as bright and cold as a meat fridge. Two people lounged around a table, Pierre and a red-faced woman with even redder hair.

"Good morning," I said. "Or is it afternoon already?" God, I was making myself cringe.

They looked up, then returned to their phones, and I felt like a substitute teacher thrust on skeptical teens. A round white clock on the far wall staggered through the seconds. I sat in an enormous chair upholstered in plastic masquerading as leather, and pulled out my laptop.

"So, I'm Nadia," I said, as my eggy breakfast tried to climb back up my throat. "I'm here to lead the rehabilitation program. Pierre and I met briefly in the cafeteria, and you must be Sherri?"

"Sherri Anderson," she said in a petulant Australian accent, putting her phone down and opening a spiral-bound notebook. "I'm the psychosocial support specialist, and I'd like to voice my concerns about the proposed program."

The sunburn on her nose had started to peel and my eyes fixated on the tiny, white curls of skin unfurling from her. I was grateful not to be the least attractive woman on base.

I smiled at her and opened a blank document. "Right, yes, please go ahead."

"The proposed rehabilitation program is unethical and problematic," said Sherri, reading from her notebook. "I object on moral grounds."

She looked over at Pierre, who was scrolling through Grindr in plain sight. I later learned that Grindr has a very active user base in Baghdad.

"Do you mind?" she said. "This is serious."

Pierre ignored her, and she barreled on. "It's illegal for the ISIS women to be detained in camps without charge or access to due process. Any program the UN offers in the camp is tantamount to condoning a violation of international law."

"OK, thanks, Sherri, I appreciate your honesty. That's a valid perspective. Erm . . . it would be helpful to know why you joined the rehabilitation team?"

"I didn't have a choice! I was working for the development agency, but this program's been given a load of money from New York, and I've been forced to move teams. Why you accepted the role, that's the mystery. It's career suicide. We'll be ridiculed by the humanitarian sector and lambasted by the press, deservedly so. We're on the wrong side of history and we'll never live it down!"

Well, shit. I obviously hadn't given the job enough thought. Desperate to escape London, I'd accepted it on a whim, but the implications were becoming clear. Merely writing an article had earned me a vitriolic response from the press, yet here I was, blithely putting those ideas into practice. Of course it was going to generate controversy. My insides dropped and shifted, my organs playing a fleshy game of *Tetris*. When I counted all the ways Rosy had fucked me . . .

Pierre looked up, grinning. "You know they chose a name for our agency? It's the UN Deradicalization Organization, or UNDO."

He guffawed. "Half the UN doesn't even believe in deradicalization, so we have to say 'rehabilitation,' but the agency name stayed the same. It makes zero sense."

Suddenly, the lights went out and I could see nothing but solid black. My mind filled with images of hissing explosives, shredded metal, twisted bodies.

"Stay calm!" I shrieked.

Pierre's laughter mocked me through the darkness.

"It's just the mains electricity switching to the generator," said Sherri. "It happens every four hours."

When the lights came back on, Pierre was wiping tears from his eyes, and my palms were pressed against my hot cheeks.

"Anyway . . ." I trailed off. No words could dispel my shame; I had to move on. I tried to remember the purpose of the meeting. What had Lina told me?

I looked at the words scribbled on the back of my agenda. *Team. Camp. Ministry.* Did this count as getting my team together? I ticked it off, because I deserved a treat.

"Shall we go to the camp?" I said.

Pierre groaned. "All the way to fucking Ninewah? You haven't even got ministry sign-off yet. And you won't get it. The Iraqis aren't going near this. There are protests in the streets, angry Shi'a kids with no jobs—the minister can't pander to Sunni Islamists right now, it's politically impossible. A qualified person would know this."

I pulled my laptop closer toward me and surreptitiously googled "Iraq protests." Thousands of results popped up, including several breaking news alerts. Fuck me. He may be a certifiable twat, but he was much better informed than me.

Hang on, didn't Tom say Pierre had applied for my job? If it were career-ending lunacy, he wouldn't have gone for it, this progeny of the French elite, and he wouldn't be so angry about being passed over—

Sherri's voice interrupted my self-soothing. "We can't possibly design the program without first visiting the camp. We've got to assess conditions, see if the women would even accept our intervention. You're putting the cart before the horse, Pierre."

I was relieved that Sherri's assiduousness had already overtaken her moral objections. "That sounds sensible, Sherri," I said. "Could you organize the trip logistics?"

"That sounds sensible, Sherri," said Pierre, mimicking me. "You know, Sherri, having a personality wouldn't expand your carbon footprint."

"Well . . ." she stammered, "if you stopped . . . farting out of your mouth, we could significantly reduce methane levels." She smiled, delighted by her comeback.

At least they hated each other. It would be even worse if they were in cahoots against me.

Pierre stuck out his tongue at Sherri, then turned to me. "It'll take forever to get security authorization to visit the camp. You'll have to fill out a lot of forms." He mimed throwing dollar bills at strippers.

"It's fine, just give them to me," I said, rubbing my temples with my fingers. "Pierre, can you arrange a visit to the ministry for when we get back from the camp?"

He blew air into his cheeks. "I know the minister well, of course; she is a family friend. But who knows if she'll agree to meet you? She doesn't normally take meetings with random strangers."

I was wrong about him. He wasn't a twat; he was a grade A cunt.

"Sure, well, give it a go, yeah?"

I closed my laptop, and by the time I'd packed my handbag, they were both gone.

4

THE EVENING DRAINED THE HEAT FROM THE AIR, BREATH-
ing cool ripples through my demure wrap dress as I
searched the grounds for the tiki bar. I'd only packed one
dress, filling the rest of my suitcase with modest cotton shirts,
panic-bought suits, and an optimistic gym kit. Quite a contrast
with my normal summer wardrobe, which comprised hipster
jumpsuits for days at UCL and bodycon dresses for endless nights
out with Rosy.

Rosy and I had met as graduate students at Warwick. It was
the first day of my master's and I'd forced myself out in search of
friends. But the Dirty Duck was silent: isolated postgrads sipping
half-pints, surrounded by stacks of books, studiously avoiding eye
contact. I looked at the books with envy. When reading lists were
released, they'd raced to the library to check them out. It hadn't
occurred to me. Now the shelves were empty, and I was being
fisted by Amazon.

"Those tits are magnificent!" Rosy's voice pierced the bar.

Everyone looked up and I looked down at my chest. My breasts, juicy and wobbly as caramel panna cottas, swelled over the V-neck of my jumper. I was having a great tit day. I turned and found Rosy looking straight at me, pretty and open-faced, her lipstick a vintage red, her skin lorry-driver white. She seemed so tall, though I struggled to separate her physical height from her self-assured, straight-backed confidence.

"Thank you," I said, my voice thin from underuse. "They're making up for lost time."

"Oh, but they look so natural. Was it expensive?" She sat next to me on the torn pleather sofa and her thigh brushed against mine. It was the most I'd been touched in a year.

"Nah, they're real, but they've been covered up most of my life. I've only just stopped wearing hijab. I'm Nadia, by the way." My hand rose and found itself suspended awkwardly between a wave and a salute.

"Rosy," she said. "And I'm officially intrigued." She picked up my Coke and took a sip. I thought of her saliva meeting mine on the wet glass. "There's no vodka in this?" she said with a grimace. "Give me two secs." She walked to the bar, ordered a shot, and tipped it into my Coke.

"OK, I'm all yours. Spill the beans." She sat down, and the movement released wafts of stale beer from the wizened couch.

"Erm, I guess I've transitioned out of being Muslim," I said, scanning the bar for beards. The penalty for apostasy is still beheading. Although probably not in Warwick.

She handed me the vodka Coke. I'd never drunk alcohol before, but I was too embarrassed to say that. It tasted like bleach.

"So, you're a trans-Islamist?" she said, tapping her chin with her Tipp-Ex white fingernail. "No, I guess that would be a trans person who joined al-Qaeda."

I raised an eyebrow. "Imagine al-Qaeda having a trans battalion. That would be peak rainbow-washing."

She snort-spluttered and I watched with satisfaction.

"You're just a regular heretic, then? Well, I commend your bravery." She bowed in my direction.

Bowing, except in prayer, was considered blasphemous in our house. Mum was once invited to a garden party at Buckingham Palace in honor of some charity interfaith tripe and she spent the entire lead-up excitedly preparing her refusal to curtsy. The queen only stayed ten minutes in the end, and Mum didn't get to meet her. Sounds like karma. Couldn't say that to Mum, though; karma's blasphemous too.

"Tell me more." Rosy pulled her bleach-blond hair into a pony-tail, surplus tufts erupting around the elastic with careless beauty. "Why'd you leave Islam? Is it, like, the standard Catholic sob story? Pedo imams?"

I swallowed and crossed my arms. It was all so recent, the pain liquid and fresh; I couldn't look directly at it.

"Mate," I said, "I had a monobrow and mustache topped off with a headscarf. Pedos looked straight past me. Honestly, it hurt."

"Aw, poor baby! An unloved, hairy little vole." She stretched and her belly button winked at me.

I forced a laugh. The irony. I was loved back then, when I was young and formless, easily fitting into the mold laid out for me. The perfect little Muslim girl who enjoyed nothing more than racking up heaven points: extra prayers, extra fasts, extra helpful to

Mum and Granddad. Sweet and shiny as jelly that dissolved on contact with the outside world.

Rosy went to the bar and returned with two double vodka Cokes, signaling, to my relief, that I'd earned an extended audience with her. As I drank, vodka sloughed cells from my pink virgin throat, and my inhibitions contorted and dissolved.

"It's really nice to meet you," I said, peering up at her with pathetic desperation. "I've had a tough year. Mum was livid when I stopped being Muslim . . . she's sort of disowned me."

"For real? Well, fuck her." She pulled me into a hug, her chest warm as an electric blanket. When she released me, I saw my brown foundation had smeared onto her T-shirt.

"Oh, God." I sucked my finger and tried to rub it off. "I'm literally leaking onto you. Promise I'm not normally such an oversharing loser."

She held my fingers still, her palm hot against my skin. I looked up and our eyes met.

"I like it," she said.

I clung to Rosy from that day, infatuated by the differences between us. She expected love, believed in its abundance, attracted it everywhere she went. While I'd retreat into corners, spiky and defensive, Rosy effortlessly created intimacy. She made perfect eye contact, listened with rapt attention, laughed generously—Rosy embodied charisma and everyone wanted her.

The first time Rosy and I kissed was at a house party. We'd been dancing for hours, winding our bodies around each other in a culturally appropriative manner. Toward the end of the night, she pushed me against the chipboard wallpaper, her chest pressing into mine as she kissed me. I barely noticed all the eyes trained on us.

Ever so briefly, I'd become part of her, and my life reoriented itself into a single-minded pursuit of that feeling.

In the weeks that followed, Rosy christened me her "main ho" and I unfurled and shone under the title. I devoured our friendship and cherished the drunken sex she sometimes offered. We shared everything—the mundane details of our lives, the tiny frustrations, the inconsequential victories—until her emotional landscape became as familiar as my own. It was a togetherness I'd always longed for, that I'd never felt I deserved.

After we graduated from Warwick, we rented a flat together in London and she founded a succession of businesses while I struggled through a PhD. She taught me that sexual possessiveness was passé, so we occasionally dated other people. But they were never serious, just fresh material for the conversation that threaded between us year after year.

When I told her my mum forbade birthdays at home, declaring them ungodly, Rosy threw me a surprise birthday extravaganza. Eighteen candled cupcakes and eighteen wrapped gifts, one for every birthday I'd missed while living with my mum, each present referencing a joke from the lengthy repertoire we'd crafted together. In the card she wrote: "Remember when you farted so loudly that Zoom asked if you wanted to unmute?" I'd never felt so seen and so loved.

Four years after disowning me, my mother abruptly reappeared in my life. She'd ring me sporadically and invite me to community events back in Leicester, trying to pick up where we left off. I obliged without enthusiasm or trust. Rosy was my family now. She'd built me a home when I didn't have one. Had loved me because of who I was, not despite it.

Our twenties tipped over into our thirties, and still Rosy and I grew more densely intertwined. I drank her up, forever unquenchable, dreading the moment I would lose her.

Then I lost her.

THWACK! MY BARE SHOULDER STUNG, AND I TURNED TO SEE Tom standing behind me, lit by a ghoulish beam of white light. Square metal lights were affixed throughout the compound, their beams intersecting like lasers against the darkness.

"Mosquito." Tom opened his palm to reveal a tiny corpse, legs askew.

"That sneaky little motherfucker." I rubbed the reddening bite on my shoulder.

"I've been waiting in the tiki bar, pet. Are you standing me up?"

I looked up at Tom's neck, which was so thick he couldn't button his polo shirt all the way. How did one acquire neck muscles? I imagined him tying a dumbbell to his neck and nodding.

"Sorry, I've been wandering around looking for it," I said, ashamed to be such a poor ambassador of my gender.

"Allow me." He took my hand, and we walked through the cafeteria and out the back door. At the top of the steps, we looked down at a tiny Hawaiian paradise. People in shorts and T-shirts were drinking and chatting around brightly colored picnic benches in a clearing flanked by artificial reeds. On the far side stood a bar under a triangular bamboo roof, plastic floral leis hanging from exposed beams. I almost cried with relief when I saw the bar stocked all the normal brands of alcohol. After ten years with Rosy,

I'd come to appreciate a drink. I ordered a double Hendrick's and tonic while he got a lager, and we both leaned back against the bar. Reggae music percolated through the air, and I smiled, feeling a bit like I was on holiday.

"You should smile more," said Tom, watching me. "You look pretty when you smile."

I stared at him but decided against violence.

We found an empty picnic table and sat down, our hands wrapped around our drinks, palms growing pink against the cold glass. I took a sip, flooding my veins with glorious floral gin. This wasn't so bad.

A serious expression came over Tom's face and I braced myself, expecting to hear dire moral concerns about the concept of de-radicalization.

"Who d'you think would play me in a movie?" he asked.

It's interesting, lowering your standards for someone, only to find them valiantly remaining subpar.

I considered his improbably square jaw, his curly blond hair, and could only think of cartoon characters.

"Prince Charming from *Shrek*? Or maybe Kristoff from *Frozen*?"

He nodded gravely. "I prefer Kristoff, because of my military service values."

"Right." I looked over his shoulder to see who else was in the bar.

He squinted at me. "You'd be played by Malala Yousafzai."

"Malala fucking Yousafzai? She was literally shot in the face."

"I mean, because of her Nobel Prize. I could see that happening for you one day."

"Oh, fuck that. I want to be played by Priyanka Chopra."

Tom reached over the table to stroke my arm. "I think you're really banging, you know."

I moved my arm away and put my hands in my lap. It was my first day, and I didn't want everyone to think I was a total hussy. Well, to know it.

"Sorry," I said. "I'm just worried about how it'll look."

He nodded, gulped down a third of his lager, and wiped the foam from his lips. "First time in Iraq for you, love? I've been here twice before, with the army, down in Basra. When this job came up, it felt natural like, coming back here. I already knew the place, could hit the ground running. It's a good fit for me. I get on with the Iraqis, got some good lads on the team. Don't even mind the heat. How about you? Why'd you choose Iraq?"

I sighed and looked up at the starless night sky curving over Baghdad, a tiny plane flashing as it cut through the darkness. "I barely thought about it, if I'm honest. Just didn't want to be in London anymore."

Tom nodded, and I caught a glimpse of my reflection in his blue eyes. "Aye, we're all running from something."

"Including you?" I drained my glass and the gin slid through my spine, displacing the stress in my back.

He shrugged, his shoulders rippling like a minor mountain range. "Left the army, hated civvy life, fucked up my relationship. It's simpler out here. The only thing I really miss is my nana. She's my best mate. And the squaddies, like. The money's good here, I've not had to pay rent in years. I managed to buy a little flat for my nana in South Shields. Best thing I ever did. Family's everything, you know."

What's with the working-class love of a nana? Though I couldn't relate, I found it endearing. This hulk of a man, his muscles straining against his clothes, openly emoting about his grandma. What's not to like?

"It's how Jordan Peterson says, a man's gotta look after the family. That's the problem with all this woke rubbish, women are forced to be men nowadays."

Oh, there it is. Maybe that's how he got into Lawrence of Arabia. *Seven Pillars of Wisdom* sounds a lot like *12 Rules for Life.*

I shook my head slowly. "You probably think I'm too masculine. Coming to a dangerous place, all on my own, to run a big UN program?"

He looked wounded, as though I'd bitch-slapped him with my oversize labia.

"That's not what I meant. It's impressive, like, what you're doing. I just think lasses deserve to be taken care of."

I wondered how he'd react, knowing I was last taken care of by another lass. "That's why it went tits up," he would say. "Too many tits!" No. No man would ever say that.

I glanced around the bar, which was mostly empty now, dark palm trees swaying high overhead, low-slung fairy lights casting dots of color over the last patrons, their shoulders rounded as they leaned into hushed conversations. There was no opening for me.

I imagined walking back to my room alone, opening the door, and falling into a cavernous void. It felt surreal to exist without being loved. The universe would realize its mistake, swallow me back into clay, use my molten parts to create a new, superior person.

So when Tom asked if I wanted another round, I agreed.

"How's your first day been, then?" he asked, setting another gin and tonic in front of me, perching his bum on the bench and swinging his legs over.

"It's a fucking disaster." I caught an ice cube between my teeth and channeled my anxiety into it as I crunched. "I don't know what I'm doing, Lina's got no time to teach me, and Pierre and Sherri think I'm incompetent, which I am. We're meant to be visiting the camp up in Ninewah, but apparently it's impossible to get security authorization. I reckon it'll be a week before everyone realizes I'm a total impostor."

"Doll, you know I'm head of security? I'll do your authorization. Give me the paperwork at breakfast."

I dropped my head into my palms, then looked up at him with simpering gratitude. "Really? Thank you."

When the bar closed, Tom walked me back to my room, and we stood outside the plywood door as insects swirled around the ceiling light above our heads. We remained for a moment, suspended at the threshold, abandoned by conversation, newly conscious of our bodies. Yearning for intimacy, settling for proximity. He pulled me into a hug and I squeezed my eyes shut, replacing his massive red arms with Rosy's delicate alabaster ones. My legs wobbled, as though full of all the tears I'd refused to cry. No one would ever replace her.

He tilted my head toward him, his thick fingers rough on my skin, his mouth dry and chapped against mine. I felt nothing. Still, I clung to his weighty body, tethering myself like a balloon nearly lost to the sky.

5

A BULLETPROOF VEST DESCENDED ONTO ME. MY KNEES dipped, surprised by the weight, and the distance between my shoulders and toes contracted; five foot eight in heels, five foot four in body armor. I stuck my arms in the air, like a child being helped into a school jumper, and Tom fastened the straps around my sides. The noon sun was infernal above the car park at Erbil airport in northern Iraq. I hoisted myself into an SUV, scorched particles of air fighting to escape my vest, boils of sweat bubbling on my face.

Tom leaned over me, trying to click my seat belt into place, his dry face close to my molten skin. When you're assigned close personal protection, they assume you've become incapable of putting on your own seat belt. The task is outsourced to a security guy who's done ten thousand hours in the gym only to spend his working life slotting metal tongues into plastic grooves. I found it both infantilizing and titillating, sitting there limp-armed while Tom tucked me in. He appeared not to share the sentiment, staring at the sweat erupting from my forehead, dribbling down my nose, and pooling into a salt lake mustache.

"How are you already this fucked?"

I stuck out my lower lip, ashamed of my weak constitution. "I'm hot."

"It's a sign of insufficient cardio training," he said, like a knob.

Is this what menopause feels like? I thought of my mother, who went through the change when I was a teenager. She would scream at lone socks whose partners had absconded between the washer and the dryer, sob when she got stuck behind a learner driver, maniacally laugh at the price of kitchen roll in Sainsbury's. I thought she was unhinged. Maybe she was just on fire.

Sherri sat next to me and wittered on about talking points for the camp focus group. Pierre had wangled his way out of the trip, and in that moment, I envied him.

Outside the city limits, we reached a series of checkpoints where control passed from Kurdish to Arab paramilitary groups. A few years earlier, these groups had battled ISIS, then they had battled each other. Now they spent all day in narrow booths by the side of the road battling their own PTSD. I wondered if they missed the fighting. We handed over rafts of permission documents, handpicking different papers for each officer. They didn't recognize each other's authority, so giving the wrong document to the wrong guy could have forced us to suspend the trip.

Over the ramp past the final checkpoint, the Ninewah countryside expanded into view. We swept along a highway, bombed-out craters erased with fresh tarmac, the surrounding hills feigning innocence. Mile upon mile of green. Not the brazen, verdant green of England, but a gentle, halting green, grateful for sparse rain.

Desert dogs, majestic like sand-colored huskies, nosed through rubbish thrown from passing cars. We overtook a white pickup truck, like the ones ISIS fighters used to ride, but instead of black-clad men holding AK-47s, there were only piles of giant ripe watermelons on the back.

The grass dissolved into a bleak, rocky terrain as we approached the camp. Abundance had no place here. About a hundred curved blue-and-white tents stood behind a mesh fence topped with curls of barbed wire that stretched out like a tangled Slinky. It was oddly regimented, with identical, equidistant tents and periodic toilets. As planned as Milton Keynes, if Milton Keynes was designed to indefinitely detain ISIS wives.

Camp guards dragged open the gates and pointed to a parking space in front of the portable cabin that served as reception. I squirmed around in my bulletproof vest, struggling to unlatch my seat belt, then pushed open the heavy door, dangled my legs out, and jumped.

A white gazebo had been erected to host our focus group, and as we walked toward it, my stomach stayed behind in the car, my torso a whistling void of fear. I was about to meet real-life ISIS women. The gazebo creaked in the wind, white tarpaulin fluttering, empty plastic chairs arranged in a circle. It looked like the setting for a Mafia wedding, the kind where guns are drawn and the bride ends up dead. My sweat turned cold as a group of women walked in wearing long abayas and headscarves. They were dressed no differently than my mother, but still, I was terrified.

The women faced us, then took their seats.

"What bait spying shit is this?" said a girl from East London. The familiarity of her accent drained the tension from my body.

There's nothing scary about a hijabi rude girl from Mile End. Nostalgia summoned an image of Whitechapel Market, Rosy and me weaving through, eating our Brick Lane samosas after a Saturday at Spitalfields. I used to think it was the biggest dump on Earth, but that was before I came to Iraq.

The girl leaned on her forearms, her severe facial expression incongruous with her diamanté-trimmed headscarf. I too had loved diamanté headscarves, back when I was religious, bringing a hint of the nineties WAG to my glamourless Islamic life.

"Erm, not spies, I promise," I said. Not the most professional way to open a focus group. I took a breath and started again. "Hello, everyone, thanks for joining us. We're from the UN, and we'd like to share some ideas and proposals with you today. But first, we'd love to hear from you about your immediate needs and concerns. Everything you say is confidential, and we encourage you to be open and honest." I tried to shift my gaze around the room, but East London girl had me transfixed.

"Oooh . . ." She rubbed her hands together. "Obviously, I should trust you. The UN is definitely not a colonial conspiracy that gives fake legal cover to Western war crimes."

I covered my mouth to hide a smile. I'd used those exact words as a teenager. God, my teachers must have thought I was such a prick.

Despite my urge to clap back at East London girl, I had to give other women a chance to speak. I ignored the girl and looked around the circle, nodding encouragingly. "So, how can we help? Does anything come to mind?"

A pretty white woman with hazel eyes and angular cheekbones

pointed at the kids running in the dirt outside. "The children need education," she said in an Australian accent. "The authorities have been promising us for a while, but we've seen nothing yet."

I cocked my head at Sherri. "Isn't UNICEF doing that?" I whispered. Even I knew UNICEF was responsible for kids.

She shrugged. "Interagency drama."

"If you really wanna help, bruv," said East London girl, "let us out of the fucking camp."

Everyone turned to look at me, and Sherri nodded her treacherous little head.

"Well, yes, I was coming to that. We're designing a rehabilitation program that could help send you home, and we'd love your feedback on our proposed plans." I glanced down at my notes. "There would be several steps. First, we'd need to interview you in detail about how you entered ISIS territory, and any role you played—"

"Yeah, thought so," East London girl interrupted. "You're here to interrogate us and get us arrested and hanged. Admit it!"

The other women started murmuring among themselves, and I tried to tamp down the dissent with my hands.

"No! Not at all. Nothing like that!"

The girl's chair clattered backward as she stood up and left the gazebo, whacking a floppy piece of plastic sheeting on her way out. There was a moment of silence, as though a performance had just ended.

Then a chubby woman with blotchy patches of rosacea raised her hand.

"Could we get some sanitary towels? And crayons and coloring books for the kids?"

"Ja, and get that Sara girl executed, will you?" said a taut German woman, and they all laughed. "We would be happy for any program to send us home."

Sara, I thought, that's her name.

Sherri pointed to a stack of containers on the far side. "We've brought some supplies with us," she said. "There are definitely sanitary towels in there. But I'm keen to hear what else you need."

I couldn't concentrate. Sara had captured me. That bolshiness, the vulnerability it undoubtedly masked, the way she reminded me of my teenage self—right down to the diamanté headscarf and the postcolonial-theory-based backchat. Without deciding to, I rose from my chair, excused myself, and walked out in search of her. I spotted her turning in to a tent and followed her in.

THE TENT WAS CURVED, LIKE A GARDEN POLYTUNNEL FOR GROW-ing vegetables. Woven mats covered the wide, long space; thin foam mattresses stacked on one side, neat piles of clothes and plastic bags in the far corner. Half a dozen women must have shared the tent, though Sara was the only one there. It was darker and a few degrees cooler than outside.

"What, you gonna stalk me now?" she said, turning around.

"Listen, I'm British Asian, like you. Could we chat, just informally?"

She raised her hands to her open mouth. "No shit. That must mean you're on my side." Her hands dropped back to her sides. "Nah, you're a coconut sellout, for real."

My cousins called me a coconut on my rare visits to Leicester, making the trips even rarer. I hated the assumption that eschewing your entire culture, heritage, and religion made you white on the inside.

"Come on, Sara, I'm only here to help."

Her eyes took a sharp left. "How d'you know my name? Spy."

"The other women mentioned it. They don't seem massive fans of yours, by the way."

She huffed and walked to the back of the tent. "Well, you ain't gonna catch me blabbing to a bunch of foreign agents. We'll end up on trial, with you lot testifying against us."

"Sara, that's literally the opposite of what I'm trying to do. I promise." My back ached from being stooped at the entrance. I took a couple of daring steps into the tent, where the ceiling was high enough for me to stand straight.

She looked over her shoulder at me and paused.

"Just give me two minutes. Please."

"Well, take your shoes off," she said eventually. "Don't be bringing that dirt up in here."

It took forever to unlace my heavy-duty leather boots, which I'd stress-bought just before leaving London.

"Bro." She looked at the boots. "You thought you was joining the army or something?"

"I didn't know what to expect," I said lamely, as I extracted one sweat-sodden foot after the other, blisters already starting to form.

Sara rustled around in a blue plastic bag, plucked out a packet of local-brand gummy bears, then pulled down two thin mattresses for us to sit on. I lowered myself onto one, slowly, like a pregnant woman, the bulletproof vest restricting my range of motion.

"I know about the law and testifying and that." She tore open the packet. "I did mock trial at school."

I was thrilled by the conversational opening. "For real? Me too!"

"I lost, obviously," she said. "Judge wasn't about to let a scarfie win a terrorism case. Racist."

I studied her face for traces of irony, delighted to find her eyes disappearing into a smile. The balls on this girl.

"Well, I had to defend a flasher in my mock trial," I said. "Put me right off the law."

"Swear down? That's gross. My best mate Jamila's husband flashed me once. His pink thing looked like an uncooked sausage. Haram upon haram, you get me?"

I laughed, despite myself, then tried to arrange my face into a sympathetic expression. "That must've been horrible. For you and your friend."

She shrugged, tossing a gummy bear into her mouth. "They're both dead now."

The air became static, tinny, like when an audio lead is pulled from an amp. Though she tried to project nonchalance, I saw the contraction of her body, the darkening of her eyes.

"I'm sorry to hear that, Sara. That must have been really hard."

"I've had worse happen." She gazed at the tent opening as though expecting someone to walk in. "Anyway," she said, with a dismissive tilt of her head, "you aren't sorry. Jamila was in ISIS, so you probably think she deserved to die."

I sighed and rubbed my eyes. "It depends. If she killed people, enslaved people, tortured people, then yeah, I would say she deserved to die."

Sara arched her thick, unplucked eyebrows. "All right, so you're gonna tell the truth, is it? I'm sick of you people pretending you don't despise us. I want it straight."

"I'll give it to you straight," I said, looking her dead in the eyes. "You're stuck here because people are afraid of you. Should they be?"

"Nah, I never done nothing violent." She tore the head off a gummy bear and chewed its body. "What, you think I'm gonna shank you?" She pointed the gummy's head at my Kevlar vest.

"Are you?"

"They don't let us have knives in here," she said, looking wistfully around the tent.

She suddenly pointed the bag of gummy bears at me and I jumped. Her head tipped back as she laughed. I took a yellow gummy, squeezed it like a stress ball between my fingers, my brain trying to decide whether it was afraid or excited.

I watched her revel in the reaction she'd caused, her eyes wet with laughter, her cheeks a pinched red. She was sitting cross-legged, wearing an enormous black abaya that made it hard to discern her figure. It was probably a hand-me-down. I dared not imagine what had happened to its original owner. Beneath the folds of the abaya, Sara's naked little feet stuck out, tiny shards of pink nail polish visible on her toenails. It looked like it had been deliberately scratched off.

"What happened there?" I pointed at her toes and she tucked them under her bum.

"Some of the other women got angry. They said it's haram."

I smiled. "Didn't you know that already? My mum never let me wear nail varnish. Apparently, it stops you from being clean for prayer."

She chewed and looked up at the daylight straining at the blue ceiling. "Is that why? No one ever told me. My parents aren't that religious, so I don't know all the rules."

"You weren't even brought up religious?" I said softly. "How did you end up here?"

She exhaled heavily and put down the sweets. "Jamila, innit. She was wicked. My ride or die, you know? Until she fucked off to join ISIS. School was so crap after that. I didn't have no other friends, and my parents don't get me, they're bare traditional, act like we're still in Pakistan, never let me go out or nothing. Then Jamila started messaging, saying 'Come to Iraq, it's paradise here,' and I got excited, like I finally had something to look forward to. And I wanted to help other Muslims; the West has been bombing them for time. I watched videos and got irate, thought I could do something."

That's it? She was just a normal kid who rebelled against her parents, looking for some excitement in her life? A teenage idealist who believed she could change the world. Why was she still trapped here?

"Hasn't anyone tried to get you out already?" I asked, my forehead rippling with incomprehension.

She shook her head. "Nah, it's all fucked-up, fam, everyone thinks I'm some criminal terrorist. My parents disowned me and I never heard nothing from the British government. But I swear I never hurt no one."

I extended my hand toward hers, but she shifted out of reach. "Trust me, Sara, I totally understand. I know what it's like to lose your best friend. People don't get it, but that grief is real. And my mum was strict too; I couldn't wait to get out of that house."

"Yeah, but you didn't join ISIS and end up locked in a camp without your . . ."

I shook my head as she trailed off. "I've just been luckier than you, that's all."

Sara fell silent, and the mood in the tent felt heavy and oppressive. She looked up at me, her eyes framed by luxuriant thick lashes.

"Are those fake lashes?" I asked, trying to lighten the mood.

She snorted. "Imagine. I'd wake up at night with the fundys snipping them off my face. 'Your eyes' hair too beautiful,'" she said in a mock Arab accent.

We both laughed, and I caught the scent of her gummy bear breath, the sweet undertones turning sour at the edges.

I cast my eyes around our sparse surroundings. "So, what do you do all day?"

She leaped up, like a kid at show-and-tell, and fetched a plastic bag from the back of the tent. Its contents tipped onto the floor in front of me: a comic book, a few sticks of gum, colored yarn plaited into bracelets, and a sock with doll's eyes and bunny ears sewn onto it. She immediately picked up the sock and stuffed it back into the bag.

"What's that? A toy?"

She paused, searching my face. "It's . . ." After a moment, she abandoned the sentence and picked up the comic book, handing it to me. "I'm reading *X-Men* right now. We swap, so sometimes I get different ones, but *X-Men* is my favorite. I know it's a bit childish, but there's not that much choice. It's comics or the Quran, and I can't understand the Quran by myself, I have to watch preachers on YouTube to help me."

She unwrapped a stick of gum and folded it into her mouth as

I leafed through the comic, tracing my fingers over the familiar illustrations. "I used to *love* the X-Men! I always wanted to be Storm."

She leaned over me, blowing a sticky pink bubble, and turned the pages until she found a large drawing of Storm. The gum snapped and she tucked it back into her mouth.

"She looks best in this scene, don't you think?" she said.

Storm was flying through the sky, her body powerful and commanding, her swirling mass of hair at one with the wind.

I nodded and smiled. "She looks amazing."

She turned the pages again, stopping at an image of Rogue, her full-bodied auburn hair framed by signature white locks. "I know she can't use her powers that much, but Rogue's my favorite. It's mad that she can't touch people or get close to anyone."

I wondered when Sara had last been held, when she'd last been looked after. Next to hers, my loneliness felt petulant and entitled.

"You shouldn't be here," I said, placing the comic book on the floor and reaching for her hand. She let me take it. "Let's get you back home."

She hesitated and averted her eyes. "You really think you can help? I need . . ."

I could see words catching in her throat, and I gave her space to continue, but eventually she closed her mouth.

"Look, if we do a security assessment, that should persuade the British government you don't pose a threat—"

She flinched, yanking her hand away from me, her entire body snapping shut. "So you *do* work for the security services." She stood up and beckoned for me to stand. "You're clapped, bruv."

I levered myself up with great difficulty. "We have to demonstrate that you aren't dangerous, surely you can understand that. Or have you got a better idea? I'm all ears."

"I bet you're wearing a wire under that straitjacket." She tapped her forefinger on my vest.

"Don't be ridiculous, this isn't *The Sopranos*, of course I'm not wearing a wire." I struggled against my vest, but I couldn't budge it.

"Get the fuck out of here."

She watched me as I fumbled with all the laces on my boots, her face completely still.

I stood up, hovering by the entrance. "Just think about it, Sara—"

She pushed me and I stumbled out of the tent into the harsh daylight. A sea of identical tents surrounded me, and I had predictably lost my bearings. I started walking toward the fence, with a vague plan to trace the perimeter until I found the reception cabin. A hand grabbed my shoulder and I almost shat myself, thinking it was an ISIS woman coming to stab me in the face. But it was only Tom.

"What d'you think you're playing at?" He gripped my upper arm and marched me back toward the focus group. "Everyone's looking for you. Do you have any idea how dangerous these women are? You could have been killed, you absolute idiot."

Tents streamed past us, little faces watching us through cracks in the blue-and-white plastic sheeting. I'd thought nothing of going after Sara. Despite the lack of supporting evidence, she made me feel safe.

"A girl ran out of the focus group and I just wanted to talk to her. Sorry, I wasn't thinking."

He shook his head, refusing to look at me. "I'm not gonna lie, Nadia, I'm raging."

Did he . . . care about me? I looked at his comically large stature, his face an explosive red. He looked like a cartoon Hercules who'd just saved a kitten from Mount Vesuvius.

I didn't hate it.

6

I SCOURED THE INTERNET FOR EVERYTHING I COULD FIND about Sara and her friend Jamila. Channeling the spirit of a brilliant yet undervalued CSI detective, I set out likely timelines and pieced together possible narratives. Everything pointed to the same conclusion: the girls were young, naive, and reckless, but they weren't terrorists.

Here's how it went down. Jamila met an intense Belgian man on a dating app, a convert called Wilbert. Friends told the papers he'd love-bombed the shit out of her (and later got her bombed for real). He said they were soulmates when they'd never met, sent her creepy teddy bears with hearts on their outsides, and texted her every hour of every day. He was clearly a sociopath, with a face carved from a red flag, but Jamila was a teenager. She would have only seen the attention, the devotion, and the melodrama she'd always craved. I dared not imagine what I'd have done if dating apps had existed when I was young. My self-esteem was so low, I'd have self-immolated for a man who called me pretty.

Wilbert told Jamila that the media coverage of ISIS was fake, disinformation and propaganda concocted by Islamophobes. But he needn't have bothered. Jamila's love-addled brain was so far gone, she'd have followed him anywhere. And what could I say? Where wouldn't I have gone for Rosy? Well, probably not Mosul, but maybe somewhere equally shit, like Dubai.

Wilbert traveled to Syria, but ISIS quickly transferred him to Iraq. Once he'd settled in Mosul, he planned every detail of Jamila's trip, sending smugglers to meet her at the border, marrying her as soon as she arrived. Those first weeks were euphoric. Liberated from school, from parents, from the banality of teenage life, Jamila had become the star of her own romantic drama. Amid that heady rush, she persuaded Sara to join her. Just two months after Sara arrived, Jamila was pregnant and calling her parents from stolen mobile phones, begging to be rescued. She told of daily beatings at Wilbert's hand, of women stoned to death in the public square, of bloody, severed heads left in the street. Sara never contacted home, and little was known about her time in Iraq, but, harangued by the press, her parents disowned her. They wept openly, telling reporters they couldn't understand why she'd left, vowing never to forgive her.

Jamila, her husband, and their unborn child were killed in a drone strike on Mosul in 2016. She was just sixteen years old.

I closed my laptop and rubbed my eyes. It was three a.m. and I'd been researching the girls for six hours straight. Though I'd read similar cases as part of my academic work, it felt completely different now I'd met Sara. Stories that once seemed so distant now felt visceral and real, their narrative threads snaking toward me, weaving into my own. I was devastated for the girls, but there was another feeling too, a gnawing discomfort that I struggled to place. I switched off the desk lamp and climbed into bed without bothering to undress. That's when I realized, suddenly and with absolute certainty, the reason I felt so moved and so disturbed by Sara's and Jamila's stories. The truth was, it nearly happened to me.

When I was fifteen, I spent the summer at Muslim camp. On a wet July morning, I huddled with my best friends, Fatima and Usrah, outside Central Leicester Mosque waiting for the coach, our rucksacks between our legs, imagining the boys we would meet.

As we settled into the coach, a woman with a teardrop face and ginormous wobbling breasts said a prayer.

"We ask you, Allah," she said, standing in the middle of the aisle, her palms turned up to the heavens, "to grant us the honor of a martyr's death."

I didn't think death by traffic accident would count as martyrdom. Shouldn't she be praying for us to arrive safely? And what exactly would it feel like to bury my face in those breasts?

I said *Ameen*, like everyone else.

Our first class was Islamic Jurisprudence, and we sat at the back parceling out the boys between us, drawing sketches on the back of a glossary of Arabic terms. Skater Boi, in his baseball cap and baggy jeans, was mine, a nod to my obsession with Avril Lavigne. Usrah chose Witch-Hazel, a Pashtu man with a pointy chin and hazel eyes. It made for a confusing moniker because Usrah also spent the entire summer rubbing witch-hazel gel over her acne-ridden face. I shuddered when Fatima picked Brother Bear, a thickly bearded guy who looked exactly like my uncle.

It was odd, studying Islam at a conference center in rural Lancashire. Vertical planks of pine clad the walls of a room normally used for corporate away days, middle managers abandoning their suits for mufti. Today there was a real mufti, and rather than role-playing sales pitches, we were discussing the admissible sources of Shari'ah law.

We stayed awake the whole first night, sharing a Travelodge-style bedroom, Fatima in the only bed, Usrah and I wedged into sleeping bags on the floor, talking about the loaded glances we'd received from our new loves. At no point that summer did we actually talk to the boys. Fantasies levitate higher without the burden of real interaction.

A week into camp, we emerged from our room to an electric atmosphere that buzzed from one person to another like a fat bluebottle. The organizers stood whispering by the tall green hedges that encircled the large-windowed 1970s conference center. It was lunchtime before we finally heard the news.

"He's here!" said Usrah, sliding into the seat next to us in the dining room.

"Nah, for real? Anwar al-Awlaki?" said Fatima, smearing butter onto a piece of white bread that disintegrated further with every swipe.

I craned my neck, looking around.

"Not *here*, here. At the airport."

Anwar al-Awlaki was a celebrity Yemeni-American preacher whose lectures were sparky and funny. It was a stark contrast to the garbled, sleep-inducing monologues we were getting from the Egyptian cleric who'd been covering for him. Awlaki had been the planned camp headliner, but mysteriously canceled at the last minute. Now he'd arrived, and the excitement was contagious.

The next morning, Awlaki floated into the classroom wearing

a simple white thawb and round, gold-rimmed glasses, his curly beard trailing down his neck. He didn't look like a superstar, but when he spoke, our fingers froze above our doodles and we stared. He told stories about the prophet Muhammad and his followers, the charm of their foibles and the humanity of their doubts. He described heart-wrenching defeats, grinding years of suffering, and ecstatic victories. His words spun vivid images of the utopia they fought to create, the world as it could be if we emulated their self-sacrificing ways. A place that thrived in the service of God, where fairness and generosity prevailed, where communities of faith overcame isolation, disconnection, and ennui.

The more he taught, the higher we rose above our petty, ordinary lives. Concerns about parents, boys, excessive body hair, all the mundane chatter in our minds quietened, then melted away.

During one session, he stopped and pointed at us, three girls sitting behind a desk in the middle of the room, watching him with rapt attention.

"You know what gives me hope?" he said, in his lilting Arab-American accent. "These young sisters, sitting and listening with devotion, the light of Allah inside them. They are the future mothers of Islam."

A collective blush spread between us, the youngest participants in the course, and we dared not move an inch for fear of dispelling the moment. After that, and without discussion or intent, we stopped wearing makeup, scrubbed the varnish off our nails, and started waking up for dawn prayers.

One morning, I walked out of the prayer room into the ethereal violet twilight, running my hands along the dewy leaves, my heart in the heavens, my body a vehicle for the fulfillment of God's will, and I felt a wholeness so precious that I longed to hold on to it for eternity.

That day in class, an older woman asked Awlaki if it was OK to be friends with non-Muslims.

"Look at what the unbelievers have done to us," he said, a rare anger twisting his voice. "Muslims in Bosnia and Chechnya subjected to genocide while the rest of Europe stood by. Tens of thousands of Afghans slaughtered by indiscriminate bombing. Hundreds of thousands murdered in the invasion of Iraq. Our resources stolen today, just as they were stolen by the West's colonial ancestors. They changed their laws so they could persecute us, they used extraordinary rendition so they could torture us, they created Guantánamo so they could imprison us. You want to befriend them? You should be asking how to defend your brothers and sisters in faith."

One year later, Anwar al-Awlaki joined al-Qaeda. Had it been that summer, I would have gone with him.

7

A SANDSTORM DESCENDED UPON BAGHDAD, TRAPPING us on base as billowing orange clouds drowned out the daylight. I stared out my bedroom window, watching solid granules of sand lash against the panes of glass. Outside, visibility had reduced to a foot, but my vision was clearer than ever. Learning about Jamila's story, glimpsing Sara's misfortune, and realizing how easily their stories could have been mine, I knew my purpose now. It was obvious. Rescuing these women was what I was put on Earth to do. I no longer gave a fuck about the controversy, about the implications for my career, couldn't care less about impressing my colleagues. If a rehabilitation program could free these poor women, I would make it happen. I had to.

Intoxicated by my mission, I put on desert-compatible linens and strapped myself into army boots, before remembering that the entire city was in a weather-induced lockdown. I sat on my purple bedspread, clothes and cosmetics strewn around me, like a toy soldier air-dropped into a doll's house. I felt emasculated, the sensation arising synchronously with an urge to bully my colleagues. The cafeteria, I thought. I'll stalk and harass them there until they come up with a goddamn plan. There'd be no more pissing about; I was deadly serious now.

I pushed outside, stumbling through the opaque, rust-colored air, sand-laden winds sloughing dead skin cells off my face. Does this count as microdermabrasion? I wondered. Or is this a trailer for the apocalypse itself? A displeased god churning up the earth and whipping it into the sky.

I made it over the grass quad and ran into the cafeteria building. While I waited for the others, I picked over a miserable, carb-laden breakfast, my energy dissipating with every bite. Sherri was the next to arrive, sand sprinkled like cinnamon on her pumpkin hair. She was wearing a gray boiler suit, like a sewage worker. For the life of me, I couldn't figure out why.

"This is evidence of escalating climate change," she said, shaking sand off herself like a wet dog. "Desertification has annihilated vegetation cover, making sandstorms more frequent, and it's becoming economically debilitating. Something must be done."

Jesus Christ, can we focus on one impossible task at a time?

"Yeah, that's shit." I stood up, took hold of her elbow, and steered her away from the buffet, pulling her into a chair. "Listen, Sherri," I said, taking a seat across from her, the detritus of my breakfast strewn in front of me. "If we get the rehabilitation program off the ground, will countries actually take their women back?"

She looked up at the square ceiling lights, which were buzzing faintly. "Hmm . . . you'd need to get the embassies on board. They'll have a big say in the final decision."

Thinking of Sara's flimsy tent cowering beneath this vicious sandstorm, I was furious that the British government hadn't already repatriated her. "Let's start with the Brits. Can you arrange a meeting with them?"

She sighed and drummed her fingers on the table. "When I get a moment."

I plucked a dehydrated croissant from my breakfast tray and kneaded it with my thumbs, impressing my rage into its limp skin. "Don't you work for me? What are you doing with all your other moments?"

"You know how I feel about the program." Sherri crossed her arms, the fabric of her boiler suit growing taut around her shoulders. I realized she looked like a Ghostbuster. "And the focus group was clear," she continued. "The women's priority is for camp conditions to improve. I made a list of the supplies they requested, and I'm procuring items ready to distribute. I'd like to return to the camp soon, if you'll agree to it. Offering material help is a practical, unimpeachably positive thing we can do."

It never fails to surprise me, the myopia of the self-righteous. "Yeah, I'm happy to do that, Sherri, but we aren't here to furnish a prison. The point is to get them out." I shredded the croissant, flakes splintering over the table. "Get me a meeting with the British embassy and let's gauge their interest in repatriation. We can return to the camp afterward."

She turned up her peeling red nose and sniffed. "Fine."

She tried to stand up, but I caught her by the sleeve and dragged her back down.

"Hang on, you're an expert on psychosocial support, right?" I pulled a pen and notebook out of my bag. "In theory, what would be the most effective program we could offer?"

She started talking, reluctantly at first, but soon she was in full flow, enjoying the opportunity to show off her knowledge. She explained how we'd assess the women's needs, offer counseling, and reconnect them with their families back home. I wrote everything down, ready to compile into a formal program design document.

"How would the security clearance process work? And how do we get sign-off from the Ministry of Humane Affairs?"

She stood up. "You'll have to ask Pierre," she said, turning toward the buffet. "That's not my purview."

When people start using the word *purview*, that's when you know you're working with cunts.

I waited an hour for Pierre to show up, shifting my chair to face the door and staring at the dark entryway. My mind wandered back to the previous night, cuddling in bed with Tom. I'd been seeing him so frequently that the sex had already become comfortable and familiar. Sometimes it's easier to find pleasure with a person you don't care about. I was completely relaxed and uninhibited around him, my body quickly finding ecstasy against his. With Rosy, part of my brain was always switched on, recording every detail, afraid it'd be the last time.

My chin had lolled onto my shoulder by the time Pierre walked in, and I had dribbled onto my top. I jumped up and tried to grab him, but he shrugged me off.

"Mademoiselle, first I take my breakfast."

I followed him around the cafeteria as though he were a flight risk, my face inches from the back of his tailored suit. The moment he sat down, I unleashed.

"Why haven't you arranged a meeting with the Minister of

Humane Affairs? Have you even requested one? There are vulnerable women in the camp relying on us; we've got to start the program ASAP."

He took a leisurely sip of his black coffee, peeled a banana, and sliced it over his bowl of cereal.

"You came back, how they say, twisted in the pants? Perhaps you should take your time, enjoy the place a little."

I stared, willing him to choke on his cornflakes. "I don't know why you're here, Pierre, but I didn't move to Iraq for shits and giggles. We've got a job to do."

He stretched and leaned back, cracking his knuckles. "Ah, this is a better question, why are we here? The UN overlords decide they look impotent in the matter of ISIS brides, so they create a shiny new agency. But why? The Iraqis don't want it. The home countries don't want it. They just need to be *seen* to act. Of course, you don't understand this; you are a baby chicken who thinks it can fly."

He wasn't wrong. Live poultry probably grasped the political dynamics better than I did. On the other hand, I had only been in Iraq for a week.

"Goddamn it, Pierre. I don't care about the whole political backstory. We've got UN backing and a big budget. There must be something we can do!"

He laughed, a cynical, villainous laugh. "She doesn't care about the politics," he said to an imaginary audience. "She's even more stupid than she seems." Shifting his gaze back to me, he jabbed a finger toward the window. "This is the fourth sandstorm this month. It's a national crisis; crops are failing, flights are grounded, no one can go to work. You think the Iraqi government will prioritize you and your *petit* program? This is no longer a British protectorate, mademoiselle."

I considered his smug, blemish-free face, the elegant drape of his suit, the silent movement of his Swiss watch. How could he empathize, this coddled son of the French establishment—when had he ever been left wanting?

"Well, I'd better tell Lina that the famous Pierre, son of an ambassador, can't secure a meeting with the minister."

The smile slid off his face, and his spoon clattered as he dropped it into the bowl. "Who told you about him? Do not ever mention my father, you hole of ass."

Ah, that's the spot.

I stood up, plucked a slice of banana from his cereal, and put it in my mouth.

"Set it up."

THE GREEN ZONE WAS HAUNTINGLY QUIET, ITS NATIONAL MON-uments cavernous and empty, would-be visitors shunned by swaths of concrete blast wall topped with cut glass. We pulled up next to an anonymous metal gate, a lone Gurkha idling outside the only indication that this was the British embassy. He walked to the window demanding our IDs, and we collected them together, handing them over in a wad. A walkie-talkie crackled on his belt, and he unlatched it and barked out our names. We waited there for thirty minutes, exposed and stripped of our IDs, like refugees floating on boats, locked out of Fortress Britain, the walls towering above us like the White Cliffs of Dover.

The gate slid open, and we entered a gravel parking lot. Dogs circled, sniffing for bombs, and armed guards followed, disemboweling the vehicle as we walked toward the security cabin. Inside, a woman with garlic breath caressed every inch of my body, paying special attention to my bra, then pushed me through a metal detector. Sherri followed shortly after. Our mug shots were snapped, passports copied, retinas scanned, and fingerprints taken. They confiscated our belongings, giving us pale green raffle tickets in their stead, and attached large badges to our chests, the letter *V* in bright red. It was more like being processed for prison than visiting the embassy of your home country.

"If you think that was bad," said Sherri, as we waited on round-bottomed plastic chairs in a reception area that looked like a regional bus station, "you should see how they treat the locals."

How could I explain a deradicalization program to a place whose entry procedure was literally a radicalizing experience?

A woman entered the reception. Wispy mouse-brown hair gathered into a bun and gold-framed spectacles on her sharp nose, she looked quintessentially civil servant.

"I'm Hannah, Counterterror," she said, shaking our hands. She had a home counties accent, a hint of smugness in her voice.

"Nadia and Sherri," I said.

We followed her through an intensively watered garden toward a large swimming pool, the potent smell of chlorine intensified by the heat. I wondered whether the drought in the southern provinces could be solved by reallocating this embassy's water supply. A pudgy, red-faced diplomat was doggy-paddling with vigor, spraying drops of water onto the flagstone. Hannah directed us to a bench by the pool, and we sat.

"I'm afraid the meeting rooms are out-of-bounds. Some big movers and shakers in today!"

I couldn't help but feel insulted. We must be pretty low down in the pecking order to be meeting by a pool.

"Thanks for seeing us," I said, as I watched a blond woman walk out of the bar opposite wearing a tropical-patterned bathing suit. "We're keen to get UNDO up and running and we'd like your guidance."

"And please let us know," Sherri interjected, "if you have any legal or ethical concerns."

I looked at Sherri, bludgeoning her with my eyes.

"Oh yes, we heard New York approved UNDO." Hannah opened a notebook and balanced it on her lap.

"We visited the camp," I said, "and I spoke to a young British girl there. I'm keen to understand how she, and others like her, could be repatriated. Would a rehabilitation program help her return to the UK?"

The blond woman lowered herself into the pool and started swimming laps.

"HMG hasn't given us a policy steer yet, but I don't see how it could hurt."

"OK, could you keep me posted if you hear anything?" I said, cycling through acronyms in my mind. HMG . . . Her Majesty's Government.

"I'm off on R & R next week, but I'll leave a note for my replacement." Embassy staff were constantly leaving on rest-and-recuperation breaks to manage their stress. I looked at the substantial swimming pool and the bar beyond, which had enormous TV screens affixed to the wall. It didn't seem that stressful.

"Any advice on how we can maximize chances of repatriation?" I tried to rearrange my legs on the wooden bench, but a slick of sweat had stuck them together.

She sucked on the end of her pen and flipped through her notebook. A drop of water landed on an open page, turning it translucent.

"Take it easy, Angie!" she said to the blond woman, who raised two wet thumbs.

She scanned through her notes. "Oh yes. HMG's new inclusion strategy commits to centering the marginalized and giving voice to the voiceless. We urge you to create a program inclusive of all genders and none, of all faiths and none, and of all sexualities and none."

I gaped at her. "Erm . . . ISIS wasn't particularly diverse, so that's not really relevant to the women in the camp."

"Peoples socialized as women," she corrected me.

"Right, people socialized as women in the camp . . . are cisgender, straight, and Muslim. Otherwise, they'd have already been beheaded."

"I'm afraid your approach does not meet the strictures of our inclusion policy. It limits my ability to offer future support." Her spectacles had steamed up in the heat, and she wiped them on her skirt, covering the lenses in tiny fibers.

Jesus Christ on the rainbow flag, was I being punk'd? It'd be difficult to find anyone in the world more marginalized, more despised than an ISIS widow. But even if they were innocent, even if they were victims of exploitation, we couldn't support them unless we found a secret pansexual lurking in one of the tents? The logic of HMG's civil service, that's the true harbinger of Britain's decline.

"Well, of course we have a robust inclusion policy," I said, smiling at Hannah as though she weren't a brain-dead automaton. "Sherri will send it over in the next couple of days. Absolutely nothing to worry about."

Hannah nodded at Sherri. "Good. I'll look forward to reviewing the document."

If Sara needed this bellend to get her home, she'd be stuck in the camp forever.

When we returned to the car, Sherri opened her mouth before I could say anything.

"I'm so pleased they've finally instituted a serious gender sensitivity policy," she said, clicking in her seat belt and grinning at me. "I've been campaigning for it my entire career."

Rosy would have wept laughing. "It's brilliant! You suddenly get superinvested in the job, only to discover you're surrounded by morons. Didn't I say it'd be a shit show?"

I gave Sherri my most derisive look. "I'm glad you feel that way, since you'll be writing the imaginary inclusion policy that I've just promised. But don't expect me to go searching for gay intersex Jews next time we're in the camp, because, news flash, *there aren't any there!*"

The car dropped us back at the UN compound, and I retreated to my room, my frustration dripping like dye into the gallons of empty time that flowed around me. I'd already forced Pierre to explain the security clearance process to me, and using that information, together with Sherri's description of psychosocial support, I'd been able to complete the program design documents. But implementation required permission from the Ministry of Humane Affairs, and Pierre still hadn't secured a meeting with the minister.

It felt torturous, the lack of agency, the endless waiting. It must have been even worse for the women in the camp. I thought of Sara's blue tent, like a plastic bag over her head, the air fast diminishing, her resistance only magnifying her powerlessness.

At moments like this, I missed prayer. It had been a gift. Tilting my head toward the sky, luminescent as though backlit by God himself, silently unburdening myself, inhaling the expansiveness of his deliverance. It had been a relief to surrender, to accept my smallness, to merge into a sacred whole. But you have to like God for it to work. These days, my attempts to pray devolved into expletive-filled rants. What's the point of you, I would say, if you let believers craft toy-shaped land mines that blow up little kids, you absolute knob?

I wondered if Sara could still pray, after every fucked-up thing she'd seen done in his name. It's one thing to be captivated by the theory: follow God's guidance and peace will reign on Earth. But, as with all utopian ideologies, the implementation had involved stuffing humanity into a concrete mold and chopping off every head that didn't perfectly fit. Only the truly callous could keep the faith after seeing that.

8

WE DROVE TO THE AIRPORT AT DAWN, THE CITY OF BAGH-
dad pink in its half sleep. The occasional taxi meandered
past us, its pace leisurely, its horn silent. A white van
pulled ahead, no doors on the back, and I glimpsed weighty meat
carcasses swinging from metal hooks. We turned onto a bridge,
the Tigris River stretching out on either side, its waters the color
of the sky, the gentle flow interrupted by a wooden boat, a man
casting his nets.

"Samoon," said Farris, as we idled at a set of traffic lights. Farris, who'd searched my suitcase on the first night, was a security
officer on Tom's team. He pointed toward a shop, where a man in
a scuffed apron stood shaping dough into spheres. "He is making
the traditional Iraqi bread. They use yogurt to make it lighter, and
put sesame seeds on top. It's very beautiful, especially fresh in the
morning. Shall I bring it for you?"

I looked at Sherri, my mouth salivating, saw the tremble of
desire in her eyes.

"That would be amazing, Farris."

He turned the car, mounted the pavement, and jumped out. Somewhat stretching the definition of "close personal protection," he locked us in the car and walked into the shop. We watched him talk to the baker, all the hand gestures in the world apparently necessary for this simple transaction.

"Don't tell Tom," said Farris, swinging the bag of bread over the headrest and starting the car. "This was an unauthorized stop. But I love to show you the best things of my country."

We tore the bread apart with our fingers, steam rising from the soft middle, its scent comforting and homely. My teeth met a little resistance from the crust, before sinking into the warm center, the salty flavor offset by full-bodied notes of sesame. It tasted so delicious, it was almost brazen—for a cheap, basic bread to achieve these heights, what a flex.

"Why can't we have this on base?" I said, stuffing another piece into my mouth.

Sherri grunted, bread pressing against her cheeks. "We prefer to be extorted by foreign contractors," she said, once she'd swallowed. "They import bleached, sliced bread for fifty times the price of this. That's our procurement process for you: rewarding foreign charlatans and shutting out honest, hardworking Iraqis."

Farris watched us through the rearview mirror, above the sway of his dangling prayer beads, smiling as we enjoyed the bounty of his motherland.

"Anytime you want, I will bring it for you," he said.

"You're a sweetheart, Farris," said Sherri. "The best Iraqi I know."

"The only Iraqi, I think, Miss Sherri," he said, laughing.

We flew to Erbil, drove to Ninewah, and arrived at the camp in the early afternoon. Though supplies had been sent ahead by road, Sherri insisted we personally distribute them to generate goodwill. I agreed readily, hoping to see Sara again, and keen to learn more about the other women.

Cardboard boxes were laid out along one side of a large white tent, ready for our arrival. We crouched over them, peeled off the Sellotape, and turned the items over in our hands: toothbrushes, socks, sanitary towels, boxes of crayons. A kid peeked through the plastic sheeting, spotted us, and ran off. Seconds later, a stampede of women swept through the tent and they filled their arms with goods, tearing them from each other's hands. The commotion almost lifted the plastic roof into the sky, panicked footsteps creating clouds of dust that filled my nose and throat. I turned around to cough, and when I looked back, every cardboard box was empty, and the women were gone.

I stood up and slapped the dirt out of my clothes.

"Right, well . . . I guess that's done," I said, as I scanned the space one last time. Sara wasn't there. Disappointment congealed in my gut, and I was surprised by the weight of it.

Sherri was livid, hands on her head, wrist-deep in her frizzy mane. "I made it absolutely clear to camp administrators that equitable distribution was a deal-breaker for us! They promised to organize the women into orderly queues, priority given to those with verifiable needs. This is just outrageously poor management!" She stormed off toward the reception cabin, looking for some unlucky administrator to chastise, while I started to break down the empty boxes, gathering them into a pile.

Farris, who'd been watching us, walked over to help. "We would all behave the same if we were needy," he said. "It's very sad, the situation of these women. Every day, I pray for Allah to help them."

We finished with the boxes, and I straightened up, looking at Farris: the dimples that gave him a permanent smile, the strength packed densely into his lean body. I wondered if his appetite for rule breaking extended beyond the illicit purchase of bread.

"Listen, Farris, there's a British girl here called Sara. I'd love to talk to her, but Tom went mental last time I wandered around on my own. You think you could get her for me?"

He looked around the empty tent. "I'm not supposed to leave you unprotected. But if it's important to you . . . ?"

"Yeah, it is. She's very young, and I'm worried about her."

He beckoned me to follow. "I will leave you in reception with Sherri and boss lady, it's safe there."

Stepping into the windowless Portakabin, I was assaulted by the din of the human-size air-conditioning unit and the vulgarity of the fluorescent strip lights. It was fair comeuppance, being stuck in these graceless spaces after spending my academic career dismissing advocates of rehabilitative design. I'd never thought architecture deserved a greater proportion of dwindling prison budgets, but I could see now that I was wrong. Being in this hideous reception cabin was inspiring in me a nihilistic hatred of humanity. I mean, would it kill them to plug in a lamp?

Several camp residents sat on chairs that lined the walls, waiting for their turn with boss lady—who was behind a desk on the far side, yelling back at Sherri with impressive confidence.

Farris walked over to boss lady and asked her a question in

Arabic, pointing at a large map of the camp tacked onto the wall. She stood up and tapped her finger on a spot before resuming her tirade against Sherri. Farris winked at me and left.

I scanned the room before opting to sit beside a Slavic-looking woman. As I sat down, I noticed burn scars on her left cheek, new ridges of skin shiny and exposed.

"Hello there, I'm Nadia from the UN," I said loudly. "You speak English?" I told myself I was projecting over the air-conditioning, but I was just using my embarrassing talking-to-a-foreigner voice.

She eyed me suspiciously and nodded.

"Nice to meet you!" I stuck out my hand, but she just looked at it.

"OK, then." My hand dropped onto the cold plastic chair. "Well, I'd love to discuss our proposed rehabilitation program. You weren't at the focus group, but perhaps you've heard about it from the other women?"

"Whatever you do, Russia will not take me back," she said, her accent made even rougher by an obvious smoking habit. "Program is waste of time for me. Maybe for those from Western Europe, you can do something."

I thought back to my research. "But a Russian woman was recently repatriated from Syria."

She laughed derisively. "Her. She was kidnapped by her husband. I came of my free will."

The air conditioner seemed to intensify its frigid blast. Would it be a faux pas to ask why, I wondered, like asking a prisoner what they were in for?

"Erm, so, what brought you here?"

"I'm Chechen," she said simply.

Fair enough, mate, I thought. We both looked up at the gold plastic clock, its numbers obscured by a thickly painted rooster. Functionless and without aesthetic merit. A Nordic prison would never have allowed it.

I turned back to her, somewhat pushing my luck. "So, what do the other women think about the program? Do any of them like the idea?"

"Some will do anything to return home," she said, her voice edged with disgust. "Desperate and weak women. But many do not trust international; they will not participate."

I found myself praying that Sara was weak and desperate. Just then, Farris popped his head round the door.

"She's outside, but refuses to come in."

I said goodbye to the Chechen woman, who scowled, and I left the cabin. The afternoon had begun its retreat and solid white clouds drifted together, forming barren sculptures in the sky. I walked toward Sara as she shifted from foot to foot, her abaya haphazard over her clothes, a glimpse of green T-shirt beneath.

"What's happened?" she hissed as she pulled me round the back of the cabin. Farris followed but hovered at a distance. "Why you bringing me to boss lady? Swear I've done nothing."

"Oh, sorry, I didn't mean . . . you're not in trouble." I touched her arm and felt it tremble. "I just wanted to check in, see if you're all right?"

She blew out a long breath. "I'm shook. You about gave me a heart attack."

Her face was thinner than I remembered, the skin around her eyes darker.

"Why are you so scared of boss lady? And why do you look so tired? Is something going on?"

"Yeah, Layla's going on."

"What's happened? Is she hurting you?" I wondered if I needed a rag doll. Show me where she touched you.

Sara rolled her eyes. "Nah, she snores like a mad ting. Every night, it sounds like the fucking invasion of Mosul. And she's on the mattress right next to mine. I kick her in the back, but she snorts like a fat bastard and carries on."

I exhaled for the first time since catching sight of her. "Is that all? Well, thank goodness for that."

"Why've you brought the feds?" She tilted her head toward Farris.

"Oh, it's just protocol, in case you attack me with your comic books or gummy bears."

She narrowed her eyes at Farris and he took a single step back. Then she turned to me. "I've run out of gummy bears, you got any? Or chocolate would be even better." She smacked her lips. "You know how long it's been since I had a Dairy Milk?"

"Dairy Milk's my favorite," I said, smiling. "Haven't found any in Iraq yet."

"I brought, like, ten multipacks with me when I came. Jamila was so excited when I opened my suitcase; half of it was just chocolate."

My heart broke thinking of Sara at fifteen, showing up to a war zone armed only with chocolate.

"You know what I miss more, though?" she said. "Saag gosht. It's been years since I had a proper curry. I tried making one in

Mosul, but couldn't find the spices. What's Arabic for garam masala? Still haven't figured that out."

"I know, I'd kill for a Tayyabs right now."

She laughed. "You've been down my ends, is it? Nah, Tayyabs is dread, my mum's lamb chops are much better."

"Better than Tayyabs? How could you have left?"

I regretted it the moment I said it. The million-dollar question. It silenced her.

"Erm . . ." I stuttered, trying to row back. "So . . . what else do you miss about London?"

She surveyed the bleak, colorless landscape around us: the dry earth, the barbed-wire fencing, the dreary repetition of portable cabins, cheap gazebos, and fraying tents.

"You know what, yeah, you'll think I'm basic, but I miss parks. I haven't seen a tree or grass or nothing since I came to the camp. But London's bare green. I used to Rollerblade round Victoria Park, music in my headphones, didn't even appreciate it, fam. Can't imagine being free like that now."

I grabbed her hand. "I've got Powerslides, three-wheelers; I used to blade around Hampstead Heath."

"Swear down?" She grinned. "You got Powerslides? I always wanted to try them, I only had four-wheelers. But Hampstead's got mad hills, bruv, I was hella scared going down those, sometimes I swerved off and fell on the grass."

"Mate, half my clothes are covered in grass stains."

Her smile lifted the skin around her eyes. "You're kinda jokes, you know. I've not met anyone from back home since Jamila died. All the other British brides are in Syria." She paused, grinding her foot into the dust. "I miss her, innit. She wasn't just my best mate, like, she was the only person I had left."

I felt a swell of empathy. She was too young to be this alone, her surroundings too dangerous to countenance it.

"I hope you'll give the program a chance, Sara," I said. "Let me try to get you home."

She dropped my hand. "It's not that easy. It's not just about getting me out."

"Is it your parents? I know they've been hard on you, but maybe we can change their minds?"

She shook her head, and her eyes briefly met mine. Just as she opened her mouth to speak, we heard the heavy tread of feet on the Portakabin steps, and Sherri rounded the corner toward Farris.

"Let's get out of here," said Sherri, pushing up her shirtsleeves. "That incompetent woman is trying to blame the whole debacle on me. It's totally unacceptable—"

"Just give me a moment," I interrupted, but Sara had turned on her heel and was fleeing back toward the tents.

I stared at Sherri, imagined nailing her to a cross.

"What did I do?" she whined, as I shoved past her and walked toward the car.

9

THE MINISTRY OF HUMANE AFFAIRS WAS A DUMP. EX-
posed electrical cables slung down the front of the building, cracks spread like varicose veins through the brick
facade, and globs of bird crap dried on the Iraqi flag at its entrance.
I stepped out of the SUV into a pothole filled with an unidentifiable liquid; it hadn't rained since I'd arrived in Baghdad, just over
a month ago. My ballet flat was soaked through and covered in an
oily residue. I swore so profusely that even Pierre was offended.

"*Mais arrête!*"

Easy for him to say. His Italian leather shoes were buffed and
unscathed.

The smell of rubbish shimmered in the air, foil wrappers tumbling over the dirt car park. An Iraqi security guard with a thick
chevron mustache and olive-green uniform sauntered toward us,
a cigarette hanging from his lips.

"Good afternoon," I said. "We have a meeting with the minister."

He walked past me and spoke to Pierre. "You have appointment, sir?"

As it was in the beginning, is now, and ever shall be, misogyny without end—that's the real Gloria Patri.

The guard showed us to a waiting room on the second floor, where wonky blinds hung like broken accordions and framed Quranic calligraphy shed glitter onto the floor. Four local men sat waiting for their turn with the minister. One looked like he'd come straight from the camp, hiking trousers coated in dust, head buried in his hands. I wondered whether there'd been a crisis since I'd visited the week prior. Was Sara OK?

The minister's assistant walked in. The seam of her pencil skirt strained to contain her rotund ass, and a thin viscose sweater stretched over her hard, spherical tits—the type of fake boobs favored in this region. There are many Domes of the Rock in the Middle East, with varying degrees of holiness. Lip fillers, cheek fillers, and Botox made her face as shapely as her body.

"A little *démodé, non?*" said Pierre, studying her outfit with a furrowed brow, as though we were on an episode of *Queer Eye.*

We'd been last to arrive but were first in to see the minister. Foreigner privilege. She sat behind a shiny mahogany desk that was completely empty: no computer, no pens, no paper. She wore a pink-and-black Chanel two-piece suit, her hair dyed an ethnically incongruous platinum blond.

"Ah, Pierre." The minister looked up from her phone and surveyed his navy suit. "Beautiful tailoring, like normal."

"Your Excellency," he said, "Chanel is made for you."

She stroked her lapel. "I bought it on the UNICEF trip to Paris last week. Wonderful shopping. You should have come."

They both looked at my black Primark suit in silence. I'd bought a designer handbag as a treat, but it hadn't occurred to me to drop thousands of pounds on a suit. Looking back, that was a mistake. I had zero credibility, and dressing like a used car salesman was not helping my case. The minister gestured for us to sit, and we took the two leather chairs facing her desk.

"What is your take?" she said, twisting a chunky, pear-shaped diamond ring around her finger. "The Americans raised threat levels, they even evacuated some staff, but we don't see rising militia activity; the Iranians are holding their position. Is this a pressure tactic? They want the prime minister to move against the militias, but that would be a disaster, don't you think? He's not strong enough."

Pierre leaned over the desk and spoke in a hushed tone. "The Americans want a more aggressive stance against the Shi'a militias, but they won't provide meaningful support. They don't have the political will to seriously engage. The French, however, are more interested than ever. President Macron made a personal commitment to recenter Iraq in his geopolitical strategy; my father discussed it with him directly. We believe Iraq must take its rightful place in the gulf, so it can enjoy the vast economic benefits of regional integration. But political stability is critical for that, and a civil war between the government and the Shi'a militias cannot be allowed to happen."

A civil fucking war? Since when was that in the cards?

"You're right, Pierre. The prime minister was pleased by his discussion with Macron. Perhaps we can do more together. Tell your father I'll see him in New York next month."

I couldn't fathom why we were talking about this; it was so far outside our remit. The minister's phone pinged, and she tapped the screen with her acrylic-tipped fingers.

"Minister," I said, deploying all my courage. "I'm Dr. Nadia Amin. As I'm sure you're aware, the UN has created a new agency called UNDO with a mandate to rehabilitate ISIS brides. We plan to conduct rigorous security assessments, to provide psychosocial support, and to repatriate those women who don't pose a threat. I have personally visited the camp twice now, and I'm keen to get the program started. All we need from you is formal permission to begin work. I have a detailed presentation about the processes—"

"Let's do this in Beirut," the minister said.

Pierre shrugged. "Why not?"

"Make it Mövenpick this time," she said. "The Kempinski's laundry ruined my Armani."

I squinted in confusion. Beirut, as in Lebanon?

"*Tamam*," she said, waving us away. "Send my assistant the details."

Pierre stood up. "Thank you, Your Excellency," he said, effecting a bizarre curtsy, before tugging me out of the room.

I stumbled behind him through the waiting room, curious faces peering up at us, past the assistant as she swiped through Snapchat filters, and down the wide institutional staircase.

"What's going on?" I said, panting, as we reached the car. "Why hasn't she signed off on the program?"

Pierre opened the car door and pushed me in. "We'll take her to Beirut and discuss it there." He shimmied in beside me and slammed the door shut.

"But . . . why?"

He slowed his voice right down, as though talking to a toddler.

"The minister has leverage because we need sign-off from her. She will use that leverage to get an all-expenses-paid holiday at a nice hotel in Beirut. It's no problem, we have a big budget."

I gasped. "Pierre, that's corruption!"

He sighed the deep, burdensome sigh of an elder mentor, though he was definitely younger than me. "We'll say that because of political sensitivities, this topic should be discussed abroad, in a highly private setting. *Bof*, why can't you enjoy anything? It's a pleasure to visit Beirut, and still you complain. From where do you derive enjoyment in life?"

I stabbed at the car window, pointing at a girl by the roadside; she must have been nine or ten years old, her face scuffed from prolonged exposure to car exhausts, trying to sell individually wrapped chewing gum to drivers, and begging when that failed. "We're supposed to be helping people, Pierre, not going on jollies to the Med. This is despicable."

"Ah, I see. You believe you are Mère Teresa. Soon you will see, the job is impossible. If you don't take the little delights, you will have nothing."

We merged, uninvited, into heavy traffic. A camouflage truck bullied cars out of the way, soldiers staring out from the tarp-covered back, while a yellow taxi slowed to a crawl, studying the gestures of every passing pedestrian.

"Will there really be a civil war?" I whispered, as though speaking quietly would deflect from the scale of my ignorance.

He laughed. "You don't know the proper name of this country? The Republic of Iraq on the Cusp of Civil War."

"How do you know all this stuff?"

He looked closely at my face. "The question is, why don't you?

If you want to get meetings with the minister, you must bring her value. Useful information and interesting insights. Not about pointless ISIS women, something about political dynamics, about international actions, intelligence she can take to the prime minister, to make her look smart."

It sounded obvious when he spelled it out, but it had never occurred to me. My state-school brain painted by numbers, doggedly carrying out the tasks itemized in my job description, while failing to intuit those sneaky implicit requirements. I'd focused on planning the rehabilitation process itself, honing the details, perfecting it—in the naive belief that a sensible, quality program would sell itself. But people like Pierre, raised as part of the elite, understood that success came through relationships: cultivating them, rewarding them, and, at the right moment, leveraging them. He knew instinctively that your actual job doesn't matter, that you're better off working an angle, creating value for people in power. It was galling to discover that straightforward hard work wasn't enough, that being a slimy, semicorrupt, brownnosing knob-head was a prerequisite for success, yet here I was, all out of ideas, forced to follow Pierre's lead.

WHILE PIERRE ORGANIZED THE TRIP TO BEIRUT, THERE WAS NOTH-ing for me to do. I lay under my bedcovers in the middle of the day, meditating on my impotence. I'd been thrilled to get a meeting with the minister, but in the room itself I'd failed, had walked out limp and defeated. Is this how it feels to have a permanently flaccid penis? Each moment of hope, every glimpse of excitement morphing into wretched disappointment and self-loathing. It's not your fault, people would tell you; it's out of your control, they'd say. But every day you'd be reminded, deeply and intimately, of the magnitude of your failure. Mere months ago, I had been a Lothario, famed for my publication, the darling of my department. I longed to talk to someone who knew me back then, someone who'd seen me thrive. My resolve weakened, and I picked up the phone to call Rosy.

She declined the call.

It was like being left all over again. How humiliating to imagine that she still cared. There was nothing I hadn't given Rosy. I'd disassembled and laid out every part of me, and she'd inspected the pieces, turned them over in her hands, before declaring them insufficient.

My phone pinged; it was a text from her: hey sorry, can't talk, got meeting with a major investor, v exciting!

I furiously typed a reply: Omg just met a top government minister, and about to take high-level delegation to Beirut, my job is incredible! Got a boyfriend, btw, Tom, insanely hot, you'll die when you meet him.

I sent the text, then got back under the covers and cried. An hour later, I forced myself to get up, switched on the bathroom light, and leaned over the sink, considering myself in the tiny mirror bolted to the breeze-block wall. The sun had deepened the brown of my skin and I looked meaty and strong.

"Now you listen to me," I said to my reflection, suppressing the cringe that burned like acid reflux in the back of my throat. I needed this pep talk, cringe be damned. "Legitimately, who gives a fuck about Rosy? She's just some grasping, trashy Instagram white girl whose every vapid business has failed. You're on another level,

Nadia. You work at the actual UN. You could change the course of history. You're trying to save lives. This is some real, legacy-defining shit."

I washed my face and felt better. The entire world was grappling with the issue of ISIS brides, all those women discarded at the caliphate's end: Were they safe, should they be repatriated, what was legally, ethically, and politically possible? And here I was, at the forefront of this global crisis, trying to forge a groundbreaking solution. Pretty cool, no? It was hard to believe I'd originally turned the job down—because of her.

I had told Rosy about the job almost six months ago, at our weekly hump-day lunch. She'd booked us a table at a brasserie in Holborn, but we weren't given a table, it was a communal bench situation, and we sat on one corner, attempting to screen out a raucous group of barristers.

I glanced over at them, wishing I had fun colleagues. I imagined sitting here with my work frenemy Lydia. We'd discuss something tiresome, like lack of compensation for peer review, and then complain about the departmental printer.

Rosy had ordered every small plate off the menu, and they arrived with ascending extravagance.

"My treat, courtesy of the VC gods." She put her Versace crossbody purse on the table, next to her cutlery. Her designer wardrobe had grown suspiciously large, even as her company languished in the red.

"Really? You expensing this?"

She cut a ricotta-filled aubergine in half. "Of course. I'm sure there are valuable business insights to gain. For instance, in how you tricked your department into making you a lecturer."

"Ooh, say lecturer again. I like how that sounds."

"*Lecturer,*" said Rosy seductively, enunciating every syllable.

I moaned in mock orgasm, until a male barrister looked over at me, and like most men, he suddenly and prematurely halted my pleasure.

Returning to my food, I tried not to grimace at the taste of aubergine. My palate had not kept pace with my social climbing. I wished we could just have peri peri chicken; it was what we both wanted. But Rosy was trying to manifest success through her culinary choices.

"Oh God," she said, dropping her fork into a butternut squash puree that looked and tasted like baby food, "I haven't told you about my date last night."

My stomach tightened at the thought of Rosy going on a date. Agreeing not to be sexually possessive was one thing in theory, but the practice of it cut my insides until I was full of secret lacerations, each one deeper than the last.

"I was on my period, badly," said Rosy. "I told him, and he dipped his fingers into my vagina and spread the blood under his eyes, like tribal markings."

"Wow, that is rank."

"Yeah, but more importantly, is it cultural appropriation?"

I snorted and a drop of Chablis traveled up my nose. "Well, was he Cherokee?"

"Inevitably. One eighth, like Elizabeth Warren."

We laughed and I felt more relaxed; this pervert was no threat to me.

Rosy paid the bill, snapping a photo of the receipt with her accounting app, and we walked to the Tube, arm in arm.

"The strangest thing happened," I said, staring at splodges of gum and cigarette butts on the pavement. "I got an email from the UN. A woman called Lina read my journal article and has offered me a job in Iraq, leading a deradicalization program for ISIS women."

"No shit, that's amazing." Rosy dropped my arm and walked a little faster. "But you're not considering it, are you?"

I dodged a flower stand and quickened my pace, trying to keep up. "Nah . . . I just can't believe someone outside of academia read my article. The UN, I mean, that's pretty epic."

"It's a niche topic. There's probably not much written about it. Anyway, you can't go, you just got the lectureship you've always wanted."

"Yeah, I know. It's only . . . Professor Fletcher thinks it's a great opportunity to put my theories into practice. She'd give me a sabbatical."

Rosy stopped dead. A commuter bumped into her and growled, while a guy in a beanie handed me the *Evening Standard*.

"You've already asked your department for permission?" She snatched the newspaper from my hand. "Isn't Iraq a war zone? You'd be crazy to put yourself in danger like that."

I thought of all the drugs Rosy had forced me to take over the past ten years. "Sorry . . . I was just thinking . . . it's cool to be asked." I tugged her arm, and we entered Holborn Underground station.

"As if you'd leave me," she said, as we tapped our cards on the ticket barriers.

"No, of course I wouldn't." We disappeared down the escalators.

10

ARRIVING AT THE MÖVENPICK HOTEL IN BEIRUT, I FELT BET-
ter about the corruption that had brought us here. The
hotel perched on cliffs over the Mediterranean, views
stretching up the northern coastline, stairs leading down to a private beach and Olympic-size swimming pool. As we walked into
the elegant marble lobby, our bags were lifted from our shoulders,
glasses of champagne placed in our hands, and we were escorted
to oceanfront bedrooms, where elaborate fruit platters had been
laid out: wedges of orange with pineapple horns and skirts of wa-
termelon.

Tom and I had dinner on an open-air patio, the black waves
surging ten feet below, the salty air mingling with fragrant smoke
blown from glass shisha pipes. Liberated from the UN canteen, I
salivated over the menu and egregiously overordered.

A tabby cat appeared at my feet, looking up at me with round,
pleading eyes. I handed down a scrap of warm flatbread and out

of nowhere, another cat raced over and grabbed it from my hand. The two cats fought, screeching like mating foxes under the table. I was such an aid worker cliché, well-meaning but out of my depth, accidentally sparking a cat civil war on my first day in Lebanon.

The sea breeze flicked through Tom's blond curls.

"Your hair is quite cherubic," I said, eating chicken wings with a knife and fork.

"Should have seen me as a kid." He dipped a cheese sambousek into a bowl of oily hummus. "I was proper cute, in my Church of England school uniform."

"You're lucky it wasn't a Catholic school," I said. "You'd have been on page three of *The Catholic Times*."

His eyes widened as he snorted. "Wow, that's dark, Dr. Nadia."

I picked a juicy pomegranate seed off the baba ghanoush, let it burst on my tongue. "So, how did you wangle coming on this trip?"

"Ah, my manner looks insubordinate, but it isn't." He popped three slimy grape leaf rolls into his mouth in one go.

I sighed inwardly. Whenever he got close to being bearable, he'd immediately back away. "Can we nip the *Lawrence of Arabia* thing in the bud? I'm sort of over it."

His mouth fell open, revealing churned-up rice and leaves. The ick suggested itself to me, but I dismissed it. Beggars can't be choosers.

"Sorry," I said, touching his arm. "I haven't seen the film in a while, so I don't get it."

After dinner, I took him to my hotel room, its porthole windows, anchor cushions, and decorative bowline knots somewhat overegging the nautical theme. Tom unbuttoned his shirt and stepped into the bathroom while I checked my phone, scrolling through the latest messages from my mum. Rosy still hadn't replied.

Had I imagined the past ten years with Rosy? The days when something funny happened and we'd rush home to reenact it for the other, saving up our laughter until it could be shared. The way she'd imitate my nemesis Lydia or my boss, Professor Fletcher, with devastating accuracy, prompting fits of hysterical laughter that would dissolve into hiccups that tormented us for hours. The notoriously shit dinner parties we'd thrown, where people would announce cigarette breaks and order McDonald's to the front stoop. The nights we'd drink tequila on the kitchen floor and play truth or dare, starting by running naked around the garden and ending with drunken confessions as we spooned in bed. In the darkness, we confided every debilitating self-doubt, every hideous flaw, and the more we spoke them aloud, the less they stung, until they no longer seemed to matter at all. We'd built a life together, a life I cherished, and she'd pissed it up the wall.

Mum had tried to warn me. One Saturday, Rosy had dragged me to a free trial at Barry's Bootcamp, and I was sprinting between two corporate Lara Crofts when my lungs took a voluntary leave of absence and I fell off the treadmill. I limped to the changing rooms and sat on a bench, waiting for Rosy to finish. When I stopped hyperventilating, I returned a call to my mum.

"What's up, Ma? I've got, like, three missed calls from you."

"*Assalamu alaikum,*" she said. "It's such a beautiful greeting, I don't know why you won't use it. Peace, that's what Allah wants us to wish one another. Isn't that a nice thing?"

"Yep." I put the phone on speaker and peeled off my sweaty gym gear. "So, what's happening on your end?"

"The Aqiqah's tomorrow, for Gulnar's baby boy. I hoped you'd come."

I pulled on my jeans and tied my hair into a topknot. "Er, yeah, I don't think so. Circumcision creeps me out. Bleeding baby penises . . . gruesome twosome. Barbaric, even?"

"Stop that. It's good for the baby's health, even the Americans do it. Anyway, the Aqiqah is not the circumcision, you should know that. It's sacrificing a sheep and weighing the baby's hair for silver."

I looked at my mottled face in the mirror and tried to apply CC cream. "Right, well, there's still blood involved, so I'm not feeling it."

"Are you being deliberately ridiculous? You won't see the sheep die, you'll just have a nice dinner with the family."

I paused, looking at my anorexic purse. "Will I get any of the silver?"

"Absolutely not, it's for charity. You should donate too, as good tidings for the baby."

"Nah, not this time, Mum. I've got plans." I packed up my bag and looked at the clock, wondering if I could persuade Rosy not to bother changing before brunch.

"Who've you got plans with? Your *gori* friend? Your priorities are all wrong, Nadia. Family is important, why can't you see that? When it really counts, that silly girl won't be there for you, it'll be your family who comes through."

"Are you for real? Rosy didn't disown me for four years—you did that."

Rosy jogged into the changing room. I mouthed the word *brunch* and she nodded.

"Sorry, Ma, I've gotta go," I said, hanging up before she could respond.

Four months later, I sat in that Beirut hotel room, listening to Tom brushing his teeth, thinking about my mother's words. She'd been right about Rosy—that two-faced skank did abandon me. But Mum had nothing to gloat about. She had wounded me first, had deserted me for years—just because of her stupid, poxy religion. She thought it'd make me reconsider, would restore me to the ranks of the believers, but it had only hardened me, turned my agnosticism into hatred. What kind of faith prompts a mother to ditch her daughter, to eject her into the world, alone and emotionally bereft? Mum was trying to make up for it now, with her lame texts, sporadic phone calls, and occasional invites back to Leicester, but it was too little, too late. Our relationship remained fragile, and we skimmed its surface with casual, innocuous chats, the threat of derailment ever present, fermented rage and resentment straining against every crack.

Tom switched off the bathroom light and walked over to me.

"You all right there?" he said.

I stood up and put my arms around him, pressing my cheek against his naked chest, his heartbeat solid and even. My tears puddled as I crushed my face into his body, little drops escaping in trickles down the side.

"Is anything the matter, pet, or are you just nighttime sad?"

I shook my head. "Nighttime," I managed to say, between sobs.

"It all hits right before bed, doesn't it? You're OK, love, just let it out."

We stood there for a while, holding on to each other, before he picked me up and carried me to bed.

OUR MEETING WITH THE IRAQI DELEGATION WAS SCHEDULED for nine a.m. in the hotel's stateroom. The floor was laid with regal carpet, marble columns flanked the room, and a colossal chandelier hung from the ceiling, its crystals reflecting light that shimmered over the sea. It was the perfect space, its scale and grandeur creating a sense of gravitas, instilling a seriousness of purpose. You could negotiate international peace treaties in this room, pull off one after another, until war became an anachronism and charity had no supplicants to sate.

"Let's get this over with," said Pierre, propping his feet on the U-shaped conference table. "There's a beach party at EddéSands."

Sherri stood opposite him, her shirt an upsetting shade of orange. "Our job is to protect vulnerable women, Pierre, we're not here to pick up Lebanese men."

"Right, are we ready for this?" I said, plugging in the projector. "Can you lay out the agendas, Sherri? Pierre, get your legs down."

He ignored me. "The men here are beautiful, with their big steroidy muscles. You should get some, Sherri. Perhaps it will relax you."

Sherri snatched the handouts from beneath his feet. "I'm married. And the abuse of steroids is no laughing matter, it causes myriad health problems, including infertility."

"And this concerns me how? I am making love, not babies."

"I'd hardly call it love," said Sherri, laying out the agendas. "If we have free time, I'm going to visit the ancient ruins at Byblos and Baalbek."

Pierre rolled his eyes. "*Bon*, and how can you justify this? Shouldn't you go help the poor children in Sabra and Shatila?"

I checked my watch. It was twenty past nine. "Where the hell are the Iraqis? Will one of you go find the minister?"

Sherri left the room, and ten minutes later, she came running back in.

"Knocked on her door," she panted. "Man answered . . . not her husband."

I had been pouring a glass of water, and the tumbler overflowed, darkening the tablecloth. "Jesus Christ. Are we paying for her to have a dirty weekend away?"

"Perhaps we can take a discreet photo," said Pierre, stroking his chin. "That could prove useful for many eventualities."

"Shit, shit, shit," I said, shuffling through my notes pointlessly. "She'll be so stressed now that you've caught her. Should we start the meeting with an icebreaker? Defuse the tension?"

"Please do," said Pierre, "I beg you."

The Iraqis entered the conference room, and we stood up to welcome them.

"Thank you for making the journey here," I said, nodding my head profusely. "I hope you are comfortable with your accommodation."

"Yes, it is nice," said the minister, without looking up from her phone. Her assistant took a seat on her right, wearing a silk floral jumpsuit and neon-pink heels. An older Iraqi civil servant called Omar sat on her left, wearing a pin-striped suit and an aggressively large mustache. He seemed embarrassed to be subordinate to these women; it was a humiliation Saddam Hussein would never have allowed.

"Perhaps we could start with an icebreaker?" I said, thinking through exercises I'd used on my students. "How about two truths and a lie? You say two truths and one falsehood, and the others guess which is which."

The Iraqis looked confused, and my team covered their faces with their hands. The minister glanced up from her phone.

"Palestine, Palestine, Israel," she said.

Pierre was shaking with silent laughter, tears spilling onto his face.

"OK, never mind." I straightened my notes. "So, the purpose of this meeting is to discuss the ISIS women's rehabilitation program." I gestured toward the PowerPoint projected onto a large screen. "I'd like to take you through a detailed presentation—"

The minister interrupted. "You are UNICEF, UNDP, or IOM?"

I looked blankly at Pierre. "*Merde,*" he said under his breath, "you don't even know the names of the UN agencies?"

I cleared my throat. "Sorry, we represent UNDO, the agency established to deradicalize ISIS women. We came to your office recently, about sign-off for our program?"

The minister yawned and put down her phone. "There are many programs now. And some UN staff tell me deradicalization is illegal."

I looked wildly at my team, but they offered no help. "What do you mean? What other programs?"

"Something for children, something for local reintegration, there are many ideas, every day UN people visit me. You must come see me together, or I cannot decide."

The minister stood up.

Fuck me, not again. "Minister, we really need to move forward, if you can just take a seat—"

Her assistant interrupted me. "We must return to Baghdad

tonight. The minister does not have time for these trips, she is busy. Please change flights."

The absolute gall of it, as if this were our idea!

"Of course, we will arrange new flights," said Pierre, practically cooing. "Thank you so much for coming, Minister. It has been an honor to host you."

"We have time for Givenchy," she said, beckoning him over. "Come, Pierre." He stood up, walked into her outstretched arm, and they left the room together, the older civil servant trailing behind.

The demonic assistant was still hovering at the table. "We need the certificates," she said, snapping her fingers in Sherri's face.

"Yes, I will leave them at reception, with your new flight details," said Sherri, as the assistant turned on her neon-pink heel and left the ballroom.

Silence settled over us, disjointed expletives firing through my brain but failing to emerge from my gaping mouth. Instead, a fly flew in, and I gagged and spat it out. Does the universe's capacity to humiliate me know no bounds? As I smeared its soggy black corpse onto the white tablecloth, I saw Sherri editing a certificate on her laptop. She replaced the words *Microfinance Conference, Kirkuk* with *Deradicalization Training Event, Beirut.*

I pointed at it. "Why . . . ?"

She shrugged as she pasted our logo onto the document. "It's a certificate-driven society."

"This is an absolute piss-take." I stood up and swiped the untouched agendas off the table. "Certificates? They haven't done a single fucking thing! We've achieved jack shit and hemorrhaged thousands of dollars for the privilege. And now we're buying them new flights? That money is for the women in the camp! Is this for real? Is that woman genuinely a minister?"

Sherri sat back in her chair and furrowed her brow. "Nadia, she's the only female minister in the Iraqi cabinet, it can't be easy for her. She must have faced some extraordinary misogyny."

"Right, and extorting humanitarians for a weekend shopping trip in Beirut is really proving the haters wrong."

Sherri nodded slowly and tapped her lip. "Perhaps it was a conspiracy, by the awful misogynistic men, choosing somebody unsuitable in order to block future women from office. How terrible."

I groaned and buried my face in my hands.

After a moment of paralysis, I remembered the minister's words and turned to Sherri. "What's the deal with these other UN programs? And who the fuck is telling her that deradicalization is illegal?"

"Deradicalization *is* illegal," she said, picking up the scattered agendas from the floor.

I stared at her Judas back, welding my mouth shut.

As I turned to leave, Sherri shouted after me, "Can I go to Byblos now?"

"Do whatever the fuck you want," I said, as the enormous gold-studded door to the stateroom shut behind me.

11

W HEN WE RETURNED TO BAGHDAD, THE CITY WAS ON
fire. Barricades of burning tires blocked our usual entrance to the Green Zone, and choking plumes of black
smoke rose above thousands of protesters blaring Klaxons and
flying Iraqi flags. A teenager in a stained T-shirt stood on a concrete post, shouting chants into a megaphone. The crowd repeated
after him, calling for jobs, for an end to corruption, for the over-
throw of the government. They had covered the blast walls in mu-
rals. One painting looked like Sara: a young woman wearing an
abaya, crouching beside a tent, her palm outstretched. Another
featured the UN globe-and-wreath symbol in blue and white, and
above it were the words *Where Are You?*

I looked at my hands, which were soft and smelled of Molton
Brown orange and bergamot hand wash, from the bathroom of
Beirut's Mövenpick Hotel. A sickly feeling rose through me, the
unmistakable sensation of being in the wrong.

I wished I was out there with the protesters. I'd been going to demonstrations ever since I was a toddler: demanding intervention in Chechnya, cheering on the intifada, excoriating the invasions of Afghanistan and Iraq. It was the first time I'd smelled weed, on the coaches we'd take from Leicester to Hyde Park, dreadlocked white guys lying on the back seats smoking joints. We made for a funny group, walking together through central London: women in burqas hoisting Socialist Workers Party banners, queer teenagers dressed as though en route to Coachella waving glow sticks and beating drums, *Guardian*-reading Karens urging roadmen to refrain from violent tactics.

It felt shitty being on this side of the bulletproof glass, institutionalized, feckless, and corrupt. I slid down in my seat, hiding my face from the crowd. Our convoy skirted around the Green Zone and crept in from the other side. As soon as we pulled into the compound, I jumped out of the car, hugging my rucksack in my arms, and ran to Lina's office.

As I opened the door, the budgie flew beak-first into my face and I screamed.

"Bulbul is not dangerous," said Lina, her eyes narrow. "Loud noises are frightening for her." The bird flapped onto her arm and she tipped it into the cage, the bottom of which was covered in dropping-stained newspaper.

I filed away my disgust and took a breath. "Lina. I just got back from Beirut and the minister has refused us sign-off. She said other UN agencies are proposing alternative programs for the camp. And someone's telling her that deradicalization is illegal. It's chaos; I don't understand what's going on and I don't know what to do."

Lina literally growled, stomping her little feet on the floor, and my frustration receded as I gawked at hers.

"They promised me this would stop! What's it going to take? It's outrageous that they won't move on—they refuse to admit defeat. I'm done with them, I'm just completely done."

I stayed silent, still hovering by the door, totally perplexed. She slumped onto the sofa, gesturing for me to sit beside her.

"Do you know how rare it is for an Arab woman to direct a flagship UN agency? They all fought me, and I won. It was in the news back home, and my father—who's a famous writer—published a column about my appointment that was syndicated across the Middle East. It was a big deal. But they keep trying to take it from me; they've been relentless. I'm so tired of it."

I strained to understand. "Sorry if this is a stupid question, but who's trying to take UNDO away from you?"

"The other agency heads!" she snapped. "Priya from Migration, Charles from Children, and Frank from Development. They think UNDO shouldn't have been created, that our remit should've fallen within their existing departments."

She sank back into the cushions, her reflection faint and uncertain in the glass coffee table, the suggestion of moisture in her eyes. She pressed her thumb and forefinger together until they turned white and her tear ducts dried out. It felt awkward, even voyeuristic, this proximity to her emotion, and I was embarrassed by the shift between us.

"I'm sorry it's been hard," I said, trying to look sympathetic while avoiding eye contact. "I really believe in this program, and I'm ready to fight for it. But I'm not sure what to do next."

She exhaled, tipped her head back, and rested it on the sofa's edge. After a few moments of silence, she straightened up.

"Sherri might be the answer. My relationships are so fraught right now, but a lot of people owe Sherri. She's worked in every agency, she knows everyone, and she's . . . well, not liked, but sort of grudgingly respected. If anyone can bring them to the table at this point, it's probably her."

"OK, got it," I said, standing up. "Leave it with me."

She stepped off the sofa and, to my astonishment, gave me a hug. I cautiously allowed my arms to encircle her, expecting her to flinch or jerk backward, but she leaned in closer, dropping her head onto my shoulder. Her budgie jealously eyed our embrace, before Lina stepped back and then turned away.

I LURKED IN THE HALLWAY OUTSIDE THE CAFETERIA, PRETENDING to study the noticeboard, while I waited to ambush Sherri. A green flyer advertised an interagency quidditch match, BYOB. Did that refer to booze or broomsticks?

I'd plotted the seduction of Sherri with a creepy level of intensity, stalking her Facebook and LinkedIn, reading the articles she'd self-published on Medium, including a book review of *Queering the Ocean: New Vistas in Hydro-Feminism*. Pierre had taught me a thing or two about the art of sycophancy, and I was determined to put it into practice.

Sherri walked up the steps wearing overalls with a flannel shirt underneath.

"Oh heyyy." I twisted a strand of hair around my finger. "I

wasn't expecting to bump into you. Should we sit together at dinner?"

She looked around suspiciously, as though expecting to find a hidden camera.

"Might be nice to get to know each other, just us girls." I was unsure whether, politically, she would embrace or reject this sop to female camaraderie.

"Oh, right, yeah," she said.

I put my arm around her and we pushed through the cafeteria doors.

After the culinary delights of Beirut, the cafeteria's offering was even more distressing than usual. Everything was yellow: potato waffles, fried fish cakes, boiled sweet corn, like school lunches before Jamie Oliver. We clanked our trays down and sat opposite each other.

"I'm intrigued by you, Sherri," I said, stabbing at the sweet corn with my fork, trying to impale one kernel on each prong. "You're so passionate and idealistic, I think it's awesome. Where did you work before the UN?"

"Oh, thanks." She smiled and sat up straight. "I wasn't sure if you . . . Anyway, I was doing a master's degree in psychology, and I taught yoga on the side—to people in need. I think yoga is a basic human right, you know? People facing poverty or domestic violence just need a chance to release all that anxiety."

I could think of other things they'd need more.

"That's wonderful," I said. "Out of interest, how could the needy people afford yoga classes?"

She waved a dismissive hand. "Oh, I didn't charge."

That she was rich enough to work for free was an interesting insight. Her parents were probably oil-guzzling, sweatshop-owning, tax-dodging hypercapitalists, and Sherri's entire personality was just a constellation of reactions against them.

"How generous of you," I said, ignoring Tom, who'd entered the cafeteria and was miming a head explosion behind Sherri's back, mouthing the words *What the fuck?*

"This was in Australia?" I asked, as I tore apart a fish cake and poked at the unidentifiable species inside.

"Yes, but I actually lived in London for a year. It was amazing. I lived on a shared canal boat at Hackney Wick as part of a collective on the river. We did everything together: planted an allotment, did batch cooking, sewed our own clothes."

I would literally rather live in the ISIS women's camp.

"Must have been a dream," I said. "Why did you leave?"

She put her cutlery down on the table. "I got into a closed marriage, and the community was polyamorous. They were stringent about being open. It's a shame, I loved it there."

I tried to keep my face neutral, like a psychotherapist. "That sounds hard."

"I get where they're coming from. Heteronormative relationships are an outcome of Western capitalism's obsession with productivity and cisgender hegemony. I wish I could've risen above it. I've been trying to decolonize my sexual preferences, at least. There's a great podcast about it, I'll send you a link. Who we're attracted to, it's all racist."

"Really? People are racist?" It's my favorite thing, white women lecturing me about race.

"Oh, sorry, of course you must be a survivor of that. I'm doing my best to change my own attitudes."

I couldn't stop myself from going off-piste. "You're already married, Sherri. How will it help the world if you're suddenly madly attracted to Gurkhas?"

She pouted. "It's still important I do the work."

I sighed. "Of course, I admire that." My eyes wandered over to Pierre and Charles. They were trying to build a structure out of condiment bottles and waffles, screaming with laughter every time it collapsed, scattering bottles of ketchup over the floor.

"What about you?" asked Sherri. "How are you finding Baghdad so far?"

This was my moment. "Honestly, it's been tough. You and me are the same, Sherri, we just want to help people. I'm trying to support those poor women in the camp, but I'm not getting anywhere. Do you remember that girl Sara, with the East London accent? She was just fifteen when she came here; one silly mistake and her whole life's been ruined. A rehabilitation program could help, it really could. If we persuade the Brits that she's not dangerous, maybe she could go home, back to her family. I mean, what else can we do?"

She blew air through her lips and watched a bottle of ketchup roll past. "The girl is a victim; she shouldn't be detained and forced into a poxy program."

"I agree with you, but this is the reality. They're stuck in the camp, and no one else is trying to get them out. It's our moral duty to do something, don't you think?"

Sherri nodded her head slowly. "If our program helps to release the women sooner, I suppose that is ethically justifiable."

I almost leaped out of my seat. "Yes! Absolutely. I agree with you. So . . . how can we get the program approved?"

She stretched out her legs and looked at the ceiling. "Well, the minister made it clear she wants a joint UN approach, so we'd need to collaborate with the other agencies."

"That makes sense, but I've never met the other agencies. I wouldn't know where to start."

"Oh?" She seemed surprised and slightly pleased. "Well, I know all the agency heads. Would you like me to arrange a coordination meeting?"

I leaned over the table and touched her arm. "Gosh, could you? That would be incredible. Thank you, Sherri, I'm so lucky to be working with you."

She smiled and started blathering about how no one on base had asked for her preferred pronouns. They were she/her, but still, it was offensive to assume that a cis straight white woman was a cis straight white woman. I felt like a man (he/him) after a one-night stand: now that I'd got what I wanted, I prayed she would shut the fuck up and leave.

12

I SAT AT THE HEAD OF THE CONFERENCE TABLE, WATCHING AS
Sherri circled: battling with the aluminum blinds, straightening
chairs, constantly checking her watch. It was the first time I'd
seen her in a suit and I marveled at my leadership skills. Over one
fish cake and waffle dinner, I'd transformed her from a conscientious objector into a full-throated advocate. To make this meeting
happen, she'd run around the compound for days, bullying and
cajoling agency heads, calling in every favor, expending every bit
of social capital. Her stress was just as palpable as ever, emanating
from her like a virus, but at least this time, I was its beneficiary.

A commotion gathered pace in the hallway, and Frank Taylor III
charged into the room, surrounded by a huddle of junior staffers.
He was a large man who straddled the cusp of physical fitness,
undoubtedly through a committed golf practice.

"Hello, I'm Nadia." I stuck out my hand, and he shook it so
vigorously that all the loose flesh on my body jiggled.

"Frank. Pleasure to meet you." His voice pounded the ceiling. "I assume Lina's sent you in her place?"

Why do Americans operate so many decibels above the rest of the world?

"Yes, she's indisposed, I'm afraid." I gestured for him to take a seat. He took my spot at the head of the table, and his staffers rippled toward the extra seats along the room's edge.

"Indisposed." He guffawed. "That's nice. Don't worry, kiddo, she's often indisposed around me."

"Hello, Frank," said a quiet voice. A petite woman, brown with a pretty face, maybe in her forties. She wore a delicate gold necklace with the distinctive twenty-four-carat hue beloved by the Indian subcontinent.

Frank stood up. "Priya!" He put his arms around her, squishing her into his blazer. "How goes it? Did you get the Dutch on board?"

"You know me," she said in a cultivated Delhi accent. "Got them in for double the original ask."

"That's my girl." He slapped her on the back and she staggered forward.

Last to arrive was Charles, famous for his bromance with Pierre, coconspirator of cafeteria japes, doctor of asteroids.

"What up, what up?" He kissed Priya on both cheeks and gripped Frank by the forearm.

"Good to see you, Charles," said Frank. "When did you get back?"

"Three days ago now," he said. "It was epic, bru, you should visit."

Priya batted her eyelashes at him. "It's been so quiet without you."

"*Hayibo*, I think not, darling." He put his arm around her. "But I missed you as well."

I shrank further into myself as they started chatting about an upcoming donor conference that I knew nothing about. They were the real deal: smart, experienced, proper grown-ups who deserved their big UN jobs. I'd never felt like more of a charlatan. If Lina couldn't get through to them, why on God's crumbling, overheated Earth would they listen to me?

Sherri tugged on my sleeve, an enormous smile on her face. "They all came!"

"Well done," I said, patting her on the shoulder. She'd done her job; it was time for me to do mine.

I cleared my throat, but no sound came out. "Hello, everyone." I waved my hands above my head like a child. "Shall we get started?"

They looked at me with derision but took their seats.

"Where's Lina?" said Priya to Frank.

He shrugged and pointed at me. "She's sent this woman in her place."

I forced a smile. "I'm Dr. Nadia Amin. Unfortunately, Lina is not available, but I'm pleased to convene this meeting on her behalf."

Priya wrinkled her perfect baby nose. "No offense, but you're not an agency lead. Lina should be here."

Of course it would be the other brown woman who'd immediately undermine me. There's no room at the top for more than one of us.

"I rate we get on with it," said Charles, looking at his watch. "I haven't got much time."

"OK, thanks," I said, gripping a pen so tightly that its barrel became imprinted on my palm. "So . . . we've met with the Ministry of Humane Affairs, and they're confused about who's doing what on deradicalization."

"Deradicalization, what a ridiculous notion. It's like we're in Xinjiang," said Frank.

I wedged my shaking hands under my bum. "Sorry, I mean rehabilitation. Either way, I know it's not ideal, but we can't just leave the women there. A program could help get them out."

"Or we could adhere to international law," said Charles, doodling on his agenda. Was he drawing . . . an astrolabe? "If the women have committed crimes, they should be given fair trials. Otherwise, they should be free to go home."

"Trial? In Iraq?" I thought of Sara on the stand, infuriating the judge with her mock-trial-based backchat. "According to Iraqi law, they'd all be hanged for 'association' with ISIS." I did air quotes with my fingers when I said the word *association*, like a dickhead.

"So, we should focus on revising the law," said Frank, stabbing his girthy red finger at me, "rather than colluding in a massive contravention of human rights."

I thought back to my research. "Hasn't the UN already tried to amend the Counterterror Law? The Iraqis didn't seem up for it."

There was silence apart from the scratching of Sherri's pen. She was dutifully taking notes for me, rather than interjecting with her own obstructionist beliefs. At least I'd done one thing right.

"The Iraqi women in the camp don't need rehabilitation," said Priya. She spoke so quietly that we had to strain to listen. It was a power move I'd read about but had never seen in action. "They didn't cross oceans to sign up: ISIS tore down their homes and forced them to marry fighters. Now they're stuck in the camp because of social stigma. We should work with local tribal leaders to change attitudes and facilitate returns."

I nodded with enthusiasm, as though this were original information. I'd already designed separate provisions for local women. But this meeting wasn't about proving myself; it was about getting them on board. "That's really smart, Priya, thank you. And what about the foreign women? Most countries are refusing to repatriate them."

"Countries are abnegating their responsibilities to their citizens," said Frank, hitting the table with his fist, causing a cascade of pens to tumble onto the floor. "The UN should be holding them to account!"

"We can do both," I said, my voice becoming pleading and whiny. "Pressure countries to accept returns while also implementing a program that demonstrates the women aren't dangerous."

Charles added a final flourish to his astrolabe drawing, which looked technically accurate, then dropped his pen and pushed back his chair. "I can't support you running programs for the children. You don't have the specialized skills, no matter what mandate HQ gave you. Now, if you'll excuse me—"

"Wait, Charles!" I slammed my hand over his, pinning it to the table. The shock made him sit back down, and everyone looked at me with newfound respect. "Listen," I said, pulling back my hand, "what if you ran the kids' program in the camp? It makes perfect sense for UNICEF to do that. I was surprised, when I visited, that you weren't already there."

Charles and Priya exchanged a look, and I finally understood what was happening. Frank had genuine ideological objections to the program and would never support it. But Charles and Priya? They just wanted a piece of the action.

"How about this?" I sketched out a diagram on the back of my agenda. "Charles's agency works with the children, Priya's runs community outreach for the local women, and UNDO focuses on the foreign women."

"Our own programs in the camp?" Priya smoothed down her caramel balayage hair, trying to underplay her excitement. "Without Lina's interference?"

Frank stood up and threw a plastic bottle of water against the wall, making the entire room flinch. "You're missing the point, you shit-for-brains hacks! The families are illegally confined in camps, and your stupid programs are going to legitimize that!"

"Bru, don't be accusing me," said Charles, rubbing his bald head. "I'm not putting kids in camps, but if that's where they are, I'll help them."

"What exactly are you proposing to do, Frank?" said Priya, indifferent to his anger. I, by comparison, had slithered down in my chair, my eyes swiveling agog on stalks above the table.

Frank crossed his arms stiffly, his blazer growing tight around his shoulders. "We're going to change the Counterterror Law."

"Good luck with that," said Priya, tapping her pen against the table's edge. "You'll forgive us for getting on with our realistic interventions."

Oh shit, I thought, mic drop.

Frank beckoned his staffers with a single hooked finger. They stood in unison and all walked out. We could hear Frank shouting "Fucking fuckwits," as they scrambled down the corridor.

My torso inched back toward an upright position.

"I think we have an agreement?" I said, turning from Charles to Priya.

Silence.

"Come on. Charles does kids, Priya does local women, and I do foreign women. This could really work."

"I want to see it in writing," said Priya, "signed by Lina."

"I'm on it. Then the three of us will go to the ministry to get the Iraqis on board?"

Charles shrugged, and Priya didn't move. I was elated.

LINA WASN'T IN HER OFFICE, LEAVING MY BREAKTHROUGH burning in my hands. I roamed the grounds, pulsating with adrenaline, wondering what to do with all my excess energy. Is this what causes voluntary gym attendance? I jogged to my room, leaping up several steps at a time, and squeezed my substantial thighs into workout leggings.

The gym was in a battered shed. Daylight sliced through the uneven planks of wood while the stand-alone air conditioner, large as a fridge, pumped cold air into the porous space. What would Sherri say if she saw this wanton waste of electricity? I climbed onto the creaky treadmill and pressed the plus button. The belt whined beneath my feet and little scenes arranged themselves in the air as I ran. The day of my damehood; me receiving the Nobel Peace Prize; my ascension to secretary-general of the UN. Rosy would rue the day she left me.

I had been in the bath on the day she left, watching droplets of condensation cling to the window. Their bellies swelled, and they lost their grip, dribbling down the glass in defeat.

"Knock knock! Don't mind us." Rosy walked in and used a towel to screen the bath. "He needs a quick wee."

Blood Man sidled up to the toilet. "Sorry, mate."

It was unfortunate that Rosy's date, the one who'd smeared period blood onto his face, had become a regular sleepover guest. His presence made me sick with jealousy, but I worked hard to appear nonchalant. He couldn't possibly last much longer.

"We've reached the final frontier," I said, as I shaped bath foam into modesty shields. "Are there any boundaries left?"

Blood Man flushed the toilet, kissed Rosy goodbye, and left the flat. Rosy threw the towel screen onto the floor and sat down on the closed toilet lid. Potted plants and strewn cosmetics masked the bathroom's disrepair in our crumbling period rental. Warmed by steam, it was the coziest place to be, since the rest of the flat hemorrhaged heat from the cracked single-glazed windows.

"How was your date with that student on Friday?" said Rosy.

"God, he was so young, my breasts tried to lactate when he sucked on them."

She laughed insufficiently.

"What's up?" I asked.

She paused for a moment. "Erm . . . he's asked me to be his girlfriend. Blood Man. Well, we should probably start calling him Andy."

I sat up and bathwater slopped over the side. That sniveling, vile degenerate. How dare he.

"What? When? You're not serious."

She didn't answer, and we both watched the towel on the floor darken as it absorbed the spilled bathwater.

"We're going to move in together," she said. "I'm sorry."

The bath foam had dissolved, leaving my stomach naked, protruding, grotesque. I covered it with my hands. I thought about Andy, wondered what it would be like to cut his throat and mark his face up with the blood, the way he liked it.

I hoisted myself out of the bath and wrapped myself in the sodden towel, Rosy looking up at me from her toilet lid perch.

"It'll be good for me," she said. "He's helping me cut down on drinking, go out less, focus on the business."

My mouth fell open. "He helps you *drink* less? I'd never drunk in my life before I met you, you're the fucking alcoholic. You think I want to be hungover every single morning? I do it for you, because that's what you want. And we can stop. We can live clean or whatever, I'd like that too."

Rosy stood up and placed a hand on my wet, naked shoulder. "I know it's difficult for you, Nadia, but I love him. I want this. Don't you think it's a bit juvenile, the way we live? We're not in our twenties anymore. It's time to grow up and get real partners, create homes of our own."

I stepped backward and whacked my hip against the porcelain sink, the pain sucking the anger out of my voice. "But we *are* real partners," I whispered. "We love each other. And we've already got a home, an amazing one."

"Don't be pathetic, Nadia," she said, her nose wrinkled in disgust. "You're so fucking clingy, can you stop being a beg for once in your life? I'm sick of having your sucky little tentacles all over me, it's suffocating and claustrophobic and I need you to get the fuck off me!"

In Baghdad, I stepped off the treadmill, prematurely winded, the painful memory compounding the lactic acid burning my sides. If Rosy had ever loved me, she'd done so casually, only when it was convenient, while I'd manipulated and crushed myself to better fit her. I'd never debase myself like that again. Sara, and the other women in the camp, they were my mission now, and there was dignity in devoting myself to a cause, relief in finding something worthy of my heart.

13

LINA HAD RETURNED TO HERSELF. SHE SAT MOTIONLESS BE-
hind her desk as the twig-legged budgie sauntered over her
paperwork. A curved black Nespresso machine dripped coffee into a china cup and water dripped from my wet hair onto her
deep-pile cream carpet. I couldn't waste time drying when I still
hadn't told her.

"Yes?" she said, as though she hadn't been whimpering in my
arms three days prior.

"I've sorted it." I stood with my legs astride, ready to absorb the
impact of her praise. "Charles and Priya will take care of children
and locals, and we'll do foreign women. The Iraqis are bound to
sign off now we're a united front. We're finally getting somewhere."

"You did what?!" Lina slammed a ring binder shut and swept it
into a drawer. The budgie panicked and took flight; one of its feath-
ers dislodged, floating in spirals back down to the desk. "You just
gave away our budget? To our competitors?"

Shame colored my cheeks, and I wrapped one leg around the other until I wobbled like a limbless pole.

"Um . . . we never talked about budgets. Just about dividing up the work . . ."

She let out a short, derisive laugh. "You thought Charles and Priya would use their own funding? It's about money, Nadia, it's always about money. I fought tooth and nail for UNDO, and here you are, tearing up my mandate and decimating my budget. What a disappointment you've turned out to be."

A kernel of rage ignited in my stomach and began to tear through my veins. How the hell was I supposed to know? She'd never explained anything to me. And why the obsession with budgets? Lina didn't mind us hemorrhaging money in Baghdad, even in Beirut, as we endlessly sucked off Iraqi bureaucrats. Why did nobody care about our actual mission?

"With all due respect," I said, my voice struggling to maintain an even keel, "if we don't start implementing soon, UNDO's going to be a joke. It's been a month and a half, and I'm no closer to sign-off. We'll be folded, and our budget will be redistributed anyway."

She hit her forehead with the heel of her palm and swore profusely in Arabic. Farris had taught me some Arabic curse words, and I listened hard, picking out the words I understood: *dog, shoe, donkey, gassy fart, pimp, fuck the souls of your dead family* . . .

Eventually, she stopped and looked up at me. "Are you even ready to start? You've got the security clearance process worked out? The psychosocial support program fully prepared? Accommodation for the team up in Ninewah?"

I nodded. "We've been ready for weeks."

She sighed and leaned back in her chair.

Anxious not to lose her, I started plumbing the depths of the inspirational business podcasts that Rosy used to mainline instead of doing any actual work.

"Have you ever heard the saying 'Perfect is the enemy of good'? And . . . 'Life is ten percent what happens and ninety percent what you make of it.' Also, erm, 'The secret of change is not to waste time fighting the old, but to use your energy to build the new.' . . . I could go on?"

Lina smiled and held up her hand. "Please stop." She leaned back in her chair. "Is this the best you can do?"

"It is."

"Fine."

THAT EVENING, I SKIPPED THROUGH THE CORRIDORS, THE CO-signed agreements held high in my hand. It reminded me of rushing home from school with my end-of-year report. "Nadia is a smart, dedicated and conscientious student," my teacher had written. I was so conscientious that I looked up the word *conscientious* in the dictionary. Mum had been very proud; she'd hugged me tight and ordered us a stuffed-crust pizza as a special treat. Would she be proud of me again, if she knew what I'd achieved in Baghdad? I went back to my room and picked up the phone to ring her.

"Oh, so you're alive, then?"

"I've texted you every day since I got here," I said, immediately regretting making the call.

"Forgive me, I didn't realize it was such a terrible burden to speak to your own mother."

I retreated into my bathroom without switching on the lights and sat on the tiled floor. "Mum, it's been really overwhelming, and I haven't had time. Don't you want to ask me how I am?"

"I could've been in a terrible accident, I could've died, and you wouldn't even know. I used to call my mother every day."

"Yeah, but you didn't have a job, so . . ." I leaned against the bathtub, bracing myself for the inevitable response.

"You think raising you wasn't a job?! You screamed for years with that colic. Not to mention all the cooking, cleaning, shopping, and ferrying you around like a taxi driver. And for what? You don't appreciate anything. . . ."

I fiddled with the bathtub as she continued to rant. The white plastic side panel was coming away, and I stuck my finger into the gap and felt a sharp cut.

Mum arrived at her closing statement: "You wouldn't understand, because you're too selfish to get married and give me a grandchild."

"You haven't exactly sold it to me," I said, as I sucked on my bloody finger. "The idea of having kids."

"What do you mean?" She sounded genuinely perplexed. "It's the best thing in the world."

I grappled around the floor for my laundry pile and stuffed a dirty T-shirt into my mouth to suppress a scream. Oblivious, as ever, to my emotional state, Mum started chatting about a maxi dress she'd bought in the John Lewis sale. I wondered how to explain my work in Iraq and why it mattered so much to me.

"Mum," I interrupted, spitting errant sand and lint from my mouth. "Do you remember the summer camp I went to taught by Anwar al-Awlaki?"

"Yes, it was so sad what happened to him. The Americans killed him with a drone, the cowards."

I looked up at the dark bathroom ceiling and imagined a bomb smashing through it. It was odd to think that someone I knew had died like that.

"Right, but he did join al-Qaeda," I said.

"So they say."

"Looking back, he was pretty radical that summer. He told us not to be friends with non-Muslims. He used to say, 'You might think they're friendly. Let's say Bob, your white neighbor, seems nice, right? Bob's going to stab you in the back.'"

"He was right. Kevin, from two doors down, reported my kitchen extension to the council. Anyway, what's your point?"

"I met this girl, Sara, in the ISIS women's camp. She's just like I was at her age, even looks like me. I've just been thinking . . . I could've been radicalized and ended up like her."

"Don't be ridiculous. You're being brainwashed by your job. I never taught you Islam like that. And look how you turned out. I clearly gave you too little Islam, not too much."

"I wonder how Sara's parents feel now, about how much Islam they gave her."

"I'm sure it wasn't their fault. It's the internet and You're Tube. Silly girl got carried away."

What would happen if Mum finally learned how to use a browser? She was only a Reddit thread away from joining Boko Haram. Nah, that wasn't fair. Mum had never been interested in beheading-centric versions of Islam, instinctively repelled by the gore, the vulgarity, and the total lack of manners.

After the call, I kicked around my room, feeling restless and emotionally spent. The day's euphoria had dissipated, leaving a residue of low-lying anxiety, and I ruminated over everything that could still go wrong. Even if we started work in the camp, would the women agree to participate? Would they pass their security assessments? Would their home countries be willing to repatriate them?

I thought of Sara, but my memory of her face was uncertain and merged with images of myself at her age: a skinny brown girl with enormous eyes, vulnerability masked by precociousness. She didn't deserve to be trapped in that camp forever; she needed someone to care about her, to advocate for her, to try to get her home. I hoped someone would have done the same thing for me.

14

EVENING DROPPED OVER THE UN COMPOUND WITHOUT warning. Every day it surprised me, the sudden disappear-ance of the sun, as though God had shouted, "Alexa, night mode!" The outdoor lamps, activated by sensors, flashed on in unison. The shadows by my feet widened, and I looked up.

"Hey there, superstar," said Tom.

I wouldn't have admitted it, but I'd grown fond of Tom, or had become habituated to him, at least. I'd retreat into his bed late at night, leaving the humiliations of the day outside his door, and I'd nestle under his big, protective arm. He was vocal about how much he fancied me, how much he admired me, and it was nice to feel adored without risking my heart. His deficiencies only made me feel safer; I could never love him, and after Rosy, it was exactly what I needed.

"You're the lady of the hour, aren't you, pet?" said Tom. "I heard you worked miracles."

I grinned and flexed my tiny biceps at him. "I've only gone and done it! The program's officially approved. Once I got Charles and Priya on board, the ministry had to give in. Turns out the UN is mad influential when it works together, though apparently that never happens."

"Aye, you're a legend, doll," he said, crushing me against his chest. "Why don't I take you out to celebrate?"

"But . . . are we allowed?"

He raised a finger to his lips. "Farris'll take us. It'll be our little secret. Now go get ready and meet me out front in ten."

Baghdad brimmed with danger on our unauthorized mission. It felt different, being outside the Green Zone without proper approval. Our conspicuous UN SUV got stuck in traffic and pedestrians mobbed the streets, crossing the road in front of and behind us, hemming us in. So many bombs had exploded in this city, on evenings just like this, on streets just like this.

I thought back to the Hostile Environment Awareness Training the UN had forced me to complete before I came to Baghdad. I had traveled to Hereford, an English–Welsh border town, to learn from two retired SAS guys, both of whom were attractive, despite their age. They taught me what to do if taken hostage (shut the fuck up and wait to be rescued) and I fantasized about them bursting into a dark room, shooting my attackers, and dragging me to safety, preferably by my hair. They told me to memorize emergency phone numbers, and I realized that apart from my current mobile, the only number I knew was the landline of the house I'd lived in when I was twelve. I practiced tying tourniquets and learned how to stuff gunshot wounds with tampons, before they drove me blindfolded to a village in the Brecon Beacons and made me plot my route home using a map and a compass. It took me four hours, and I still got it wrong. They showed me how to spot IEDs—improvised explosive devices—but I kept thinking of IUDs, intrauterine contraceptive devices, and imagined my womb exploding over Iraqi highways. I leaned over plastic dummies and arched my back suggestively as I gave them CPR to the tune of "Stayin' Alive." After all that, neither course instructor asked me out.

A young boy tapped on the bulletproof window and jolted me from my daydream. He held up a cardboard box full of packets of tissue, gesturing for me to buy one, but Tom waved him away.

We inched along Abu Nawas Street, beside the sweeping black waters of the Tigris, the trees along the promenade wrapped in aggressive red fairy lights. Eventually, we turned in to the parking lot of the Baghdad Hotel, which was dark except for a light-up plastic palm tree. Dwarfed by real palm trees, its purpose was unclear. The car stopped and Tom opened the door.

"You not coming in, Farris?" I asked.

He shook his head from the driver's seat and gave Tom a look. "Nah, you guys go ahead."

"He disapproves," said Tom, punching Farris on the arm.

We walked through the hotel lobby, up a silent flight of stairs, and through a white metal door. On the other side, Arabic music played at an incredible volume. I glanced back at the door and wondered how it had restrained all this noise. Iraqi waitresses thronged down the center of a large wooden balcony, a dozen cushioned seating areas on either side. Men lounged in their seats, foreigners and locals, smoking cigars and shisha pipes, drinking whiskey, and eating hummus with freshly baked bread. There were no female patrons, only servers, and they were voluptuous, their round flesh wobbling under crop tops and miniskirts.

"I didn't know Iraqi women dressed like this in public." I twisted around to look at them.

"They're prossies, like," said Tom as he ushered me toward a table.

A girl came over to take our order, her young face smeared with heavy makeup, like a child left unattended at her mother's dressing table, an undersized tube top and a short skirt digging red lines into her flesh. For an Iraqi girl to prostitute herself in a society this regressive, she must have been absolutely desperate. Her father and brothers had probably been killed in the war; perhaps she had a disabled mother to care for, younger siblings who needed feeding. How do men get hard for such abject vulnerability? How can anyone enjoy a drink looking at this spectacle of utter misery? I thought of Farris, who'd chosen to stay in the car. That's what a real man looks like.

"They only have whiskey, I'm afraid," said Tom, after placing our order, "but it's fun to be out, right?"

"Isn't this depressing?" I said, the menu hanging limp from my hand. "If the women leave the camp, will they end up in places like this?"

"Aye, some will," he said, as a waitress placed a bottle of Johnnie Walker, a couple of crystal tumblers, and some fresh bread and hummus on the low, carved wooden table in front of us. "But some won't."

I thought of Sara, stripped of her clothes, forced to yield to these degenerates. "But . . . it's unconscionable."

He shrugged. "Sex work is work."

"Fuck off. Who told you that? Sherri? Having your fragile and vulnerable body abused because you have no other options is not work, it's exploitation."

He picked up my glass and gave it to me. "Calm down, pet. Here, have a drink. Didn't realize you were such a conservative."

"I'm not conservative. I'm just not some idiot white girl who thinks selling pictures on OnlyFans is the same thing as being repeatedly raped in a war zone. Sex work, my arse."

I drank the entire glass of whiskey until my throat burned with the same intensity as the rest of my body.

Tom reached over to stroke my leg and I flinched.

"At least you're trying to do some good," he said.

"I don't even know if the program's going to help, Tom, and I'd rather the women stay in the camp than be forced to work here."

"Relax, Nadia, you've already achieved so much. Even Lawrence—"

"I swear to God," I interrupted, "if you mention Lawrence one more time . . ."

"Oh, sorry," he said, his mouth full of bread and hummus, "my bad."

A man walked past and stared at the cleavage peeking from my open shirt. I buttoned it up to the top and scanned the room. Men leered at me from every direction, like feline predators, their eyes yellow in the low light.

"Does everyone here think I'm a prostitute?"

"It doesn't matter. You're with me, bought and paid for." He laughed.

I wondered how it would feel to reach down for a fork and stab it into his eye.

15

THE FINAL DAYS IN BAGHDAD WERE CHAOTIC AS WE PRE-
pared for the big move up to Ninewah, and amid this surge
of activity, Pierre threw me a curveball. I was in the cafeteria, slopping macaroni and cheese onto my plate, when he cut the
queue, shuffling my tray forward so he could slot his own in.

"I have an imam for you," he said.

I cocked my head, holding steamed broccoli suspended in
tongs. "What the fuck do I want an imam for?"

Pierre took the tongs off me and loaded his own plate with
broccoli. He rarely ate anything except greens. "The minister insists we provide religious education to the women."

I stopped and turned around, the queue backing up behind us.
"You're kidding. You know as well as I do: forced religious reeducation massively backfires in situations like this. Anyway, we don't
have time. We're about to leave."

Pierre pushed me forward. "This isn't optional. And she has a
preferred imam: Hussein Ali Abbas."

I found a place to sit, expecting Pierre to join me, but he just stood beside the table, scanning the cafeteria for better options. "Hang on," I said. "The imam's called Hussein? Isn't that a Shi'a name?"

He tutted. "*C'est très grossier.* You cannot reduce a person to their sect."

I could feel my eyes literally boggle. "Mate. We're talking about *ISIS brides*; they think Shi'as are heretics. They'd never accept religious teaching from him. And stop looking at me like that! I didn't draft ISIS's apostasy rules."

"No matter. The minister wants us to seriously consider him, so we must. I've given the imam your number; he's going to call you."

I raised a fork to my mouth and caught a whiff of the cheese sauce. It smelled of old people and the NHS. I chewed slowly, feeling anxiety solidify alongside the macaroni sludge in my tummy.

"Fuck's sake, Pierre, why can't you deal with it?" But Pierre was already on the other side of the cafeteria, sneaking pieces of broccoli into the hood of Charles's sweatshirt.

Later that evening, I received five missed calls and eleven WhatsApp messages from the cleric.

Good evening Miss, read the first message.

I didn't recognize the number, so I tapped on the profile picture, which was a painting of two deceased Shi'a religious leaders. Their disembodied heads floated on elaborate floral wreaths, and golden minarets rose through the misty background. I vaguely remembered them from my preparatory reading; they were called something something Sadr and something else something else Sadr.

The phone rang and I recoiled. I couldn't have felt more invaded if he'd teleported into my bedroom.

Another message arrived: I am Imam Hussein Ali Abbas.

What was I supposed to say? We couldn't possibly have a Shi'a imam teaching Sunni extremists— The phone rang again. Christ! If I said the wrong thing, I'd piss off the ministry and they could pull support for our program.

Ping! I am pleased to work for UN, the message read.

Fuck, fuck, have the Iraqis already promised him the job? The phone buzzed around my purple bedspread, as though possessed. Oh God, make it stop. Stop calling me!

A message: Where we shall meet?

In hell, I thought, if I'm not already there. I locked my phone in my bedroom and fled to the tiki bar, where a dozen people sat drinking around picnic tables and the chords of "Sweet Child O' Mine" filtered through the air. In the middle of the clearing, Charles and Pierre used a bamboo stick to play limbo.

I ordered a tequila and sat alone, watching a group of people I didn't recognize enter the bar. Pierre went over to greet them.

"Sharp sharp, darling." Charles had appeared at my table. "You must be buzzing, sign-off at last." He gestured at the empty seats beside me. "Can I join?"

I nodded and watched Pierre gather his posse around a picnic table on the far side.

"Who are they?" I tilted my head toward them.

"Eish, they're journalists." Charles pushed a wedge of lime into his Corona. "Pierre loves to be in the know; journos have the best gossip. Can't be bothered, myself. To me, hanging out with them is work. I prefer to have fun in the evenings."

Charles smiled a gummy, baby-cheeked smile and I wondered how old he was. Completely bald, but wrinkle-free; agency head, but committed prankster . . . My computations went nowhere.

"You're all about the fun, aren't you?" I said, like a total grandma. "Your cafeteria larks do liven the place up, I suppose. I'd be too worried about people not taking me seriously."

He smirked and held the cold bottle of beer against his face. His black skin glistened beneath the trickles of condensation. "Never had that problem, darling. Married at nineteen, first kid at twenty, PhD at twenty-two, it's unbelievable, no? I accidentally grew up, I was serious too quick. Now I look for joy, and Pierre's my bru. He has an intense family, like mine, very ambitious for him. We're both happy to be outside, away from that pressure. This is practically a holiday for us."

I searched for angst amid his relaxed features but found none. "You've got kids? Isn't it hard being away from them?"

"I rate it's better like this," he said, rubbing his bald head sheepishly. "I was going crazy back in Jo'burg; my responsibilities drowned me and I wasn't being a proper father. This way, I can send good money back to my family. That's what I can do just now."

I tried to hide the judgment from my face; I'd never been a fan of parents who abandon their children. My eyes drifted toward Pierre's table.

"Wait!" I grabbed Charles's arm. "Isn't that guy from the ministry? He was in Beirut with us, a civil servant."

"Saddam? Yeah, him and Pierre are sleeping together."

My eyes grew wider than my head. "What?! But he's Iraqi. And, like, fifty years old."

"Pierre loves a zaddy, everyone knows that. Anyway, how do you think your program got approved?"

"Erm . . . a cross-UN approach exerted irresistible pressure on the ministry?"

Charles laughed until he fell off the bench.

I pushed out my lower lip. "Unbelievable. One fucking achievement in all this time, and it's not even mine."

He clambered back onto his seat. "Don't take it personal, sister. It's the outcome that matters, ey? And it's happening now. We're almost ready to move to the camp."

My eyes were fixed on the civil servant, who was giggling into his enormous mustache. "What? Yeah, moving to Ninewah, at last. Can't wait."

"It'll be a jol." He stood up and collected our empties.

Charles walked to the bar and Pierre stumbled in the opposite direction, his fingers awkwardly crooked around a triangle of three drinks, alcohol sloshing over the sides.

I collared him as he walked past.

"Hey, Pierre!"

He slid onto the bench and set down the tumblers. "Nadia, the great, undeserving boss. Tell me you're happy at last. I bring you the victory you want. No more sad complaining, I hope."

"Are you really sleeping with Saddam?" I whispered, leaning in toward him.

"Saddam . . . ?" He shook his head and wagged his finger in my face. "That is very racist, Nadia. His name is Omar. You can't call every Iraqi with an erogenous mustache Saddam."

I felt myself flush. When the *French* call you racist, you listen.

"Oh, sorry, I didn't know . . ."

He bopped my nose with his sticky finger. "I love dating Iraqis," he said. "I've learned so much. For instance, Shi'as are bottoms and Sunnis are tops."

I choked on my own inhale. "How have you not been murdered yet? You fully deserve it."

He laughed, absolutely delighted with himself. "It's part of the Shi'a culture, martyrdom and bloodletting. Have you ever seen Muharram? They hit themselves with metal spikes. And Sunnis, you know, are the conquerors, the oppressors. It's the logical conclusion."

A journalist wandered over to us, rescuing me from the diabolical conversation.

"Peter Banks," he said in a slightly affected English accent, the voice that northern grammar-school boys adopt when they go to Oxford. "I hear you're the lady with a real passion for ISIS brides?"

That cheered me up, and I needed it after the day I'd had. "Nadia Amin," I said. "And yeah, I'm the person who actually cares about those women."

He sat beside me and asked lots of smart, eloquent questions about the camp. I relaxed next to him, grateful to resume my position as an expert, and we drank and talked until the bar closed. Then I went looking for Tom, desperate to avoid my demonic phone for a little longer, but he was on a night shift and I was forced to return to my room. I tiptoed through the door, shielding my eyes from my phone's urgent flashes, swaying drunkenly as visions of Shi'a martyrs apparated on my bedroom walls. Eventually, I surveyed the damage.

[Missed Call]

I ready at your service.
Good cooperation for us

[Missed Call]

Hello?
??
Why you not reply for me?

[Missed Call]

Imam Hussein Ali Abbas.
????????????
I call the minister for this disrespect.

I put my phone in a drawer and got under my bedspread fully clothed, cowering under all my layers before I fell into the anxious, wakeful kind of sleep that tequila allows.

16

THREE IMAMS MADE THE SHORT LIST: THE MINISTRY-recommended Shi'a, a local Sunni, and an American convert. We decided to interview the Shi'a cleric first, since he was already disqualified. After my brazen silence, he'd managed to contact Lina, and she'd absolutely bollocked me for blanking him.

Farris showed him in. Despite the humidity that wrapped its wet, sticky fingers around Baghdad that day, the cleric was dressed in dark, heavy robes. He extended a limp hand toward Pierre and nodded at Lina and me. There was no flicker of recognition when he looked at me, and my body resumed its respiratory functions.

Lina, Pierre, and I sat in a row, like talent show judges, while the cleric took a seat opposite us.

"We are very appreciative of your offer of support," said Lina, in an obsequious voice. "Our esteemed colleagues at the ministry have highly recommended you."

"Yes, I am esteemed," he said, adjusting his black turban.

"On any other project, we would have immediately hired you."

She smiled ruefully. "But, you understand better than us, working with ISIS brides is very sensitive."

"They are killers of all Iraq." He tapped his fat, globular prayer beads on the table.

"Yes, exactly," said Lina. "But our goal is to persuade the women to become moderate, and we're concerned they won't accept teaching from a Shi'a. Excuse me for being blunt."

"There is no Shi'a and Sunni, we are all Iraqis!" He shook his prayer beads in our direction. "You internationals created sectarianism in Iraq. Before Americans come, we were all united."

"Be that as it may, we must work with the situation as it stands." Lina had tired of the exchange and handed over to me by kicking me under the table.

Avoiding eye contact with my colleagues, I decided to make a bold play. "Imam. We'd be delighted to work with you, and we're grateful for your extraordinary sacrifice." My leg had developed a nervous bounce, and I held it down with one hand. "Not many are prepared to live in the camp. We only have a trailer for you without air-conditioning, and some of the women may try to stab you. We will provide a protective vest, but you know how they are. It is honorable to risk your life to teach the women of ISIS, and we thank you."

He coughed, and his voice got quiet. "I will try my best, but my schedule, I am very busy, I will hope to make time."

As Pierre showed him out, Lina couldn't help but smile. I lifted my palm, and she gave me a reluctant high five. I caught sight of my reflection on a snoozing laptop screen. The blurry blackness had airbrushed my face, making me look perfect.

Pierre returned with the Sunni Iraqi cleric in tow. His turban was white rather than black, and his robes were lighter than the Shi'a ones. These outfit differences made a pointed theological statement, though one I struggled to remember. Something about levels of guilt felt by the opposing sects toward a couple of tragic deaths in the seventh century.

Lina and I stood up to welcome him, but he recoiled, indicating that we should not attempt to touch him with our vile female hands. I wondered whether, later, he'd be sidling up to the waitresses at the Baghdad Hotel.

The cleric was no older than me, but he slowly descended into his chair in an approximation of gravitas. He cleared his throat. "In the name of Allah, most gracious, most merciful," he said. "The people of our blessed nation have been through a terrible trial. We must lead the repair of our devastated lands and reverse the tragedies that befell us from the hands of the Americans."

OK, I thought, that's not a terrible start. It's only Corbyn-level anti-Americanism.

I flipped open a notebook. "Sheikh, it's a pleasure to meet you. As a distinguished Islamic scholar, you are well-placed to lead the religious education program in the camp and we'd love to hear more about your approach. How would you tackle the beliefs of the ISIS women?"

He patted his upper lip with a folded handkerchief and carefully placed it back into his breast pocket. "Daesh, they made some mistakes." He shook his head gravely. "They were young men, eager for a quick change. They did not listen to the wisdom of the traditional leaders. This is not the right path. It must be gradual to change the society. I will teach the women the Quran and the Shari'ah in the correct way."

"The key problem with ISIS was . . . pace?" I put my pen down.

He sniffed. "Your questions are not appropriate. Who else have you spoken to?"

I looked at Lina, and she shrugged. "We met with Imam Hussein Ali Abbas earlier today," I said.

"*Astagfirullah!*" he exclaimed. It was a religious expression of disgust I'd last heard when my mother found a Lil' Kim CD hidden under my bed.

"The only thing worse than a Jew," he said, "is a Shi'a."

Pierre tried and failed to suppress a snigger, while Lina and I slowly deflated. We continued the meeting for a respectable thirty minutes, then got him the fuck off our base.

"Christ, we don't have time for this!" I said, banging my head against the table. "Who recommended this guy?"

Pierre thumbed through his Moleskine notebook. "The Sunni Endowment. They said he was a moderate."

"He is moderate," I said, "the way al-Qaeda is moderate compared to ISIS."

Lina scrolled through her phone, her lips vibrating. "There's plenty of decent imams in this country, Pierre, how's it come to this?"

He shrugged. "It is not a desirable posting."

Because of the time difference between California and Baghdad, we broke for a few hours and reconvened later that evening for the final interview. I brought a packet of digestive biscuits with me for moral support, while Lina produced a vodka soda with lime for each of us, disguised in mugs. The Zoom call connected and our last clerical candidate appeared on the wall. He was a white guy, with shoulder-length shaggy hair and a goatee. A bit of a skater-boy aesthetic, filtered through several Ayurvedic retreats. The only visibly Muslim thing about him was his red kufi prayer hat, like a fez without the tassel. He sat cross-legged on a patch of grass, lit by the early-morning sun, dense maple trees swaying gently behind him. The scene was ostentatiously beautiful, and we leaned toward it from our cramped, windowless conference room in our beige and dusty compound.

"Good morning from sunny Berkeley . . . or good evening, where you are? It's a blessing to be with you folks. I'm Sheikh Jason, as you know, since you dialed me." He giggled.

I summoned my last shred of positivity. "Thanks so much for joining us. I know it's early in California, so we're grateful for you making the time."

"No problemo. I was stoked to hear from you guys. Deradicalizing ISIS women, what a gnarly problem. I'm superintrigued."

"Great." I clicked my pen on and off absent-mindedly until Lina snatched it from my hand. "So, as we explained in the email, we're looking for a religious figure to teach moderate interpretations of Islam to ISIS brides."

"Sounds like the Lord's work." He opened his arms wide, like a megachurch preacher. "It would be an honor and a privilege to bring the message of universal love into these women's lives. The seeds of hate are planted through experiences of neglect and suffering. Terrible things grow forth, and some think they are weeds, but they are wrong! God calls on us to nurture all his plants, to nourish and heal them with the power of our collective humanity and with the force of our positive vibrations."

Pierre swallowed his laughter and gave himself the hiccups.

"Right," I said, as I stared down Pierre. "Did you have in mind any specific approaches you'd like to try?"

"We must create interlocking experiences to open the heart, the body, and the soul." He closed his eyes and placed one hand over his chest. "Communing with nature, receiving the energy of crystals, yogic breath work, and movement." He took a deep, cleansing breath and became very still.

I squinted at him, my mouth agape. Was that the wi-fi or had he slipped into a trance? I ran my eyes down our list of questions, while Pierre hiccupped like the frog he was.

"You still with us, Sheikh Jason?"

He made prayer hands and bowed at me. What kind of a Muslim . . . ?

"So, as a convert, have you experienced challenges to your religious authority? Do you anticipate any problems working with the women because you weren't born Muslim?"

"We don't say convert." He pursed his lips and wagged his finger. "I am a revert. I reverted to my natural state of being, in harmony with our Lord. We are all born in blessed communion with God, and I was honored to return to the path of peace and enlightenment."

When the call ended, our portal into the Golden State snapped shut, and we adjusted our eyes to the dim conference room, which looked more miserable than ever.

"This man is a Buddhist," said Pierre.

"It's out there." Lina tapped her hands together, her rings clinking against each other. "But do we want to start over?"

I massaged my cheeks. He was a terrible choice, but I couldn't countenance delaying the program any longer. The religious studies classes didn't matter anyway, I reasoned to myself, we were only providing them as a sop to the ministry.

"I guess . . . a bit of yoga never harmed anyone?"

And that was how we decided to bring Sheikh Jason of Berkeley to the women of ISIS.

THE LEAVING PARTY WAS MESSY, OUR LAST CHANCE TO DRINK, dance, and fuck before moving to camp chaste. Charles ransacked a conference room for microphones and a projector, rigging them up in the tiki bar while everyone else wolfed down dinner and ran to their bedrooms to change. Sherri and I didn't have suitable outfits, so we tried sexing up our work clothes, knotting shirts under our busts, rolling skirts at the waistband, covering our earlobes and clavicles in jewelry. I wore delicate amethyst earrings and a thin gold chain, but Sherri had replicas of colonial-era Maasai shields hanging from her ears, and an ostrich shell necklace handmade by bushwomen in Nhoqma village, Namibia.

The prospect of leaving had induced a collective hysteria in us, and we started downing tequila shots at eight p.m. Compound life had been intense and stifling, forcing us to live and work in relentless proximity, until the boundaries between us weakened and collapsed. We fought like siblings, drank like college girls, and worked like deckhands. It was exhausting, insane, and unhealthy, and moving to the camp was bound to be even worse. So, on our last night, we forgot our drama, left our dignity in our rooms, and showed up ready to get lit.

Tom poured liquor across a row of shot glasses. "Let's. Get. Mortal!" he yelled as we tipped them back.

Charles hit play on "You Sexy Thing," and Tom grabbed a microphone and sang about believing in miracles as he sidestepped through the bar. He dragged his hands down his torso, trying to channel male stripper energy, but his thrusting was comical and robotic. The girls stood back, giggling, but Pierre was beside himself. He launched onto the dance floor and gyrated against Tom's crotch before fluently lowering into a slut drop, bouncing on the floor with one arm raised high.

Lina and I ordered more shots and sat beside each other on high stools. She took hold of my forearm and licked it while I shivered with excitement. Then, she tapped a saltshaker over the glistening spit and placed a wedge of lime in my mouth, the wet side facing her. She licked the salt off my arm, took the shot, and sucked on the lime while I held it in my mouth. Tom stopped dancing and trained his eyes on us, wiping the sweat from his brow with the back of his hand. Lina winked at him. Whatever she was trying to do here, I was down.

Priya took her shoes off, climbed onto a table, and sang into an imaginary microphone because the boys were hogging all the real ones. Her hair flipped back and forth, and she spilled a drink over her shirt, which gradually turned translucent. I could see the lace of her bra, the wet swelling of her breasts. Alcohol makes everyone so fuckable. Well, everyone except Sherri, whose curly hair had grown alarmingly frizzy in the humidity.

Wait, was Sherri crying . . . ?

"He did terrible things," she sobbed, pointing at the speakers.

It was R. Kelly, singing about his mind telling him no, but his body telling him yes.

I ran to the Spotify, switched to "Girls Just Want to Have Fun," and dragged Sherri, Priya, and Lina onto the dance floor. Pierre joined us, squealing, "Yas girls, they wanna have fun!" Arms around one another, we jumped up and down, and I suddenly loved these idiots, even felt loved by them.

Charles grabbed a microphone off Tom, stood on a chair, and raised his glass. "A toast. To this mad adventure, to our crazy family, and to saving the world!" Everyone cheered, and Pierre fell over.

I pushed out of the stifling bar and into the clearing, where the night air cooled my skin, and the sky hung low and comforting in its darkness. Lina wandered over, and we sat side by side on a bench, leaning our backs against a rough concrete wall, close enough that I could smell the tequila on her breath. I wondered if she was about to kiss me, and how Tom would feel about a threesome with the birder in chief.

"Thank you," she said, without turning to look at me. "It can't have been easy, pushing me like you did, but I'm glad it's happening. It was the right thing."

I don't often prefer professional validation to sexual overtures, but in this instance I was relieved. Lina's approval meant I had succeeded, and for the first time in Baghdad, I felt a profound sense of contentment and optimism about what lay ahead.

I leaned my head on her shoulder. "Thanks for taking a chance on me, Lina. I'm grateful to be part of something that matters."

She nudged me and pointed to the other side of the clearing. I followed her line of sight and saw Charles and Priya making out in the shadows. That naughty little philanderer.

Back inside, Tom slow-danced by himself while Sherri stood behind the bar, pouring tequila straight into her mouth, her hair as large as a hedgerow. Pierre had passed out, his two legs stuck out on the floor, his torso obscured by a table.

The back door of the cafeteria building swung open and Frank Taylor III barreled down the steps in blue-and-white-striped flannel pajamas. Everyone stopped dead.

"Turn that music off! It's four a.m.! ISIS has a point—you are a bunch of degenerates!"

He spun around and stormed out. The silence held for a moment, before it was splintered by giggles, then shattered with laughter.

17

I'D ALWAYS IMAGINED LIVING IN THE CAMP ITSELF. PERHAPS setting up a caravan park for ourselves, like those at the seaside, perched on an adjacent bluff, where we'd benevolently watch over waves of blue-and-white tents. But Sherri had coordinated with UN operations to rent us a secure villa in the nearby town of Qayyarah. It was mid-June, nearly two months since I'd arrived in Iraq, when our convoy pulled up to our new home. A custodian rose from his three-legged stool and dragged open the gate.

We spilled out of the vehicles and stood around on the scrubby grass, beneath the intermittent shade cast by palm trees, and looked up. The villa was tall and wonky, its uneven stone facade elevated by the ornate detailing that framed the windows and doors.

"Very history," said the custodian, pointing at the building. "They build use the stones from ancient."

We gathered the villa had been built in the 1970s, using re-claimed stones and carvings that hailed from different eras. There was something haunting about the structure, living its life anew while nursing the secrets of previous souls. I wondered what we'd impart to those stones, how we'd compare to what they'd witnessed before.

Pierre moved first. He slung a rucksack over his shoulder and ran into the villa, his footsteps pounding up the internal staircase. Realizing Pierre was about to call dibs on the best room, Charles hotfooted it after him. Priya wandered around the garden with her phone at arm's length as she searched for a signal, while Sherri cornered the custodian and interrogated him about techniques for the preservation of historic masonry.

Tom picked up our bags and nudged me inside. We climbed the stairs and walked past a large primary bedroom, where Charles and Pierre wrestled on the bed as Pierre yelled something in French—probably a variation of "finders keepers." Tom and I chose two small bedrooms next to each other, and he dropped our bags before lifting me up, my legs flailing in the air as he tried to kiss me. I wriggled free; it was all too exciting to be stuck with Tom, and I ran off to explore the rest of the house.

Sherri had selected a room, and I briefly watched as she emptied her suitcase onto the bed and pulled a tangle of wire hangers out of the wardrobe. Charles and Pierre had struck an agreement and raced down the stairs. When he reached the bottom step, Charles crouched down and Pierre leaped onto his shoulders. Charles carried him around the ground floor, and Pierre shouted "touchdown" as he tapped the top of every doorway.

In the living room, Priya bent over the wi-fi router; she turned it over and removed and reinserted wires before trying to turn it back on. Against the wall stood an aging mustard sofa with a wooden frame, and I wondered if it had sat there since the 1970s, coughing dust out of its cushions after each war, startled to find its limbs intact.

I heard the whine of metal gates and walked outside, beneath the grapevines wrapped around wooden trellises overhead, as a white SUV pulled into the driveway. The passenger door swung open, and a pair of bare, skinny legs covered in blond hair emerged. Then I saw his board shorts, gray Nirvana T-shirt, brown goatee, and aviator sunglasses.

"Hey, hey! I'm Sheikh Jason." He held out a hand, and I looked at it. What type of Muslim cleric shakes a woman's hand? I gingerly shook it. Maybe he thought the limp-wristed action he gave me was a fair compromise.

"Welcome, I'm Nadia, we met on Zoom. I hope your journey was OK. Let me show you inside."

Farris, who must have collected him from the airport, followed us in, struggling with Jason's gargantuan rucksack.

"It was a long flight," said Jason, as he rubbed the rose quartz pendant hanging from his neck, "but it gave me time for a deep and meaningful convo with our Lord. I needed to check in with him about our plans here, and I felt his blessings upon our sacred mission."

We entered the living room, where Priya was running network connections diagnostics on her laptop.

"Priya," I said, gesturing between them, "this is Sheikh Jason. He'll be teaching the religious education classes."

She looked at him. Laughter rippled up her body and, finding her mouth squeezed shut, rippled back down again. She removed the laptop from her knees and stood up.

"Good to have you with us," she said, opening her mouth slightly.

"Priya will be running the tribal outreach program," I said. "She's hoping to facilitate returns for the local women in the camp."

Farris, trying to rebalance the monster rucksack on his back, fell forward and lay splayed on the floor, his limbs thrashing like those of an overturned turtle. I ran over to help him while Jason stepped toward Priya.

"Great to meet you," said Jason, taking hold of her startled hand. "We should get together for a confab. I'd love to find a way to support our Iraqi sisters."

A dialogue box flashed open on Priya's laptop screen with the words *connection failure.*

I ushered Jason toward the stairs, and Farris heaved up the rucksack and followed us.

Jason inspected his new bedroom, pointlessly opening all the drawers and the wardrobe before sticking his head out the window. Farris dropped the rucksack on the floor and bolted before I could thank him. It took a lot to irritate Farris, but in one airport drive, Jason had clearly succeeded.

"The light of the Lord will cleanse us all," said Jason, struggling to retract his head from the window.

"You must be exhausted," I said, "so I'll leave you to rest. There's food in the kitchen if you're hungry."

He sat on the bed, bouncing on his flat bottom, palms outstretched on either side.

"Dang. I'm so eager to get started. Can we just go to the camp?"

"Um, your classes don't start for a couple of days," I said. But then I thought about Sara. It had been nearly a month since I'd seen her and I was excited to tell her we'd arrived. "You know what . . . maybe we can go say hi."

"Do we need a translator? I've been studying, but my Arabic isn't quite there."

I shuddered thinking about Jason trying to speak Arabic; never had a whiter man existed. "No, you'll only be with the foreign women. The camp says most of them have passable English."

"All right, ma'am, let's rock and roll." Jason stood up and I looked at his appalling outfit.

"How about you wear clerical dress? It'd be good to establish your authority early."

"We are all equal before Allah," he said. "I claim no authority, only the desire to heal."

"Even so, some consider shorts un-Islamic, and Nirvana . . . well, it's a lot for women who think music is haram."

He shook his head slowly. "It's very sad, the concept of the haram being abused in this way. It's going to be quite a journey for these poor, misguided souls. But, with grace and the guidance of our Lord, we'll surely get there."

"Yep. I'll leave you to shower and change." I closed the door behind me, my suspicions hardening into knowledge.

We had royally fucked this up.

18

THE URGE TO IMPRESS THE ISIS WOMEN TOOK ME BY SUR-
prise. But as I entered the camp next to Sheikh Jason, I felt
concern for my street cred. He had changed into a long,
white robe and the red prayer cap he'd worn on Zoom. It was all
too big and too ethnic for him, and he looked like he was in fancy
dress on his way to a frat party. He point-blank refused to wear the
bulletproof vest. "I need to establish trust and openness," he said.
After a long argument, Tom gave up, preferring Jason's stabbing to
a continuation of the conversation.

Though we'd shown up unannounced, and several days early,
the camp administrators agreed to let us meet some of the foreign
women and showed us to a prefab classroom. It was a gray, windowless cabin with a white uPVC door, three metal steps leading
up to it. I made a beeline for the air conditioner affixed to the far
wall and stood directly under it, the cold air slipping indulgently
beneath my bulletproof vest. I wondered how many women would
attend these classes solely to cool down. Should we start a control

group? One group just sits in a cool room, while another group receives moderate religious teaching. Who ends up more deradicalized?

I heard a squeaking sound and turned to see Jason writing his name on the whiteboard in green marker, before drawing lots of little hearts. The door opened and a dozen women filtered in, a smattering of children in their arms or running around underfoot. They eyed my Kevlar vest and studied Sheikh Jason's cheesy grin. Some lowered themselves into seats, while others stood at the back, ready for a quick escape. I scanned the faces, wrapped in bright headscarves or hidden behind black niqabs. Not Sara, not Sara, not Sara. Is that Sara under the face covering?

Jason beamed and, in a self-conscious display of informality, sat on the teacher's desk. "*Assalamu alaikum,*" he said, butchering the Arabic pronunciation. My stomach cramped into itself with cringe.

"I'm Sheikh Jason all the way from sunny California. The glory of Islam was gifted to me ten years ago, and I reverted with joy in my heart. Since then, I've had the honor of learning at the feet of great Islamic scholars. I'm truly delighted to be with you, and I'll be providing a space here in the camp for open conversations about our beautiful faith."

A woman wearing a glittery headscarf burped, making the others giggle. A constipated expression came over Jason's face. With great effort, he produced a tiny burp and smiled victoriously. The women stared at him in disgust.

"Suck-up," said a voice from behind a niqab.

Jason clasped his hands together. "So, I'd love to learn about your journeys here. Is anyone willing to share their story?"

The long silence was interrupted by a toddler knocking over a chair and wailing. His mother rushed toward him, glaring at me as though I'd willed it to happen. I made a face that said: You're mental, I'm not the god of plastic chairs.

Eventually, Jason pointed at a young woman with a fuzz of upper lip hair and a substantial Middle Eastern nose. "How about you? What's your name?"

She sighed and looked at the others. "Aisha from Switzerland."

"Welcome, Aisha, it's nice to meet you. And how did you come to be in Iraq?" He folded into a cross-legged position on the table, which looked even more childish than having his short legs dangling.

Aisha stared at him as he rearranged himself. "Sajjad brought me."

Jason nodded profusely. "Great, and how did you know Sajjad?"

"He was my youth worker. Started grooming me when I was thirteen."

Jason froze, immediately out of his depth. "Oh wow, that's terrible. . . ."

Aisha grew bolder as Jason trailed off. "Yet I'm still not allowed back. All I want is to go home. Sajjad is dead, and I'm glad he's dead! Why won't they let me go home?"

Some of the women tutted and shook their heads, and one of the niqabis trained her eyes on me. "I'm going to be honest," Aisha spat. "Even if I get murdered for apostasy, I regret it all."

I hurried to the front of the room.

"If I can interrupt," I said. "I'm Dr. Nadia Amin, from the UNDO team. Aisha, I want to reassure you, and everyone else, that our mission is to get you home. We'll interview each of you and liaise with Iraqi intelligence services to get you security clearances. Then we'll work with your home embassies to enable your repatriation. In the meantime, we'll also be providing psychological support in the camp. If you want to participate, please sign up in the reception cabin."

I stepped away and gestured toward Jason. "Sorry, back to you."

Jason turned to Aisha and manipulated his features into an expression of deep empathy. "Thank you, Aisha, for so bravely sharing your truth with the group. It's important that we create a safe space so we can honestly process our feelings together. Now, can you all promise not to physically attack Aisha later?"

"Off with her head!" said a woman in a French accent. The others laughed, and Jason's eyes widened in panic.

"Relax, monsieur," said the Frenchwoman. "We come here to prove we are not radical, so our countries will take us back. It's the women who refuse to meet you that you must worry for."

"Well, goodness." The red splotches on Jason's face dissolved back into white. "Thanks for that reassurance, you had me worried there. And what is your name?"

"Khadijah." She smoothed down the pleats of her neatly ironed headscarf, removed an errant pin, and reinserted it flat. There was dignity in the way she held herself, in the quality and cleanliness of her clothes. She had committed to her appearance, despite the restrictions of camp life, and it spoke highly of her tenacity and self-regard. To have gotten hold of an iron, that was a feat in itself.

"Would you be open to sharing your story with us, Khadijah?" Jason shifted his buttocks until he was directly facing her.

"*Bof,* what can I say? I was frustrated, as French Algerian we are treated like the second class. In culture, in public life, even in the university, our experiences are ignored—we are erased, reduced to stereotype, we are just a problem to be managed, expected to shut up and be grateful. After reading about the exploitation of Algeria, I entered online forums to discuss my anger, and I found people there, intelligent and knowledgeable. I start to see Muslim can be powerful, not only victim. It gave me purpose, the chance to build an Islamic state, instead of only begging from the white master."

Jason nodded so vigorously that I feared he would snap his thin neck. "Absolutely! I completely understand, seeking empowerment after generations of colonial oppression. And how do you assess the experience now?"

"Bah, ISIS are savages. They should not be leading the Islamic Ummah, stupid, uneducated, backward men."

"Very good," said Jason, moving on to the next woman.

Several others spoke, but none of them were Sara.

An hour later, Jason wriggled his legs out from under him and jumped off the table. "Allah is all-loving and kind, and he wants Muslims to rise with generosity and hope, not with killing and war. Great sharing, everyone. I recognize the sacred trust you have offered me today and I respond with gratitude and a promise to honor your inner light. It would be wonderful to end with some big cleansing breaths."

The women would've been less horrified if he'd handed round AK-47s and told them to form a firing squad against Swiss Aisha. They gaped as he closed his eyes and inhaled loud ocean breaths and exhaled exaggerated aaahhhhs. At least he omitted the namaste.

The women rose, most of them giggling and clutching at each other's abayas as they drifted toward the exit. The air shifted behind me, and I turned around, coming face-to-cloth with a niqabi.

"Your sheikh is a pussy," she said, the movement of her niqab suggesting the contours of her mouth. My face swallowed itself in a smile.

"I know," I said, trying to act casual. "You should have seen our other options."

"How could they have been worse?" Sara scratched her toe with the bottom of her blue plastic slipper. Her naked toes were the only part of her body I could see, apart from her eyes.

"One was Shi'a, and the other was basically Osama bin Laden." The room was empty now, except for Jason. He gestured he would meet me in the car, and I waved him away.

"I vote for Bin Laden," she said without missing a beat.

"I know. That's the entire problem, babe."

She laughed, and her niqab flapped outward with the extra breath.

"You think Yogi Bear is going to convince us of anything?" She pronounced think "fink" and I found it charming.

"I wish he was a bear," I said, arching my eyebrows. "He's a yogi-twink."

"A twink," she repeated, giggling. "See, that's why I vote Bin Laden; he was a bear, with that big beard."

"Is that what his adoring recruits would say? Oh my, what a big beard you have?"

"I would have gone with: oh my, what a big weapon you have," she said, her eyes creasing.

"Ha! That is perfection."

I looked at the black cloth covering her face and tugged it gently. "You weren't wearing this last time. Have you literally become more radical?"

"Nah, I've got a rash." She lifted her niqab to show me the bumpy red spots. "Can you get me a cream for it?"

"Yeah, sure." I hovered my fingers over her raw skin, and her breath, warm and moist, tickled my hand. "I'm glad you came today."

She snorted and dropped the niqab back over her face. "Why? You in love with me already?"

I leaned toward her and whispered, "So what if I was? Would you chuck me off a building for being a lesbian?"

Her eyes met mine, and framed by layers of black cloth, they seemed larger and more seductive. "Are you actually a lesbian?"

I broke eye contact. "Depends on the girl." I shrugged. "You're not my type. I'm not a doppelbanger."

"Gross," she said like a nineties teen. "You eat fishy fanny?"

"I'd rather do that than suck ISIS dick."

"You'd be surprised," she said, a wicked look sprinting through her eyes. "There was some decent dick."

"Oh, Jesus mother," I groaned, covering my face with my palms. "How in God's name did we get onto this?"

"It's facts." She shifted from one foot to the other, looking mighty pleased.

I heard a distant Tom call my name, and I picked up my handbag.

"You going?" she said, a slight edge to her voice.

"Yeah, my team's waiting for me, but the program starts in a couple of days. I hope you'll sign up?"

"Erm, it's just, I was gonna ask . . ." Her eyes grew small and squinty as she examined my face, assessing me for something.

"You got fat," she said finally.

I had put on a few pounds since discovering the UN tuck shop sold Snickers bars.

"Yeah, well, you got scabies."

Her black cloak shuddered with laughter as the cabin door opened, and Tom beckoned me out.

IT FELT LIKE THE START OF THE SUMMER HOLIDAYS, THE DAYS STILL undefined, everything to look forward to. Sunlight leaked through the wooden shutters, pooled like molten glass on my bedroom floor, and the smell of fresh Iraqi bread filtered through the air. I opened the shutters and the oak slats gave way to palm trees, overlapping crosshatches of green, their chins laden with immature dates. It was mid-June, a month before they'd ripen. I sat at my dresser and turned cosmetics over in my hand, wondering what Sara might like, before setting aside an eyeshadow that Rosy had bought me. MILF was the name of its glittery gold shade, which I thought would make Sara giggle.

At lunchtime, I found myself delighted by the food situation. Farris walked in carrying platters of grilled kebab, deep-fried falafel, and stuffed grape leaves. He wore a white T-shirt that read "Free Britney, Free Palestine" across the front. It was surprising, the way Britney's plight had touched the hearts of the Iraqi people.

"Howdy," he said, setting down the food. Farris had learned English by endlessly rewatching a pirated copy of *Die Hard*. He perfected his accent by working for the US Marines. It was fortunate, the strong overlap in vocabulary between the two. Legend has it he said, "Yippee-ki-yay, motherfucker," in the interview and they hired him on the spot.

"Hey, Farris." I took a seat at the square kitchen table, which was covered with a plastic Mickey Mouse tablecloth. "That looks amazing. You eating?"

"No, Doctor, I have Friday prayers." He set out a plate and cutlery for me, even though that was definitely not his job, and left the kitchen.

I was grateful to be alone, preferring privacy for this moment of self-pleasure. I lifted a steaming, delicate kebab to my mouth—

"Oooh yeah!" said Tom, bursting into the room. He put four falafels into his mouth at once. "This is fit."

Could I not even have a food orgasm without Tom being there?

He stood over the kitchen counter and stuffed his face for three straight minutes. Then he was done. Priya walked in as he kissed me goodbye.

"You guys are cute," she said, her face contorted with disgust.

"Sorry." I stared longingly at my kebab. Would we never have a moment alone? "Didn't mean to be PDA."

She walked to the fridge and retrieved a bottle of orange juice the color of nuclear waste.

"You're a lucky bitch." She tipped the juice into her mouth without touching the rim.

I surrendered to my kebab and gasped when the spices hit the back of my throat.

"What, because of Tom?" I said, in between urgent mouthfuls.

She nodded and took a seat at the table across from me.

I picked at some kind of animal tendon trapped in my incisors. "I don't know. He does half piss me off sometimes."

"At least he's not skulking around like he's ashamed of you." She bit into a stuffed grape leaf and green juice dribbled down her chin.

"Oh, are you having a . . . with Charles . . . ?" I avoided eye contact, worried I'd crossed a line. Did she know about his wife?

She lowered her face into her palms. "Is it that obvious?" Her voice was muffled now. "He'll be pissed, he wants to keep it private."

Private, I thought. That's smart, a better word than *secret*. This was clearly not his first rodeo. Priya leaned toward me, her thin gold necklace swinging like a pendulum between us.

"Thing is, he's so hot and cold, it's confusing. I'm not putting any pressure on him, I'm happy to keep it casual, he's the one bringing the drama. Like, every two days, he's trying to pick a fight. What's the need? We're both stuck here, why can't we just enjoy it?"

I dropped the last piece of kebab onto my plate and wiped my greasy hands on a Star Wars napkin, trying to absorb this unexpected overshare. She obviously didn't know about his wife and kids, and I wasn't going to be the one to tell her.

"He's an idiot," I said. "You're gorgeous, and he doesn't deserve you."

I stood up to wash my plate, darting my hands between freezing and scalding streams of water; there was no mixer on the taps. When Farris had washed up earlier, he'd used the taps to explain the difference between Arabs and Europeans.

"The Arab is the hot tap—starts warm, you piss him off, he is quickly boiling. The European is the cold tap—starts normal, you make him angry, he turns to ice. And the two cannot be mixed."

I had wondered whether to slip him a copy of *Orientalism*.

"Hey," said Priya, "you've got a couple of days before your program starts, right? Could you help with the 'Come and See' visit tomorrow?"

"Sure, what's that?"

She produced a nail file and started excreting skin cells over her half-finished plate of food. "We're bringing tribal leaders to the camp to introduce them to the local women. It's like: hey, they aren't scary, take them back home, won't you?"

The scrape of her nail file emitted tiny clouds of human matter, making my kebab repeat in my throat. Why are people so compulsively vile?

"Sounds high stakes," I said. "What's the plan?"

She bent her fingers and blew. "We'll have a formal lunch, and I'll give a speech to encourage them to accept the women back. After that, it'll be like a careers fair. The women will talk to tribal leaders from their area. Ideally, the leaders will sign sponsorship agreements on the spot. With those, the women will have formal protection, and we can send them home. Charles will be there once he's done with the kids' program, but I could do with another set of hands."

"Sounds good, happy to help."

My phone buzzed with a message from Rosy. My thumb hovered over it, then pressed delete.

Priya stood up and tipped her detritus into the bin, while I found Gaviscon, Imodium, and rehydration tablets in the first-aid box and took them up to my room. It was becoming clear that the kebab I had so loved did not love me back.

19

THE NEXT MORNING, I WAS FANNING MY BURNING ARSE-
hole when Priya knocked on my bedroom door. I froze, my
vulnerable buttocks raw and exposed, as the doorknob
turned.

My voice returned in the nick of time. "I'll meet you downstairs," I yelled.

I shimmied into a pair of pants and descended the stairs at a
geriatric pace, trying to spare my ravaged cheeks further chafing.
Pierre was lying face-down on the living room floor as Jason hovered his palms over him, his curly brown hair scraped into a
topknot.

"Reiki," said Jason, glancing over at us. "It's energy healing."

"He's raking my aura," said Pierre through the rug. "Proximity
to ISIS is infecting my chakras."

Priya and I exchanged a look and left the villa, where Farris
waited, ready to drive us to the camp. I requested a stop at the
pharmacy.

Priya lowered her sunglasses. "What do you need?"

"Scabies cream for a girl in the camp and, like, Pepto Bismol or something. I need to mainline that shit if I plan to keep eating." Farris started the car, and we pulled out of the villa onto a pulverized asphalt road.

Priya's voice ululated as the car bounced over the uneven surface. "It's always a toss-up. I try to stick to plain bread. If you eat for real, you will pay."

"Exposure therapy," said Farris over his shoulder as he drove us into town. "Keep eating, and your body will adapt to the new bacteria. But you may get a tapeworm."

"I'd love a tapeworm," said Priya, sucking in her tiny belly. "Imagine, being able to eat all day without getting fat."

I wished I could disagree, but the truth was I'd trade all my professional accomplishments for the body of a third-tier Only-Fans star.

The pharmacy staggered under a massive billboard advertising the skin-whitening brand Fair & Lovely. A woman lovingly caressed her own face, her skin as pale as a White Walker's. I wondered what Sara would have made of it. I'd heard that ISIS considered white converts to be the most desirable brides. Imagine fleeing Europe for the land of Islam, and you're still second fiddle to some white girl who's lost control of her gap year.

Farris helped me pick out my items in the pharmacy before we got back on the road. The car careened into a pothole, and Priya and I bumped our heads on the ceiling.

"So, you're already doing special favors," said Priya, rubbing her head. "Be careful. They can be a manipulative lot. It's not my first time in a refugee camp."

"Come on. She's a kid with fucking scabies. It's not a big deal to buy her a cream."

Priya rifled through the plastic bag, extracted the slim cardboard box, and waved it in my face. "It starts with cream, and before you know it, you're committing wire fraud."

I raised an eyebrow. "Oh yeah? How exactly did your Ethiopia posting end?"

She put a single finger over her mouth. "Let's just say I learned my lesson. Well played, Aklilu, well played."

At the camp, the sky looked vast above the cowering tents, a startling blue, clouds drifting from dense opacity to threadbare whimsy, like stretched felt. The wind tumbled through the dirt pathways, lifting stony fragments before dropping them back down.

We didn't have our bulletproof vests on, and my steps felt light and effortless. Priya had argued it was a bad look, trying to persuade tribal leaders that the women weren't dangerous while skulking around in body armor. Tom conducted a new security assessment and concluded it was probably fine, but we all had to sign waivers saying that if we got stabbed, it was our own fault.

Priya handed me a roll of gaffer tape and a stack of paper signs. I labeled the five white gazebos by province and put up signs for different towns on the tables inside. The wind surged through the gazebos and their plastic sides rose like sails, the flimsy tables skittering to the side. I hunted for rocks on the dirt floor and used them to weigh the tables down.

As I crouched to pick up a sturdy rock, I felt the earth shudder and saw tiny stones jumping like fleas. I walked outside and watched a convoy of black GMCs enter the camp. Larger than normal SUVs, they looked like fat, shiny beetles crawling over the sand-colored ground. Women poked their heads out of the tents to watch the commotion, as dozens of tribal leaders emerged from the cars, holding on to their heads as the wind lifted their keffi-yehs. Priya walked toward them and they greeted her, one after another, by lifting their hands to their chests. The rising and falling hands gave the impression of the wave.

Priya showed the guests into a large tent, where she and Charles had laid Bedouin-style embroidered cushions around the perimeter. Reed mats covered the rest of the floor. Everyone crowded onto the seating, and Priya and I poured endless cups of tea and coffee while Charles held forth as though he, rather than Priya, was in charge.

The food was delayed, so we inadvertently provided the pro-tracted hospitality expected by tribal leaders. Eventually, Tom and Farris brought in steaming platters of rice and lamb and placed them at regular intervals along the floor. It smelled fragrant and rich, but my stomach tied itself into a knot, refusing entry. While the men dug in with their hands, Priya stood up to make her speech, Farris beside her, poised to translate.

"Welcome, honored guests." Index cards trembled in her fin-gers. "We are delighted to have you with us. It is time to bring Iraq's daughters back to their homes. We hope you will be reas-sured and comforted by your visit today. With your help, we can restore these women to their lives and heal this country."

Farris dutifully translated her speech, and a gap-toothed tribal leader in a black-and-gold cloak yelled something in Arabic, rice spilling out of his mouth. Everyone laughed, and Farris looked at his feet.

"What did he say?" asked Priya.

"They'll take the pretty ones."

I looked around at the men, as they shoveled restaurant food into their mouths, meters from where the women eked out stale rations from polystyrene boxes. You want the pretty ones? I guess you'd also prefer them to be young, traumatized, and helpless? I imagined handing out white-hot branding irons to the women. "All together now," I would say, as we applied them to the men's genitals. Is there an NGO that would fund that?

"Sorry," said Farris, sitting down next to me. "They are rural people. This is not Islam."

I gave him a wry smile. "I know."

After lunch, the tribal leaders dispersed to the various gazebos, where the women were waiting. At each table, one female suppliant would cower in front of three or four men, their bodies casting great, looming shadows over her as they determined her fate.

From the back of the Anbar tent, I watched a woman in a forest-green headscarf. She was sitting at the Ramadi table, and her shoulders shook as tears slipped through the fingers covering her face. The tribal leader waved her away with the back of his hand and she ran out, her long black abaya sweeping across the dirt floor.

I hurried after her. "Hey, are you OK?" I said.

She turned around, gasping through hysterical sobs. "He says I am terrorist and my children are terrorist. We did nothing. ISIS came, ask for marriage, what can I do? I had no choice."

I tried to assemble some words of comfort, but she scurried away, disappearing into the rows of tents. I rubbed my eyes and lifted my face to the sky. The late-afternoon sun wobbled like a naked yolk on the horizon, and the heat of the day fled toward it. I took a deep breath, but like everywhere in this country, the air was filled with diesel from the generators, and it scraped through my throat, noxious and harsh.

A slight figure in a niqab wound its way toward me, plastic slippers thwacking against the dirt.

"Wah'gwan?" she said.

I smiled and felt around in my pockets for the cream.

"Hey, Sara. Look, I got you this." I handed her the slim cardboard box, and she tucked it up the sleeve of her abaya.

"Safe, thanks, bruv." She stood on her tiptoes and looked over my shoulder. "What's going on?"

"We've brought tribal leaders to meet the local women."

"Is there anyone here from Mosul?"

"Yeah, over there in the Ninewah tent. Why?"

She took off toward the gazebo, and Priya stormed past me in the opposite direction, swearing loudly. I looked one way, then the other. I went after Priya first.

"What's happened?" I said, trotting beside her.

"They're extorting us, the fucking pricks—two hundred dollars each, or they won't leave. We can't just let the tribal leaders stay here overnight; it would be incredibly unsafe. They've got us over a barrel."

"Christ, that's so messed up."

"I tried to negotiate it down to a hundred dollars. Farris translated their response; it was something like, 'Our horses wouldn't even shit for a hundred dollars.'" She bit her hand to suppress a scream.

Charles was waiting for us in the reception cabin with a brown envelope full of hundred-dollar bills. He patted Priya on the back.

"I'm sorry," he said. "You tried."

Priya took the envelope and returned to the tribal leaders to distribute the money as the light began to fade. An hour later, the black SUVs were gone and the gazebos were desolate, A4 signs littering the floor, chairs overturned and tables askew. The women had flocked to the tent where we'd hosted the fancy lunch and were picking apart the leftovers.

As I walked back to the car, I spotted a hunched figure sitting on the ground by the fence, niqab hanging low over her knees, plastic slippers sticking out. I recognized those slippers.

"Sara?" I walked over to her.

Her cloth-covered face looked up, then returned its gaze to the ground. Violent strokes of pink colored the sky, casting a blush over the curve of her back.

"I know it's you." I sat down next to her, wincing as the rocks stabbed my ruined arse. "What's happened?"

Her voice, corroded by tears, came out thin and small. "They're such bastards," she said.

My eyes immediately filled with unearned tears and I threatened them until they returned to their ducts.

"Who's upset you, love?" I said.

She started hyperventilating, sucking the black niqab in and out of her mouth. I pulled it over her head, grabbed her hand, and put my face in front of hers.

"Listen to me, look at me. Breathe. Here, do it with me. Exhale . . . one, two, three. Inhale . . . one, two, three."

Her gasps began to slow as darkness washed the color from the sky and her silhouette retreated further into the dusk.

"Sara, tell me what's going on."

Her bony hand shook like a terrified rodent in my palm.

"I've got a two-year-old," she whispered, tears running over the sores on her face. "And they've taken her away."

"What?" I struggled to make sense of it. Sara was just a school-girl in my mind, but she . . . had a baby? She seemed to age suddenly, in fast-forward, shadows creeping up her face, elasticity melting from her skin.

"Who took her? Where is she?"

She exhaled and brought the back of her sleeve to her scabbed cheeks.

"Her Iraqi grandparents came to the camp a year ago. My husband died in the invasion, and his parents wanted the child. They took her right from my arms; I was screaming like hell but no one stopped them. I've got no rights here; everyone thinks I'm just some foreign whore. The worst thing is, she's only in Mosul. She's so close, I can feel her all the time, every part of my body feels her, it's like she's calling for me, and I can't go to her."

She brought up her knees, pressed her face into them, and cried. I stroked her back, my mind barely able to stretch over the scale of her grief. She'd lost her home, her parents, her future—and now her child. Torn right out of her arms. Who the fuck had let that happen?

A ferocious protectiveness unlocked inside me, and it felt primal, as though I'd become a parent myself. I started strategizing in my mind, trying to figure out how to bring the child back.

"You spoke to a tribal leader from Mosul today?" I said. "Could he help?"

"He told me to get lost. Said the child is where it should be."

I shook my head. "I'm so sorry, Sara, this is incredibly fucked-up."

Her voice was high-pitched now and her words tumbled out fast and breathless. "It's my own fault, I should've run away, I should've protected her, but I was just so scared after Mosul. You don't know what I saw. The bombings were constant, so many people dead on the streets, mothers like me, babies with their heads in bits. Every time I close my eyes, I can still see it, I can smell the bodies burning. When they brought us to the camp, I couldn't move for days, I stayed in the tent, I couldn't do anything except feed her. But I should've run, gone to the border, got somewhere further than here, somewhere they couldn't find us."

I put my arms around her and held her close. "It wasn't your fault, Sara, there's nothing you could have done, there was no right choice to make. You kept her safe, I know it must be unbearable that she's not with you, but you kept her alive."

She pulled away and tipped her head back, leaning it against the fence, the breeze spreading tears into tributaries across her face.

"She's the best little girl, she hardly ever cried, and we used to cuddle the whole time. Her hair is really dark and curly, and she's got these fat cheeks, I'd stroke them all day with my thumb. I only had one toy for her, a sock bunny that I made myself, but she loved it, and she'd get all excited and giggly when I took it out."

She grabbed my hands. "You've got to help me find her, Nadia, you've got to bring her back, I'm begging you."

She didn't need to ask; I was already consumed.

"I swear to you, Sara," I said, looking her dead in the eyes, "I'll do every possible thing. There is nothing I won't do."

She folded into me, my body where her daughter's should have been, and we stayed there until I heard Priya yell my name through the darkness.

I dabbed under Sara's eyes, absorbing her tears with my fingertips, before standing up. As I turned to walk away, she called after me.

"Her name is Habibah."

20

THAT NIGHT, WE GATHERED IN THE LIVING ROOM TO
nurse Priya's wounds. After the day I'd had, my body ached
for the support of solid surfaces, so I sat on the tile floor
with my back against the wall, legs outstretched. Charles stepped
over me, walked into the kitchen, and returned with a foil tray of
spinach sambousek and two glass bottles of Coke. He handed me
a bottle before sitting on the mustard sofa. The cold glass felt sharp
against my hand, and as I drank, the sugary bubbles floated up-
ward and burst in my brain. Why does Coke taste so much better
from a glass bottle?

Pierre ran down the stairs, waving a quart of whiskey. "I have
the emergency supply!" He skidded into the living room in his
socks and sat beside Priya, who was lying in the middle of the
floor.

Priya sat up, took the bottle from his hand, and glugged.

Pierre watched her. "It was so bad?" She nodded, handed back
the whiskey, and lay down.

The back door opened and Sheikh Jason walked in.

"Beautiful stars tonight," he said. Somewhat belaboring the point, he was wearing solar-system-themed pajamas that covered his body with little round planets.

He stood over us. "Oh man, heavy vibes in here. Should I lead a guided meditation?"

"*No!*" we all said with one breath.

"OK, OK." He sat on the sofa opposite Charles. "So, what happened today?"

"Wait for me," yelled Sherri from upstairs. She came down slowly in a bathrobe, her face painted with a thick green mask that brought out the green in her eyes, her curly hair tied in a round bun high on her head. She perched uncertainly next to Jason, as though any sudden movement would cause the mask to fall straight off her face.

"There's a lot of pollution," she said, even though no one had asked. "This extracts the impurities from your skin."

Everyone trained their eyes on Priya, who sighed and stared at the ceiling. "I've fucked it. The tribal twats extorted me and they didn't sponsor a single woman to return."

"It's a process, it takes time as well," said Charles through a mouthful of pastry. "You can't expect results just like that."

Priya covered her eyes with her hands. "But I hate every single one of them. I never want to see them again!"

Pierre took a sip of whiskey, then offered it to Jason, whose whole body shrank away.

"*Désolé*, I forgot you are a holy man." Pierre handed the bottle to Sherri, who cleared gloopy face mask from her lips before taking a drink.

I watched quietly, waiting for an opportunity to bring up Sara. Learning about Habibah had changed everything. I felt enclosed by a glass cloche, my focus solely on my mission, the world beyond muffled and irrelevant.

During a break in the conversation, I moved to the middle of the room and cleared my throat. "I need your advice, guys. There's a young woman in the camp, Sara, and her baby's been taken off her. It's with its grandparents in Mosul. How should I go about getting it back?"

"She's a terrorist," said Pierre, pulling Priya into a seated position so he could examine her hair for split ends. "The child is better off without her."

"Oh, fuck off, Pierre. How can you say that? You don't know her."

He took a strand of Priya's hair and bit the end off. "*Ma chérie*, you don't know her either. She could be the slitter of many throats."

"Don't be ridiculous, she was just a housewife. She came here as a teenager, following her best friend. One stupid decision and her whole life's been destroyed. She doesn't deserve to be separated from her child, on top of everything else. It's already been traumatizing enough."

Priya nudged Pierre off her and tied up her hair. "Wait, is this the girl you bought scabies cream for? I told you this would happen. You're getting attached, and it's totally unprofessional."

"My job," I said, jabbing my Coke bottle in her direction, "is to deradicalize these women. What could be more radicalizing than having your child stolen from you?"

"They were fucking radicals when they came here," yelled Priya. "ISIS wouldn't have succeeded without all these mental foreigners showing up. The local women, they're the real victims. They didn't have a choice!"

"Oh my God, Priya, it's not a zero-sum game. I'm not saying the local women aren't victims, but can't you accept some of the foreign women are too?"

Sherri knelt on the floor between Priya and me. "Come on, you two," she said. "You're both on the same side. You share a passion for supporting victims, and that's wonderful. Priya, maybe one of the tribal leaders from Mosul can help this girl access her child? Even just a supervised visit?"

Priya pushed her away. "Back off, Sherri. Don't you understand what happened today? I'm a colossal failure, I can't influence tribal leaders even though my job depends on it. And if I could, a foreign fucking jihadi would not be my top priority."

I looked around the room, at everyone's useless, gawking expressions, at Charles blithely stuffing his face with pastry.

"Hey, Mr. UNICEF," I said, knocking a spinach sambousek out of his hand. "You're in charge of kids, why don't you have an opinion? You think it's OK that children are being stolen from the camp?"

He laid the foil tray on the ground, wiped the greasy crumbs from his face. "Eish, calm down, Nadia. The child's with its grandparents, living in the community. Who's to say that's a bad outcome? Life in the camp isn't great."

It was probably the "calm down" that did it. My vision was temporarily obscured by a searing white light. "I'm not surprised you think that," I said, practically hissing, "seeing as you've abandoned your own children. You imagine all parents are as callous and heartless as you are."

The room fell silent and Charles gripped one fist with the other, skin taut over the knuckles. Priya stood up and walked over to him.

"Got a wife at home too, I guess?" she whispered.

He looked away. She picked up the foil tray and smacked it across his face, pastries scattering across the floor. Sobbing, she ran upstairs, and Charles trudged after her.

Everyone was staring at me, mouths open, but I struggled to care. This was such petty bullshit compared to what Sara was going through.

"*Putain!*" said Pierre, his hands a storm of gestures. "You are a total bitch, Nadia. For what have you done this? She already had the worst day."

"Priya deserved to know," I said, before turning my attention to Jason. "You've been very quiet. Surely you agree that it's evil to separate a mother from her baby like this?"

"Dude, it's a toughie." His finger traced circles around the green planet on his leg. "Islamic Shari'ah tends to favor the father's family. I'll have to pray on this one."

I scoffed. "What would you know? You fake fucking sheikh."

"*Arrête*, Nadia, enough!" said Pierre, producing a pack of cards from his pocket. "Why don't we play a game of poker? Perhaps we can rescue this terrible evening."

My Coke bottle clattered against the tile floor as I stormed out.

I lingered in the upstairs hallway, my face pressed against the wall, my breathing sharp and shallow.

"Oh, goodness," I heard Jason say downstairs, "gambling's off-limits for me."

What a despicable little rules gimp. Oh no, God says I can't play cards. But tearing a child from its mother's bosom? Nothing in the rule book about that.

I heard scampering on the stairs and turned to see a slimy green face.

"You're right about the girl," said Sherri, patting my arm. "It's totally unconscionable what's happened to her. We should talk to Lina; she's got powerful connections in Mosul, I'm sure she could do something."

I grabbed her and pulled her into a hug, her body limp with surprise, her face mask smearing onto my shoulder. "I'll call her in the morning. Thank you, Sherri."

Tom was in his bedroom doing jumping jacks in a white vest and boxer shorts, as though he'd forgotten his PE kit.

"Hey, doll." He wiped his brow with a withered flannel.

I stumbled toward him, my hands outstretched. "It's all fucked-up, Tom."

He surrounded my body with his and cradled my head against his chest. I inhaled the smell of his sweat, and my balled-up fists weakened, then dropped. I staked my fury ashore and stepped away for the night, letting the sadness take me.

21

THE DAWN POSTED SHARDS OF PALE LIGHT THROUGH THE angled shutters, and I lay in clammy sheets, my mind on the cusp of consciousness, thinking about Sara and Habibah, about being separated from my own mother. I'd last visited home the previous summer, the day after a debauched festival weekend with Rosy.

That morning, I had awoken wedged into a sleeping bag. I was wearing every item of clothing I'd brought with me, while Rosy was splayed out naked. During the night, my liver had sucked the alcohol out of my bloodstream, leaving behind particles of ice that unfolded and duplicated. At a cellular level, Rosy belonged here; binge drinking, camping, underdressing. This was her heritage, and her body was fortified against it. I may have been born in the Midlands, but I wasn't meant for these climes.

A spasm through Rosy's foot awoke her suddenly. "What?" She blinked in confusion.

"Morning, babe." I stood with my sleeping bag stuck around me. "Should we get going?"

"Oh, yeah." She yawned. "Sunday, Family Funday, gotta get back to London."

Rosy rarely went a week without seeing her parents. They used their meager resources to pile mattresses into her life, one on top of the other, ready to break her falls and to launch her back up, cheering her on all the while. If she murdered someone, her parents would put together a playlist to accompany the grave digging. They'd make a day of it.

An unformed idea drifted through my mind. "I was thinking maybe I should visit my mum."

"Doesn't she hate you?" She rolled over and opened Instagram on her phone.

"She doesn't *hate* me. It was hard for her, my dad dying so young, and I didn't exactly turn out the way she wanted, but she's softening. At least she talks to me now—"

"OMG, look at us here." Rosy waved her phone in my face, a photo from last night, me giving her a piggyback ride, a flower crown falling from her head. "I don't even remember uploading that. Ah, it's been wicked."

We packed up, pouring out earwigs drowned in gin-filled plastic tumblers and licking the insides of crisp packets for residual salt. I tried to wrestle my sleeping bag back into its carry case, but it was like trying to stuff a baby back up a vagina. When I called my mother, she said, "Oh, yes, come!" with such excitement that I doubted my version of our relationship.

I sat behind the wheel of my hire car, squinting through my comedown brain. Rosy had masked her bloodshot eyes with oversize sunglasses, the disguise of A-listers who can't actually bear to relinquish attention. I drove her to the train station in a quaint Suffolk village that looked like the backdrop to a hate crime. She hoisted up her rucksack and blew me a kiss, which I caught with a flourish, pressing it against my heart. I watched for her laughter, but she'd already turned away.

The car had steamed up, and I peeled myself until I was in a crop top and hot pants. I tapped "home" on Google Maps, but it pulled up my London address, so I had to type it in. I started to drive and as I merged onto the motorway, Cat Stevens's "Morning Has Broken" played on the radio. A rare crossover between my two worlds. Cat Stevens's conversion to Islam was much celebrated in our household. Mum loved the dreary Islamic music he produced under his new name, Yusuf Islam, but she also allowed "Morning Has Broken," it being sufficiently godly. My favorite, "The First Cut Is the Deepest," had been banned.

After three separate service station stops, a bright-blue sign descended into view, the word *Leicester* written in white, the universal color of ceasefire. This time will be different, I thought.

I turned in to our neighborhood, a dense grid of redbrick terraced houses, wheelie bins standing guard next to each door. Immigrants don't fit easily into class categories, resources forever undermined by foreignness, but my family was broadly middle class, and since my father's death, my mother had been generously supported by her brothers, who owned a small chain of travel agents specializing in hajj and trips back to Pakistan. This meant my mother was free to take on low-paying work teaching kids at the mosque. I parked half a block from my mum's house and got dressed in the back seat, jeans and a blouse buttoned to the top. I left the car there, a crime scene of hedonism, and walked to the house. The windows were veiled with lace net curtains, originally white, now off-gray. I let myself in. My house keys, once torn from my hands as my mother pushed me out, had since been restored to me.

"Mum!" I shut the front door behind me, and the breeze dislodged a musty smell from the beige paisley carpet, unchanged since the seventies. It was both comforting and suffocating in its familiarity.

She came out of the kitchen wiping her hands on her apron, the tips of her fingers yellow with turmeric. "Salaam, darling." She hugged me into a cloud of airborne onion bhaji. "What a nice surprise."

"Are you making pakoras?" I dropped my bag, turning up my nose to sniff.

"Yes, I know they're your favorite." Her thin gray hair was twisted up into a knot. She'd given up coloring it with henna, and a couple of reddish-orange streaks at the bottom were all that remained of her brief foray into beautification. "I didn't have any of the ingredients, so I had to go out, then I decided I might as well do a big shop, so I went to the cash-and-carry." She returned to the kitchen, and I followed, looking at her pastel-colored shalwar kameez, which was crumpled at the back. She loved to cook in the lightweight, cotton ones. "I saw Auntie Asmaa there, and she asked about you. You remember her son, Hayder, he was in the year above you. He's getting married. You know he had a nose job. I don't like to say, but it made a world of difference. Found a wife easily after that."

"Oh yeah, honky Hayder. Good for him."

She tutted. "You lot were so mean about it. It's your fault he had a complex, poor lad."

"You just said he needed a nose job!"

"Yeah, well, it was massive, wasn't it? It's good for Auntie Asmaa. She's been dying to get her kids married. She got her wedding outfits last time she went to Pakistan, on the off chance, but that was three years ago now and she's put on two stone since then. The tailor's gonna have a job with that."

She scooped the onion bhajis out of the pan and onto a plate covered in paper towels that turned yellow and translucent. She plonked it in front of me and fetched a can of Rubicon mango and a tub of mint chutney from the fridge.

"Eat." She sat across from me as I tore apart tendrils of battered onion, dipped them in chutney, tossed them in the air, and caught them with my mouth.

"Delicious, Mum," I said with my mouth full. The grease spread through me, absorbing the poison of the weekend.

Mum sighed. "Stop doing that. You'll drop it."

"No, I won't." I launched another one into the air, but it missed my mouth and hit me on the cheek. Mum pursed her lips.

"You jinxed it!"

"That's a terrible thing to say." Her arms jingled as she pushed the plate closer to me. She'd worn the same set of solid gold bangles ever since I could remember, a gift from her mother, who showed love solely through the distribution of precious metals. "The evil eye is no joke. Ruksana's terrible neighbor cursed her after she refused to pay half for a new fence. Nothing wrong with the original fence, mind you, but the neighbor got a dog, disgusting thing, and wanted it sealed off. Anyway, she lost her job after that. Took her ages to find a new one."

"Ruksana got fired because she did literally no work." I glugged sparkling mango from the can and burped.

"Don't be awful. She was trying to get her NVQ in childcare. The poor thing had a lot of reading."

"Oh yeah, poor her. Remember when I did a PhD in criminology and worked the entire time?"

"No one likes a show-off." Mum stood up to clear the plates. "Not everyone finds it so easy."

"You think I found it easy? I had no family at the time. Thanks for all the support, by the way."

"Go get ready," she said, scrubbing the pan with a wire scourer. "I'll drive you to the hospital to visit your granddad." Mum often used selective hearing to leap over the ravines that separated us, and to refocus on the minutiae that we could both bear. I thought about grabbing the scourer out of her hand and forcing her to acknowledge what she'd done to me. But I just put my plate in the sink and went upstairs.

I sat on the toilet, scrolling through my phone. Rosy had sent me a selfie with her parents in an adult ball pit, grins wider than their faces. What did I have to look forward to? An afternoon in geriatric care. I washed the crumbs off my face and went back downstairs.

"Ready when you are." I held on to either side of the kitchen doorframe and leaned in.

Mum dried the last plate with a tea towel and took her apron off. She turned around to survey my outfit and I stiffened, though surely I'd done enough to pass the inspection.

"Aren't you going to cover your arms?" She tugged at my short sleeves with her damp fingers.

"Mum, it's too warm for a cardie." I shook her off me, wishing I'd stayed in the fucking hot pants. She was impossible to satisfy, why did I even bother?

"It's hotter in hellfire." She crossed her thick brown arms as though she were heaven's bouncer.

I rolled my eyes and leaned against the frosted-glass kitchen door. "Jesus Christ, not this again."

Mum gasped with pantomime-level drama. "Language! If you're going to act like this, get in your car and drive home."

I turned away. "I've been here for thirty minutes," I muttered, "and I'm already being attacked."

Mum grabbed my shoulder. "My father is dying and you care about your outfit? You're a disgrace!"

I pried her fingers from me. "He's not dying, he's having an IV drip for dehydration. And I'm not being a fashion victim here, I'm wearing something reasonable and comfortable. Stop being so controlling."

"It's called mothering. I sacrificed my whole life for you, and all you do is throw it back in my face. I wish I never had you."

She said the words often, but that didn't temper their impact. It's hard to believe you're worthy of love when your own mother wishes you didn't exist. On the other hand, she had made me pakoras, so she couldn't be fully committed to my annihilation. It always surprised me how swiftly her nurturing dissolved into vitriol.

"I didn't ask to be born!" I winced even as I said it; what a teenage line. Mum stood square in front of me, limbering up for another round, but a wave of exhaustion crested and broke over me.

"You are—" she began, before I interrupted her.

"*Fine.* I'll put a cardigan on."

I stomped upstairs, found the most hideous cardigan in my mum's wardrobe, and put it on. When I returned, she was filling Tupperware containers with curry and rice. Granddad's refusal to eat hospital food was a bigger threat to his life than his latest ailment. Mum looked up at me and nodded.

"Good girl."

Once the food was ready, she put a black abaya over her clothes and pinned on a floral headscarf, and we got into her car. The Tupperware was hot resting on my jeans, alcohol sweat bubbled from my pores, and the wool cardigan itched against my arms. Spending a comedown with my mother in Leicester—I must have been a sadist in my past life.

"How is that girl?" Mum asked as we drove past the local butcher. A neon green "Halal" sign flashed in the window. Nothing about my relationship with Rosy was halal and Mum often blamed her for dragging me further into the ranks of the unbelievers. She wasn't wrong.

"Yeah, she's fine. Her start-up is going well."

"At least one of you is making money. When will you get a proper job?"

"Academia is hard, Mum," I said for the umpteenth time. "It's tough to get a lectureship."

The car slowed, and the indicator clicked on before we rounded a corner.

"All that education and you earn less than your cousin Saif, who dropped out at fifteen. You know, he just bought a Mercedes. And he gave his mother a Gucci bag." Mum's obsession with designer brands was incongruous with her religious devotion, more Calvinism than Islam; the wealthy are also the elect. And people say Muslims fail to assimilate.

"I'm sorry, but Saif is what, thirty, and he still lives in his childhood bedroom? That is spectacularly lame. At least I'm a grown-up who takes responsibility for her own life."

"You? A grown-up?" Mum's voice was elevated in both volume and pitch. "You hold on to Rosy's coattails like a lost child, following her around, getting friendship tattoos and doing God knows what every weekend. You should be married by now, not shacked up with some *gori* girl as if you're still at uni. Nothing grown-up about either of you."

I was stunned, as though she'd cut off my heroin supply and was lambasting me for taking methadone. Maybe I'm obsessed with Rosy, Mum, because you took my fucking family away from me. I drafted several responses in my mind, but each was more provocative than the last, so I kept my mouth shut.

We walked into the hospital, over rubbery linoleum floors that were patched up with gaffer tape. The smell of disinfectant and the sight of empty gurneys made me think of babies covered in gunk tearing out of screaming women, and victims of car accidents pulsating blood through open wounds. I wondered whether, one day, I would lie here, watching the yellowing ceiling tiles blinking in and out of view, as life was dragged from my wretched body. We reached my granddad's ward and stepped behind the thin paper curtain surrounding his bed. Saif and his parents were already there. Granddad looked tiny in the hospital bed, his head swallowed by the double pillows, and I felt guilty for resenting the visit.

Mum pushed me toward Granddad. "Talk to him," she said, as though I'd traveled all this way planning to ignore him.

"Salaam." I showed him the depressed carnations I'd bought from a petrol station. "Sorry you're not feeling well." I pressed my hand into his, and he looked up at me. He said something in Urdu and I looked at him blankly.

"It's Nadia, your granddaughter," said Mum. He looked down at my hand, still in his, and I gently squeezed it.

"You're going to be OK," I said. "We all love you."

He said something else in Urdu and Saif sniggered.

I moved aside to let Saif's parents come closer and placed the flowers next to the stacks of food on the bedside table. Mum put her arms around me and gave me a hug; a cessation of hostilities. She told me to get her a coffee and Saif joined me as we wandered the hospital corridors. He was wearing an oversize beige Nike tracksuit with a gold chain, and in my mother's green wool cardigan, I looked like his head teacher.

"I heard you got a Mercedes," I said, grateful for this tidbit from my mother. It was a challenge to make conversation with my cousin; we barely shared a language, let alone a lifestyle.

"Yeah, it's sick." He shook his fingers as though he'd burned them on his shit-hot car. "I got the S-class G-Tronic with a V-6 engine."

"Didn't understand any part of that," I said.

"What you riding now? The Tube, innit?" He fell about laughing, delighted by his witticism.

"Mostly, yeah." To expend energy on this conversation felt unjustifiable. I held a cup under the coffee machine, and we watched it whirr and spit.

"Hey, listen," I said, as we strolled back toward the ward, tepid cups in hand. "Did you understand what Granddad said to me?"

"Oh yeah! He saw that tattoo on your wrist. Can't believe you let him see that. He asked your mum why she'd raised such a whore."

Of course. I closed my eyes to absorb the scale of my defeat. Of course he did.

22

ALL JOBS, NO MATTER HOW LOFTY THEIR GOALS, ARE composed of repetitive component parts, and the rehabilitation of ISIS women was no exception.

Every day, I'd wake up late and drag myself to the shower, which was usually being hogged by Charles, and I'd yell at him to hurry up, before sneaking into Sherri's room to steal clean underwear because I'd forgotten to do a wash. Then I'd shower and dress in five minutes flat and rush out of the villa, grabbing a pastry and packed lunch on my way, only to end up waiting in the car for that last person (inevitably Pierre) who still wasn't ready.

At the camp, Sherri and I spent our mornings in a tiny Portakabin carrying out psychosocial assessments. For each woman who'd come in, we'd ask a set of questions to determine the psychological and social assistance they needed, before drawing up a personalized support plan.

At lunchtime, I'd find Sara kicking around outside and we'd slip into an empty cabin to share my lunch. Lina had promised to locate Sara's daughter, so we felt confident and hopeful. In the meantime, we enjoyed hanging out, and in that first month, we became proper friends. She was sharp, witty, a real Londoner, forever cracking me up with imitations of her tentmates: stinky Sujood's fear of dissolving in the shower, Nafisah's Chewbacca-scale hairiness, and, worst of all, sweet-thieving, monster-snoring Layla. And she loved listening to my stories about Pierre and his Iraqi zaddy, Lina and her demonic budgie, and the evolving soap opera of Charles and Priya's affair. Together, we'd daydream about London, waxing nostalgic about discount handbags at TK Maxx, McDonald's Filet-O-Fish (the staple Muslim order), and our love of Whitechapel Gallery (not the art, only the gift shop). Sometimes, she'd tell me about her daughter. The startled expression on her face when she hiccupped, the edible quality of her skin, the way her hair felt downy soft even when it looked like twigs.

In the afternoons, Sherri would provide one-to-one counseling while I contacted the women's friends and family members back home and occasionally supervised Jason's classes.

Once Sherri and I had completed a psychosocial assessment, we'd ask Sheikh Jason for his observations, then we'd write a report and pass the case on to Pierre. His job was to liaise with six competing Iraqi intelligence agencies to uncover any dirt on the woman in question. The intelligence agencies would check their mad and disorganized records to see if the woman had actively supported ISIS; for example, by joining the brutal morality police, or by participating in recruitment or propaganda efforts. If she was cleared, Pierre would send that clearance together with our report to the relevant embassy. The embassy would handle repatriation.

Charles and Priya ran their programs separately from us, and we'd only hear about them over dinner in the evenings. Charles often returned to the villa ashen-faced, clutching horrific pictures drawn by the children in his care, while Priya disappeared for days on end—usually after an epic fight with Charles—when she'd tour Iraqi towns and villages trying to change attitudes toward the camp.

While Charles and Priya struggled to make headway in that first month, the UNDO team had an early success. French Khadijah, a beautiful and self-possessed intellectual in her early thirties, had a straightforward assessment with Sherri and me. She was in close contact with her family, who owned a high-end jewelry store on the rue de la Paix, and who had the means to support her if she returned to Paris. The family had already paid a French PTSD specialist to give her therapy over Zoom, and it had proven remarkably effective. Though she'd experienced torture in an ISIS prison after attempting to escape, Khadijah was adept at managing her day-to-day mental state. Once Sheikh Jason confirmed she'd been a constructive participant in class, Sherri and I completed our report and handed her over to Pierre.

It quickly transpired that Pierre and Khadijah had both studied philosophy at the Sorbonne, just a couple of years apart, and they nattered endlessly about the professors they hated, the course materials they considered antiquated, and the examination system they labeled crass and reductive. Pierre declared her "chic" and "the right kind of French immigrant." Of course, he had no sympathy for the other French girl in the camp, Marie, a visibly troubled young convert and former drug addict, who he left to fester.

Pierre devoted himself to procuring Khadijah's security clearance and used his political connections to get expedited responses from all six intelligence agencies. When the Iraqis cleared Khadijah,

Pierre personally visited the French ambassador. He emphasized Khadijah's contrition, evidenced by her early attempts to flee, and described her torture in ISIS detention in such graphic detail, it brought the ambassador to tears. Then, he worked his contacts in Paris until he found civil servants to guide the embassy through every step of the repatriation process. When he returned to the villa, the repatriation order in hand, we celebrated like never before. We'd proven the program could work.

23

I WAS CURIOUS TO SEE HOW LINA WOULD DRESS FOR THE camp. Sitting on the living room sofa, my knees angled toward the stairwell, I watched for her descent, as though awaiting the first glimpse of a bride. The tan Jimmy Choo sneakers came first, white laces sparkling as they tapped against each step. Then, green wide-legged slacks, high-waisted, a cream satin blouse tucked in, a thin gold necklace against her collarbone. Her dark hair blow-dried into its signature bob, Audrey Hepburn sunglasses perched on top. I glanced down at my Matalan linen shirt. I looked like a used tissue.

Pierre followed her down the stairs, and I stood up to offer them my plate of fresh Iraqi bread and grilled halloumi. They looked at it with disgust.

"*Beurk*," said Pierre, putting a protective arm around Lina. "Fat *and* carbohydrates. *Dégueulasse!*" He ushered Lina into the kitchen, where they poured two coffees before going outside to smoke.

The camp yielded to Lina as though she were a celebrity. Gates opened before we reached them, guards and staffers stepped aside, women stared from gaps between the tents. We were shown to a special cabin with cloth-covered tables, upholstered chairs, and glass tumblers. I didn't know the camp had a VIP section, and I resented that it had been whipped out for Lina.

As we settled in, we heard a metallic creaking. Something heaving up the steps. A belly entered the cabin first, the rest of him followed. The man was enormous, and I wondered if his stature helped or hindered his role as a preeminent local dignitary.

He was wearing a starched, blinding white thawb, an equally white keffiyeh on his head, held down by a circular black band. How did these guys achieve such bright whites? My socks always turned gray, no matter what detergent I used.

His thick, crescent mustache made him look like a walrus, and the bristles looked so sharp, I could imagine them cutting which-ever poor woman had to kiss him. A clean-shaven young man followed him in, wearing a baseball cap and black T-shirt.

We stood up and Lina placed her right hand on her chest. "Sheikh Abu-Bakr al-Obeidi, it's wonderful to see you again."

"My Lina!" His smile lifted his entire face, making him look ten years younger. "You are still beautiful, but very thin. We will pre-pare a great feast for you."

"Thank you, Sheikh, I would be delighted." She offered him a seat, but he pulled a phone out of his pocket and waved it at her.

"We do TikTok together?" His eyes were wide and hopeful. "I did some practice."

I looked at Pierre, but his face was stone.

"How about we do it properly when I visit your home? The space here is small." She gestured at the surrounding walls with a sweep of her arm.

"OK, OK." He selected the largest chair and sat down. "We do it in my garden, where I plant many flowers for my lovely Lina."

Lina took a breath and opened her notebook. "Sheikh, I'd like to discuss the possibility of returning local women to their homes. You are powerful and respected in the community, and your support is crucial to us."

I wondered why Priya wasn't here, since local returns were definitely her jurisdiction.

The sheikh nodded and stroked his amber prayer beads. "Yes, one word from me, and all of Iraq listens."

Pierre noticed a scuff on his leather shoe, and he bent his right leg over his left thigh so he could rub it off. His suspended right foot was pointing at the sheikh.

The young mafioso accompanying the sheikh whispered in Pierre's ear, "In Mosul, you would be killed for this disrespect." Pierre's leg abruptly dropped to the ground.

Lina turned to me. "Before we start, Nadia, why don't you get the Sara issue out of the way?"

I jolted. The scene was so engrossing, I'd forgotten my physical presence in the room.

"Um, yes, Sheikh, thanks, you are honorable and . . . glorious?" I've never been good at obsequious preamble. "We'd be very grateful if you could help us reunite a young mother with her baby. Sara is here in the camp, and her late husband's family have the child in Mosul."

The sheikh looked at me with curiosity. Perhaps he'd have liked to do a TikTok with me too.

He nodded. "Bring her."

I scrambled to my feet, but my arse was wedged into the chair and it rose with me. I plucked it off and vowed to stop eating halloumi.

At the reception cabin, I breathlessly asked someone to go find Sara. A camp administrator set off, walking so slowly that she appeared to be stationary. It took all my restraint not to go myself, but I'd received several formal warnings by that point for failing to observe security protocol.

I stood there and watched the camp, observing the industriousness of the women. They scrubbed, dunked, and wrung their threadbare clothes before hanging them from long plastic washing lines. They beat foam mattresses, shook reed mats, and carried shower caddies to and from sanitation stations. They huddled together in pairs and furtively exchanged tiny rolls of cash for bags of sweets, cards of phone credit, and plastic handheld fans.

But if I'd closed my eyes, I wouldn't have known the women were there. All you could hear was children. The din of an ordinary primary school playground, except they were locked outside, and not one of them had a father.

Sara wound her way toward me, wearing a jaunty pink headscarf; her scabies had cleared, and she'd stopped wearing the niqab. The bottom of her abaya was covered in mud. Metal taps around the camp leaked water, which mixed with the earth and made it soft and sticky. The moisture spread through the pathways between tents, and the bottoms of most abayas were dip-dyed in mud. Washing out the mud was a Sisyphean task; they'd rarely stay clean for more than a day. Some women held up their abayas, their hairy, bare shins poking out as they walked. But many were too religious to expose their legs. I wondered if, in the end, the Iraqi authorities would arrest those with muddy abayas and pardon those with tanned shins. As fair a way as any to determine who was still a fundamentalist.

"Oi oi!" I said, as Sara approached. "Got your face out for the lads?"

She smiled and lifted a palm to her cheek. "It's much better now, isn't it?"

I nodded and reached out my hand like a relay stick. She grabbed on.

"Lina's here with some big shot from Mosul," I said, pulling her into a jog. "We've told him about your situation, and he wants to meet you."

"Oh shit, thanks, bruv."

When we reached the cabin, we stood in the doorway, wheezing.

"This is Sara," I panted.

She took a breath and lowered herself into a chair opposite the sheikh, her fingers gripping the underside. "*Assalamu alaikum*, Sheikh," she said, pronouncing the Arabic correctly. "Thanks for meeting me, I really appreciate it. It would mean everything, if you could help me see my baby."

"How old?" He pointed at Sara but looked at me.

I did a brief calculation; if she left at fifteen, she must be . . . "She's nineteen," I said.

"Only one child?"

I nodded, still hovering in the doorway.

"How many marriages?"

I looked blankly at Sara.

"Three," she whispered.

He flinched. "Very bad."

The sheikh gestured for her to stand up and twirl. She looked at me, startled, but I was too flabbergasted to offer any direction. She did as instructed and quickly sat back down.

"*Tamam*, OK." He fingered his mustache. "I will marry her, and bring the baby."

"Hang on!" I interjected. "With all due respect, Sheikh, marriage is not an option. We are humbly requesting your help to bring the baby to the camp."

His face started to burn up. "I offer her a great honor!"

I stared at Lina, but she just shook her head.

Sara spoke, a tremor in her voice. "I beg you, Sheikh, please help me, in the name of Islam. The prophet Muhammad said: 'Whoever separates a mother and her child, God will separate him from his loved ones on the Day of Resurrection.'"

The sheikh's entire body convulsed. "This Daesh prostitute tells me what is the religion!"

"That's enough." I rushed over to Sara and pulled her out of her chair.

The mafioso staffer rose to his feet and whispered in my ear, "In Mosul, you would be killed for this disrespect."

"Well, we're not in fucking Mosul, so back the fuck off."

I dragged Sara out of the cabin, and we stumbled down the steps, dazed and bewildered in the appalling sunshine. The midday sun had incinerated the delicate morning clouds, and noxious heat descended from the sky and rose from the earth. I wondered whether, in truth, both heaven and hell burned just the same: the molten core of the Earth for the unbelievers, the livid blaze of the sun for the believers.

Sara was crying silently, and I put my arm around her as we

walked toward the large square of shade cast by the reception cabin. There, we sat together in the dust, our thighs touching, her head heavy on my shoulder.

"I'm so sorry," I said, stroking her headscarf and stabbing my fingers on all the pins that held it together. "I shouldn't have put you in that position."

"Should I have said yes?" She dragged a sleeve across her nose. "What if it's my only chance to get Habibah back?"

"There's got to be another way," I said uncertainly. I'd put all my hopes on Lina and hadn't anticipated that she'd fail to deliver. "Erm, I'll . . . you know . . . I'll go to Baghdad. Yeah, I could ask the British embassy for help, or the Ministry of Humane Affairs." I traced my fingers across her cheek, over the fading scars of her scabies. "It's disgusting that he's even asking. He's forty years older than you, already married, no doubt. He's the goddamn whore."

"He's so fat, I could die under him," she said with a blubbery smile.

"Yeah, let's agree, that's not plan A."

Tom hurtled around the corner, wearing cargo trousers and wraparound sunglasses. He looked unconscionably fit, his T-shirt stretched taut around his muscles, his skin glistening with sweat, his chin strong and masculine. The real reward for not joining ISIS, I thought, is getting to fuck Tom instead of being raped by perverted geriatrics. I should pitch the concept to Prevent.

"There you are! Been looking all over for you, man. Pierre called, said you're to go back to the villa immediately." He reached out his hand and I took it, while offering my other hand to Sara. We both staggered to our feet. I hugged Sara and lingered for a moment, waiting for her to disappear behind the washing lines slung between the tents.

Tom kissed the top of my head and ushered me toward the car. "You scared me, pet. Again."

"Sorry, but you won't believe what happened today."

I told him everything as he helped me into the SUV and pulled my seat belt over me.

He stuck the keys into the ignition, and we moved out of the camp. "Probably not a lot you can do," he said. "You've gotta pick your battles."

The gates were dragged open for us. "Yeah? Well, I choose this battle."

"Why?" He raised a hand to thank the camp guards.

I leaned back in my seat, asking myself the same question.

"This will sound stupid, but you know the theory of the multiverse? How every possible version of your life is taking place in parallel? Well, Sara is living one version of my life."

Tom's face furrowed in concentration. "Oh, you're . . . what's it called, reincarnated?"

"What?" I banged my head against the car window. "No, Tom, I'm not some time-traveling yogi on a mission to rescue distressed Islamists. I just empathize with her, for fuck's sake."

"Well," he said, looking hurt, "don't go doing anything stupid."

I loosened my seat belt and inched forward, resting my chin on his shoulder. "Maybe stupid problems require stupid solutions. I thought I was so clever, back at UCL, designing the perfect de-radicalization program. I didn't know shit back then. I didn't realize repatriations would be so difficult; even when we prove a woman is innocent, that she's been manipulated, lied to, abused—it doesn't guarantee she'll be allowed to go home. We've not repatriated a single person since Khadijah."

The windshield framed a patch of clear blue sky and a tiny plane chugged into view, leaving behind white contrails, like the track marks left by our UN vehicles on camp soil. I hoped to leave a more enduring legacy than that.

WATER CASCADED OVER MY BACK AS I SAT IN THE SHOWER, knees tucked under my chin. I imagined it diluting my rage, bit by bit, until my blood ran clear. But even as the scalding water scoured my skin, fresh anger bloomed within. I thought of Sara trussed up like the prostitutes at the Baghdad Hotel. Over my mutilated, dead body.

Sitting at my dressing table, I dried my hair and wrapped it in a towel turban. I wondered how my turban differed from the Sikh ones. In the days after 9/11, when I was still wearing a headscarf, a Sikh man handed me a flyer for an "Alliance of the Headgear," Sikh men and Muslim women, united by the violence their head coverings inspired against them. It moved me to tears. I cried a lot in those disorienting weeks, my mind replaying images of tiny silhouetted figures throwing themselves from the burning towers. It wasn't the Islam that I knew. But what did I know? I tore through an English translation of the Quran, its lyrical passages alternating between grace and vengeance. Whatever you were looking for, you could find it there.

I heard Sherri knocking on Priya's door, trying to coax her out with the promise of soup. Priya and Charles had broken up again, and she hadn't eaten all day. The door opened, and they went downstairs. I got dressed and followed them to the kitchen, but paused before going in. It was awkward being around Priya, after the way I'd hurt her.

Sherri noticed me standing there. "There'll be plenty if you want some," she said as she dribbled chopped carrots into the pan.

I looked at Priya.

"It's fine," she said, sighing. "You can come in."

I shuffled into the room. "Erm . . . I want to apologize again, Priya. I'm sorry for what I said about Charles."

She interlaced her hands and placed them on the kitchen table. "I guess it's better that I know. But you shouldn't have done it like that."

I grimaced as I thought back to my outburst. "It was shitty of me. I really am sorry."

As I waited for Lina to return from the camp, my anxiety was too intense even for soup. I walked to the medicine cupboard, grabbed a couple of paracetamol, and washed them down with a swig of sticky pink Pepto Bismol. What's the opposite of a breakfast of champions? Dinner of the defeated.

The front door opened, and I ran out of the kitchen and found Lina standing next to Pierre.

"Lina, can I grab you for a second?"

Pierre rolled his eyes, and Lina followed me into the living room. She sat on the edge of the sofa opposite me, holding her bag in her lap like a shield.

"Nadia," she said, blowing air into her cheeks. "Your behavior today was unacceptable. The sheikh is powerful and we need him.

I can see Sara matters to you, but she's not the only woman in the camp."

The smell of vegetable soup wafted into the room, causing a bubble of Pepto Bismol to rise from my stomach and pop in my throat.

"I apologize, Lina," I said, with all the fake sincerity I could muster. "It'll never happen again. But . . . can I ask, do you have other local contacts who could help Sara?"

She spluttered. "After that performance today? You'll never get a leader from Mosul to meet with you again."

I thought back to earlier in the day. What could I have done differently? It was Lina's silence that was outrageous; would she have just let them get married?

"I understand," I said, trying to keep my cool. "Just one last thing. Can I have permission to visit Baghdad? I'd like to ask the British embassy and the Ministry of Humane Affairs for help with Sara's case."

She shook her head. "You have some nerve, Nadia."

I pressed my palms together. "Please, this is important to me. She's just a kid, and she needs our help. I promise I'll never ask for anything else." I sounded whiny, like a teenager begging for pocket money.

Lina gave me a look of disgust. She stood up and wedged her handbag onto her shoulder. "Fine, you can travel back to Baghdad with me next week. But that'll be the end of it. I don't want to hear another word about that girl."

She disappeared upstairs, and I thought about her words. "That girl." It was how Mum used to refer to Rosy.

I felt better now I had a plan, and my appetite returned. I wandered into the kitchen, where Sherri was holding out a spoonful of soup. Pierre took a sip.

"You are too shy with the salt," he said.

Sherri shook table salt into the pot and stirred, before ladling out portions for Pierre and me. Priya had already retreated to her room.

"You were a drama queen today, *non?*" Pierre raised the bowl to his face and slurped the soup like a dog. He finished and placed the bowl on the counter. "Nadia told a senior local leader to fuck off," he said to Sherri.

"Was he a dreadful misogynist?" asked Sherri, tilting her head.

Pierre licked the vegetable residue on his lips. "That's like asking if he is Iraqi."

"You're so racist!" Sherri crossed her arms. "What about Farris?"

Pierre sniggered. "Farris wishes to bed you."

"He's a devout Muslim," said Sherri, "and I'm married!" She took out her phone, surreptitiously opened Farris's WhatsApp picture, and scrutinized it.

"It's grotesque, what happened today," I said. "An elderly leader tried to marry Sara in exchange for access to her baby." I raised a spoon to my mouth but, in my anger, I missed, and soup dribbled down my linen shirt.

"That's terrible," said Sherri, stuffing her phone back into her pocket. "Which one's Sara again? We've not assessed her, have we?"

"She's the British girl," I said. "She's refused to have an assessment until she's got her child back. But these venal local leaders are no help."

"Actually, we made progress after you left." Pierre dabbed his mouth with a silk paisley handkerchief. "We agreed on several returns."

Sherri furrowed her brow. "For the local women? Does Priya know? Is Lina trying to take over her program?"

Pierre looked over his shoulder. "You must not tell. Anyway, it is her own fault; Priya's performance has been catastrophic."

Sherri shook her head. "Poor old Priya. This is the last thing she needs."

"Hang on," I said, staring at Pierre. "You've struck deals for other women without forced marriages? How did you manage that?"

"Sure, for the old, ugly ones. Finally, it pays to be unfuckable."

Sherri clipped him around the ear, and I whacked him with the back of my hand.

"*Putain!* Where is your humor? It's only a job."

It had long since stopped being a job to me.

24

J ASON'S TEACHINGS MADE ME LONG FOR THE COHERENCE of fundamentalist Islam. As I sat in the car waiting for him, I thought about the futility of rehabilitating women who were still being actively traumatized. What could Sara learn about moderate Islam while separated from her baby?

What is moderation in religion, anyway, other than a tolerance for dissonance? God's instructions, issued over a thousand years ago, will always be extreme by contemporary standards. We protect religious freedom, but we expect people to cherry-pick which religious teachings they observe. Luckily, the vast majority of believers abide by the easy, sensible rulings and sidestep the rest. It's quite a hard skill to teach. Ignore that part, you have to say, I know God's word is infallible, but obviously that bit is mental.

Jason, dressed in his long white robe, drifted toward the car with all the energy of a ghost with anemia.

"Blessed day," said Jason as he climbed into the car.

Blessed day? Is this the fucking *Handmaid's Tale*?

He pressed through my silence. "Beautiful weather."

I looked out the window as the car eased onto the road, the sun a blinding white against the relentless blue sky.

"The weather's literally the same every day." I rifled through my plastic lunch bag and extracted a za'atar croissant.

Farris looked into the rearview mirror, biting his lip.

"Sorry." Flakes of pastry erupted from my mouth. "I'll be tidy." I rolled down the window and tried to hang out for my next bite.

Clusters of men in the street jeered and pointed at me, and Farris yelled to shut the window while Jason waved grandiosely as though he were the pope.

I yanked Jason's hand down. "Stop that. They aren't exactly well-wishers."

"My love spreads forth in abundance for all of God's children."

I wondered if his madrasa had dispatched him to Iraq in hopes he'd be murdered.

That afternoon, I stopped by the teaching cabin to observe Jason's class and to check in on Sara. I'd been busy planning my trip to Baghdad and hadn't seen her for a couple of days.

"Hey, I've got news," I said, grabbing her as soon as she walked in. "I'm off to Baghdad tomorrow. Got meetings with the Minister of Humane Affairs and the British embassy, so fingers crossed."

She beamed. "Thanks, Nadia," she said, as I tucked a strand of baby hair into the side of her headscarf.

"And that's not all. . . ." I rustled around in my lunch bag and pulled out a purple chocolate bar, tucking it up my sleeve. I furtively passed it from my sleeve to Sara's, trying to obscure the naked favoritism.

"Oh. My. Days." Her eyes widened. "A fucking Dairy Milk? Swear down?"

"I sent Farris on a mission, and he delivered." I briefly squeezed her hand. "Enjoy."

The last few women walked in and drifted around, picking up the handouts, turning them over, and putting them back down.

Jason wrote the word *peace* on the whiteboard in bubble letters. "*Assalamu alaikum*, my blessed sisters." He pressed the air down with his palms, indicating the women should sit. They circulated for a little longer, as though playing a leisurely game of musical chairs, before they settled.

He smiled over the class. "Islam comes from the root word *salaam*, which means 'peace.' *Salaam* is also the beautiful word we use to greet one another. At its core, Islam is a religion of peace."

The women's eyes collectively rolled to the backs of their heads, like dolls being turned upside down.

"Sheikh J.," said Sara, folding her handout into a paper plane. "I'm not being funny or nothing, but if Islam was peaceful, it'd just be eight guys and a camel in the desert."

"OK, yeah, I hear you." He perched his flat bottom on the corner of the desk. "Islam did spread partly through conquest. But that was normal at the time, and it was congruent with the broader cultural and historical context."

Fatihah, an older Tunisian woman in a plain white headscarf, raised her hand. "We were taught, since we were children, that the Quran is timeless, sound, and complete. It is not context-dependent."

Though Sherri and I had completed Fatihah's assessment, her

case had ground to a halt after the Iraqis revealed she'd recruited two other Tunisian women into ISIS.

Sara's paper plane flew through the air, and German Hanna caught it with one hand, crushing it.

"Hey!" Sara swiped a handout from a neighboring table and folded a fresh plane.

"Of course the Quran is timeless, but it doesn't preach violence." Jason picked up a small green book and thumbed through its pages. "Here, look. The Quran says, 'Whoever kills a soul . . . it is as if he had slain mankind entirely.'"

"I'm not so interested to do a battle of Quranic verses," said Fatihah, "though I could quote many against this. But do you seriously say Islam is pacifist?"

"Not pacifist in all circumstances," said Jason, "but peace-loving and peace-seeking."

Swiss Aisha half lifted her hand. "When is violence allowed?"

We'd submitted Aisha's case to the Swiss embassy. It was a no-brainer, she'd clearly been groomed and trafficked, but the embassy had stopped communicating with us.

"Violence can only be a last resort," said Jason, flicking rapidly through his lesson plan. "Against invasion or oppression, for instance."

"Oh, like when the Americans invaded Iraq?" said Sara in a sarcastic drawl. "Or when Assad genocided Sunni Muslims in Syria?"

"There are legitimate ways to defend against such violence." Jason was repeatedly scraping back his hair. "But ISIS took it too far. They killed innocent people, enslaved women, and persecuted other faiths."

"This is normal in war, throughout history, including by Muslims?" said Fatihah. Her voice was calm, interested rather than defensive.

"There is a difference between what people have done historically in the name of Islam," said Jason, sweat bubbling along his brow, "and what Islam itself calls for."

"Right, and you're the guy to tell us the difference?" Sara pushed her chair back and lifted her feet onto the desk. "Are you even Muslim?"

"The Lord guided me into reverting ten years ago." A droplet of sweat fell from Jason's brow and landed on his eyelashes.

"The Lord," snorted Sara. "It's Allah, bruv. Get your religions straight. Where exactly did you study Islam?"

"I was fortunate enough to study at a wonderful madrasa in Berkeley, California." Jason walked over to the whiteboard and wrote out a Quranic verse: "There shall be no compulsion in religion, Surat al-Baqarah, Verse 256."

"In California?" said Sara. "You can't make this shit up. I bet you're one of those guys who thinks Muslims can be gay and trans and feminist."

Jason turned from the whiteboard. "Well, yes, as a matter of fact—" he began, but he was interrupted by an audible ripple of discontent.

"Nadia." Sara swung her legs off the table and stood up. "Is this for real? The guy is an American PsyOp." The women were murmuring between themselves and a few walked out.

I launched myself into the fray, standing between Jason and the women. "OK, relax! Let's take a five-minute break."

A few of the women plucked cigarettes out of the black folds of their abayas and stepped outside to smoke. The others broke into small groups, huddling together and conferring in hushed tones.

I bundled Jason into a corner. "Mate, what are you playing at? Can you just stick to the lesson plan? They've been brainwashed for years; you've got to ease them into it. Don't get baited on *trans* issues—there are Tory MPs more radical than this lot."

"Yes . . . sorry . . . I didn't." He wiped his cheeks with the back of his hand.

"Jesus Christ, Jason," I said. "You're not crying, are you?"

He shook his head, snuffling.

I stood with him and leafed through the lesson plan we'd hastily drafted together in the week before his arrival, pointing out the key teaching points. Then I called the women back in.

"Right, then," said Jason with a watery smile. "Let's talk about our personal commitments to peace."

German Hanna leaned back in her chair and sighed, the marker-scribbled whiteboard reflected in her light brown eyes. "ISIS is finished, and anyway, the women never fought. Why would we start now? I wish for a normal life in Berlin and, for sure, I will not shoot up the Brandenburg Gate and enslave the tourists. How can we persuade you of this? You judge us for crimes we have not committed."

The other women nodded, and a red-faced Finnish girl called Elli said, "I never left my home in Mosul, except for the market. I didn't shoot guns; I just made a lot of stuffed aubergines. Really, a lot. I couldn't kill anyone, except with cholesterol."

Elli's husband had taken her and their two sons on holiday to Turkey and arranged for them to be smuggled into Syria without her prior knowledge. The family was later transferred to Mosul, where her husband died in battle. Her younger son was now suffering from severe PTSD, and Sherri and I were trying to fast-track their case.

"If only I murdered Sajjad with an oily vegetable," said Swiss Aisha. "But no, a drone got the satisfaction."

Some of the other women tutted and shook their heads.

"*Fick di!* You didn't live with him! You don't know what he did to me."

"We all suffered our burdens," said Tunisian Fatihah, staring down the disapproving women. She placed an arm around Aisha as she cried.

Jason walked to Aisha's table and crouched down, his face exuberantly sympathetic. "How can I safeguard you in this moment?"

"Mate, leave her alone," said Sara. "Is this trauma porn to you? Why are you getting off on this?"

Jason's expression slid to the floor. I coughed and made a circular motion with my fingers that said "Move the fuck on."

He stood up and handed out blank sheets of paper.

"Now, if you feel comfortable, I'd like you to write your own personal commitments to nonviolence."

"I would stab him in the butthole!" yelled Aisha. Fatihah shushed her, and she resumed her crying.

Sara started scribbling with her blunt pencil, then she paused and looked up. "Can I make an exception for Nigel Farage?"

"You can chuck a milkshake," I said from the back of the room. "Nothing more."

"Fair dos." She resumed her writing.

25

RETURNING TO BASE IN BAGHDAD FELT LIKE VISITING MY alma mater after graduating. It had been six weeks since I'd moved out, and there were new people here now, striding around, looking purposeful and important, oblivious to my presence. I'd been allocated a temporary bedroom, which was bare, and I haunted the cafeteria and the tiki bar feeling irrelevant and obsolete. I missed the others, my frustration with them dissipating in the distance between us.

It was odd to visit the ministry without Pierre, and I wondered whether I was becoming more important or less responsible. The glamorous assistant was waiting for me outside, dressed as a dominatrix that day, and she ushered me upstairs, past the queuing supplicants, straight into the minister's office.

The minister stood as I entered the room, and I turned around, thinking a dignitary must be behind me, but there was no one there.

"Nadia!" she said, gripping me with both hands. It felt surreal hearing my name come out of her mouth. I blinked, adjusting to my new and undeserved status, as though I'd been upgraded to business class on a flight. "Let me show you this beautiful painting I commission."

She led me to the room's far side, pointing at an enormous, extremely flattering oil painting of her face. "You like it?"

"Oh, wow, that's . . . startling."

She watched me, waiting for more.

I reached back into the depths of my art GCSE. "Great use of color and, erm, shade and . . . texture?"

"Yes!" she said, flashing her icy veneers at me. "You can see. My husband says waste of money, all my beautiful paintings. He doesn't understand art."

"Is he a bit of a philistine?"

"No," she said, frowning. "He is Iraqi."

She ushered me to the seating area, where she settled into a gold-encrusted, high-backed armchair that could only be described as a throne.

"Nadia, good to meet you." She folded her pink-shellacked hands on her lap. "We like to make collaboration with UN, but many of you left to the camp, we don't see you anymore. I have good project ideas, you can bring funding, yes?"

"Of course, Your Excellency." I noticed a crystal bowl of Werther's Originals on the coffee table. Looking at those creamy little drops of homesickness, I had an overwhelming urge to nip into a Tesco.

"Please take," said the minister, following my line of sight. I'd been staring at the sweets like a malnourished child. I took one.

I peeled the clear plastic wrapper and gripped the sweet in my palm. "We're always open to exploring new projects. However, I wanted to ask for your help today."

"Yes?" She sat back on her throne and her diamond chandelier earrings shimmered.

"There's a young woman in the camp who's been separated from her baby. Her late husband's family, in Mosul, are keeping the child from her. I wondered if you could help return the child."

She leaned forward, her arms heavy with gold bracelets not dissimilar to my mother's. "You should ask local sheikh for this."

"Actually, we met with Sheikh Abu-Bakr al-Obeidi, but he insisted on marrying the girl."

"Ah! Al-Obeidi is honorable tribe, powerful in Mosul. It is a very fortunate match. She is lucky girl." The minister twisted around her watch and examined the clockface.

"But she does not wish to marry," I said, the sweet growing sticky in my hand. "She only wants her baby back. Minister, you must understand, as a mother, the pain of this separation."

The minister snapped her head toward me. "ISIS girl is not mother, she is criminal. The sheikh offers kind and generous chance for her. She must accept."

She took a breath and retrieved her smile. "So, the funding. You can bring donations to us?"

I strung together a bunch of meaningless words until she was satisfied, and I trudged out of the decrepit building, its missing windows staring after me like hollow, pitiless eyes. In the car, I realized my right hand was stuck into a fist by the molten Werther's Original. In a state of abject despondency, I sank low in my seat, pried open my palm, and sucked the sweet off my hand.

I GASPED AND SAT UP IN BED. THE ROOM FELT UNFAMILIAR, AND it took a moment to remember I was visiting Baghdad. The curtains resisted the weak morning light, the gloom interrupted only by the flashing of my phone. I picked it up and saw dozens of notifications. My immediate thought was: I'd been canceled on Twitter and my life and career were over. Except I hadn't logged in to Twitter in months. . . .

I'm so sorry, wrote Sherri.

You chose bad horse, wrote Pierre.

Hope you're all right pet, wrote Tom.

Told you the foreign women are evil, wrote Priya.

Silly girl has just misunderstood, wrote my mum.

Everyone had sent me the same news article. The headline read: BRITISH ISIS GIRL THREATENS LONDON. It was an interview with Sara, a huge photograph of her in a black abaya, her face curled into a sneer. A British tabloid reporter had visited her in the camp, and she had talked—my God, had she talked. She said East London was "clapped" and the best way to improve Stratford Westfield was to "drop a bomb on it." I knew she was joking, but who said that to a journalist? She said Western governments were hypocritical for banging on about international law when they'd illegally invaded Iraq and Afghanistan. "One rule for ISIS, and another for you lot. Not exactly fair, is it?" She did say living in Mosul was "bare crap," but admitted to enjoying the local aviary, where she was "impressed" by ISIS's bird conservation program.

Why are Arabs so obsessed with birds? Also, fuck, fuck, fuck. What in God's name had she done?

My appointment at the British embassy wasn't until the afternoon, but I couldn't wait. I collared a driver at breakfast, insisting he take me there at once, while he grumbled about paperwork and security protocol.

"It's two streets away, for Christ's sake, inside the Green Zone." I slammed my fist on the table. "Come on, it's urgent."

He wedged a stack of toast in his mouth and led me to the car, spinning a set of keys around his forefinger.

We pulled up outside the embassy, and a Gurkha checked his clipboard for my name.

"Your appointment this afternoon." He batted us away with the back of his hand.

I wormed my torso out of the passenger-side window. "Tell the Counterterror team I'm here about the British ISIS girl who's all over the news."

His nostrils flared, and he walked away, shouting into the walkie-talkie. I watched his eyebrows rise, and he rapidly pulled open the gate and beckoned us in.

"Sorry, ma'am." He gave me a salute as the car passed, and I briefly enjoyed the shift in power between us.

I was rushed through the ten-stage security process, and when I emerged in reception, a man was waiting for me. He had a deeply receding hairline and his skin was deathly pale; he'd either just arrived or he had one hell of an SPF routine.

"I'm Ian." He stuck out his hand. "Hannah's replacement."

"Nadia, UNDO." I wondered where Hannah had gone this time. The Maldives? Dubai? Thailand? I'd heard this was her seventh rest-and-recuperation trip of the year.

Ian led me toward a wooden bench in the rose garden. Yet again, the meeting rooms were reserved for people of consequence.

"You'll have to forgive me," he said. "I'm not fully across the handover yet. But there have been developments in London. The girl, Sara, we're revoking her citizenship. It's not public yet, so you need to keep shtum, but we could use your help managing her, since you're on the ground, as it were."

I squinted, trying to remember an international law module I'd once taken. "Her citizenship? That's illegal, you can't do that."

Ian patted his pockets and found his phone. "Let me get the exact wording for you."

I shielded my eyes with my hand, as though watching a horror movie, his face torn into strips by my fingers.

"So . . . she is a member of a proscribed terrorist group and has made a credible threat to UK security; as such she has lost her right to British citizenship."

"A credible threat? She was kidding around, lots of people hate Stratford Westfield, it's . . . gauche. She's obviously not planning an attack!"

Ian locked his phone and slid it into his pocket. "Well, that's neither here nor there. It's sufficient to make the legal case."

"Is there anything she can do?" I lifted my face until my eyes were level with his. "Literally anything that could change this decision?"

He crossed his arms and clicked his pen on and off. "No. There's a legal appeals process, blah, blah, blah, but she won't get anywhere. It's done. Politically, it's impossible to take her back."

I raked my fingers through my unwashed hair. "She's just

young. Quite stupid, a bit reckless, but mostly young. You know she isn't dangerous."

He shrugged. "Not really relevant, is it? Anyway, it's out of my hands."

The sprinklers switched on in the garden, spraying precious droplets of water over the rosebushes, and a cool fragrance drifted over us. That was it. Sara's life, forever paused, stuck on a freeze-frame of its most wretched moment.

Ian tapped his pen against his leather-bound notebook. "So, we'd like your help containing the fallout. It wouldn't do to have her hysterical all over the media. Perhaps you can persuade her to keep quiet and take it like a champ?"

My eyes fixated on his pen as he jerked it up and down. I wanted to snatch it from him and drive it up his arsehole.

"She's got a child." I pursed my lips, forcing myself to measure out each word. "Can you at least help us reunite her with the child?"

He flicked through his notebook. "The child's in the custody of local family members," he said, pointing at his scribbled hand-writing. "So that's an Iraqi decision."

"But I'm not getting anywhere with the Iraqis," I said through gritted teeth. "Can you apply political pressure?"

Ian slammed his notebook closed and pulled the black elastic around it. "No can do. We've spent quite a lot of political capital dumping the girl here. Can't ask the Iraqis for any more."

I crossed my arms and gripped my sides. "Let me get this straight. You want me to tell Sara that she's staying in the camp forever, that she'll never see her daughter again, and that she shouldn't make a fuss?"

"Yes, exactly. That would be great, Nadia. Thanks for helping us out." He stood up and offered me his hand. I did not take it.

As I made my way out, through layer upon layer of foot-thick concrete blast wall, I wondered how I'd feel if the embassy were blown up. I think I'd shrug. "Not my decision," I would say. "Afraid it's out of my hands."

The driver returned me to the UN compound, and I hauled myself out of the car. Before I could close the door behind me, I saw Lina charging round the corner, coming right at me.

"What the fuck have you done?" She slammed the car door shut, and it missed my fingers by an inch.

I stepped to one side. "Er, what . . . ?"

"Peter Banks, the journalist, called me asking for a comment. He said you both hung out at the tiki bar. Apparently, you told him about the camp, the program, and all the reasons it was controversial. Then, and this I will never understand, you told him—a British reporter—that there was a British woman in the camp?! You've absolutely fucked us, Nadia. UNDO is all over the news, being accused of whitewashing terrorists. All those countries who were considering taking their citizens back, what do you think they'll do now? How could you have been so stupid?"

Peter Banks, Peter Banks. I repeated his name in my head. Then it came back to me. That night at the tiki bar, Pierre's journalist friends, me drunk on tequila avoiding the Shi'a cleric's texts, upset that Pierre's shenanigans—rather than my hard work—had gotten the program approved. I'd been flattered by the journalist's interest in me, keen to demonstrate my status, my passion, and my expertise. . . .

Holy shit. I did this. This was me.

26

ARRIS PICKED ME UP FROM THE AIRPORT AND I INSISTED HE drive me straight to the camp. I curled up on the back seat, unclean, sleep-deprived, and strung out. My bloodshot eyes drifted between open and closed, and I caught glimpses of Erbil as it flicked by like a series of still shots. An ornamental park, fountains arching high, dedicated to a politician killed by a suicide bomb. Apartment blocks, their perilously cheap construction masked by decorative strips of fluorescent light. The twisted debris of an enormous mansion, blown up by Iranian ballistic missiles. Much of the city was newly built, naff, and nondescript, like a midrange retail park. The Kurds had planned to create a capital as ritzy and as glamorous as Dubai, but couldn't resist stealing public funds.

"Wassup, Doctor? You good?" Farris glanced at me through the rearview mirror.

Even being called Doctor couldn't cheer me up today. "I'm miserable," I said.

"Let's have music, it will help." He put on Boyz II Men's "End of the Road" and started crooning along.

I sat up. "For real, Farris? I'm already depressed, and now I have to claw out my eardrums."

He swayed in the front seat. "It's very beautiful song, my favorite. It makes me think of my love for my country, how I belong to her."

The Iraqi capacity for cheesiness truly has no limits.

"How can you stand it here?" I pointed at an old woman, cross-legged on the pavement, wearing a soiled housedress, her hand outstretched for change. "Everything is so fucked-up."

"Ah, it's nothing. I lived through the invasion, the civil war, then ISIS." He lifted both hands from the steering wheel, his fingers imitating guns. "Bam, bam, bam!" He blew away the imaginary smoke and holstered the weapons. "Now, it's OK. The killing has stopped."

"You must think I'm so pathetic, losing my mind after barely three months here."

We passed a makeshift pitch, kids playing football in different Premier League shirts. A barefoot child tackled the ball, obscuring the view with clouds of dust.

"You compare it to London, it seems bad." Farris returned a single, relaxed hand to the steering wheel. "You didn't see Iraq before; it's a miracle we survived. Foreigners get frustrated and leave, but this was the home of my mother, and every time it is destroyed, we thank God we are alive, and we rebuild."

The city retreated behind us, giving way to a deserted no-man's-land. Farris hit play on Celine Dion's "My Heart Will Go On" and I whacked the back of his headrest.

"Do you know what a corn fest is, Farris? Your playlist is like Quavers served with a tin of Green Giant."

He ignored me and sang every word, his voice breaking over the high notes. The soundtrack made the view even more woeful. Abandoned sites with rusted metal tanks and pipes, half-dismantled hamlets bleeding mud bricks, empty squares of scrubland, fences erected around them in anticipation of future worth. Who had the energy to rebuild this place, over and over again?

We arrived at the camp in the early evening, and I waited in the teaching cabin while Farris went to find Sara. White paper haunted the room: handouts, worksheets, and notepaper drifting beneath gusts of air-conditioning. I leafed through a few sheets. A handout of Gandhi quotes, speech bubbles coming out of his mouth, a penis drawn on his head. A handwritten chore list, signed by two women who shared a tent. Jason had forced them to write it after they pulled each other's headscarves off in a fight about a moldy sandwich and a colony of ants. And scraps of paper on which the women had played snog, marry, kill. Jason always ended up dead, while Tom and Charles alternated between snog and marry. I felt smug thinking about Tom's residence in my bed.

Then there was a letter, Swiss Aisha's words, in Jason's handwriting.

Dear Mr. Ambassador,

I'm Aisha Al-Jumaili, born in Zurich in 2001. When I was fourteen, I made a terrible mistake. I trusted the wrong man. Sajjad was my youth worker, and he made me feel special. He was thirty years old and already married,

*but he had a car, and snuck me out of the house and took
me on adventures.*

*After a while, he showed me pictures of Islamic State,
only nice ones, and told me that's where we belonged. He
said Switzerland would never accept us, because our
parents are foreigners. I was very stupid to agree, and I
regret it with all my heart. I am Swiss, and I love
Switzerland. Believe me, Mr. Ambassador, I have been
punished for the choice I made. Every time I close my
eyes, I see the crimes of ISIS. My mind is always hurting. I
can't tell you what Sajjad did to me, it's too shameful. I cry
every night for my mother, for the pain I caused her by
leaving, and I'm desperate to come back home. Please
could you*

The next few lines were crossed out, then nothing. They must
have started again on a fresh sheet of paper.

This was my job, not Jason's, and I felt guilty for dropping the
ball. The Swiss embassy had stopped responding to us weeks ago
and I should have escalated the case by now.

I drafted an email about Aisha, then Sara walked in and I put
my phone down. She looked like she'd shrunk, her body a thin
cardboard spool wrapped in layers of black cloth. She started talking before she sat down, her words tumbling out in a panic.

"He said he'd help me find Habibah, that's why I chatted to
him, but I didn't know the interview had started when I said the
Westfield thing, we was just joking around, obvs I'm not gonna
blow it up, it was banter. But now everyone's calling me a terrorist
and saying I shouldn't be allowed back. And the dickhead broke

his promise, he didn't do nothing about Habibah, the article didn't even mention her!"

I thought about Peter Banks, the manipulative little fuck. He deserved to be flayed. Sara wasn't technically a juvenile, but ISIS had arrested her development, and in many ways she was still the fifteen-year-old who'd shown up here. She obviously hadn't understood the implications of the interview, and he'd exploited her, even used her missing child as bait.

But I directed the brunt of my anger at myself. How could I have been so careless, so irresponsible, so unprofessional? I'd sat in the tiki bar, a drunk little show-off, blabbing to a journalist, and now Sara was paying the price.

She slumped over a desk and started crying. I rummaged through my handbag, looking for a Snickers bar. All out of options, chocolate was the only comfort I had to offer. It was a relief to focus on the sloppy innards of my bag instead of looking at Sara. She thought it was bad now, but she didn't know about her citizenship, didn't know how spectacularly I'd failed in Baghdad, didn't know she had nothing left to live for.

I unwrapped the Snickers and handed it over. Her tired chin jerked around as she chewed, and I considered whether to confess. This was my fault, not hers. But I couldn't risk losing her trust. As I reached out to wipe smudges of chocolate from her lips, I made a vow to myself. I would do every earthly thing to make this right.

I took a notebook and pen out of my bag and turned to her.

"Tell me everything you know about your husband's family, about where Habibah might be."

THAT NIGHT, MY BODY WAS UTTERLY EXHAUSTED, LIMBS SO heavy they fused with the mattress, but my mind remained wide-awake. I couldn't stop self-flagellating. And as I mulled over Sara's separation from Habibah, I remembered the years my mother and I had spent apart. I was a year older than Sara when my mother disowned me.

During my final year as an undergraduate, I had returned to Leicester for the Christmas holidays, only to spend every possible minute revising in Central Library. Opening hours grew shorter every day, preparing us for the moment when everything would close and we'd be left alone to face our families.

I walked home through town, festive lights blinking through the temperate drizzle, snow elusive yet again. As I turned in to residential streets, I peered through living room windows at overstuffed stockings and extravagantly large presents. Every year I felt robbed. People used to say, "Well, you've got Eid," but it doesn't compare. It has none of the collective anticipation, none of the licentious partying, none of the fiscally irresponsible gift giving—at least not in my household. Eid falls on a random weekday, so you nip home for twenty-four hours, painfully conscious of normal life carrying on without you, and stuff your face with biryani while hoping for twenty quid off your granddad. It's not the same.

I comforted myself by judging other people's Christmas tree decorations. Most were about as classy as a *TOWIE* gender-reveal party, decked out with striped candy canes, novelty baubles, Santas abseiling down the side. At least I had taste.

I jimmied my house key into the lock, but the door swung open, pulling my outstretched hand into the paisley-carpeted hallway. Mum, her hair a tangled mess around her shoulders, wrestled the key from the lock. It would be four years before I got that key back. She placed her palm flat against my chest and tried to push me back outside.

"Wait! What are you doing?" I braced myself, resisting her.

"Get out."

I wriggled past her and ran into the stifling living room. The heating had been on all day, but I didn't dare take off my coat.

"Mum! What the hell is going on?"

"Hell indeed, that's where you're going."

She stormed past me and grabbed her phone from the mantel. The only other thing on the mantel was a plastic mosque-shaped alarm clock that played a muffled call to prayer five times a day. Mum turned her phone to me, a screenshot from Facebook, a photo of me sans headscarf, arm around my friend Matthew. I took the phone and sank into the sofa, my coat bunching up around me. It looked worse than it was. Matthew was just a friend, I was still a pathetic virgin, and I did wear my headscarf 98 percent of the time. Only very occasionally did I take it off.

"Where did you get this?" I said.

Mum towered over me. "Auntie Asmaa sent it to me, shocked and disgusted she was, she felt sorry for me. I'm so ashamed, I can't even look at you."

Auntie Asmaa, you treacherous bitch, wait until I spill the

beans about your hideous sons. You think I'm bad, you should meet Ruth and Mandy, the crackheads your kids are dating.

"What have you got to say for yourself?" Mum tugged at my headscarf, pulling it tight against my neck. "Is this just for show? Is it all a lie?"

The truth was, I didn't know. My religious devotion had thinned so gradually, I'd barely noticed its ebb. Tiny experiments, like praying dawn prayer at nine a.m. instead of five a.m., gave way to bigger transgressions, like turning my headscarf into a bandanna and dropping low to Blu Cantrell on a night out. University exerted such a strong pull toward the mainstream, it took a lot of strength to resist being like everyone else. And it ground me down, searching for reasons to stay different.

When I was a schoolgirl, being religious had broadened my horizons, enabled me to travel to camps and conferences, to make new friends, to be exposed to grown-up books and ideas. It gave me an intensely idealistic outlook, one that felt empowering, that made my life seem important.

But at university, religion only held me back, its desperate arms clinging to my leg, resisting every step forward. It hated the new books I was reading, complex and challenging philosophical texts instead of trite meditations on God's will; it hated the new people teaching me, ferocious critical thinkers instead of vacuous orators; and it hated the new friends I was making, cerebral yet hedonistic creatives instead of prudes engrossed by their own arrested development.

Sometimes it was hard to kneel on my prayer mat and believe the words I was reciting. Was there really some big daddy in the sky who massively wanted me to abstain from getting down to Flo Rida on Thirsty Thursdays at Oceana?

Most of the time I blocked it out, refusing to acknowledge that my faith was weakening, unable to countenance the implications of leaving. I knew my mother would disown me, that I'd lose everybody who mattered to me, that I might never feel at home again.

But that day, when Mum asked me the question, straight to my face, I felt an overwhelming urge to be honest. I'd spent years deflecting and avoiding, lying to myself and to everybody else, and in a moment of blind, reckless courage, I decided to stop.

"I guess . . . if I'm honest, I don't think I believe anymore."

"No." It came out long and slow, a guttural wail, her face falling into her hands.

My body was numb, dissociated, devoid of emotion, the realization only coming to me as I spoke the words. "It's unoriginal to say, but if he could create any world . . . why this? Nobody would . . . you know. Choose this."

Mum knelt before me and grasped my arms. "Darling, please, you've lost yourself. Please don't do this. It's not for me, I promise, I want this for you. I know in my heart, it's the only way to feel peace, it's the only way anything makes any sense. It's who we are. It's a blessing, my darling, please don't let go."

I watched the tears fall from her eyes one by one before merging into currents, and a distant part of me hated the pain I'd caused. She genuinely believed, without equivocation, and it meant everything to her. And I understood—I'd once felt the same way; faith had nourished and sustained me. But over time, it had curdled, my insides recoiling as I continued to ram it into myself.

Now there was an incredible sense of relief. To let go of the dissonance that had split my mind in two, that forced one side to constantly dissimulate to the other. I hadn't even realized the strain it had caused, the constant inauthenticity, pretending to everyone, to myself, to be someone I wasn't. A new life was possible now.

"I'm sorry that it hurts you, but I don't want this anymore."

"Get out!" she screamed.

She staggered to her feet, grabbed her favorite crystal vase, and smashed it against the wall. I went upstairs to pack.

27

I T DIDN'T TAKE MUCH TO ENLIST FARRIS.

"Everybody needs their mother," he said, when I explained Sara's situation.

"Thank you!" I said. "I don't know why everyone finds that so hard to understand."

While Farris bunked off work to search for Habibah, I tried to carry on as normal, conducting new assessments and following up with embassies, but the negative media coverage had turned the program to shit, and no one was being repatriated. I veered between depression and anxiety, sleeping more and more, and occasionally coming up with harebrained schemes before being talked down by Tom and Sherri. "Give Farris half a chance," they would say. "He might find her." So I showed up at the camp every day, needled away at my job, and I waited.

One Tuesday afternoon, two weeks after my disastrous trip to Baghdad, I sat in Jason's class and watched listlessly as the women role-played ISIS recruiters and damsels in distress.

Aisha took to the floor, her upper lip and chin covered in black marker, her voice absurdly gruff. "Pretty lady, you are so fine. Won't you be mine?" She presented her hand to Marie, who slipped out from behind the desk.

"*Quoi, moi?*" She fluttered her eyelashes and fanned her face coquettishly with a handout.

Aisha stroked her imitation facial hair and licked her lips. "I take you to the funfair, and buy you candy, and we enjoy the rides."

They skipped around, hand in hand, throwing back their heads in fake laughter. It wouldn't have won them places at RADA, but we got the gist. They repositioned themselves at the front, and Aisha peered into Marie's eyes.

"Allah joined our souls in heaven," said Aisha. "That's why it feels so good, so natural to be together."

Marie did a little swoon. "*Mon beau, mon amour . . .*"

"There is a place where we can serve Allah together as faithful Muslims. I wish to take you there."

"Where is this magical place?" asked Marie, cocking her head.

"The Islamic State of Iraq and al-Sham."

Marie did a pantomime gasp and pretended to slap Aisha across the face. "You lie! That is not a good place. This is a trick. I will not go!" She stormed off, briefly leaving the cabin for dramatic effect, while Aisha bowed to scattered applause and laughter.

Sara sat silent and hollow-faced at the back. She knew about her citizenship by then, and the news had eviscerated her. I'd spent an entire afternoon outside the cabin with her as she gasped through one panic attack after another. Part of her had always believed she'd end up back home, that eventually she'd resume the life she'd left behind. It was impossible for her to dream now, to fantasize about the future; even if she got Habibah back, what kind of life could she provide? A darkness came over Sara during those weeks that scared me, and I'd subtly turn over her hands, checking for marks on her wrists. I became convinced that finding Habibah was the only way to keep Sara alive, and I grew agitated and pushy with Farris as he returned home every evening with nothing new to report.

When I walked back to the car that Tuesday, after class, I saw Farris leaning against the SUV, smoking a cigarette. There was something different about him, about his posture. . . . I broke into a jog.

"You've found them, haven't you?"

He flicked his cigarette onto the dirt, blew on his fingernails, and rubbed them on his stripy polo shirt.

"Yippee-ki-yay, motherfucker!"

I shrieked and threw my arms around him, but he stiffened and stepped back.

"Muslims do not touch like this," he said gently.

"Sorry, Farris, I keep forgetting, no touchy. So, can we go right now? Can we?"

He checked his watch and looked up at the position of the sun.

"We'll be cutting it close. . . ."

I pressed my palms together and raised them to my mouth.

"OK, *yallah*," he said, spinning around to open the passenger door for me. "Let's go!"

The afternoon dragged across the sky like a filter, softening the light. We sped down the highway, past a drab, rocky landscape interrupted by clusters of mud-brick homes, petrol stations with single rusted pumps, cemeteries with low, uneven headstones bearing hand-painted inscriptions.

I looked over the headrest at Farris's marine-style close-cropped hair. It was unusual for an Iraqi of his age; most of his peers grew out their hair, using mounds of gel to shape it into elaborate styles. I wondered how Farris straddled his two worlds, working with foreigners and living among Iraqis. Perhaps it was like growing up Muslim in Britain.

"You're staring, Doctor," said Farris, catching my eyes in the mirror.

"No, yeah, sorry. Just . . . I'm so grateful for this. It means a lot."

He sighed, wedged his elbow against the door, and rested his head on the palm of his hand.

"I lost my mom," he said, fixing his eyes on the road. "They bombed her house in 2003, during the invasion. I still worked for the Americans after that." He snorted. "And I enjoyed it. Imagine. How fucked-up."

I edged closer to the back of his seat.

"I'm so sorry, Farris, I had no idea."

He sniffed roughly and wiped his nose with the back of his hand.

"I admire what you're doing for Sara. If someone could give me another day with my mom . . ."

We gazed out the window as we approached the old city of Mosul, on the western bank of the Tigris. The closer we got, the more dramatic the destruction. The buildings went from mostly intact to half-clothed to completely naked, until we found ourselves amid a scene of monumental devastation.

As the car slowed I saw exposed timber frames jutting out of collapsed homes at odd angles, like bones sticking out of flesh. An internal stairway climbed to a missing second floor, the surrounding house bombed into the dirt. A pile of rubble, thick chunks of stone mixed with colorful scraps of clothing, the blackened head of a doll, a single leather shoe. The car felt light on oxygen, as though we were at altitude, and my lungs worked hard to pull in each breath. The road narrowed and disappeared into a crater ahead of us, so we parked and continued on foot. We meandered through alleyways, past crowds of people living beneath the few surviving roofs, through the smell of cooking, of burned plastic and gasoline. We reached a doorway covered with a dirty floral cloth. A number was etched on the outside wall with white chalk.

Farris stopped and pointed. "This is it."

I looked at him, suddenly terrified. I wasn't prepared, didn't know what to say, couldn't afford to fuck it up.

"Help me," I said, as we stood there, our arms limp, beside each other. "Translate my garbled words into beautiful and compelling Arabic?"

He nodded and called out into the doorway. We heard the squeaking of internal doors and a few moments later an elderly woman pulled the curtain aside, a loose headscarf draped over her sparse gray hair. She and Farris exchanged words in Arabic, and her eyes scanned me from head to toe as she gripped the edge of the curtain. Turning to the side, she allowed us to step in.

We hovered in the squat corridor, with its peeling lino flooring, a white bulb hanging overhead. She bustled past us in her long housedress and flip-flops, and showed us into the dim living room.

And there she was. Sitting on the traditional floor seating that edged the room, a chubby toddler, her fat little arms poking out of a denim pinafore, turning a yellow plastic tumbler over in her hands, bouncing up and down. She looked at me, her huge dark eyes an exact copy of Sara's, babbling and thrusting the cup in my direction. She patted the maroon cushion with one outstretched arm, her spongy cheeks puckering into a dimpled smile, the wild spirit of Sara palpable within her.

It felt so wrong that I should be the one to see her. I imagined hiding Sara inside my body, letting her watch Habibah through my eyes. I could feel her willing me to scoop up the child and run.

Farris gestured for me to sit, while Habibah's grandmother lowered herself onto a canvas foldout chair and called to her husband. He walked into the room and picked up Habibah. She dropped the cup and squirmed against his hip, poking her fingers through his gray beard. He released her and sat cross-legged next to Farris on the floor cushions. Habibah crawled over their knees, slapping her stubby hand on Farris's jeans as he ruffled the shiny black curls that tumbled over her head. I realized I'd never seen Sara's hair.

Everyone was looking at me, so I coughed hard and began.

"Thank you for inviting us in, we are very grateful. I've been working with Habibah's mother, Sara, in the camp for almost two months now and she misses her daughter desperately. She's a kind person who knows she made a mistake, and she longs to be reunited with her child."

Farris translated at length with lots of beseeching hand gestures, but the grandparents' faces darkened and they interrupted him, speaking in rapid, angry bursts. Wrinkles burrowed deep into their foreheads, ripples of skin swayed beneath their chins, and I wondered how many years they had left, what would happen to Habibah once they were gone.

Farris turned to me, his shoulders already rounded in defeat. "They say they lost everything because of ISIS. Their boys, their home, their savings. Habibah is all they have left."

I focused on the grandmother. "You understand, more than anyone, the pain of losing a child. It's unbearable. Sara can't live like this, it's more than she can take."

The grandfather stood up, yelling, jabbing his finger toward me, his eyes wet.

Farris's lip trembled as he spoke. "He says they lost their sons because of ISIS, because of women like Sara. Their sons were good men, only looking to get married, and the foreign women tempted them, led them to their deaths. She shouldn't have come to this country. They will never allow her to see Habibah again."

The grandfather picked up Habibah, and she squealed as she swung through the air. He left the room with her. I turned to look at the grandmother, at her misty eyes, the stillness of her repose, the weathered fingers interlaced on her lap. She spoke quietly, staring at the wall opposite, where the plaster had been gouged out to reveal a crumbling expanse of brick.

"All of us are suffering now," translated Farris. "Sara must suffer for what she did. We must suffer for what we failed to do. You will find no escape from the pain here."

Farris stood up, but I ignored him.

"What about Habibah?" I pleaded, my hands in tight fists. "She doesn't deserve to suffer this separation from her mother. What will happen to her when you're gone?"

Farris translated, and the grandfather stormed back in, shouting and pointing at the door. Farris wrestled me to my feet and dragged me out, and we stumbled together through the dark alleyway outside, our heels kicking up the debris. We reached a bright clearing, the early-evening light streaming through the gaps in the dismembered buildings that surrounded us.

I broke down and Farris gathered me into his arms, his humanity overriding his faith as he held me.

"You tried your best, Doctor," he said, as my tears soaked his T-shirt. "You can tell her the child is happy, is safe, is cared for. You saw the child with your own eyes. That will be something. It will be a comfort."

I TOOK TO MY BED, PULLED THE SHEETS OVER ME, AND LAY STILL, held down by an imperceptible force. Sunlight penetrated the shutters; the beams lengthened and widened, crept across the ceiling, climbed down the walls, then gave up and pulled back, leaving me in darkness. I knew I was being ridiculous. The loss wasn't mine, I wasn't entitled to this pain, but there was nothing I could do; my body had stopped working. Tom and Sherri crept in and left plates of scrambled eggs and cups of tea on the bedside table. They tried to talk to me, but my muscles appeared to have atrophied and I couldn't move, couldn't speak. I crawled to the bathroom on my hands and knees, a being but not a human.

This wasn't the first time my body had shut down. When my mother threw me out, I took the train back to my student bedroom in Oxford. It was three days before Christmas, and everyone else was home with their families. I bought a dozen energy bars from the station and dragged my suitcase through the bitter wind, gaudy angels strung up in lights across the high street. Opening the front door, I found it wedged against piles of post, as though snowed in from the inside. I turned on the heating, got into bed, and stayed there. Dark days merged into darker nights, my body unmoving, a corpse waiting to be claimed by the earth. I failed to get up for my five daily prayers, and despite the thousands of prostrations I'd made over the years, God let me go without a second glance. One week became two, then three, and my curves shrank and fell away, until my body was as thin, as featureless, as unrecognizable as my mind. My phone sat blankly next to me. Nobody called.

I woke up in early January and heard a voice. It was a part of myself I'd never met before.

"Get the fuck up," it said.

My body obeyed.

"Get into the shower, you absolutely reek."

So I did. I listened as it took me to the library, as it forced me to apply for the master's at Warwick, as it got me a job, as it wrestled me through my final year. Cowering under its stern, loveless commands, I survived, but I did not live. Until Rosy, until I gorged on her luminescence, I survived, but I did not live.

A sharp knock on the door brought me back to Iraq. Lina walked in and stood over me.

"Nadia. Is this a joke? You've been in bed for what, three days? I know the program's gone to hell, but you've still got to show up and do your job. If you're not at the camp tomorrow, you're fired."

I opened my mouth, but no words emerged. Lina gave me a final, withering look before she turned around and walked out.

Sherri, who'd been hovering outside, came in, sat on my bed, and stroked my hair.

"Sara's been asking after you. She says it's OK about the baby, she knows you tried your best. She just wants to see you. I think her exact words were 'Bruv, get that bitch back here.'"

I smiled weakly and rolled over onto my front. My voice came out faint. "Does she forgive me?" I propped my torso up on my elbows.

"Of course she does, silly." Sherri picked up a morsel of egg from the plate beside my bed and held it against my lips. I opened my mouth and chewed it slowly, feeling a rush of energy through my body.

The next morning, I sat up in bed and used my hands to drag each leg over the side, tentatively touching the floor with my toes. The tiles felt deliciously cold against my bare skin. I leaned my whole weight onto my feet and stood up, swaying slightly. I shuffled toward the bathroom, clutching the walls for balance. Toothpaste felt sharp as fire in my mouth, the water shocking against my face. I dressed, the seams of my clothes sturdier than those of my body, and descended the stairs, my fingers gripping the banister.

"*Alors*, she lives," said Pierre, downing a shot of espresso in the kitchen. "You had an attack of the nerves, yes? Like a Victorian housewife."

Sherri hit him with the back of a teaspoon. "Good morning, Nadia, how are you?" She spoke loudly and slowly, as though I had Alzheimer's. I couldn't decide which reaction I hated more.

"I'm fine." I leaned heavily against the counter. "What's been happening?"

"Pierre broke Charles's nose," she said, handing me some bread. I pulled it apart and steam rose from the spongy middle. "They were playing Frisbee with plates. Have you ever heard of anything so stupid?"

"And yet," said Pierre, "he did not make a spectacle and go to his bed for a week."

In the car with Jason, I shut down inquiries about my well-being and asked about the classes I'd missed. Jason had let slip that he'd holidayed in Tel Aviv and the women toilet-papered the teaching cabin in protest (leading to a severe shortage of toilet roll in the camp). A jihadi cat video had been doing the rounds, raising doubts about the efficacy of our deradicalization efforts. The video was a compilation of cats performing heroic feats, leaping up ten-foot walls and springing between rooftops accompanied by a backing track of rousing jihadi anthems. Jason had tried some sand therapy, encouraging the women to process their trauma with toy dolls and trays of multicolored sand, but the women had a water fight, leaving the sand ruined and the dolls drowned.

"It's tougher than I thought," he said.

I watched the town of Qayyarah through the window, every home the same shade of beige, like photographs blanched by the sun.

"Are they dangerous, though?" I turned to look at him. He'd been growing out his beard to enhance his religious authority and his goatee now looked pubic and unkempt.

He thought for a moment. "They'll have lifelong difficulties, trying to process the horrors they've been through, rationalizing the roles they played, no matter how small. But dangerous? No, I don't think so."

"To strip Sara of her citizenship, that was crazy, right?"

He looked concerned and nodded at me slowly. "It was a disproportionate response, yes. But, Nadia, you know it's out of our hands."

"You sound like the embassy." I crossed my arms and legs so they pointed away from him.

When we arrived at the camp, I saw Sara leaning against the teaching cabin. She jumped when she saw me but tried to recover her cool, kicking the dirt ground with her slippers. Jason and the other women went inside, leaving me and Sara alone.

She looked at the floor, the peak of her headscarf casting a triangular shadow on her forehead.

"Where've you been, dickhead? I heard you got all dramatic and fainted."

I put my hands on her arms, and she lifted her eyes to mine.

"I'm so sorry, Sara. I did everything I could. But I saw her, and she is beautiful and healthy, and I wish with my entire soul that I could have shown her to you."

She smiled through bleary eyes. "Is she fat, like a juicy little dumpling? Doesn't she have the maddest smile with those dimples? Is her hair still long and curly? Can she talk yet? Was she walking?"

I nodded and squeezed her arms. "She's the fattest, juiciest dumpling. Her hair's curly, her dimples are glorious, and she babbles and toddles around. Her eyes are just like yours. She's everything."

I hugged her as she whispered under her breath, "My baby's OK. Habibah's OK."

She pulled away, wiping her tears with the sleeve of her abaya, and turned back toward her tent.

28

A MELODIOUS JINGLE FILTERED IN FROM THE STREET AND woke me up. The promise of whipped ice cream, drizzled with raspberry syrup, topped off with a chocolate flake. But the Middle East loves to disappoint. I threw open my shutters, and instead of an ice cream van, there was a wagon selling cylinders of household propane gas.

I was angry all the time. Not only had I failed to reunite Sara and Habibah, but progress had stalled in every single case. We watched helplessly as politicians squirmed and equivocated, worrying about the impact of repatriations on their electoral prospects. It felt futile to carry on, but what else could I do? I couldn't exactly leave when the whole thing was my fault.

I went downstairs and found Charles and Pierre bowling in the living room.

"Strike!"

"No! That's cheating!"

Six empty juice bottles were strewn over the far end of the room.

Pierre pointed at a row of cushions on the floor. "You must stand behind this line."

He righted all the bottles and Charles picked up the ball, polished it on his trousers, and positioned himself to bowl. I plucked the ball from his fingers, ran outside, and hurled it over the garden wall. The boys came after me and I screamed in their faces.

"Get in the car! Every single day you make us late for work. Don't you care at all?"

They backed away slowly, and in my unhinged state, I found some catharsis in their fear.

Sara didn't show up for lunch that day, and she didn't attend class that afternoon. I sat there, methodically tearing Jason's handouts to shreds as he convened a manifestation session. The women were asked to make vision boards and to direct psychic energies toward the futures they wanted to create. But the session descended into mayhem when Aisha thought she saw a jinn, prompting the women to run screaming from the cabin, accusing Jason of witchcraft.

Sara wasn't in class the next day either, when Jason droned on about historical methodologies for the derivation of Shari'ah law. By the end, only two women were still awake, one of whom was busy making an intricate origami frog.

During the car ride home, I asked Jason if he knew where Sara was. He shook his head and kept his eyes fixed on the road. That night, I checked with everyone in the villa, but no one knew anything.

On day three, I slipped out of class to visit the reception cabin.

"She's fine," said boss lady, without looking up from her paperwork. "She does not want program anymore."

It made sense, I supposed. There was no point coming to class—she'd never be allowed to go home anyway. And she probably couldn't bear to see me after I'd so spectacularly let her down. Still, I worried about her, feared for her safety, for her mental health.

On the fourth day, I collared Layla, Sara's tentmate.

"I know she's upset with me," I said, trapping her in a corner as the women filed out of the cabin. "But is Sara doing OK? She's not hurt herself or anything?"

Layla stared at me. "You joke?"

"Why would I be joking? I've not seen her for days and I'm getting concerned."

"Are you truly so stupid?" Her lip twisted into a sneer as she pushed past me.

I grabbed her arm and spun her back.

"Layla! Tell me what's going on!"

"You gave her to the old, ugly sheikh," she yelled, little droplets of spit spraying over my face. "You people tell her she must marry to have her child. It's the same as before—to have our rights, we must give sex. You preach at us, but you are no better than ISIS."

"What?" My voice sounded squeaky and small. "She's married the guy from Mosul? She's gone?"

"The Lebanese lady and the blond army man came. The girl was desperate for her baby, and they insist this is the only way. It's disgusting what you do to her."

Layla shook me off and left the cabin, while I stayed completely still. She'd married the sheikh. Lina? And Tom? They'd gone behind my back to do *this*? Then, like a freight train, my senses came rushing back to me and I ran after her.

"Wait! Layla!" I caught up with her and dropped my voice to

a whisper. "I know you aren't allowed phones in here, but does she have one? Please tell me she has one."

She rolled her eyes. "Of course she has a phone. We aren't cavewomen."

I took Sara's number and hurtled back toward the car, where Jason and Farris were waiting. I pushed Jason into the side of the car and his arms flapped wildly in the air.

"Did you know? Sara's been given to that vile sheikh!"

"Sorry, dude, we weren't allowed to tell you."

I pushed him again and his scrawny back hit the passenger window. "You let them do this? What kind of holy man are you? You think this is moral?"

"Perhaps it's for the best?" He dug his Birkenstocks into the ground. "Love may blossom between them."

"Who are you, Harvey Weinstein? She's being raped in return for access to her child. You think that's moderate Islam, do you, you California cunt?" My face was inches from his and I could see white streaks of SPF on his skin.

"And rub that sunscreen in," I said, practically touching his eyeball with mine. "You look like you've cum on your own face."

I backed away as Jason's hand rose to his face and Farris walked toward me.

"They didn't tell me," said Farris. "I would never have allowed it."

When we got back to the villa, I threw open the car door and tore through the house, violently cursing every person in my path. I stormed up the stairs, into Lina's bedroom, and found her placing folded clothes into her carry case.

"Please, Lina," I said, my side tightening into a stitch. "Tell me you didn't."

She patted her bed, but I refused to sit down.

"We partly did it for you." She held a pair of folded slacks suspended over her case. "You were very distracted. She's with her daughter now, which is what you wanted. You're finally free to move on."

"No." I was winded and struggling to speak. "Don't say you did it for me. Don't say that."

"Calm yourself, Nadia." She lowered the slacks into her case and picked up the last items of clothing. "It's over."

I shook uncontrollably, my body burning from the inside out.

"She's being raped! As we speak, that hideous troll is raping her!"

Lina let out a sharp laugh, zipped up her case, and hoisted it onto her shoulder. "Raped. She's an ISIS bride, that's literally what she signed up for."

I grabbed the case off her shoulder and dropped it onto the floor. "She's a child, you fucking psycho. Can you hear yourself?"

"Get a grip. She's not a child anymore, she's nineteen years old. Oh, and you're fired, obviously. You've done me a favor, actually— we were about to get rid of Priya, but there's a new spot for her now."

"I'll go to the press! Sara's famous. I'll tell them you've forced her to marry in exchange for seeing her child. It'll be a scandal!"

Lina sighed and perched on the end of the bed. "She's a consenting adult, and she's freely chosen to enter this marriage. Now she's with her child, in a new home, and the Iraqis have confirmed she won't be prosecuted for affiliation to ISIS. It's a good outcome, more than the British press thinks she deserves."

"You're a monster, Lina. It's a good thing you've got that budgie, you batshit bird-fucking ice queen. No one else can stand you."

I ran across the corridor to Tom's room and flung open the

door. He wasn't there, so I thudded down the stairs and found him in the kitchen.

"You helped her do this!" I screamed.

He dropped his falafel wrap onto a plate and reached his arms out toward me. "Nadia, it was the only way. She wanted the bairn badly, and the whole thing's been driving you mad, pet. This works, like, for both of youse."

I shrank away from him. "Oh, you thought it'd be better, having her raped every day for the rest of her life? You thought that'd make me feel better? Are you mental? After all this time together, don't you know me at all?"

Standing there, his mouth gaping and wordless, a bit of falafel stuck to his chin, he looked more brain-dead than ever.

"I knew you were stupid when I met you, but this? It's my own fault, I suppose. I've had smarter conversations with a toaster, I should've known you'd pull some moronic stunt eventually. I'm ashamed we were ever together, Tom, you're an embarrassment."

I picked up a glass from the counter, gripped its cold, wet surface in my hand, and, using all my force, I smashed it onto the floor. Tom and I looked down at the ice-hued shrapnel strewn between us, then I turned and ran out.

I jogged across the garden, toward a wooden shed on the far side. Sitting in the dirt behind it, hidden from view, I got out my phone and sent Sara a bunch of WhatsApp messages.

> It's Nadia
> What address are you at?
> Have you got Habibah?
> Should I get you guys out of there?

One gray tick, two gray ticks appeared, then nothing. I watched the screen for what felt like hours, until the phone slid onto the ground, and my head fell into my trembling, sweaty hands. On some level, I knew it was crazy—trying to kidnap her from one of Mosul's most powerful men. Where would I even take her? But panic gripped me, my mind overcome with appalling images of him cornering Sara, forcing his body on her, Habibah hearing her screams. My insides bled, thinking of him on top of her. How could I leave them there? It was all my fault; if I'd never spoken to that journalist, she'd never have lost her citizenship, and maybe the embassy would've helped—

From below I saw a flash of color. The ticks had turned blue and the word "typing . . ." appeared. I scrambled for my phone, and it briefly danced in the air above my slippery hands.

> Omg yes pls
> His dick is deformed
> We're three doors down from Muhammad al-Ameen
> Mosque, Zuhour neighborhood, Mosul
> There's a black GMC Suburban in the drive

I typed:

> Kk
> I'll get back to you
> Hang in there

"Nadia!" Sherri called out. "Where are you?"

I stashed my phone in my pocket and peeked out from behind the shed, as though I were already a fugitive.

"Over here." I waved.

As she hurried toward me, her hair tie loosened and coils of hair erupted from her head.

"I swear I didn't know," she said, rounding the corner of the shed at speed, halting inches from my feet. "I wouldn't have let them . . ."

Sherri slid to the ground and sat cross-legged across from me, our knees touching, her hand rubbing my dirt-stained trousers. I scrutinized her face, wondering if she could be trusted with my harebrained, planless plan.

"You know, I was almost radicalized myself," she said. "I did my master's thesis about Assad's torture of children and watched all these hideous YouTube videos. I was about ready to sign up to fight that sadistic ferret."

"You watched videos of kids being tortured?" I picked up a twig from the floor and snapped it in half. "It's pretty fucked-up that you *didn't* join the jihad."

"I know, I should have, really." She looked over her shoulder and lowered her voice. "Are you going to do something? I promise I won't tell."

I leaned toward her and whispered, "I want to get her out. Her and the baby."

"Yeah, I thought you might. Do you know where she is?"

I nodded and patted my phone through my trouser pocket.

"Maybe Farris can help? He's got a personal car. Wait, I'll go get him."

She stood up and disappeared round the other side of the shed, and I listened to the sound of her scampering through the garden.

Ten minutes later, Farris walked over and crouched next to me.

"You wanna get her out? We should move tonight. You're getting fired."

I nodded, my eyes large and baleful. "But, Farris, I don't want to ruin your life. You could lose your job, or worse."

He smiled and arched his thick, masculine eyebrows. "Are you kidding? This is what I live for. Let's fuck shit up. Hang on, I'll call my friend, maybe someone can smuggle you guys over the border to Turkey."

"Oh God, yes. Thank you."

He pulled out his phone and made seven successive phone calls, some in Kurdish, some in Arabic, none of them intelligible to me. His voice varied, sometimes rapid and urgent, gesticulating as though the other person could see; at other times he spoke softly, pleading, cajoling.

When the talking stopped, I looked at him with pitiful hope.

"We're all set," said Farris. "You need to dress official, bring ID and only a handbag. Meet me outside at midnight."

My eyes filled with tears, and my voice disappeared. He gave me a salute before leaving, and I picked up the phone to text Sara. We were coming for her.

29

S HERRI ESCORTED ME TO MY BEDROOM, CIRCLING LIKE A
one-woman entourage, telling everyone to back off and give
me space.

"*Oh là là.*" Pierre bit into a meatball as we bustled past, the
juices dripping down his fingers. "Demoiselle collapses again."

Sherri shut the door behind us and I sat on my bed, surveying
the room. The jostling cosmetics on my dressing table, clothes
clambering out of my laundry bag, the empty shoes lined up beneath the window. What should I take? The question dislodged a
stream of exhaustion and I lay back, drowning beneath it, staring
at the swirls of Artex on the ceiling. The mattress bounced as
Sherri lay down next to me, the frizzy tendrils of her hair tickling
my face.

"Do you think I'm crazy?" The repeated swirls on the ceiling
spun through my mind, nauseating me.

"You care a lot," she said, her voice full of caution. "That's not
necessarily a bad thing. I'd want you in my corner"

The chirps of crickets grew louder in the dark garden beyond the shutters, piercing and discordant.

"I've got a lectureship waiting for me in London. It took me years to get that. I like my department and my boss; it would be a massive shame to lose it. God, what am I thinking? Forget the bloody job, I could get arrested. Smuggling a suspected ISIS member across international borders, I'd spend the rest of my life in some hideous prison befriending rats until I die of bubonic plague."

Sherri groped for my hand. "You don't have to do this. It's more than anyone could be expected to do." Her warm fingers laced through mine.

"But I can't just piss off back to London and leave Sara here. It's my fault, what's happened to her. How can I live a normal life, while she's trapped here forever, with him, being violated by him? I can't do it, I won't."

We lay in silence for several minutes before Sherri spoke. "There's no right answer here. You're brave for even considering it. Braver than me."

"I'm not brave, I'm pissed off." My words stoked the embers of adrenaline that had settled in my stomach, and I sat up. "Now come help me pack."

She leaped off the bed, emptied my handbag, and held its gaping mouth open. "Let's see what we can fit in here."

I slid my laptop into the padded compartment, wound up my chargers, and chucked them in the bottom. I went around sniffing the armpits of my shirts, randomly allocating some to my bag, and packed clean knickers, socks, and a pair of linen trousers. My fingers hovered over the expensive cosmetics on my dressing table before selecting the foundation.

"It's hard to get a good color match," I said, pouting, as Sherri nodded sympathetically.

I put on a trouser suit and my UN lanyard. "Farris said to dress official. Maybe it'll help us get through checkpoints."

Finally, I dug through my suitcase until I found the envelope of hundred-dollar bills that I'd been told to bring in case of emergency. I flicked through the crisp bluish-green notes. "Never imagined I'd use this to pay a people smuggler."

"One second," said Sherri, slipping out of the room. When she returned, she pressed a roll of money into my hand. It was tied with a thick elastic band.

"Just in case you need more." She closed my fingers into a fist around it.

I pulled her into a hug.

"Who'd have thought," I said, "that it'd be me and you?"

"I knew before you did." She stroked my cheek with her thumb. "You're a good egg, underneath it all."

I hid the money in socks and stuffed them deep in my bag. It felt sexy and sort of criminal, having all this cash. I supposed I was about to become a criminal. It seemed a shame not to spread the hundred-dollar bills over my bed and writhe around on them naked. Another time.

We stood back, looking at the neatly packed handbag and the chaos strewn around it.

"Oh, I've got an idea." Sherri skipped around the room and picked up my remaining clothes, stuffing them under my duvet to create the appearance of a sleeping body. "I've always wanted to do that. It could buy you some time in the morning."

I looked at the unconvincing results. "Am I really that lumpy?"

"Only in the best way," she said, reaching out to squeeze my love handles. "Oh, I meant to tell you. You're going to Turkey, right? I've got friends in Gaziantep."

She took my phone and typed in a couple of numbers, then she turned it around to show me the time: 11:55 P.M. Sherri left the room to check everyone had gone to bed. I picked up my bag, switched the lights off, and put myself on standby. When she returned, I followed her down the stairs and out the front door. She stayed under the awning, and I waved goodbye before continuing to the gate. Farris had left it ajar, so I wouldn't have to creak it open, and the villa's security guard had mysteriously disappeared. Farris's doing, no doubt. I slipped through the gap and onto the street, where a silver sedan was parked nearby.

Farris, hands poised on the steering wheel, looked at me as I got in the car.

"Are you sure, Doctor?"

"Yes." I shut the door and hugged my handbag close to my chest. "Are you?"

He grinned and turned the key in the ignition, just as the clock struck midnight and August became September. We drove through the residential streets of Qayyarah, lights flickering behind pieces of fabric stretched over bedroom windows, and the longer we drove, the more lights were extinguished, until we found ourselves in darkness. We joined a highway toward the city of Mosul, this time approaching from the east. I messaged Sara to give her an ETA, and my phone lit Farris's face from below, making him look like the grim reaper.

We entered a posh part of Mosul, worlds apart from the devastation we'd seen on the other side of the river. It had been spared the worst of the war, the occasional bomb sites dwarfed by tacky, Disney-style villas with fluted columns, their ornate metal gates protecting shiny black SUVs. My heart pounded every time we passed a mosque, their neon green crescents flashing bright against the dark sky, as though advertising much seedier establishments. When we reached the Muhammad al-Ameen Mosque, we slowed to a crawl.

She wasn't there. I checked my WhatsApp, but my last message to her was unread and she wasn't online. We squinted at the house, past the chunky vehicle and the trees, and we couldn't see any lights or movement.

"Is this definitely the right place?" asked Farris. I showed him Sara's previous messages, and he looked up at the street and checked maps on his phone. "Yep, this should be it."

"What should I do? There's no point messaging if she hasn't seen the last one. And I can't ring—what if it wakes up the sheikh?"

Farris shook his head. "We wait."

I sat there, falling into a new dimension of time, every minute an eternity. My vision grew blurry as I stared at the wrought iron gate, decorated with flecks of gold, the hulking darkness of the GMC behind, its bulky edges shifting until it was a crouched gorilla, humongous, steady on its haunches, ready to attack.

Had she changed her mind, decided it was ridiculous, far too risky, that it'd put Habibah in harm's way? Or had the sheikh discovered her plan? What if he was punishing her, had chained her to the bed, locked her in the basement? Had I made things worse, yet again? Was I destined to ruin everything I—

Farris spotted something. "Look," he said, pointing toward a barely discernible shift of shadows in the driveway. The shadows grew larger, more defined. Sara, cloaked in black, a small bag on her shoulder, Habibah wrapped in a blanket, asleep in her arms. A flood of oxygen hit my lungs so suddenly that it almost knocked me out. I hadn't even realized I'd been holding my breath. I got out to open the back passenger door, and Sara gently laid Habibah on the seat, picked up her bag, and climbed in. We dared not speak as we drove through Mosul, afraid that the city would hear our words and pounce. The density of buildings thinned and the city's core receded until we merged onto a dark highway, the car's two headlights revealing mile after mile of emptiness. Sara broke the silence first.

"The fat fuck wouldn't go to sleep."

"You scared the living daylights out of me." I twisted around to look at her. "Are you OK? How's Habibah?"

"She's a cheeky little brat." She smiled, looking down at her daughter. "I've hardly slept these last five days, been staring at her like a creep. She's so much bigger. . . ." She swallowed and shook her head. "Anyway, what's the plan?"

"We've got a smuggler to get us across the border into Turkey."

"Sweet," she said, "that's how I got in."

Full circle. What if, by retracing Sara's exact steps, we could turn back the clocks, undoing all her mistakes, reversing her radicalization? Perhaps this would be it, UNDO's final success.

Farris killed the lights and the car swerved off the road, skidding amid the rocks.

"Checkpoint!" he said. We looked ahead and saw a distant, naked bulb, like one you'd see in a prison cell illuminating a scene of gruesome torture. What would happen if we were arrested?

What would they do to us in detention? The sheikh's transgressions would pale in comparison. He probably hadn't been using pliers.

"Nadia, get your UN badge. Sara and Habibah must get in the trunk."

Sara glanced back at the trunk. "Oh shit, for real? Are we gonna fit? What happens if he finds us?"

"It'll be fine, Sara." I spoke loudly, trying to mask the wobble in my voice.

Sara clambered into the trunk, her abaya flowing all over the place. We wound it tightly around her, but there wasn't space for Habibah. Sara shifted about, trying to fold her body in different ways. Eventually, she got into a fetal position, creating a little gap by her belly. I slowly lifted Habibah, trying not to wake her, and Sara held her tummy in as I wedged her into the rounded space.

"Can they definitely breathe in there?" I said to Farris as we climbed back into the front seats.

He nodded. "It won't be for long."

We continued up the road and stopped at the checkpoint. Farris lowered the window and cold air rushed in, mingling with the sweaty heat of my body, giving me a flu-like sensation. A soldier ambled toward us, a multitude of badges stitched onto his fatigues, a semiautomatic rifle hanging off his shoulder. His young, mustachioed face peered at me, and I looked directly at him, giving him a curt nod. He spoke in Kurdish and Farris reached over me, pressed open the glove box, and retrieved some papers, placing my UN badge on top. The soldier took the items back to his narrow guard station and examined them in the light.

We sat in that lonely car, waiting for him to return, suspended between liberty and incarceration. Then Habibah started crying. Farris and I looked at each other in a state of utter panic. The car bounced slightly; Sara must have been moving, attempting to console her.

I switched on the radio, frantically searching for music to drown out Habibah, but there was only static. Farris grappled around the side pockets, opened the glove box, found a cassette, and rammed it into the tape deck. Arab wedding music blared from the speakers, totally incongruous with the silent expanse of desert around us.

"Isn't this even more suspicious?"

Farris opened his arms, desperation on his face. "What else can we do?"

The guard walked back to the car, handed the documents through the window, and stared at us, his head cocked toward the music. He barked something in Kurdish and Farris turned the cassette off. There was a moment of completely terrifying silence, before the guard tipped his beret at us, and Farris lurched the car forward. He was gripping the steering wheel so tightly that his knuckles were white and his fingers looked welded to it. We didn't speak for several miles, until Farris stopped the car and released Sara and Habibah from the back.

"I stuck my tit in her mouth!" said Sara. "Can you believe that worked?"

We collapsed into hysterical giggles.

"Who doesn't love a tit in the mouth?" I said. "That would shut anybody up!"

The road unfolded steadily in front of us, every new square of tarmac rolling itself out beneath us like a red carpet. Every few minutes, one of us would start laughing again, setting the others off, and we basked in one another's delirium, in our relief.

After about an hour of driving, Farris announced we were nearing the handover point. He grabbed his phone with one hand, checked the coordinates, and steered the car off the road.

We debated whether to keep the headlights on and decided to switch them off. The beams disintegrated and blackness consumed the car as though we were suspended in outer space. The darkness silenced us, Habibah's purring snores the only sound. It would have been a good time to pray, but I didn't want to encourage Sara. I reached over the headrest and found her hand, and we remained there, holding on to each other. A prayer of sorts.

After about twenty thousand years of waiting, an SUV came roaring down the road, and we shielded our eyes against the blinding lights as it screeched off the road just ahead of us. Farris got out of the car, telling us to stay there, and a few moments later, he opened my door, and another man opened Sara's.

"This is Darban," said Farris, gesturing toward the man, who was wearing traditional Kurdish dress—a stiff kaftan and baggy trousers, cinched in by a wide cloth belt.

Darban grunted, picked up our bags, and put them into his car while Sara scooped up Habibah, who murmured but stayed asleep. We all looked at the child for a second, longing to inhabit her innocence.

"Thanks, bruv," said Sara to Farris. "You did us a solid."

She placed Habibah in the back of the SUV and climbed in with her. Darban sat in the front, leaving Farris and me alone on the roadside.

I stood in front of him, amid the smell of idling engines, backlit by headlights, oceans of darkness above, beneath, and around. Tears formed in my eyes, the icy breeze whipping them away.

"I don't know what to say. . . . You didn't have to . . . I could never . . ."

He stepped forward and tucked a wad of dollars into my handbag.

"It was my honor, Doctor."

We faced each other, like a couple about to recite vows. I thought of the Bible verse perpetually read at weddings, the one about love being patient and kind and not show-offy. In that moment, as the dust danced in the headlights, I wondered whether this Muslim man was the greatest love I'd ever known.

30

DARBAN DROVE US INTO THE MOUNTAINS, TWISTING around hairpin turns, every swing of the car's beams illuminating sheer drops. I held on to the door pocket, its texture gummy against my fingers, and fixed my eyes on the road, as though my concentration would save us. As we climbed higher, my stomach sank further, until it rested on the car's long metal axle. When the incline leveled out, Darban veered off the road and the car growled over chunky rocks before he flicked on the four-wheel drive, lurching us forward with fresh power. Habibah started crying, and Sara picked her up and tried to sing, but the juddering made her voice skip like a scratched CD. After dozens of miles driving off-road, our bones knocking together like flint in search of a flame, our eardrums lacerated by Habibah's screams, the car finally pulled over.

"From here, we walk," said Darban.

We had reached the deepest part of the night, but on those

mountains, straddled high between Iraq and Turkey, the sky was boundless and indecently bright with stars. Darban fashioned a sling out of Habibah's blanket, strapping her to Sara's back, and we followed him along the path formed by a desiccated riverbed, vestiges of moisture haunting the air. As we trudged up uneven slopes, our fingers grew frigid in the cold, every new vantage point revealing acres of desolation, scrubby half trees the only life for miles around. I focused on the ground, selecting the most suitable rocks to absorb each step, keeping my core tight. It was exhausting, and before long, we were stumbling, unsteady and unbalanced. At one point I fell, but it was when Sara tripped that we came apart. Habibah tumbled off her back onto the rocky ground and started screaming, her voice piercing the skin of the night. Sara was beside herself, shrieking in terror, gathering Habibah in her arms, touching her hand to the tiny cuts on her face, apoplectic when her fingers came away red with blood. I froze. What had we done? What had I been thinking, bringing them up an obscenely cold mountain, illegally, in the middle of the night? If we had hurt that child, I wouldn't survive it; neither of us would.

Darban ran toward them and crouched down to examine Habibah.

"She OK," he yelled. His words echoed up the formidable mountainside, its craggy shadows maleficent, undead.

The cuts were minor, but Sara had lost it, glued to the ground, rocking Habibah, refusing to get up. I sat next to them, surrounding them both with my arms, whispering in Sara's ear.

"It's not safe, love, it's too cold for her, we have to keep moving. I'll put her on my back, and you can walk close behind me, and you'll be there to catch her, if anything happens again, you'll catch her."

Sara was sobbing. "I can't protect her, I've never been able to protect her."

I wanted to fall apart alongside her, all the emotion of the past twenty-four hours clawing at my skin, threatening to erupt. But I had to be strong.

My palms against her wet cheeks, I held her face close to mine. "We'll do it together, Sara."

Habibah was so heavy, I bent forward with the effort, as though I were Atlas, carrying the entire cosmos on my back. For hours I put one foot in front of the other, Sara so close that our misty exhalations merged into singular clouds before they dissolved into the night. Everything hurt; my bones felt brittle as ice, my feet blistered and bled, filling my shoes with blood, a warm relief from the relentless cold.

On our next break, I looked up and saw a hazy line of gold on the horizon. We watched the kindling of the dawn, its thin, hesitant light growing stronger, pushing darkness farther up the sky, keeping back hues of purple and pink for itself. Darban pointed, and in the distance we saw a road snaking through the hills.

"Almost arrived," he said through a silver gap-toothed smile.

Sara and I looked at each other, astonished to have survived the night. We quickened our pace, as though our cells were photosynthesizing the light, and we soon reached the road. Darban looked at me, rubbing his thumb against his forefinger, and I dug into my handbag, plucked out a money-laden sock, and handed him five thousand dollars. Me, with my gum-tree furniture half-owned by Rosy, our crappy flat-shares, joint Aldi food shops; it was the most I'd ever spent. I looked back at Sara, her cheeks flushed by the climb, felt Habibah's chubby hands splayed against my back. A family rescued. I'd have paid anything.

The daylight was bright and exposing. We stood for a moment and surveyed the clean asphalt carving through the undulating landscape, the grass dry, bleached the color of sand, the pale green trees, each standing alone, mistrustful, squatting close to the ground.

Darban pointed toward some large black rings, incongruous in the scene. They were tires, so enormous that I struggled to imagine the size of the associated vehicle.

"You hide inside. Ako find you there."

I stared at him, incredulous. "You can't be serious. For how long? What if he doesn't see us?"

"It's OK." He turned back, beginning to retrace the route we'd just completed.

I scanned our surroundings, searching for emergency exits, but there was nothing, no shops, no houses, no farms. If this went tits up, we'd have no way out.

"Wait!" I ran after Darban. "You can't just leave us here. At least wait until the next guy comes? Come on, please, we're two women alone, we've got a *child* with us, it's not safe."

He refused to meet my eyes. "I go now. You OK here."

As I watched him leave, my organs slid into each other, huddling in fear.

"Bruv!" said Sara. "What's happening?"

I took a breath and plastered a smile onto my face. "It's all good! We're going to climb into these tires and wait for the next guy to collect us."

Sara walked over to a tire and kicked it with a skeptical foot.

"For real? This is some bookey shit."

"Yeah, it's normal," I lied. "I forgot to tell you about this part of the plan."

Sara untied Habibah from my back; she babbled sleepily but didn't properly wake up. I helped Sara into the first tire. The middle had been gouged out, leaving just a rind of rubber. She rounded her body against its edge, and I put Habibah against her middle. Then I climbed into a second tire, trying to reassure myself that we hadn't just been robbed and left to die.

As I lay there, pins and needles creeping through my limbs, I thought of the migrants who died every day, in the back of refrigerated trucks, thrashing their arms in the Mediterranean, falling into ravines, kicked to death by border police. I never thought I'd end up like them, but then again, they probably hadn't expected it either. One day they're selecting the least bruised apple at the market, the next they're fleeing an invading army, the earth hostile beneath their feet, smugglers calculating the monetary value of their desperation.

Barely five minutes in the tire and I was panicking, my breathing rapid and irregular, my stomach dunking in and out of nausea. I tried calming myself with a visualization, imagined I was back in Leicester, the dark-red brick of the terrace, the roughness of its texture, the white plastic front door with the frosted glass, the dodgy jiggle of the handle, the brown paisley carpet, the cracked textured wallpaper, the scent of pakoras . . . It dislodged in me a choking nostalgia, a profound yearning for home, and I wondered whether I'd always had this longing or whether it was new and inauthentic, devised by fear.

Only two cars drove past that morning. Each time I heard the slow, building growl of a vehicle, my heart leaped out of the tire, waving a white flag, but both times they just drove past. What if they hadn't seen us, had missed the spot, had given up and returned to the city? What if no one had ever intended to come for us? How long could we survive out here? I thought I'd been afraid before, but I hadn't known fear until that moment. Hadn't known how it drained the warmth from every inch of your body, made you rigid with the anticipation of pain. How it created a searing white panic in your mind that devoured every passing thought, using it as fuel. I wondered about death, how bad could it be, the coziness of being tucked into the soil, the silent reprieve of a corpse's mind.

Habibah's scream jerked me out of my spiral and I clambered out of my tire, dashing over to help Sara and Habibah get out of theirs.

Sara stuck her arm out and I grabbed on to it, heaving her up. "I'm shitting myself, Nadia, this is fucking dread, how long we meant to be down here, is anyone even coming?"

"It's all fine, Sara, just try to stay calm." I bent down and lifted Habibah out, her face a deep red, wet and snotty.

I set her down on the ground, her curly dark hair wild on her head, and she squinted up at me, at her surroundings, her crying interrupted by her surprise. We were so visible in the naked daylight. Every elevation loomed menacing in the distance, and I imagined snipers, border guards, criminals crouching in wait, studying our isolation, waiting for the moment to pounce.

I unscrewed our last bottle of water, and Sara held it against Habibah's lips, Habibah's fat little hands struggling for control of the bottle. We all drank, then stared at the tiny amount of water that remained.

"We're fucked, just admit it, Nadia, we've been had."

I shook my head and pulled out my phone. No bars.

"Get back in the tire, and I'll call Farris. I'm sure it's all fine, but I'll have to walk a bit, until I find a signal."

"Fuck that! You're not leaving me here."

She tried to pick up Habibah, who immediately started screaming, her tiny voice reverberating from the angular rocks that littered the landscape. Sara gave up and put her back down. She toddled along, picking up stones, examining each one with furrowed curiosity.

"I'll be faster on my own, just let me run ahead." I started jogging, holding my phone in front of my face, willing a solitary bar to appear.

Then we heard it, the rumble of a car in the distance. I turned and ran back, gesturing for Sara to hide in the tires, but we didn't have time. She lay flat behind one of them, pulled a squealing Habibah on top of her, and I skidded toward them, diving onto the ground. I saw a flash of yellow, heard the cutting of an engine, the slam of a car door.

"You from Darban?"

I peeked up and saw a young man leaning back against the car, arms crossed, looking quizzically at our extremely poor hiding skills. An enormous smile took control of my face, and I thanked every god that had ever graced this beautiful, majestic world.

"Yes! That's us!"

I was overtaken by a passion for life so cheesy and full-throated that I could have written dozens of greeting-card poems, one after another, unashamed and unapologetic. What an incredible, unbidden, and undeserved gift it is to be alive.

Sara was less ebullient. "Don't be giving us the stink eye, bruv," she said to the driver as she heaved herself up. "We did actually wait in those tires for bare time."

The guy lit a cigarette and inhaled. "Sorry I late, I forget. Then Farris call to check, I say, wow, I didn't leave yet."

Christ alive. How many times over would we have died if it weren't for Farris?

"I, Ako," he said, pointing at himself. "That, Amputee Mountain." He pointed at the route we'd just traversed. "Many land mines!"

Sara and I looked at each other in horror as he laughed and mimed explosions around his limbs.

"Told you we should've gotten an ISIS smuggler—" started Sara, before I covered her mouth with my hand.

We got into the car and I grappled around for my seat belt, which unfathomably had been cut off, the car continually beeping in protest. Ako eased us onto the road and we bumped through the gears, wooden prayer beads swinging from the rearview mirror, a cream shag rug decorating the space beneath the back windscreen.

"Welcome to Turkey." Ako grinned and switched on the radio, filling the car with nineties pop, first the Spice Girls, then Atomic Kitten, and then . . . oh what was that . . . God, it was Aerosmith.

The whole thing was completely surreal. One moment I'm cowering in a tire, fear dissolving my bowels, and the next I'm comfortably sitting in a car, listening to top tunes from my childhood. It was dizzying, the emotional whiplash, and I tried emptying my mind to give it a rest.

Sara and I watched the sunshine spread over the surrounding countryside while Habibah crawled around the back, hitting her flat palms on the seats out of time with the music. It felt like the start of a summer holiday, arriving at some village in Greece, the radio a time warp, the taxi driver delighted to begin a season of bountiful fares.

The drive to Diyarbakir took about four hours, including a break at a rest stop. We wandered around the convenience shop, beneath the buzzing strip lights, picking up packets of crisps, awed by the unusual flavors, loading up on strange wafery chocolates.

We snoozed the rest of the way, rocking in and out of vivid dreamscapes, the stress we'd experienced anthropomorphizing in our subconscious.

Eventually Ako tapped my shoulder and I lifted my head, startled to see that we'd reached the city. Grand historical monuments, one after another, elbowed against concrete high-rises; the crumbling expanse of Byzantine city walls, enormous, curved Ottoman fortresses, sweeping stone bridges arching over the Tigris, its streaming waters retracing our steps back toward Mosul. The scale and gravitas of the place felt appropriate somehow, a fitting conclusion to our epic journey.

"This is Kurdish city." Ako jabbed his hand toward the panorama. "The Turkish government oppresses us. They don't want Kurds to have their identity, they want to force everyone to be only Turkish."

"That's how Muslims are treated in the UK," said Sara, her nose pressed against the window, her breath steaming it up.

"Well, that's not really true. . . ." I trailed off as the car pulled up to a tall building with a white facade and large square windows stacked one above the other, the words *Plaza Hotel* emblazoned across the front.

"You stay here now, but after I can help you find apartment," said Ako.

I handed him my phone, and he tapped in his number while Sara and Habibah got out of the back. I thanked Ako and gathered up our bags. The moment I shut the door behind me, there was a screech, a bafflingly large cloud of diesel, and an empty space where the car had been. The fumes cleared and we found ourselves alone, contemplating the wide steps up to the hotel.

31

WE MADE FOR A CONSPICUOUS TRIO CROSSING THE IM-
posing marble lobby, all of us covered in dust, as though
we'd casually survived an earthquake and decided to
treat ourselves to a weekend away.

"There's bare grime on your hair," said Sara, surveying me.
"You look like Medusa innit, about to turn to stone and that."

I squinted at her. "Wait, isn't Medusa the one with snake hair?
She didn't turn into stone, her enemies—"

"Can I help you?" A woman inserted herself into our midst, a
gold receptionist badge on her lapel, a disdainful expression on
her face.

To be fair, we looked extremely suspect, and our mere presence
in the lobby was probably undercutting the room rates.

"Hello, dear," I said in my poshest accent. "Would you kindly
check us in? We've been exploring your glorious countryside, and
it's time we clean up and tuck into a hearty meal."

She sniffed and held out her palm. "Passport and credit card."

We were allocated a twin room far less glamorous than the lobby had suggested. The carpeted floor had seen only the suggestion of a hoover, and the bedspreads, covered in blue and orange zigzags, gave me an immediate headache.

We collapsed onto the beds after wolfing down some lunch, and Habibah crawled over the floor, fascinated by the evidence it bore of previous guests, putting absolutely everything into her mouth. Sara scooped her up and she screamed, kicking wildly at the air.

"Why does she do that?" said Sara, pulling a long hair and half a peanut out of Habibah's mouth. "It's so gross, and I can't get her to stop."

I thought back to a Freudian text I'd once skim-read for my psychoanalytic criminology module. "Oral fixation? She probably has anal and phallic fixations still to go, so . . . maybe enjoy this time?"

Sara dry-heaved. "Why do people still read that nonce?"

Habibah clamped her mouth onto a pillow and there was silence at last. We sat there, Sara and I, bloodied feet dangling below our respective beds, adapting to the unfamiliar stillness.

"It's mad that we survived that," said Sara, sucking her teeth. "I'm not gonna lie, man, I was *shook*. In that tire . . . I was wishing I was back in the sheikh's bed, you get me?"

"Trust me, babe, I was wishing I'd left you there."

We laughed and picked over every detail of the journey, marveling at what we'd overcome. There was catharsis in using the past tense, in turning those terrifying moments into anecdotes, practicing how we'd fit them into the stories of our lives. Eventually, Sara turned her thoughts to the future.

"So, what happens now?" she asked. "Is this it, or are we trying to get home?"

I tried to think, but my neurons were firing blanks. Could I even do this without Farris?

"Er . . . well, you've had your citizenship revoked, so I guess you can't go back to the UK. . . ."

"I'd better learn Turkish, then, is that what you're saying? Are you gonna leave me here?"

My eyelids drooped, exhaustion pressing me into the bed, its softness curling up around me.

"Fake passport?" I murmured. "But you're too recognizable because of the article."

I fell asleep before I heard her reply.

My dreams were lurid and stressful. I was Medusa and Sara was Mephistopheles, and I chased her around the underworld, trying to turn her into stone just so I could get a grip on her. Habibah suddenly appeared, a fat cupid on a cloud, but her face was screwed up and she was bawling.

I woke up to find Habibah screaming as though her fingernails were being ripped out, Sara kneeling on the floor, trying to console her.

"What happened?"

"I tried to get her to eat some real food, you know, to vary her diet from floor pubic hair, but she's gone apeshit. I'm a crap mum, Nadia, I don't know what I'm doing. She doesn't even recognize me; we've been apart for so long, I just freak her out, and everything I do is wrong, and she hates me."

I sat up and stretched my arms above my head, triggering a satisfying crack in my back. "When you put it like that, she seems like a bog-standard toddler, and you sound like every mum that's ever existed."

My phone buzzed and my heart paused, as if only one could be powered at a time. A message from Sherri: They know you're both gone. Maybe don't use phone / ID / credit cards for a while. Good luck.

"Holy shit." I leaped out of bed and wrestled myself into a change of clothes. Why had I given that receptionist my passport and credit card? I imagined the smug look on her face as Turkish counterterror police clasped metal handcuffs around our dirty wrists.

"They know we're gone. I'll get some cash and a new phone, then we'll get out of here. They won't find us, don't worry."

Sara's eyes widened, and her hands froze above Habibah as though she were casting a spell. I grabbed my handbag and fled the room, leaving the two of them sitting on the floor, Sara trying to slow her breaths, Habibah poised to devour a putrid sock.

There was a cash machine in the lobby and I maxed out all my cards, exorbitant bank fees announcing themselves with every transaction. I tried to appear nonchalant as I stashed thick stacks of cash in my handbag and exited the hotel.

It was that point in the early evening when half the cars have their lights on and half don't. The traffic surged and halted in increments as waves of people left work and eased their cars into the crush. The pavements were cracked and splintered, the curbs oddly high, the flow of pedestrians blocked by knotted groups of teenagers. I pushed past, wildly looking up at the storefronts, wondering why phone shops were ubiquitous until you actually needed one.

A shop with huge metal platters of sticky-sweet baklava, another with bald white mannequins dressed in tight polyester outfits, on and on until I saw that beautiful glass counter filled with phones, the walls lined with plastic cases of every conceivable size, a middle-aged man fiddling with tiny screws.

"I need a cheap smartphone, local SIM card, and lots of credit," I said, making up for my lack of Turkish with vigorous hand gestures.

"OK." His mustache spread across his face. "I understand." He set down the phone he'd been working on and gathered the items I needed. "I give you special price."

I sighed inwardly, confounded by the wads of Turkish currency in my purse, accepting the inevitability of being ripped off. Ten minutes later I stepped out of the shop carrying a blue plastic bag and walked to a thinly planted neighborhood park, where I positioned myself on a bench. I inserted the SIM card into the new phone and copied over some numbers: Mum, the driver Ako, Farris, Sherri, and Sherri's friends in Gaziantep. Rosy's number came up as I scrolled through my contacts, and I was startled to see her name.

I thought of her so rarely now, it was hard to fathom the immoderate love I'd once had for her, hard to remember the consuming grief that had driven me from London. Looking back at the person I was, devastated by years of unrequited love, my horizons petty and small, I was grateful to Sara. She'd given me a purpose, something beyond myself, the pursuit of an unequivocal moral good. It had forced Rosy into perspective. On some level, I'd always known that she would never love me, but I'd let myself be driven by scarcity, believing her intimacy was the only joy I'd ever know. I knew my worth now. I didn't save Rosy's number.

I removed the SIM from my old phone and snapped it in half, like people do in the movies, and I crushed the rest of the device underfoot. From my new phone, I texted my mum: New number, all good here. She wasn't the type of person who'd spot a change in country code. Then I called Ako, our local driver. As the phone rang, I looked up at the massive Soviet-style apartment blocks that bore down on the tiny park, hundreds of windows circling from every direction. From the upper stories, I must have seemed so small, bent over a little bench, a phone clutched to my ear.

"Elu?"

"Hello, it's Nadia from earlier. Can you find us an apartment in Gaziantep and take us there tonight?"

"*Basha*, Gaziantep is good. Many Westerners there. I call you back."

When I returned to the hotel, Habibah was banging on a glass tumbler with a plastic pen, while Sara struggled to plait her wet hair.

Sara stood up as soon as I walked in. "What's happened? I've been proper pranging."

"It's all good." I dumped my handbag on the bed and kicked off my shoes. "We're going to move to another city, just to be extra safe. Get your things together, we'll leave tonight."

Sara started packing up and I got into the shower, inching up the heat until the scalding water displaced my anxiety and cleared my mind. But when I got out, the hotel bathrobe wouldn't close over my wide hips, and the indignity nearly tipped me over the edge. I stabbed my fingernails into my palms, forcing myself to keep it together.

I sidestepped out of the bathroom, holding the robe closed, put on my only clean outfit, and packed up. Then we sat on a twin bed, our bags on our laps, staring at my phone, waiting for our second escape to begin.

32

O UR FIRST WEEK IN GAZIANTEP WAS EUPHORIC. A MONTH'S rent up front in cash, no questions, and no IDs got us a two-bedroom apartment in a tower block with open-air stairwells and neighbors who mercifully ignored us. The furniture was chintzy, but it felt homely and safe, and we took great pleasure in scrubbing every surface and unpacking our meager belongings, finding the perfect place for each item. Every day, we'd visit a new park or playground, pushing Habibah on the swings, or letting her toddle over the grass, eating worms and clumps of dirt with her chubby hands. On the way home, I'd buy fresh produce and Sara would show off the culinary skills of an exemplary ISIS bride. At bedtime, Sara would tell Habibah stories about gobby princesses being rescued from refugee camps by brave knights disguised as criminology lecturers. I'd sit on the floor, lean against their bed, and listen in. It was better than the damehood I'd dreamed of.

At first, I was constantly looking over my shoulder, fearful of men in dark shades and crossing roads to avoid police officers, but no one came for us, and my anxiety receded day by day. I googled our names regularly, but there were no breaking news stories, no Interpol alerts. The last thing reported about Sara was just a couple of lines about her marriage to a local man in Mosul. The press hadn't learned of her escape. I understood why the sheikh had declined to advertise his humiliation, but it was strange the UN hadn't said anything.

I realized, with considerable relief, that if the UN never accused me of a crime, I could potentially return to my lectureship in London. Still, it was hard to imagine leaving Sara, and with four months of my sabbatical remaining, there was no pressure to decide. I messaged Sherri's contacts in the city to scope out potential work, and they said jobs were plentiful, and promised to help whenever we needed. But I allowed myself a moment to enjoy the domestic reverie, to cherish the strange new family I'd created.

One afternoon, while Habibah was napping, Sara and I dumped all our clothes in the bathtub and filled it with water and detergent.

"You never talk about your time in Mosul," I said, stirring my suit trousers around aimlessly. "What was it like? Did you get along with your husbands?"

She took the trousers out of my hands and rubbed them together to create a lather. "You're doing it wrong. It's like this."

I sat back on my haunches and watched as she rinsed them.

"They were twats, except for Youssef. He was Egyptian, about my age, loved to cuddle. Sweet guy. A bit wet, which is probably why he died so quick. Fucked me up when I lost him. He was just . . . too innocent for the whole thing, you know? Like me when

I first got there. I didn't know jack shit about what was coming. It's funny to think I was just a kid. We both were."

Droplets of condensation covered her face, and I couldn't tell if there were tears hidden among them. Since we'd arrived in Turkey, Sara had been so emotionally contained, it was easy to forget what she'd been through.

I squeezed the back of her shoulder. "I'm sorry. That must have been really hard. Was that Habibah's father?"

"I wish. Her dad was a real prick. Sometimes I pretend to myself that she's Youssef's. He's the one who would've loved her."

We stayed silent for a while as I watched her scrub, abandoning all pretense of helping. In some ways, she was so much older than me: she'd run a household, managed three husbands in succession, four including the Mosul sheikh, and she had suffered so much loss. And here I was, unable to properly wash clothes or put together a decent meal, let alone provide psychological support.

She dipped her hands into the water and dredged up an enormous pair of knickers.

"Bruv! Them things are butters!" She held them aloft, stretching the sizable waistband.

I shrugged. "It's comfier when they cover your tummy. You'll see when you're my age."

She raised her eyebrows. "Can't believe you got that peng ting Tom, wearing these."

Hearing Tom's name, I felt a surprising heaviness in my body. Sadness, I supposed. Turns out you can't sleep with someone for that long without catching a vestige of a feeling. I didn't forgive him, but I admitted the stupid oaf might've only been trying to help.

"We had real sexy lingerie," said Sara. "They encouraged us to make an effort. When I first got there, Jamila gave me this book, *A Halal Guide to Mind-Blowing Sex*. It was like, you might wear a burqa in the streets, but you best be a ho in the sheets."

"What makes sex halal? Saying a prayer, draining all the blood out, and failing multiple health inspections?"

We gripped the sides of the bathtub as we laughed.

When she'd finished the washing, we wandered around the flat, hanging wet clothes on radiators and the backs of chairs.

"What was your life like before?" she asked.

"Oh, the opposite of yours. I lived with my best mate, Rosy, and we just partied the whole time."

"So, she's the devil who indoctrinated you into Western ways?"

I looked at her, confused, and crossed my arms. "You sound like my mother. You're the one who got indoctrinated by your mate Jamila. What did she say? 'It's amazing out here. You can get raped by ISIS fighters every day'?"

Sara flapped a wet T-shirt and it cracked like a whip. "I'm not some white girl who got roofied. I chose to get married, and men have their rights within marriage."

"Come on, you don't believe that." My voice, playful at first, developed an urgent edge. "No one has the right to demand sex from you, whether you're married or not. You know that."

Done with the clothes, Sara went into the kitchen and un-hooked her apron from the back of the door. It was a plastic wipe-down one covered in Beatrix Potter illustrations.

"Don't tell me what to believe," she said. "We're not in de-rad class, I don't have to listen to any more of that bullshit."

A sickly uncertainty crept through me. Surely she didn't . . . no, it was impossible. I knew her, she was me, living an unluckier version of my life. She swore like an East Ender, had a filthy sense of humor, loved her daughter ferociously—a person like that couldn't . . .

I tried to remember our conversations back at the camp, but we'd spent so much time joking around. Had I ever actually asked her what she believed?

"Hang on a second," I said, blocking Sara's path to the stove. "Tell me you know ISIS was wrong. I just need to hear you say those words."

She pushed me aside and plonked a pan onto the hob. "Wrong about what?"

My eyes widened. "About everything, Sara. They were wrong about everything. How about . . . the sex slavery? You might not think they raped you, but they sure as hell raped thousands of Yezidi women."

"I never saw that," she said, washing an aubergine, not even bothering to look up.

As I watched her nonchalance, my panic was incinerated by anger. How dare she use me to alleviate her own suffering, only to be so cavalier about the suffering of others.

"Fuck off, Sara. Get your head out of the sand. It's safe now, no one's coming after you, you won't be murdered for apostasy. Just tell the truth. ISIS did absolutely despicable things; they caused innocent and vulnerable people unimaginable pain. Whatever your version of Islam, you can't think that was the will of God."

"I can think whatever I want. You don't own me." She drizzled oil into the pan and turned on the gas.

She sounded like a teenager defying an overbearing mother.

Was she being deliberately obtuse? Didn't she understand the magnitude of what I was saying?

I spun her round before she could light a match, the gas hissing from the burner. "There were little girls," I yelled in her face. "Little girls just like Habibah, torn from their families, enslaved, left to die. Their mothers, women like me and you, captured, sold, and raped. Sold again, raped again. Tell me you know that. Fucking say it!"

She wiped my spit off her cheeks, struck a match, held it to the burner. "That's. Not. What. I. Saw."

My head spun amid the lingering gas fumes, nausea cresting in my stomach. I grabbed my handbag, wrenched open the front door, and stumbled outside. A breeze drifted through the outdoor walkways, and I bent over, dragging sharp, painful gasps into my lungs.

I fled to the local park, where I collapsed onto the grass, surrounded by the shrieks and laughter of playing children, the white sky solid and unyielding overhead.

Had I delivered Habibah to a monster? Or was Sara just in denial? Perhaps it was too difficult to accept that she'd been a part of such evil, that her husbands had likely inflicted appalling violence. Maybe she couldn't bear to think about it, the things they'd done before climbing into her bed.

I found myself missing Tom. He'd been such a consistent source of comfort, though I'd never appreciated it. Had he seen something in Sara that I hadn't? Were there signs that I alone had failed to notice? Had I been that easy to manipulate?

It was exhausting, parsing the possibilities, and I felt a desperate urge to drink. I stood up and walked through the park, googling local bars. When I reached the main road, I hailed a yellow cab to a cocktail place near Democracy Square.

As the taxi drove me through unfamiliar streets, the city felt foreign and impenetrable. I had no connection to this place, no reason to be here. I was anonymous, untethered, and, above all, utterly alone.

THE MARGARITAS WERE DISGUSTING. ARTIFICIAL LIME JUICE, dirt-cheap tequila, shitty table salt—every sip made me wince. Still, I sat there, ordering one after another, until my small mosaic table was crowded with empty glasses.

As evening approached, a band clambered onto the narrow stage, setting up a synthesizer, an oboe, a traditional drum. The lead singer, a woman in her fifties, wore a tiny polka-dot dress, and her ample flesh wobbled as she sang mournful Turkish ballads, each more miserable than the last. The bar filled with couples, groups of friends, and the occasional solitary man. I batted off a few advances, content to sit alone with my radioactive green drink. Until the American appeared.

He was a tank of a man, twice the height and width of everyone else, but blindingly friendly—a bit like Tom. From South Carolina, he was the type of person who says "Moslem" and "I-rak," his irrepressible optimism aided by his ignorance of geopolitics. The anti-Sara.

I introduced myself as Katie, and he exclaimed at my British accent, his eyes flicking between my breasts and my face as he made conversation I barely bothered to follow. We shared a shisha, passing the long silicone hose between us, our lips pressing down where the other's had been.

"Shall we go to your place?" I said, after we'd spent an hour together.

"Hell yeah." He dropped the shisha hose onto the ground and signaled for the check.

As soon as he shut the door to his apartment, he put his thick hand around my neck and flattened me against the wall.

"Do you like that?" he said, his lips wet against my ear.

I nodded, breathless.

His other hand slid down, under my waistband, into my knickers. A single finger rubbed circles into my clit until I trembled against the wall, my throat pushing farther into his grip. My brain emptied, the fucktastrophe of my life dissolving into white-hot pleasure.

Sometimes, sex really works.

Gripping my wrists, he dragged me into the bedroom, which was empty apart from a single bed and an open suitcase. He stripped me, then unbuckled his belt, keeping his eyes trained on my naked body as he shed the rest of his clothes. He bent me over the bed, pushing my face into the mattress, his hand holding taut a fistful of my hair, and he fucked me hard until my body was limp in glorious surrender.

Afterward, I lay on his massive chest, inhaling the masculine smell of his sweat as he raked his fingers through my hair.

"So, what's your real name?" he said.

"Is it that obvious?" I cranked my head up to look at him. "It's Nadia."

"Nadia," he repeated, using the correct pronunciation. "You

know it means delicate in Arabic, right? It's a beautiful name. Why don't you use it?"

I rolled off him and propped myself up on my elbows. "How do you know that, Rick from South Carolina?"

"My real name is Abu Bakr," he said, sitting up, "after the companion of the Prophet."

"Jesus fucking Christ," I groaned, covering my face with my hands. "Don't tell me you're a convert?"

He sniffed. "I like to say revert: all of us are born Muslim."

I laughed so hard that I fell off the bed.

He peered over the side and extended his hand. "Why's that funny?"

I let him pull me back up. "You remind me of Sheikh Jason. Man . . . the whole point of this was to escape Islam for five goddamn minutes."

He nodded gravely. "You cannot escape Allah. He is everywhere."

"All right, mate, if you're so holy, how come you're having sex with a stranger?"

He rubbed his face, splotches of white appearing amid his sunburn. "We all have our failings."

I fucked him three more times before I left, because I don't look a well-hung gift horse in the mouth, but I didn't take his number.

33

I SLEPT UNTIL MIDDAY, THE DEEP LEADEN SLEEP OF SEXUAL SA-
tiety, and awoke feeling cleansed and refreshed, forgetting for
a moment where I was. Awareness soon rushed back, hitting
like a baseball to the stomach. I wished I could bottle that innocent, oblivious sensation when you first wake up, before you remember you've accidentally ordered a jihadi bride.

"What time did you get in?" said Sara as I walked into the
kitchen. She was sitting at the table, a peasant-style handkerchief
over her hair, caressing a mug of tea. "I woke up for Fajr prayers
and you still weren't back. What were you doing?"

"All right, Mother." I picked up the opaque silver kettle and
bobbed it up and down, feeling its weight, and, judging it sufficient,
I placed it back on the hob and turned on the gas. "If you must
know," I said, succumbing to an urge to bait her, "I got drunk, met
a guy in a bar, and had extremely hot, rough sex. What do you
make of that?"

"Hm." Sara wrinkled her nose. "And now you feel disgusting and ashamed, right?"

I leaned back against the counter, my feet sticky against the linoleum floor. "Not really, I feel fine. He was secretly Muslim, which I found hilarious. Americans will sneak up on you like that, with their universally circumcised penises." The kettle whistled behind me, and I picked it up, poured boiling water over a tea bag. "Anyway, you've had a lot of dick for an Islamist—three husbands, four if you include the sheikh. Why are you acting like you've never had sex before?"

Sara took a sip of tea and watched an ant dart between the salt and pepper shakers. "It's not my fault my husbands kept dying. Anyway, it's different. I wasn't, like, horny for them."

I immediately felt ashamed of myself. The girl was a survivor of rape, and I was being hideously insensitive. She had so much unprocessed trauma, and I'd done nothing to help her heal. I sat down and put my hand over hers.

"I'm sorry, Sara. Sex should be enjoyable and it's terrible that you've not experienced it that way."

She pulled her hand away and my palm dropped onto the table. "You're a patronizing twat sometimes. What do I care how good the sex was? It's not like I joined ISIS to get myself off."

I crossed my arms. "Why the fuck did you join?"

She rubbed her forehead and looked up at the ceiling. "Being real, yeah, it felt powerful, crossing the world on my own, for God. Do you know what my life was like before? There's nothing cool about being Muslim in London; you just stand out, and people think you're stupid and backward. No one fancied me, cos of my headscarf, and cos I'm not thicc. I couldn't get a boyfriend, dickheads at school just took the piss out of my pancake tits. And it was so boring; my parents never let me hang out with the gal-dem, I was always stuck at home. And what did I have to look forward to? A life working at fucking Carphone Warehouse. Allow it, man, I wanted to do something *big*."

I nodded, thinking through alternative routes like a careers adviser. "There are better ways to make an impact. Couldn't you have . . . joined the Labour Party and become an MP?"

She laughed for about ten minutes straight, eventually sliding off her chair and lying on the floor, banging it with her hand. I cannot communicate with this generation, I thought as I sat there like a boomer, clinging to my faith in electoral democracy.

"I'm dead," she said as she pulled herself up, wiping tears from her eyes.

When the laughter dissipated, I asked her, "Did you do anything big, though? When you got there?"

She picked up our empty mugs and took them over to the sink. "It didn't live up to the hype, I admit. They just wanted the women at home. I was like, if I wanted an arranged marriage and to spend all day cooking and cleaning, I could've stayed in East London, you get me?"

I watched the back of her long cotton housedress as she did the washing up. "What's in it for the women?" I asked. "You know how men get seventy-two virgins when they're martyred? What do women get?"

Sara wiped her hands on the tea towel and turned around. "They get to be the prettiest virgin in heaven."

We made eye contact and both dissolved into giggles.

"That's so shit," I said, through ripples of laughter.

She shook her head, dabbing at the corners of her eyes. "Who'd want to be a virgin again?"

Habibah toddled into the kitchen and Sara picked her up and covered her cheeks in kisses while the toddler bucked and waved her hands. My cheeks were flushed, and I felt hopeful. No one with that sense of humor could be dangerous. She was a bit brainwashed, but I could fix that, I just needed time.

We all got dressed and left the flat, passing bicycles and colorful slippers strewn outside the other doors, triangles of afternoon sun falling through the open-air stairwells. At the park, Habibah squirmed and pointed at the swings.

"Wing!" she said.

"Holy shit," said Sara, setting her on the ground. "Did she say swing?"

I crouched down next to them. "She said swing!"

"Yes, Habibah!" we said. "That's a swing!"

"Wing! Wing!" she repeated, as we cooed and exclaimed.

It was possible Habibah had been speaking to us in Arabic this entire time, but we hadn't understood any of it.

Sara wedged her into the rubber swing, poking one chubby leg through, then the other. We stood facing her and Sara used one hand to push as Habibah squealed open-mouthed, her tiny front teeth catching the light.

"Prettiest virgin in heaven," I said, as the breeze caught itself in my linen trousers, blowing them out wide. "I suppose you lost your virginity to your first husband? Was it awful? Sorry, I mean, you don't have to talk about it. . . ."

She shrugged. "I wasn't forced, but I didn't enjoy it." The swing eased back toward her and she pushed it again. "What about you? How'd you lose yours?"

"Oh, you'll judge me, but it happened at a house party. Rosy and I were making out in a bedroom, and I thought it would just be me and her, but one of her guy friends joined us. It was that kind of party, pretty wild. So yeah. I don't know. Next thing, my blood was everywhere. . . . It wasn't how I'd imagined."

The swing slowed to a halt, Sara's hand suspended motionless in the air.

"Fuck me," she said. "It's so grim they took advantage like that. Your mates as well."

Out of nowhere, my stomach convulsed, and I took a step back.

"No, it wasn't like that. It's not a big deal. . . ." But even as I said the words, I knew they weren't true.

Sara was moving toward me, her arms open, and she wrapped herself around me. My hands rose to my face, shocked to find it wet with tears. She held me as the sun stretched into ribbons of pink that wove through the top branches of swaying pistachio trees. The smell of roasting chestnuts drifted over from a portable stand, the strengthening wind twisting the vendor's words as he yelled out special prices for the end of the day.

We took Habibah out of the swing and sat on a wooden bench, watching color scream through the sky as the sun took its final breaths.

"Do you think," said Sara, "your mum was trying to protect you from that?"

I exhaled and tilted my head back, the wind slipping through my loose strands of hair. "She couldn't have conceived of it, but, yeah . . . I guess. And your parents . . . ?"

She put her fingers through mine, the breeze puffing up her headscarf. "Four loveless marriages, three dead husbands, forever exiled . . . it's not what they dreamed of."

We leaned against each other as Habibah fell asleep between us, waiting for the darkness to force us home.

As I lay in bed that night, I grieved for my younger self, for the girl who believed that love meant banishing your instincts and pleasing someone else, no matter the cost to yourself. I thought about Sara's words. Had my mother been trying to protect me? Mum would've been disgusted by the way I'd lost my virginity, but the truth was, she was the reason it happened. By enforcing such rigid expectations and discarding me when I failed to measure up, she'd taught me that love was scarce and conditional, that speaking up and inhabiting your authenticity only led to rejection and pain. It left me vulnerable, alone, and desperate, with a profound belief in my unworthiness, and a servile willingness to yield to the object of my love.

Though she'd reinserted herself into my life, Mum had never shown remorse for the damage she'd done. Our relationship found a cadence she could manage, banal gossip about family and friends stemming a wellspring of pain and resentment, rogue spurts of anger circumvented and quickly plugged up. On the day she inexplicably ended my disownment, I'd tried to elicit an apology, but during that phone call, and in every interaction since, I'd failed.

One Sunday, shortly after completing my PhD, I had been eating Chinese takeaway and watching *Grey's Anatomy* as I waited for Rosy to finish up another blasted Family Funday with her parents.

Mum's caller ID flashed on my phone, and noodles fell out of my mouth back into the carton. I couldn't believe it was real. It must be a butt-dial, I said to myself, or her phone's been stolen and a scammer's trying to shake me down for money.

"Hello?"

"Salaam, darling. How are you?"

It was really her. My mouth hung open. She didn't wait for a response.

"Remember Amina, her cousin Fouzia was in your year at school? Anyway, I've just come from her grandfather's funeral. Very sad. He was such a nice man. Amina got married last year, though, so at least he saw all his grandchildren settled."

Rage curdled with the chow mein in my stomach. Is she for real? Was this genuinely how she thought it'd go down? Thought she could turn up, years later, without apology or explanation, and just continue our conversation?

"Do you still speak to Fouzia?" she said. "She's a sweet thing, though I never liked her brothers, weird they were, tattoos on their necks. I'll never understand why people ruin their bodies like that."

I stood up and paced the room, veering between fury and anguish. "Are you joking, Mum? You think I want to talk about Fouzia right now? You've blanked me for *four years*. I've done a master's and a PhD in that time, you've missed an entire chunk of my life. The last time I saw you, you said I wasn't your kid anymore, made an orphan of me at twenty, and for what? Because I had different beliefs to you? Do you have any idea what that did to me? How devastating that's been to my life? What makes you think that's OK? How dare you bring me into this world without offering me unconditional love? What kind of mother are you?"

She was quiet for a while, and I listened to her uneven breathing down the phone. "Well, you hurt me too," she said. "Anyway, why don't you come home for Eid? The mosque has been refurbished, there's a much nicer women's section now. I had to join the committee to make it happen, all those men don't think women need a space to pray. I told them!"

I shook my head, incredulous. "So that's it? You're not going to apologize? You expect me just to pick up where we left off?"

"I'm making a nice big chicken biryani on Eid, and those aubergine pakoras you like. If you come a day early, we could buy you a pair of shalwar kameez, there's a new shop down Belgrave Road, they've brought some lovely styles over from Pakistan. I went there with Auntie Asmaa, nothing fit me of course, but they'll have plenty in your size."

It was an outrage, this performance of hers. The levels of evasion, the total avoidance of accountability, the barefaced refusal to apologize, it was psychotic. She did not deserve to have me back.

I looked around my empty living room, the old bottles of wine with candles stuck into the tops, hardened wax dripped down the sides, the detritus of my lonely takeaway, McDreamy's face hovering on pause, Rosy still hours from home.

I'd known the moment I heard Mum's voice that I wasn't strong enough to reject her. That's the irony of being left by your mother—it leaves you so precarious, so devoid of emotional resilience, that you can't say no to love, wherever it comes from, no matter the conditions attached. I seethed against her internally, and sometimes that anger would surge through the cracks, but I accepted her back. On her terms, in her time frame, and only ever what she wanted to give—I would still take it.

"Well . . . what kind of shalwar kameez?" I said. "You know I don't like a lot of sequins. . . ."

34

I T WAS OCTOBER. THE DAYS HELD A STEADY HEAT, BUT THE
nights arrived with biting overtures from the distant Aegean
Sea, and the city filled with dancers and musicians attending
Gaziantep University's annual music festival. Women in traditional
headdresses, cascading silver disks framing their faces, and men in
heavily embroidered waistcoats walked onto campus alongside a
variety of student tropes: goths, jocks, sorority girls. They carried
pear-shaped ouds, slender metal drums, and sturdy black cases
coddling flutes, oboes, and violins. We watched the commotion
from the edge of a park, swinging Habibah between us, listening
as dissonant sound checks resolved into sweeping, mellifluous
concordance.

I wondered whether university would have saved Sara. It's like
the polar opposite of ISIS. Fancy dress emporiums instead of
Burqas R Us, sexual partners who ghosted you without actually
dying, and people with dissenting opinions . . . well, excoriated on
social media and driven from their jobs, but not literally beheaded.

Sara had spent her time in Mosul confined to a kitchen, ingesting nothing but propaganda, willfully ignorant of the horrors just beyond her walls. She needed to experience real life, to be challenged, to be exposed to different perspectives. It was time for Sara to get a job.

The next day, I texted Sherri's contacts, and Jan was the first to reply.

Sure, happy to help, he wrote. I'm hosting a dinner party tonight, would you like to join us?

A party? Just seeing the word was a delight; I was gagging to drink, to dance, to talk to someone with a basic appreciation of enlightenment values. I looked at the lone bottle of foundation on my dresser, the three outfits that swung limply in my closet.

"Sara, I'm going to the shops!" I yelled as I left the flat.

I tried to keep it classy, but it was tough, being on a budget in a city that loved printing birds of paradise on skintight Lycra dresses. Squeezing myself into one such dress, I pulled aside the faux-velvet curtain and stepped out of the changing room, swiveling this way and that to consider myself in the mirror. The shop assistant kissed the tips of her curved red nails.

"This is parfact!"

I looked hot, my curves voluptuous against the stretchy fabric, but it was too slutty. Perhaps I could wear an open shirt over the top, knotted at the waist? I gave the cashier a thumbs-up.

As I browsed cosmetics at the pharmacy, I had a brain wave: makeover sesh with Sara! If she remembered the total joy of getting dolled up for a night out, maybe she'd discard that hideous abaya for good. I bought hydrating face masks, a peach eyeshadow that could double as a blusher, a mascara that could double as a brow pen, and a matte ruby lipstick.

Back at the flat, I called Sara into my bedroom. "Spa day!" I said, as I tipped my haul onto the bed and tried to spread it out. What had felt abundant and luxurious in the shopping bags looked sparse and cheap against the bedspread, but Sara was thrilled.

"Sick," she said, and she leaped onto my bed and settled back against the cushions.

I wrapped her hair in a white towel, spread the moisturizing mask over her face, and covered her eyes with cucumber slices, before doing the same for myself. We lay back, slipping into a meditative trance, and I fantasized that Sara would embrace reason and we'd live together like sisters, watching Habibah grow into the smart, precocious, compassionate woman she was destined to be.

For the moment, however, Habibah was still a toddler, and she wriggled over our laps, plucked the cucumber slices from our eyes, and put them in her mouth.

"Cumber!" she said, green mash spread over her teeth.

"Yes, cucumber!" Sara grabbed her under the arms and tickled her as she squealed and thrashed around.

We washed off our masks and sat cross-legged on the floor, doing each other's makeup. I rubbed foundation into her skin, applauding her ample collagen, and tenderly swept peach shadow over her curved eyelids and apple cheeks. Watching her face, so close to mine, I thought about how few years she'd lived, how long each of those years had been.

"Me and Jamila used to do this," she said, dragging lipstick over my mouth. "Back in Mile End. We'd get all dressed up, but we didn't have no place to show it off. In Mosul, I said we should get ready for our husbands together. But we lived in different houses, and it was too scary to go outside with makeup on, even with the niqab and that. Morality police would've gone mental if they'd caught us."

She tore off a square of toilet roll and held it up to my mouth. "Blot."

I kissed it, then she did, the red negatives of our lips overlapping on the flimsy piece of tissue. She bent forward, tossed her hair over her head, and tousled it with her hands. I handed her my new dress to try on. She hid behind the wardrobe door to change, and when she came out, the dress hung loose over her thin body, but she looked pretty and young.

"Wow, come look." I pulled her into the bathroom and did a "ta-da" with my hands as she peered at herself in the mirror, touching her face, her hair, her exposed collarbone.

The colorful dress lit her up, and I watched as she enjoyed her own reflection. I'd noticed her love of color at the camp. Once her scabies era had ended, she would hover over the clothing bin like a magpie, picking out the brightest headscarves.

"You look gorgeous," I said.

"I wish I had your curves, though." She twisted around to look at her flat bottom.

"Yeah, well, I've got a bit too much, so you're welcome to share."

We hovered in front of the mirror, admiring our glow-ups, and I remembered the first time I went out without my headscarf on. The feeling of being unencumbered, the breeze through my hair, the lightness of it. It was a freedom I hadn't even known I'd missed.

"Hey, Sara, why don't you come to the dinner party tonight? I'm sure Habibah could sleep in a bedroom. I can text to ask."

"What, like this?" She pointed at her hair, at her naked arms.

I bristled but tried to keep my voice relaxed. "It'd be a waste not to, you look amazing."

She turned on the tap and lathered her hands—

"Wait! What are you doing?"

She bent down and washed the makeup off her face.

All the levity, all the optimism of the afternoon, swilled around the sink and drained away. I had nothing to offer her; she didn't want to be ordinary, didn't care about looking pretty, about having fun. What was I supposed to do? How do you heal someone who doesn't think they're broken?

She dried her face, leaving smears of brown foundation on the white towel, then she squared up to me. "When are you gonna back off, Nadia? You need to stop."

The nerve. On top of it all, she had an attitude about it? She'd manipulated me, pretended to be just like me, made me do her bidding. And now that she'd gotten everything she wanted, without warning or apology, she'd flipped the script.

"Excuse me for offering you a fun night out dressed as something other than a geriatric war widow. I can't believe how fucking ungrateful you are, after everything I've done."

She sighed and took a step back. "Don't deep it, Nadia, I am grateful, for real. I'll never forget what you did for me and Habibah. I don't want beef, I'm just asking you to respect my beliefs. Like, it's actually vexing me, you going on all the time. I'm Muslim, you get me? That's not gonna change, so stop pushing."

She turned toward the kitchen, and I followed her.

"Your beliefs are mental! Jamila was killed because of ISIS; you and Habibah could've died. How can you still believe in that shit?"

She whacked a bunch of carrots against the counter and took out a knife. "I'm not gonna strap on a suicide vest, all right, but I won't be a Kafir ho neither. I'm a practicing Muslim, I've got morals and that. You're not gonna catch me whoring myself out at 'dinner parties.' I've got self-respect, and I plan to keep it."

She opened the fridge, and I slammed the door shut in her face. "You're calling me a whore? I'm the one who saved you from a lifetime of sheikh rape! I'm the one who stopped you from getting raped!"

She returned to the counter, gripped the carrots, and cut them into batons. "Yeah, and I'm glad about that, but it don't give you the right to control my life. Or did you just want to replace his rule over me with yours?"

It was exhausting, battling the crosswinds of my emotion, trying to reach her.

"I've only ever tried to help you, Sara, how do you not see that? I'm just trying to look out for you."

She took out a Perspex dish and a packet of pasta sheets and I forced myself not to salivate. Her vegetable lasagnas were legendary.

"Why didn't you pick Aisha?" she said, cracking pasta sheets to fit the bottom of the dish.

"What?"

"Swiss Aisha, from the camp. If you wanted an unbeliever. She literally said she was an apostate, in front of everyone. She'd have gone out whoring with you."

I gaped at her. "I wasn't choosing a best mate, Sara, I was saving you. You begged me, you cried every day, asking for Habibah."

"Yeah, but I never hid who I was."

All at once, it came back to me. The snarky comments she'd made in class, the times she'd challenged Jason, her refusal to get assessed or to get security clearance, the things she must've said to the journalist. I'd chosen not to see it, distracted by my connection with her, my distress at the loss of her child, the intensity with which I'd identified with her.

And what about Aisha? She'd been groomed by her youth worker, had been beaten, abused, traumatized, she'd denounced ISIS every chance she got, and she was desperate to go home. I'd kept forgetting about her case, had failed to follow it up, and then I'd just left. Why hadn't I done more to help her? Because she wasn't funny? Because she didn't look like me? Because she didn't invoke the pain of my estrangement from my mother? What kind of insane narcissist was I? I hadn't chosen Sara, I'd chosen myself, and this was exactly the outcome I deserved.

35

JAN OPENED THE DOOR FLAPPING A TEA TOWEL, CLOUDS of smoke billowing around him, his brown hair in a side sweep above his steamed-up glasses.

"Hallo, you must be Nadia. Afraid we have a small cooking disaster. Come in, come in!"

I followed him through the smoke into the living room, awkwardly clutching a cylindrical gift box as he threw open all the windows. He eventually took it from my hands and considered the label.

"Ah, Glenfiddich, what a treat." He smoothed his finger over the gold lettering. "You must have traveled to the other side of town for this."

I smiled and nodded as my hands fiddled with the shirt I'd knotted over the cursed dress. It felt fussy and try-hard.

"My pleasure," I said. "Thanks so much for having me."

He poured a glass of champagne and handed it to me. "The others will be here soon, but I must abandon you for a moment."

"Anything I can do to help?" I said as he retreated toward the kitchen, but he waved a dismissive hand over his head.

I downed my champagne and poured myself a second glass. The white dining table was scuffed with black burn marks that splayed into copper at the edges, and it had been laid with mismatched crockery, tumblers instead of wineglasses, kitchen roll instead of napkins. On the other side of the room, two wipe-clean sofas edged a floral rug, the floor beyond laid with square terracotta tiles. It was a cross between a student flat-share and a cheap Mediterranean holiday rental: like every home ever featured on *A Place in the Sun*.

The doorbell rang, and I heard a woman's voice in the corridor.

"Look what I got! Tonight, we rage," she said in a German accent.

She followed Jan into the living room, broad-shouldered with a boy cut, wearing a black halter-neck and jeans, a bottle of vodka in one hand, a small baggie of pills in the other. Halter-necks had always fascinated me, how easily the fabric bow could be undone, how quickly the wearer could be uncovered.

"*Scheisse.*" She closed her fingers over the drugs. "I forgot we had company."

She plonked her vodka on the table, tucked the baggie into her bra, and walked over to me.

"I'm Christina."

"Nadia." I stuck out my hand, but she ignored it and hugged me, my hand flattened against her crotch.

"*Ja*, of course. They never said how cute you are." She stroked the fabric around my hips. "Neat dress, looks good on you."

I flushed and mumbled my thanks, but she'd already turned

around and started taunting Jan about his cooking. They disappeared into the kitchen together and I walked over to the window, watching the flash of blue from TV screens in the apartments opposite, the yellow halogen lights pouring over the streets below, the red braking of traffic.

"Boregi?"

Christina was standing behind me, holding a plate of blackened phyllo pastry. She put it down on the table and I took a seat next to her as she topped off our glasses. She picked up a cheese roll and took a bite, but quickly tore off a piece of paper towel and spat the half-chewed food onto it.

"He insists on cooking," she said, dabbing the corner of her mouth. "But he cannot do it. We always tell him, Jan, it's so cheap to buy it from a restaurant. Never listens. Next time will work, he says."

I drained my glass, and she raised an eyebrow but immediately refilled it. "Bad day?"

I sighed and absent-mindedly picked up a pastry. "You could say that."

She watched me put the pastry in my mouth and smiled when I spat it out.

"Tell me more. What's made you sad?"

I leaned back in my chair and selected my words carefully.

"I'm having . . . an ungrateful refugee problem."

She smirked. "Aren't we all? What do we do this for?"

"I've been asking myself that," I said, bubbles of champagne beginning to levitate in my mind. "Why am I doing this?"

Christina pushed a gold bangle up her tanned, athletic arm. "Everyone who comes to Gaziantep is escaping something. At least the Syrians are fleeing a real war; the aid workers are only running from internal battles. And together we create a mad intensity that drowns everything out."

I thought about the grief I'd felt when Rosy left me and how monumentally being in Iraq had displaced those feelings, how completely they'd been erased.

"But here's the thing," I said. "I eradicated the drama I showed up with, but I created new bullshit that's ten times worse." I ran my finger around the rim of my glass and it made an alarming, high-pitched sound.

"You had the full UN experience, I see." Christina leaned over and playfully knocked my shoulder with hers, her bare skin against my crinkled shirt. "When you were crying as a child, did your mother ever say: 'I'll give you something to cry about'?"

I nodded, wondering where this could possibly be going.

"In Europe you feel anxious and overwhelmed by pathetic first-world problems, then you come over here and replace them with big serious problems. You still feel shit all the time, but at least you finally have a good reason."

She grinned at me, delighted by her own analogy, and the half dozen earrings scattered over her lobes twinkled under the blown-glass ceiling light. As I watched her, I reached a definitive conclusion: she was hot.

Jan walked into the room carrying a fresh bottle of champagne, a tea towel spilling out of his back pocket.

"What internal void are you running from, Jan?" Christina said, waving her empty glass toward him. "We're talking about why we became aid workers."

Jan popped the cork and filled her glass. "It's early for an existential crisis, no? Let me see . . . I am escaping the soul-crushing boredom of normal life, the creeping inevitability of romantic commitment, home ownership, and ennui."

Christina nodded and tried to hide the food-filled paper towels under a plate. "Yes, what do you call it in England—normie? We cannot stand to be normies. To turn into our parents. To only repeat the same lives as everyone else."

"And we can be heroes," said Jan, wiping his brow with the blackened tea towel, leaving ash on his forehead. "Obviously not for real. Here we get robbed by the Turkish government and manipulated by the refugees, but back home we show off and everyone thinks we are noble, self-sacrificing, and brave."

There was a loud triple knock on the front door. Jan went to answer it and returned with a short Black man.

"Ronald, this is Nadia. Nadia, Ronald," said Jan, pointing between us. I held out my hand and Ronald shook it and smiled, his kooky teeth giving him an immediate charm. He and Christina kissed each other on both cheeks.

"Ronald, what brought you to Gaziantep?" said Jan, pouring a fresh glass of champagne. "What are you escaping back home?"

"Jesus," he said, as Jan handed him the drink. "What a question. Well, it's good money compared to my country." He gulped down the champagne. "And I get to be friends with you fucked-up people." He punched Jan's arm. "I feel normal in comparison."

"Speak for yourself." Christina gestured toward the burned pastries. "Jan is extraordinary. Look at his cooking."

"Oh, shit monkey!" Jan ran to the kitchen, and when he came back, he was carrying the charred corpse of a chicken.

"It's fine," he said pleadingly. "Just take the skin off."

We settled around the table, moving on to white wine, eating tiny slivers of meat salvaged from the chicken, lightheaded from the sooty air and drunk on our empty stomachs.

"Nadia's having a day of hating refugees," said Christina, using a chicken bone as a toothpick. "Let's make her feel better."

"They can really be dickheads." Jan lit a cigarette. "Considering they are needy, you would expect them to be nice."

"I feel like such a failure," I said, resting my elbows on the table. "I tried so hard, but I've made no impact. Nothing I do makes any difference."

"Ah, this is our favorite game." Christina stood up to retrieve the bottle of Glenfiddich. "The failure Olympics. Who wants to start?"

"I've got a good one." Ronald took the cigarette from Jan's mouth, inhaled, then held it between his fingers as the smoke crawled up his face in curls. "I set up a peace committee in a South Sudanese village for the UN. We trained them on conflict de-escalation, set up regular local meetings, and printed them special T-shirts, you know, so they'd feel part of a team. But the meetings got them all riled up, and they started attacking a rival tribe, literally wearing their T-shirts as military uniforms. We'd accidentally created a new militia, with UN branding across their fronts."

My mouth fell open, Christina laughed, and Jan snorted whiskey into his nose, crying out that it burned. Ronald watched us with satisfaction, grinding out the cigarette in an ashtray made of bottle tops.

"My turn," said Christina, reaching up to smooth her hair, her bracelet sliding down her arm. "I had a female empowerment program in Sierra Leone. We taught business skills to local women, like how to make a business plan, get seed funding, do accounts, and so on. Then they all set up brothels. Every single one of them became a madam. I empowered women to exploit women."

Ronald nodded sagely, as though this outcome were inevitable. Jan picked up a packet of Camel Blues, flipped open the cardboard top, pulled out a cigarette, and craned his neck as he lit up.

"My worst must be Yemen," he said, picking an errant strand of tobacco from his lip. "I helped a local NGO buy discounted food and medicine for refugees. They resold the goods at a colossal markup and used the profits to pay for holidays in the Algarve. And we helped them cover it up, to avoid reputational damage to the UN. It was so fucked-up."

I felt comforted by their confessions. My mistakes weren't so bad, not so extraordinary, a professional hazard even.

"God forbid anyone should expose the UN," said Christina, taking the baggie out of her bra, briefly revealing the side of her breast. She crushed the pills and sprinkled them into our drinks. "It's a good thing for you, though"—she gestured in my direction—"they'll never come after you. Better for them to sweep it under the rug. Especially after that dubious-as-hell marriage they arranged."

I stared at her, my drunk mind trying to compute what she knew, assembling and disassembling potential risks, drafting statements of denial.

"Don't worry, we're on your side." She placed her hand over mine. "Sherri told us you're a legend, and she has very high standards. She and Farris send their love, by the way. Besides, now you know the catastrophes we're responsible for, it's mutually assured destruction."

"So, what's the penalty for doing MDMA in Turkey?" Ronald held up his glass, the powder swirling around it like a Berocca.

"They send you to the Saudi consulate and you get dissolved in acid," said Jan, triggering a groaning chuckle among the rest of us.

"Oh, acid," said Christina, throwing up her palms. "It's been ages. I wonder how we could get hold of some."

Jan turned up the music and turned down the lights. As we finished our laced drinks, elation rose through us unprompted, and we moved to the middle of the room and danced. Christina draped her arms over my shoulders, and I held her waist, feeling her hips rise and fall, inhaling the scent of her perfume. Jan and Ronald left the room, and Christina pressed her soft lips against mine, my fingers rising up her collarbone, the taste of whiskey on her tongue. She led me to the sofa, which exhaled as she sat, and it wheezed further as I straddled her, my hair falling over her face, my palms against her cheeks as she undid my shirt. We paused for a moment and giggled as we listened to the creaking bed in the other room. Then we returned fiercely to each other, the room melting around us until we were lit by the coral shadows of dawn.

36

Y NECK COULD BARELY SUPPORT MY HEAD AS I WALKED home, repeatedly lolling forward as my eyes drifted between open and closed, my temples throbbing. I crawled into bed and stayed there all day, until thirst clawed at my throat, forcing me to the kitchen, where I gripped the metal draining board and filled mug after mug with water. As hydration dissolved the morass in my brain, I realized the flat was very quiet. Where the fuck was Sara?

I stumbled into her room and flung open the wardrobes and drawers, but her belongings were still there. You're on a massive comedown and you're paranoid as shit, I said to myself, they'll just be at the park or the shops.

Then I spotted them. Tiny curls of silver filings next to a pair of neatly folded trousers. I moved the clothes, and hidden underneath were three cards of phone credit, one of them unwrapped with the bar code scratched off, and a square of plastic with a SIM-card-shaped hole.

Who could she possibly be calling? And why had she hidden it from me? My legs sank toward the floor, and I stayed there, my torso bent over my knees, the contraband trembling in my fingers. There was only one answer, and it was devastating.

I heard Sara's keys in the door, the rustle of shopping bags in the kitchen, Habibah's cranky sobs. She came into the bedroom, Habibah on her hip, her eyes moving over the open wardrobe, the dresser drawers, and resting on the evidence in my hand.

"Let me put Habibah down for a nap before you start."

I dragged myself to the kitchen table and sat with my head in my hands, barely able to comprehend the magnitude of my failure. I'd destroyed my entire life to save hers, and it had all been for nothing.

Sara came in, headscarf draped over her shoulders, and walked to the counter, where she unwound the seal on a loaf of bread.

"Total honesty," I said, pushing the phone credit across the table. "I deserve at least that. Are you going back to ISIS?"

Her ponytail swung as she moved around the kitchen, and her back was straight, shoulders relaxed. There was no anxiety, no re-morse.

"It's not like that, fam. Some of my friends from Mosul live in Turkey now. I want to build a life with like-minded people, that's all."

So, it was true. She was planning to leave me for her fucking *ISIS* mates. Before the rage, and before the sadness, I felt the insult. What was it about me? Did I have the face of someone begging to be binned? What had I not done for her, what had I not given, in what ways had I not been enough?

"You're an ungrateful bitch, you know that? Those fuckers

313

didn't save you, they didn't rescue Habibah. I did that. I bet they're being friendly now, pretending to be normal and moderate, but they'll get a bomb on you or Habibah, eventually. How can you be so stupid, Sara? You've seen this movie before."

She buttered several slices of bread and got a block of cheese and a wet bundle of lettuce out of the fridge.

"I've been watching you," she said, "and it's pure sad, bruv. Your life is meaningless, you're always desperate for the next random shag, for a drink, anything to escape. But I've got a purpose—I'm living in the service of Allah, and that's how I'm raising Habibah."

I rubbed my eyes with the heels of my hands, trying to disentangle her words. "So, you're punishing me for going out drinking and sleeping around? Well, if it bothers you that much, I'll stop. You don't have to join ISIS over it."

Sara assembled the sandwiches on two plates, placed one in front of me, and set one next to her as she sat down.

"I'm not telling you how to live, it's just what you are, innit. But it's not gonna be my life, I can tell you that for free. We're a Muslim family, me and Habibah, and I want to raise her around people I respect, you get me? It's my worst nightmare, her turning out like you."

I buckled against her words. Did she really think so little of me? Then I thought about Habibah. What kind of life would she have? It was all my fault, going out partying, coming home bragging about my sexcapades, of course it had been too much for Sara. She was so fresh out of ISIS, so deeply brainwashed, I should've been more careful, more incremental. . . .

"Sara, please don't be rash, you're not thinking straight. You can get a job in the camp, make your own money, have friends separate to me. You can have a normal life and give Habibah the safety she deserves."

She bit into her sandwich, and I listened to the crunch of lettuce leaves, watched as her tongue dislodged a spiky bit from her teeth.

"By normal, you mean like you? A slag with a savior complex?"

Fuck me, the girl had a real one-two punch.

"Then don't be like me," I pleaded. "I'm not trying to be a role model. Don't drink, don't sleep around, don't take off your head-scarf. Just be a normal, moderate Muslim, like the two billion others in the world, like your parents."

"My parents deaded me in the media when I left. They're even worse than you. At least you don't pretend to be Muslim while siding with the kuffar against your own daughter."

It was futile; I'd lost her. If only Farris had taken my place. Quiet, humble, intensely moral Farris. He could have shown her the Islam that protects rather than hurts. How could I do that when I'd never found it for myself? I pressed my forehead into the table, my eyes welling up.

"What can I do, Sara?" I said, tears pooling over the plastic tablecloth. "Please tell me what to do."

She did not answer.

That evening I shut myself in my room and searched news sites for the moment Sara's parents had disowned her. It happened after the Christmas market attack in Berlin; the public's rage had intensified and all parents of ISIS members were hounded by the press, repeatedly asked to disavow their progeny.

There were photos of Sara's parents weeping outside their

graffitied front door, the number thirteen in tarnished brass. Photos of their neighbors shaking angry fists next to a green sign, the words *Ayltree Estate* above red-and-black symbols forbidding dogs, littering, and ball games. My hand scrambled for my phone and I called my mother.

"About time," she said, through the sound of thunder. "I've decided it's easier to imagine . . . childless . . . call for months on end."

"What? I can hardly hear you. Mum, are you eating crisps right now? It sounds like a bleeding Concorde is taking off. Can you stop eating for, like, two seconds?"

"Fine, is that better? Can you hear me now?"

"Yes, thank you. Listen, Mum, I need you to do something." I zoomed in on the photos on my screen. "Get a pen and paper."

"Why, what for?"

"Mum, please, just do it. It's urgent."

She exhaled, her lips vibrating as she shuffled around. "Ordering me around," she muttered. "Child . . . thankless . . .

"OK, got a pen," she said finally.

"Write down: number thirteen, Ayltree Estate, Mile End, London."

There was the scratch of a pen. "Right, so what's this about? Tell me you've found some bloke to marry you, and you're sending me to meet the family."

"Erm, no . . . don't freak out, but you remember that girl Sara who I met in the camp? I've brought her to Turkey illegally, and I think she's going to rejoin ISIS."

Mum gasped and swore a lot in Urdu.

"Wait, just listen. I need you to persuade her parents to come here. They might be the only people who can stop her. Hang on, write down our address in Gaziantep too."

I could hear her scrawling the words as I read them out, complaining about her blood pressure.

"What have you done, you silly girl?"

"Please, just get in the car and drive to London. I need them to come straightaway. If I lose her now, there'll be nothing I can do, I'll never find her, it'll be too late."

"You couldn't be a doctor or a lawyer, could you, nooo, you had to do a PhD, earn no money for a decade, then run around the Middle East with a lunatic criminal. What did I do to deserve this? Didn't I tell you—"

"Mum," I interrupted. "She's got a little girl. Habibah. If anything happens to her, it will be all my fault. Please, I need you."

I could hear her opening the hallway cupboard, the clatter of keys. "Forget Gucci," she said. "I want a Birkin bag for this!"

I lay back on my bed, catatonic. My unblinking eyes stared at a large moth on the ceiling, its feathery soft wings adorned with brown-and-black geometric patterns, flapping toward the hot exposed bulb, burning itself, recoiling in pain, then returning, over and over again.

I HADN'T EXPECTED ANYTHING TO COME OF SLEEPING WITH Christina. She was pretty and I liked her, but we'd both been off our faces, and I was so desperate to forget about Sara that I would've fucked a bedpost. So it was a surprise when she texted me.

Last night was hot, she wrote. You can smuggle me across borders anytime.

A blush spread through me like a tide, lifting thoughts of Sara and sweeping them away.

I had an amazing time, I typed, can't wait to see you again.

How about a proper date? Lunch tomorrow, my treat?

Abso-fucking-lutely.

My phone glowed next to me as I snuggled in bed and fantasized about my new life with Christina. We'd move into a cozy little flat, furnished with kitsch we'd pick out at the local market, and it would be tacky but in an ironic way, and every item would have a secret story that only we knew. During the day we'd work side by side at the camp, being worthy and good, and in the evenings I'd wrap my arms around her waist as she cooked delicious and hearty dinners, Lana Del Rey's new album on repeat in the background. We'd alternate weekends between house parties and road trips around Turkey, staying at charming bed-and-breakfasts with views of the domes of Istanbul or the fairy chimneys of Cappadocia.

Yes, I thought all this before our first date, because I am a massive U-Haul lesbian.

We met at an upscale restaurant that served sushi to foreigners and a few urbane locals. I arrived first, and a waitress in a tight white shirt spoke English unprompted and showed me to a table by the window. Looking out onto the street, the soft-bound menu in my hand, I watched a mother and daughter with matching blond highlights step over an old Syrian woman begging for change, clutching their Fendi bags closer as they walked toward the entrance. Christina appeared on the street and tucked a couple of notes into the old woman's cup, before waving at me, her bangles jingling against each other, her jeans beautifully cut beneath a loose, half-tucked blouse, a couple of buttons undone. She came inside and wound her way around the tables toward me, leaning over to kiss me on both cheeks. Her scent, though it held only one memory, was already intoxicating.

"Hello, gorgeous girl." She sat down and kicked her rucksack under the table. "How bad was the comedown?"

I handed her the menu and sat back in my curved velvet chair. "Oh, I was in hell, but maybe only the third circle."

"Ah, I see," she said, scanning the menu. "And what distinguishes the third circle?"

"Your brain feels like it's going to melt out of your ears, but you're periodically distracted by flashbacks to a glorious sexual encounter."

She looked up, smiling with her light brown eyes. "Is that so? Well, I'm happy to have provided some comfort."

We ordered salmon maki, tuna nigiri, and sparkling waters, and the waitress tucked the menu under her arm and took away the wineglasses. She came back with two green bottles of Perrier, and Christina thanked her with extravagant politeness.

I poured my water into a tall crystal glass. "Sara—the girl I rescued—made the comedown a hell of a lot worse."

"*Ach, nein,* what has she done now?" She pressed the backs of her hands against her cheeks, giving the appearance of a squashed blowfish.

"She bought a phone and reached out to some of her ISIS contacts." My eyes stung as I remembered the emotional turmoil of the past twenty-four hours.

Christina reached over the gray-and-white marble table, taking hold of my hand. "You know, if she continues, you must contact the police."

"It's just, she's never done anything violent. She says she just wants to live among devout Muslims. If I reported her . . . she'd end up in prison forever, and her daughter . . ."

She leaned toward me, the graceful curve of her neck exposed by her short haircut.

"It's shit, I get that. We shouldn't be convicting people based on their ideas. But what if she did get involved in a violent crime? Could you have that on your conscience? And what about the welfare of her daughter?"

My face crumpled, and I hid it with my hands. "It's so unfair. They got to her when she was so young. And I haven't done enough, my lifestyle has put her off even more. I'm such a mess, I couldn't show her a better way."

Christina looked pained. "It's not your fault, you did everything you could, Nadia. You have such a big heart, and you've tried so hard. But you're too close to this now."

I nodded and dabbed a napkin against my face. "I'm trying to get her parents over here, maybe they can get through to her. But if not . . . I'll need your help to figure out the right thing."

"I'm here, *schatzi*."

The waitress returned with our food, placing the rectangular platters in front of us.

"Anyway, let's talk about better things," I said, shaking Sara from my head. "How are you?"

She smiled, breaking apart her chopsticks and scraping them against each other. "Well, I met a sexy girl, a sweetheart too. She's a breath of fresh air. So, things are looking up for me."

Heat rose in my cheeks, and I tried to calm myself by pouring soy sauce into a saucer, swirling a lump of wasabi around in it.

"Thanks, hun," I said, grazing her shin under the table. "You're pretty special too. How's Gaziantep been so far? How long have you been here?"

"Just six months. I finished a brutal assignment in Bangladesh, at the big camp for Rohingya refugees, and, honestly, this has been a holiday in comparison. Turkey's a great place to be—gorgeous countryside for the weekends, and the camp is more operational than most. I hope you'll come and work with us. You'd fit in so well; Jan and Ronald already love you."

"That sounds fun. What kind of roles do you have?" I put a salmon maki into my mouth, and my smile dissolved into a grimace.

She giggled. "Oh, I forgot to tell you. They cook the sushi here. It's pretty disgusting. But sometimes you need a break from all the kebabs."

I raised my eyebrows, chewing the congealed rice and flaky dry fish abomination, washing it down with my bubbly water. I didn't even like real sushi, who was I kidding?

"No shit, Christina, this is vile." Memories resurfaced of the UN canteen in Baghdad.

"You'll get used to it. As for the camp, you did rehabilitation programming before, right? So, you'd be great at organizing activities, like literacy, group therapy, skills building."

I looked at her tanned arms, the gold hair lightly covering them, and I yearned to wrap them around me, to bury my life inside hers.

"Sounds perfect." I slipped off my shoe and ran my toes up her leg. "I think anything would be fun with you."

Christina paid the bill, despite my protestations, and walked me back to my flat. We held hands as we stood outside, and she kissed me on the cheek.

"Our next date will be at my place," she whispered into my ear, before turning to walk away.

I floated up the stairwell, captivated by the promise of a new life, the chance to start over. Back inside, I dropped my handbag on the floor, lay on my bed, and checked my phone. There was a message from my mother.

It was difficult, but I persuaded them. They will be with you tomorrow. Flight from Heathrow lands at 2:15pm. Please be safe, darling. I love you.

37

I HARDLY SLEPT THAT NIGHT, MY FRAZZLED MIND SPLICING IM-
ages of Christina's breasts with visions of Sara exploding in a
suicide bomb. The harrowing movie played on the backs of my
eyelids, forcing me to keep my eyes open, to stare for hours into
the darkness.

I sprang out of bed the moment I heard Sara, determined to
keep hold of her for one more day. She eyed me suspiciously as I
made cheerful conversation and followed her around the flat, suggesting we play charades, or tag, or I spy. She went along with it, I
suppose that's how dull our domestic lives had become, but she
hadn't watched enough TV for charades to work and I spy was just
as devastatingly boring as I remembered. Tag, however, was a tri-
umph; Habibah shrieked with delight, toddling after us, and falling
over as Sara and I tackled each other to the ground.

When the red numerals on the microwave hit 14:15, my jubi-
lation stopped dead, and my stomach started to devour its own
fleshy lining. Sara went to put Habibah down for a nap, and I

stood in front of my bedroom window, watching cars amble down the street, going into brief cardiac arrest every time I saw a yellow taxi. Ninety minutes later, I was still there, decoding the marital drama unfolding in the apartment opposite as though it were an interpretive dance performance. A taxi pulled up, and an older Pakistani couple eased out of the back seat, the woman wearing a black mackintosh, her green shalwar kameez flowing out of the bottom, the man wearing a fleece gilet and beige pakol hat. I peeked into Sara's bedroom and saw her sitting on the floor, her back against the bed, playing *Candy Crush* on the phone she no longer bothered to hide. Colors vibrated and exploded on her screen, reminding me of the opening credits of *Art Attack*. She would've been too young to get the reference. I crept to the front door, put it on the latch to keep the door open, and ran down the outdoor stairwell, meeting Sara's parents at the bottom.

"Salaam, Uncle, Auntie," I said as I picked up their bags, noticing parts of Sara's face in each of theirs. "I'm Nadia, thanks so much for coming."

They nodded, exhaustion heavy on their features, and they lumbered up the stairs behind me, their hands gripping the lacquered black banister. I dropped their bags in the hallway, softly closing the door behind them. We went into Sara's room and she turned briefly, then twisted around more forcefully, her phone clattering over the tile floor.

"*Ammi?*" she said, her voice high-pitched, instantly thick with tears.

"*Beta,*" said her mother. Her knees shook as she tried to lower herself, but the floor was too far away.

Sara's eyes widened, and she scrambled to get up. Her mother had not been this old the day she ran away. They put their arms around each other, and Sara's legs trembled and gave way, until she was kneeling on the floor, her face crushed against her mother's tummy, her mother cradling her head with her hands.

"I'm sorry." Sara wept, her tears slipping off her mother's mackintosh, perfect and unbroken. "I'm so sorry."

Her father put one arm around her, one arm around her mother, and they clung together, a decimated family briefly whole.

Perhaps this will be enough for her. My heart turned the words into a prayer. Please let this be enough.

I tiptoed out toward my room. When I opened the door, I was startled to find the room bathed in a warm gold light, the late-afternoon sun hitting perfectly linear, the walls awash with deliverance. I lay for a moment, basking in its warmth, until the sun dipped beneath the window ledge and shadows drew down the walls like blinds. I reached for my phone and called my mum.

"Oh, praise be to Allah," she said. "Are you OK? Did they arrive?"

"They're here, Mum, thank you. I'm so grateful for what you did, I think this could really work. She didn't need me, she needed her family."

Mum exhaled heavily. "What a relief. It wasn't easy, you know, they were very angry with her. Said they didn't have a daughter anymore. It was shocking, how they'd turned against her. I spoke with them for hours, told them I know what it's like to have a daughter who's turned away from your beliefs, who's chosen a path that you cannot understand. But you can't let them go, it isn't right to leave your child alone like that. I know . . . it isn't right."

I was afraid to respond for fear of dispelling the moment. This

325

was the closest she'd ever come to apologizing. And I knew now why I'd wanted it so much. It felt like my pain finally had a witness. I wasn't needy or hypersensitive: I had suffered, I'd been hurt, and I hadn't deserved it.

"Will you come home now?" said Mum, into the silence.

I got under the covers, lifting the blankets over my face, inhaling the sweaty residue of my sleepless night. "Not sure what I should do. I might stay here. I've met some nice people, there are jobs I could do in the camp."

"Darling, it was brave, what you did, and . . . I didn't know that about you, that you could be so brave. Although maybe I did know, because of everything you accomplished when I wasn't in your life. But I want you to come home now; you belong here."

"Do I, though?" I curled into a fetal position, letting the blanket settle over my head, the air close and stuffy around me. "I've never had that feeling of properly belonging. Wherever I go, whoever I'm with, it's never quite right."

I listened as Mum took a breath, and for a second it felt like we were in the same room. Then she spoke.

"Do you remember when those kids at primary school used to pick on you, and you'd come home and sit on my lap for ages while I combed your hair? You liked the big square paddle brush the best because it massaged your head. When you felt better, you'd pick a ribbon from the box, your favorite was the blue tartan one, and I'd cut two lengths and snip triangles into the ends so they wouldn't fray, and I'd tie your hair into pigtails. Then I'd get onto all fours and pretend to be a horse and you'd climb onto my back and ride around. I could make you happy then, I made you feel safe, and maybe I can again, if you'll give me a chance."

I pressed the backs of my hands against my cheeks. They were hot and wet with tears.

"I miss you, Mum," I ventured through sobs. "I've missed you for years."

"I know, darling, I miss you too. It's time to come home."

ON MY FINAL MORNING, THE FLAT WAS ALIVE WITH THE SOUNDS of a family: the hiss of eggs frying in the kitchen, Habibah crying in her high chair, the cascade of the shower, Sara banging on the bathroom door, demanding access.

I pottered around my bedroom, packing up my stuff, leaving anything that didn't fit neatly folded for Sara. Opening up my passport, I looked at the Turkish entry stamp that Christina had managed to get me, then I turned to the photo page. A long-gone version of me stared back, and I stroked her with my thumb. For the first time, I felt compassion for her.

The doorbell rang and I jogged into the hallway to let Christina in. I'd asked her to come interview Sara for a job in the camp, and she'd obliged like the angel she was.

"Thanks so much for doing this." I showed her into the living room and tried to ignore how casually beautiful she looked in her cotton cap-sleeve blouse and tapered slacks.

Sara joined us, wearing the suit I'd worn for our mountain crossing, which she'd patched up with her impressive sewing skills. It was too big for her, but we considered it a lucky suit, after everything it had seen us through.

I left them in privacy and went to join Sara's dad in the kitchen.

He gestured for me to sit at the table and flipped over the eggs, slid them onto a plate, and carried it over to me.

"You should eat before you go," he said.

I thanked him and shook salt over the eggs, while Habibah shredded her bread and threw it onto the floor, watching its descent with fascination.

He switched off the cooker and sat down across from me, his gray hair combed into tidy ridges that gathered into curls behind his ears. The same curls that covered Habibah's little head. He rummaged around in his pockets and pulled out two small packages wrapped in pink-and-white-striped tissue paper.

"For you and your mum." He pushed them across the table toward me. "It's not much, just necklaces. We can never repay you both for what you did for our family."

My fingers closed around the crinkly paper. "Thank you, Uncle. I know this has been difficult, but I'm so relieved you came. Sara needs you. You can help her and Habibah to be safe, to make the right choices."

He leaned back and shook his head. "It's because of your mother. We were ready to forget about her, the shame was so great, and our anger. But your mother convinced us that you can love your daughter—you *must* love her—even if she makes choices that hurt you. She is a wonderful woman and you must tell her she has healed our hearts. She, and you, repaired our family, and there is no greater gift."

Habibah flicked a piece of egg and it landed on his face. He beamed at her and reached over to pinch her fat, sticky cheek.

"And you gave us our granddaughter. This beautiful girl, already we can't imagine being without her."

I thought about her other grandparents, back in Mosul, how I'd robbed them of their last remaining joy, the guilt I would carry for the rest of my life.

Sara's mum walked into the kitchen and came over to me, a transparent scarf lightly draped over her hair.

She spoke little English but repeated the words "good girl," and stroked my face with her worn hands. I stood up and hugged her, and Sara's dad heaved himself up and kissed me on the top of my head, just the way my granddad used to.

I heard the living room door open and went out into the hallway to find Sara and Christina conferring in low voices.

Christina looked up. "My God, Nadia, you didn't tell me you had a math whiz on your hands!" She patted Sara on the back.

Sara bowed her head and smiled.

"We need an assistant in accounts, and she'll be perfect. She's going to start on Monday." Christina reached out her hand and Sara shook it shyly.

I walked Christina out of the building, and we stood facing each other, the morning sun reflecting off the dozens of windows that stretched up both sides of the street.

"I can see why you like her," said Christina. "She's funny and very sharp."

"I can't thank you enough for this." I suddenly felt awkward and embarrassed, shifting one foot behind the other. "You've been incredibly generous to both of us."

She batted my gratitude away with her hand. "Oh, it's nothing. We're in desperate need of English speakers, and the girl is more numerate than most."

"You'll keep a close eye on her for me?"

"Of course, and I won't be as squeamish as you." She took my hands in hers. "I only wish you would choose to stay."

I looked at her narrow, delicate wrists and longed to disappear into the oblivion of another soul. But I knew now that until I found wholeness alone, I'd only create codependence yet again.

"Trust me, I'm finding it very hard to leave you. But I know it's the right thing."

She smiled and kissed my cheek. "You're braver than me, but I knew that when I met you."

We hugged each other, and she walked away, the threads that had so quickly spun between us stretching and breaking, leaving only a distant ache, the memory of a home never quite created.

I checked my watch. There was time for a final walk to the park before going to the airport. As I cleared the tower blocks, the bright autumn sky stretched into view, its breeze encouraging the trees to relinquish their leaves, promising that renewal would come. Branches shook loose red and yellow confetti to celebrate the end of the season, and their rough brown limbs rose higher, unencumbered.

If Farris were with me, he would undoubtedly play "Believe" by Cher.

Back in the flat, I retrieved two wrapped boxes from under my bed and yelled for Sara. She burst into the room and came to a halt by the presents. I nodded for her to go ahead, and she tore off the paper to reveal a pair of adult Rollerblades and a pair of kids' roller skates. She squealed and threw her arms around me.

"For you and Habibah," I said, smiling as she wrestled open the larger box.

"Powerslides? You remembered!"

She sat on the floor and put them on. She'd changed out of my suit and was wearing a T-shirt and jeans, her dark hair swinging in a ponytail, fancy new Rollerblades on her feet. There was space for joy in her life now, and I felt proud to have given her that.

I hoisted my handbag onto my shoulder and said my goodbyes to Sara's parents.

She skated with me to the front door. "I don't know what to say, Nadia. Sorry I was a bit of an aggy bitch. I forgot what it was like, being together, I didn't know they . . . and Habibah . . ." She fixed her eyes on her shiny new wheels.

"Hey." I took hold of her chin and lifted it up. "Don't get soppy on me now, or you'll start me off."

She smiled. "Yeah, you can be a bit of a crybaby."

I pushed her and she slowly rolled backward. "They really love you, Sara. If nothing else, do it for them."

She nodded and skated toward me, until we were hugging each other tightly.

"Right, then," I said, opening the door. "See you in hell."

She winked as the door began to close behind me. "I won't be there."

Epilogue

I T WAS CHRISTMAS DAY IN LEICESTER, AND I WATCHED THE first and second *Die Hard*s back-to-back while polishing off the Milk Tray our neighbor Kevin had brought round. Farris and I had synchronized our watches, and pressed play on the movies at exactly the same time, sending each other a constant stream of texts quoting the most melodramatic lines, and selfies imitating the most outlandish facial expressions. It had taken a true connoisseur to make me appreciate the Christmas spirit embedded deep within the violence.

Mum walked into the sitting room, and I held up the Milk Tray. "See, Kevin's not so bad."

She scoffed. "Nobody ever wants a Milk Tray, it's the kind of chocolate you give people you hate. And now I have to give him something, only he knows I won't stoop that low, so I'll end up forking out for a box of Ferrero Rocher. He knows what he's doing."

Mum went to the kitchen to check on the potato-and-mince-stuffed rotis and the smell was so intoxicating, I regretted eating so many hazelnut swirls. I said goodbye to Farris, switched off the telly, and followed my nose into the kitchen.

"When are you off to prison, then?" said Mum, as she flipped the steaming rotis onto plates.

I checked my watch and reread the message from Tom. "Couple of hours."

Inspired by my bravery, Sherri had quit the UN and become head of direct action for Extinction Rebellion. She was arrested and given a four-month sentence after gluing herself to the M25. Sheikh Jason also spent a month in custody, after cheerfully telling a US border official that he'd been helping ISIS brides. They detained him on suspicion of aiding and abetting terrorists, and it took the UN four solid weeks to get him released. Meanwhile, I had waltzed through the e-gates at Heathrow Airport scot-free, no questions asked.

Lina had called my boss at UCL, Professor Fletcher, and screamed diatribes about my appalling behavior down the phone, but she'd stopped short of discussing the specifics. I guess the UN really had covered it up. Professor Fletcher said she was disappointed in me, which stung—though less than a prison sentence would have. Ultimately, there were no grounds for my dismissal, and my lectureship would resume after my sabbatical ended in January.

"It's nice they have special Christmas visiting hours," I said as I wiped my mouth with a square of kitchen roll. "Sherri's family is in Australia, so Tom and I are going to make it special for her. We've bought her a book she'll love: *Nonbinary and Androgynous MerPeople: A Subaltern Perspective*."

Mum asked me for a can of Rubicon mango.

"Catch!" I said, tossing it to her.

She caught it with one hand, but still moaned. "It's going to fizz over now, you silly girl." She tapped a fingernail against the top of the can and pulled the ring. When it didn't erupt, I crowed victoriously.

"It'll be fun to see Tom," I said after I'd cleared my plate, my overloaded stomach whining in distress. I suppose Muslim Christmases are not that different after all. "He's got a close protection job at Westminster, won't tell me whose detail he's on, but it sounds pretty glamorous. It's just the three of us in the UK: me, Sherri, and Tom. Pierre finally got sent to Geneva, his dream posting, so he's out on the slopes every weekend. He even managed to take Saddam with him."

Mum's head spun round.

"Obviously not *the* Saddam, it's a nickname. Anyway, Lina's been promoted to New York and slanders me to everyone she meets, so I'll definitely never work for the UN again. Charles got bored of his Rumspringa and went back to his family, and Priya's still stuck in Iraq, so she got lumped with the budgie."

Mum didn't even pretend to be interested. "Are you planning to shower today?" she said, sniffing with great exaggeration.

I sighed and dragged myself upstairs, scrolling through Instagram. Then I saw it, the prominent photograph in my news feed, doused with hundreds of likes: Rosy in a bohemian, cream lace wedding dress; Andy, who'd grown a hipster mustache for the occasion, wearing a vintage brown three-piece suit. The scene had a congruence to it, almost like I'd seen it before, the ending I'd always known. Rosy was where she was meant to be. And so was I.

When I returned, clean and dressed, Mum asked if I had time

for a walk. I conferred with my watch, then with my stomach, concluding a walk was necessary to get the digestive juices flowing. We put on our coats, and Mum pointed at my wet hair.

"You'll catch your death of cold going out like that."

"You're just saying that to get me back into a headscarf."

She smiled. "Well . . . did it work?"

It wasn't technically raining, but the air was wet, and the opaque cloud cover made it hard to discern the time of day. I'd developed a new appreciation of British weather since I'd come back: the way it slid between temperate and cold, between moist and sodden, but never burned you from the outside in. Mum said my trip had been wasted on me, that she would have loved the sunshine. I told her the sun wouldn't have been able to find her under that abaya of hers.

"Any news from Sara?" Mum asked.

"She's doing well so far. It's her first-ever job, and she loves storming around being efficacious and having a paycheck. Christina's trying to set her up with a Syrian man from the camp. He fought Assad, but with the Free Syrian Army, so he's got that strong moral vibe Sara likes, but without jihadist overtones. It could be the perfect solution."

Mum nodded approvingly, and we wandered through the narrow neighborhood streets, rating Christmas trees as though we were judges on *Strictly*.

"An eight?!" she spluttered. "It's got barely nothing on it, just a dangle of white lights."

"Don't you think it's quite sophisticated? The minimalism?"

"No, it's a waste of time. You've got to really get involved, or it's not worth it."

We paused to look at a tree so heavily decked with lights it was about to keel over. Mum confirmed this was more to her liking.

"Can't we get a tree?"

Mum gasped. *"Astagfirullah!* Of course we can't. We don't celebrate Christmas."

We continued walking for a while, then Mum turned to me. "If you like, we could put up a seasonal Ka'ba?" She said it seriously, as though yielding a major concession.

"A Ka'ba? So just a cardboard box in the middle of the room?"

She looked me in the eyes. "Well . . . we could paint it black?"

We held each other's gaze for a second before we broke into laughter.

It started to drizzle, the pavement drinking in the moisture, and I pulled out my key as we reached the front door. Me in my tight jeans and cropped jacket, Mum in her glittery (but definitely not Christmassy) headscarf, a long wool coat over her abaya. Together, we went inside.

Author's Note

I've spent much of my career clinging to the facts. For an academic, policy adviser, and peace-building practitioner, accuracy is paramount. So, writing a work of fiction has been a massive adjustment, in equal parts liberating and uncomfortable. In this novel I have striven for authenticity in character, emotion, and theme, but to that end, I have sometimes sacrificed accuracy in setting and context.

The primary departure from reality is the nature of the ISIS women's camp depicted in the novel. Though there were foreign ISIS women in Iraq, they did not end up in camps in significant numbers. The foreign women in the novel would more likely be found in the al-Hol or al-Roj camps in Syria. The camps in Iraq held largely Iraqi residents.

A second key difference relates to smuggling routes. Foreigners were usually smuggled into and out of ISIS territory through the Turkish–Syrian border, not the Turkish–Iraqi border. When foreigners did end up in Iraq, they generally traveled through Syria first.

These inaccuracies stem from my decision to set the novel in Iraq rather than in Syria. I did this because I have direct experience working on the issue of ISIS women in Iraq—albeit with Iraqis rather than foreigners. Also, the political and humanitarian situation in Syria is extremely complex, and the camps are so dangerous and miserable, I feared that setting the novel there would distract from my core themes.

Third, although much of the novel takes place in the summer of 2019, I reference a mass protest movement that did not break out until October 2019. I chose to include the protests, despite the timing being slightly off, as a means of showcasing the pervasive anger felt by Iraqis toward their government and toward international organizations—both of whom are perceived to have failed local citizens.

I worked in Iraq for ten years, though I did not live there full-time. For several years I advised the Iraqi government on the rehabilitation and reintegration of women perceived to be affiliated with ISIS. Although the UN was a ubiquitous presence during my time in Iraq, I was not employed by the organization. UNDO is not a real agency. Several different compounds in Baghdad inspired my description of the UN base.

You'll find plenty more evidence in the book that it's a work of fiction, but where I have deployed significant artistic license, I have done so deliberately and in service of the broader themes of the novel.

And if this book has been too fictional for your taste, I recommend you check out my policy reports. There's a really long one about farm shrinkage, rural to urban migration, and intertribal conflict in Iraq's southern provinces due to the breakdown of regional water-sharing accords, escalating climate change, and deleterious dam management.

Acknowledgments

Thank you to:

My US agent, Allison Malecha; her colleagues Khalid McCalla and Tori Clayton; and the team at Trellis Literary Management.

My UK agent, Florence Rees; the rights team of Sam Edenborough, Lucy Joyce, Jack Sargeant; and the entire team at A. M. Heath.

The team at Tiny Reparations: Lashanda Anakwah, Phoebe Robinson, Sarah Thegeby, Isabel DaSilva, Melissa Solis, Alice Dalrymple, Kym Surridge, and Lorie Pagnozzi.

The team at W&N: Juliet Annan, Jo Whitford, Francesca Pearce, Aoife Datta, Javerya Iqbal, Sandra Taylor, Catherine Worsley, Victoria Laws, Esther Waters, Tolu Ayo-Ajala, Steve Marking, Sophie Nevrkla, Paul Stark, Ellie Bowker, Hannah Cox, and Ilona Jasiewicz.

For reading and providing feedback on my manuscript, thank you to Jinan, RKB, Musab, Usayd, Kat, Keiran, Jazz, Daphne, Amelia, Emily, Nick, Jana, Aaron, Alex, Dons, Helena, Theresa, Larissa, Claire, Jack, and Lydia.

For industry advice, thank you to Caroline Hulse, Ali Shaw, and Laura Barnett.

Always in gratitude to my parents and siblings.

About the Author

Dr. Nussaibah Younis is a peace-building practitioner and a globally recognized expert on contemporary Iraq. For several years, Dr. Younis advised the Iraqi government on proposed programs to deradicalize women affiliated with ISIS. She has a PhD in international affairs from Durham University in the UK and a BA in modern history and English from the University of Oxford. Dr. Younis was a senior fellow at the Atlantic Council in Washington, DC, where she directed the Future of Iraq Task Force and offered strategic advice to US government agencies on Iraq policy. She was a postdoctoral fellow at the Harvard Kennedy School's Belfer Center and has published op-eds in *The Wall Street Journal*, *The Guardian*, and *The New York Times*. She has worked in Washington, DC; Dubai; Cairo; Beirut; Amman; and Baghdad, and currently lives in London.